NOT TO
THIS
LADY,
YOU DON'T

NOT TO THIS LADY, YOU DON'T

WILLIAM L. PRENTISS

iUniverse, Inc.
Bloomington

Not To This Lady, You Don't

This is a work of fiction. All of the characters, names, incidents, organizations, and dialogue in this novel are either the products of the author's imagination or are used fictitiously.

iUniverse books may be ordered through booksellers or by contacting:

iUniverse
1663 Liberty Drive
Bloomington, IN 47403
www.iuniverse.com
1-800-Authors (1-800-288-4677)

Because of the dynamic nature of the Internet, any web addresses or links contained in this book may have changed since publication and may no longer be valid. The views expressed in this work are solely those of the author and do not necessarily reflect the views of the publisher, and the publisher hereby disclaims any responsibility for them.

Any people depicted in stock imagery provided by Thinkstock are models, and such images are being used for illustrative purposes only.
Certain stock imagery © Thinkstock.

ISBN: 978-1-4759-7830-8 (sc)
ISBN: 978-1-4759-7831-5 (ebk)

Library of Congress Control Number: 2013903363

Printed in the United States of America

iUniverse rev. date: 03/01/2013

1

The squeeze in her stomach wrenched her awake. Something was twisting her insides like taffy on the arms of the old neighborhood candy store machines. Through a haze all she could see was white. Then eyes. All colors, piercing the blur, staring down on her. Now whole faces. Men, women. *Who the hell were they?*

Wake up, ninny. It's a hospital. You're alive. You made it.

She tried to groan.

Wow, it hurts. Thank God someone knew. Something was flowing into her arm. Oh yeah, that's good. It must be powerful stuff. How about blood? Were they giving her blood, too? That could be trouble. She might come out of this mess with something bad, like AIDS? She'd heard about patients being pumped full of contaminated blood. Sure, they sued the hospitals, but what good did that do?

A mouth close to her ear whispered, "You have a visitor." She hoped it was Ross. She had to tell him what happened in the basement and what she had tried to do. No, the moon-shaped face with the cigar breath, double chins, and lots of forty-year old wrinkles didn't belong to the best-looking deputy in the U. S. marshal service. The face hovering within a few inches of hers hadn't the remotest resemblance to Ross Vincennes, the man she hoped would help bail her out of the worst mess she had ever been in.

Nothing familiar about the voice, either. It wasn't as smooth as Ross's, more authoritative. And urgent.

He said, "Mrs. Velotti, I'm detective Leo Carey of the Chicago police department. I'm glad to hear you are going to be all right. Can you tell me what happened? You were found badly wounded on the basement floor of your home. Can you can tell us who shot you?. And why."

How could she tell him anything until she could unscramble a story that would work?

Her lips could hardly form the words. She whispered: "Why don't you tell me?"

Maybe the cop would give up for today, give her time to think. Right now, make him answer some questions.

"Where's my husband?"

"Did he shoot you, Mrs. Velotti?"

Good God, how could Bob have shot anyone if he was dead? Or was he dead? Cry, go into shock, but keep your mouth shut until you can talk to Ross. Act donkey dumb. Put up the blank, dead-eyed wall you once used to ward off tirades by your mom.

"Where's my husband?"

"Please, Mrs. Velotti, don't excite yourself. Mr. Velotti is missing. His car is gone and some of his clothes. Tell me, please, did he shoot you?"

Jesus God, say "no" and the cop says," then who?" Then you say you don't know and he says something like "Why were you in the basement?" and then asks lots of other questions. Good, here's the doctor. Give him a look. Get this guy out of here.

"That's all for today, officer."

"Just a couple more questions, doctor."

Look like you're in agony. Groan for God's sake.

The man in white to the rescue.

"Absolutely not. No more questions. You'll have to go officer. Now!"

Silence. She dozed as the stabs of pain subsided. She felt herself sinking into something so soft that every inch of her skin was being caressed as by a silken cloud. The critical care bed was as comforting and protective as the blue velvet-lined box she had once laid a favorite doll. How gentle she had been then, her touch conveying all of a child's capacity for unqualified love.

It wasn't anything learned from her mother. Cora Lambucci maintained a strict nine o'clock bedtime with no tucking in or bedside stories. She had the next day's schedule for her only child already posted on the kitchen wall. She would break out an extra blanket on those cold-black north Jersey nights. For anything resembling a sniffle, she delivered a steaming lemonade followed by a chest rub with some greasy stuff. Marti would never forget its awful smell.

Cora could be rough in her hands-on care, but I was a fool to ever doubt her love or question her fierce protection, even with all the nagging about posture and grammar and self improvement. Yeah, and the right kind of boys I could see.

It had prepared her for what? The attention of a lot of men, but only one she had loved. Three husbands and now a bullet in the gut. What a mess. She was alive, but had to begin a new life. Get it right. She would still be under the protection of the federal government, with another new name, but if she couldn't be the woman her mother wanted her to be, at least she could be someone she, Martina Lambucci Costello, could live with.

2

Deputy U.S. marshal Ross Vincennes was regretting the extra two hours sleep he took before getting back to his assignment at Memorial hospital. Martina Costello, renamed with her protected husband, Leland and Karen Velotti, was conscious, but a Chicago cop had beaten him to her bedside. If the protected witness's wife forgot who she was supposed to be, and blurted out her real name, Vincennes's boss, Lou Robbins, U. S. Marshal, Northern Illinois, would chew his ass. Before ordering him to the hospital, Robbins had snapped, "Get the story on what happened. Keep her in line, She can't blow her or her husband's identity."

Vincennes stood by the critical care nurse's station, unseen by Leo Carey as the tall, bulky detective rumbled head down through the Memorial Hospital hallway and disappeared in a stairwell.

How in hell did he happen to be at the hospital just as she broke out of her post-op snooze? Lucky? More likely he had a hospital contact that told him she might be coming out of it. Maybe the cop, trying to make sense of the basement shooting, didn't get much. He hadn't been with Marti for long. Whatever she told him didn't matter actually, so long as she spoke as Karen Velotti, wife of Leland Velotti.

Vincennes hurried down the corridor to critical care. He hoped she was awake. He needed a repeat of whatever she told Carey. And more. The tightly-wound Robbins wanted the entire story. Now.

"Get some rest, but get back to the hospital asap," he said at their late night meeting. "You have to keep Mrs. Costello, I mean Velotti, under control."

Marti Costello hadn't been able to use her real name since her husband, formerly Robert Costello, flopped at trying to jail his boss for tax evasion. They came to Chicago in the protected witness program. She told Vincennes, who was the Velotti case worker, that she wanted out, but he warned her she might have made a bad decision on how to get out. An hour after their meeting in a northwest side motel, and his warning that she might be in serious trouble, she was shot in the basement of the protected witness's bungalow.

Vincennes hoped she would clam up to maintain her protected status as the missing man's wife. The Chicago cops would push her hard for an explanation on how someone got into her home and nearly killed her.

To Vincennes, why Marti took the bullet was only part of the mystery. *Why shoot her? She came into the program because of Costello's deal with the feds. Why would whoever invaded that basement want her dead? And where in hell was Costello?*

A check with neighbors found a woman who saw Costello's car leave its garage. About an hour after he drove off, the same witness saw a white male leave the house, a chunky guy who staggered to a car at the curb. She said he was holding a handkerchief to the side of his head. No, she didn't get a license number and couldn't describe the car. Said it was black.

A couple of hours before the shooting, Marti, as she wanted to be called when she was alone with Vincennes, sat fully dressed on one of the twin beds in a Red Roof Inn. Vincennes stood over her, looking down her partly open blouse as he undid the buttons of his shirt. He knew something was on her mind beside sex because they were usually all over each other before the door was closed. For this meeting, instead of the usual pre-romp fooling around, she had riveted him with a this-is-important look and said, "You know, Ross, we can do better than these motel shack ups. I mean be together all the time. Permanently."

She looked up at him out of the blue pools that could easily accommodate a full gainer off the high board. The eyes dominated a face Vincennes described to himself, as high class working girl pretty. Dark, almost black hair, fluffed around good facial skin, and right-size matching teeth helped it all work, especially when she displayed them in one of her fast-disappearing smiles, the smiles that seldom became grins, fading before they included her eyes.

At less than a hundred and twenty pounds, she barely wrinkled the bed spread. Her outfit that day was simple, the usual for their trysts-skirt and blouse.

She admitted she didn't make much effort to dress well for their meetings.

"What the hell, Ross. I don't dress for you. I undress."

That afternoon, her movements were anything but upbeat. He had never seen her as intense, or more serious, unless it had been the day he moved her and her husband into their twenty-five year old bungalow on Chicago's northwest side. That look had been disgust combined with outrage.

She glared at her husband, "Bob, this dump reminds me of some of the North Jersey crap my dad paints. I expected something better than this."

His answer was pleading. "Take it easy, Marti. There's no rule that says we can't move up."

Vincennes's eyebrows lifted at this.

The protected witness said, "Maybe I'll do so well in my job we can do better."

To that Vincennes said, "Hell yes. Why not?"

Marti's face relaxed, but her husband's optimism didn't rate a smile. She turned to Vincennes.

"What can you do for fun in this town?"

Her look and what later followed the look soon made it clear she wanted someone other than her too-short, too-old, and almost out-of-hair husband to show her around. This, he decided, was a very unhappy woman.

To Ross Vincennes, it didn't fit at all. She was far younger than her husband by at least fifteen years and obviously had an itch that Costello-Velotti couldn't satisfy. It was there so Vincennes took it. He didn't have to make the first move. They danced around with phone calls and a couple of lunches over the next couple of weeks, but he thought he knew where it was headed. He hoped so, anyway.

She had made it clear over the sandwiches and ice tea that her husband was a mismatch. She didn't knock the man on a personal basis, if implying he was inadequate sexually is impersonal.

She said, "He's always tired. He goes to sleep in front of the teevee news. A big evening to him is fooling around with his woodworking tools in the basement."

After that lunch, he said, "Let's go for a drive."

Minutes later he pulled his unmarked government car into a deserted section of forest preserve off Golf road. He said, "It's beautiful here."

She stared at him across the bench seat, and said, "It sure is, but not here."

Once in the motel room on Waukegan road, there were no preliminaries. They clinched and the party was underway.

She said, "Ross baby, I think our friendship has moved to a new level."

After that first steamy session they met during Vincennes's extended lunch hours once a week in motels around O'Hare airport and in suburbs north and west. Ross was certain Costello never had a clue. The job they found for him with the help of an agency that knew nothing more than Costello's new name was eight to four-thirty in suburban Northbrook. He soon became known as a reliable worker, never sick or needing extra time off. The job with a small accountancy firm seemed adequate cover for the former big shot

But somehow they found him.

Marti told Vincennes, "He makes us a drink, eats whatever I put on the table, turns on the news, reads the Wall Street Journal, and is in bed by ten. We pass each other like Staten Island ferries in a fog."

Vincennes hardly ever saw them together, but it was obvious in his cursory visits that she didn't pretend to give priority to housekeeping in the two-bedroom bungalow. She said, "I told him to get a maid if he wants neatness. If I'm marooned in the vast wasteland of the second city, I'm going to spend as little time as possible in that dump. I told Bob, I mean Leland, that I enjoyed rattling around the area in the ancient Taurus he bought me." During the two months of her meetings with Vincennes she festooned the bungalow with cheap art and other items acquired from the area's shopping centers. Apparently, there were no discussions about finding a better place. At least Costello-Velotti demonstrated no such need in his infrequent meetings with Vincennes.

Vincennes told Robbins it was working out. The marshal's office had sought and found a neighborhood of working people and retirees whose social interaction revolved mostly around their children or their churches. After brief introductory meetings with adjoining home owners the Velotti's contact with their neighbors was limited to coming-and-going salutations. The home selection was based on the agency's experience in placing people. The small two-story house was supposed to an appropriate front for a man with a small accountant's job.

The Velottis were the official home owners, with a mortgage, utility bills, taxes, and all. The former financial officer for New Jersey's $50,000,000 Stanton Corporation had swapped his important job and huge income for a reasonable chance of staying alive. When he told

Vincennes he had a small amount of untraceable cash from his savings, Vincennes warned him.

"You and your wife can't run up expenses beyond those expected of someone at your income level. That is, if you want to block that route to finding you."

Vincennes had been reawakened sexually by Marti. It was a fantastic break after a fifteen-year marriage in which sex had become infrequent and ritualistic. He didn't think Marti had fallen for him, but the sex was better than good. He prided himself on his performance, and he was sure she wanted their meetings as much as he did, but while they both murmured compliments during the enthusiastic sessions, the word love, that is love for each other, wasn't mentioned. There was little post-coital talk, and neither of them smoked. She hurried into the bathroom, and he pulled on his clothes. He followed her into the shower once and she chased him out.

He hadn't given much thought to the future. He was satisfied that he'd gotten lucky in a major way. He hoped the liaison would continue indefinitely. Then, that day, staring up at him from the Red Roof bed, arms folded under her breasts, Marti said, "I'm expecting to come into some money, I mean a lot of money."

He stood there, fingers on a shirt button, waiting for the rest.

"Oh yeah. Mind telling me from where?"

"You'll know soon enough. How do you feel about taking off with it. I mean there would be enough for us to live the good life for a long, long time."

He had smiled, still not moving.

He thought, "What a weird twist to what began as simply fooling around. She knew he was unhappy in his marriage, but he thought their affair would wind down when they faced the inevitable "Where do we go from here?" decision. The kiss off would be made less painful by his noble proclamation of obligations to his wife and two kids, bullshit, etcetera, but this could be a whole new ball game. A properly funded future with this honey pot could be another matter, the end of job and home boredom."

The idea of living with this woman full-time had never occurred to him, but the situation with his wife was terrible. She was on his ass constantly about one thing or another, and the demands of two teen-age daughters by her first husband was making him think of any kind of escape other than a divorce he could never afford.

He considered himself living in subservient misery. He thought the Thoreau observation he'd picked up in English Lit, the one about most men leading lives of quiet desperation. It, described his situation perfectly. A buddy had recommended he try for the government job and as with most things in his life he had gone along, letting whatever unfolded carry him like a leaf in stream rather than seeking out some goals he could claim as his own. He knew he was bright enough to do better than duty as a federal cop, a judgment amplified by his wife. The small college degree could have led to something requiring more enterprise than law enforcement. The job was okay. In other circumstances, such as a different household environment, he would have been happy enough, especially when a fringe benefit like Marti Costello came along.

He had accepted the sexual bounty with no unease over his luck even though the consequences of getting caught were obvious. The situation was already dangerous. He couldn't let it make him reckless. He had no expectations beyond their next meeting, and suddenly she stunned him with her invitation. It brought him to a level of alertness Lou Robbins might have applauded in situations more appropriate to his job.

He didn't believe in luck. There were no free lunches, the cliché adage first laid on him by his career army noncom father. The other shoe might be about to drop and he had to be careful.

The lady could have her say so long as it didn't get into dangerous areas. There might be things he didn't need to know, didn't want to know.

Maybe it was cash from insurance.

He said, "Are you sure you're the beneficiary? The sole beneficiary?"

One of her quick smiles. She understood. "Oh yes, I'm sure."

It would take an idiot to misunderstand where she was coming from. If she was inheriting from an aunt Nelly or uncle Fred she would have said so. She was talking about stashed money, most likely her husband's money, possibly cash stolen from Phil Stanton, the boss Bob Costello tried to send to prison.

She hadn't inferred she was going to steal it. The lady must have had a better avenue to the loot. Something very unkosher might be hatching here.

He wanted to hear it all, but as he looked down on the lady he could sense her mind right now was clearly on something more important to her than love making. He remembered his dad's warning about free food.

She could have been a teacher but she didn't need to put the answer on a black board. She knew her husband wasn't going to stop her from taking his cash because he would be out of the picture. The little darling with the ice-blue eyes had dropped the proverbial dime on her hubby, although the call may have cost more than a dime. A lot more in this case. The lady had surely called long distance.

He reached for the room's straight-back desk chair and pulled it to the bed so they were knee to knee. The move gave him a few seconds to think about how he would handle this. When he looked into her face again they stared into each others eyes, sitting motionless for several seconds. No words spoken. She didn't look away.

Yeah. Now she knew he knew.

He was as horny as usual, but his cock had gone limp. The subject was murder, a real prick deflater. His mind was spinning like a Vegas slot.

Could the tiny brunette personally kill her husband?

Good God, maybe she wanted him to do it. Was the man hated that much, or had her boredom become desperation. Why she had suddenly seen him as a permanent partner required some explanation.

As if anticipating his questions, she looked down at her hands, now in her lap.

"I have to get away, start a new life. Living like this is driving me crazy."

Yeah, she just missed the good life, the life Bob Costello's money and connections had provided in the Big Apple area. She had a way of getting the money, but it had to include the elimination of Bob. Was she capable of doing it herself? The soft body had to have a core of steel plate if it could manage to kill a man she had shared a bed with for years. No way. She was simply going to tell someone back home where her husband was hiding out.

The full implications of her words flooded his mind like water gushing through a busted levee. However he reacted to what was coming, there was no way he was going to walk away untouched.

He could nip this in the proverbial bud, but there was no way he could save his job, either by anonymous tip or direct intervention. He could kiss goodbye to the arrangement with Marti, too. Robbins would move the suddenly unprotectable Costello to a new location, then turn the screws on the witness's wife. Maybe she wouldn't crack, but if she thought her lover was the whistle blower, she might implicate him. Shit. Goodbye to sixteen years of ass-kissing boredom and simple options in a life that had no real direction, but a retirement that could at least be comfortable.

To Ross Vincennes, Robert Costello was a New Jersey scumbag, however well-educated and employed. Shacking up with his wife had not only been a pleasure. It was as if he were exacting punishment on the crooked financial expert, deserved but not delivered because of Costello's government deal. He had made no effort to know the man. Understanding what made him tick wasn't his job. As far as he cared, Costello was just another sleaze, however brilliant in his machinations with money and computers, whose greed got him in deep shit. He should have taken his talents to Wall Street instead of joining the Stanton corporation.

Would I give a shit if his murder gave Marti a shot at some getaway money. Hell no!

He thought it wasn't all that hard to understand how Marti's mind was working. Wives of protected witnesses often wanted out. The change of location was just one of the contributing factors. Wives missed friends and family, ached for old haunts and the normal shape and focus of their lives. Mates perhaps incompatible to begin with were thrust even closer in uncomfortable exile.

The government discouraged divorces among the protected flock. It meant redoing the entire process, new identities, new and separate environments. The government also knew former wives might prove vengeful, or if found by their husband's enemies, could be forced to reveal a witness's location. Suicides, often involving alcohol, or drugs, weren't all that unusual among unhappy and desperate wives, but Ross Vincennes was certain that the woman who had as good as announced the upcoming execution of her husband would never contemplate killing him herself. Her route to amending a bad situation was betrayal.

He reached for her hands. They were usually cool and dry, but now while still cool they were moist.

"Where is all this cash, or whatever?"

She had turned her head down and took her hands away to concentrate on a button at the top of her blouse. Her head snapped up. It was as if the question was obtrusive.

"I don't know. I'm going to get the money. I'm not sure how soon, but let it go at that." Then softer and slower, "I just want to know if you'd like to get out of here with me. I'm going to leave Bob and I know you aren't happy with your own life. This could be a chance for both of us to start over. Together."

He stood up, tugging at his shirt. She raised her eyebrows, wanting his response to all this. The look was more meaningful than the one-word question.

"Well?"

He said, "Hey, baby, I'll go to the goddamn moon with you, but I won't jerk you around.

"We'd want to do it right, and we'd need a lot of money. You're sure you are going to get all this cash, but you're not sure about the where and when?"

Her hands were back in her lap, her eyes boring into his. He thought whatever he had dropped into Marti's mind was being reviewed with the concentration of an analyst over a computer printout.

She said, "Wait a sec." She stood up and maneuvered around him to the room's small desk where she left her purse He watched as she pulled a small black booklet from the bag. Turning back to him she dropped the booklet in his lap.

He read, "North Shore National Bank."

"Open it."

"Okay."

It was a disappointment. *They wouldn't get very far on this.*

He said, "Oh boy, one hundred thousand dollars."

She sat down. She saw he wasn't impressed.

"That's just a part of what I'm going to get."

Oh shit, she had accepted a down payment.

He closed his eyes for a second. He had to say it right, but on the face of it, this girl was in way over her head. Like in getting drowned.

He said, "Marti, I don't want to know anymore about this, but I think you may be in danger. Whoever gave you this money expects a service of some kind. We aren't going to talk about it, but I think you have a better chance to win the Illinois lottery than you have of collecting the rest of your money."

She exploded, uncomprehending. "You're kidding. What do you mean?"

He shook his head. "Look. Whoever promised you the money probably doesn't have it right now. They have to get it from somewhere—or someone. Isn't that right?"

A delayed nod, face flushed. She was breathing in quick short takes.

"He said, "Okay. You expect it to be turned over for something you can give in return?"

She looked at him in a way that reminded him of himself in fifth grade, when he didn't have the answer to a grim teacher's question. She took a stab at it.

"Negotiation. There'll be negotiations."

Negotiations, huh? She had never looked as intense to him, nor as vulnerable, with a portion of her lower lip held by her beautiful teeth. He had almost laughed.

Who told her that shit? Not one of the old neighborhood wise guys back home? Those assholes didn't negotiate. They broke knee caps. Even to con her they wouldn't use a word like negotiation, but someone with some education might have. Whoever it was, the negotiations still might include a lighter held under Bob Costello's balls.

"Marti, look. They know where you are, don't they? They have to if you are going to get the rest of the money."

"Yes."

"Okay, then please listen. I don't know about our future together. My marriage is crap and running away with you would be like going to heaven, but we'd still be looking over our shoulders wherever we'd go. I've seen a lot of that in the program. You never really feel safe. You never are safe."

You never are safe."

He shook his head. *This was going to hurt. In a way it was like saying goodbye to someone with whom you never wanted to use the word.*

"I want you to try to call off this deal, and I want you to get your hundred thou out of that bank and get the hell out of Chicago."

She stared at him, then shook her head. Unbelieving.

He said. "I hope it's not to late to run because I think you've put trust in someone who will double cross you for sure. And possibly do you serious harm. Like kill you. There is no way in the world that money is going to be negotiated short of torture, stuff you don't want to think about—and even if you showed me a signed contract, I don't see why the ultimate holder of the money would honor any deal to give you any more of it. They'd probably force you to give back the down payment. Then they wouldn't need you anymore. Understand?" She flinched at the words, "down payment." The fingers of her right hand were squeezing the fingers of the left, something Vincennes had never seen before. She stared into his face, but there was no focus in it. She might have been looking through him at the wall. She bounced to her feet, head down, brushing at some creases in her skirt.

"Ross, I'm sorry, but there's something I forgot to take care of. Now. I have to go."

He had no intention of holding her, learning more than he wanted to know. He had told her what she needed to know. She wasn't stupid. Far from it, but she was moving too fast.

She had to sort out her thoughts. Decide what to do now. She had clearly had enough of him and his pessimism. Words of doom would be more like it.

He remembered saying, "Sure, sweetie. I'll call you tomorrow."

She had scooped her purse and was gone. No kiss. Not even a wave. He breathed what was left of her perfume. *God, he hadn't realized how much he wanted her.*

3

Lou Robbins was a career federal lawman. At fifty-five, and after thirty years service he longed for retirement and an end to many of the chores he hated. Baby sitting social misfits who had ratted on other undesirables topped his list.

He had summoned Vincennes to meet him at a Denny's restaurant on Milwaukee road late in the evening of the basement shooting and Costello's disappearance. There wasn't another customer in the place.

Vincennes had left the hospital while the woman officially known as Karen Velotti was still in surgery. Per his orders from Robbins, he was to be there when Velotti woke up.

He said, "If she wakes up, Lou. I never thought a human being could lose so much blood and live. I got to a head nurse, but she would only say Velotti was still in surgery. I'll get back there as soon as I get a few hours sleep.".

Over the rim of his coffee cup, Robbins stared unblinking into his agent's face. Vincennes recognized the look. Robbins's, whose career including running alongside presidential cars in motorcades, and years of risky foreign service, wanted answers to a nasty situation. His face was unlined, his hair still dark brown, and he exuded a take-charge strength in the mold of the old movie star, Spencer Tracy. With his retirement coming up in a few months, Lou Robbins didn't want to leave with this kind of unfinished business. He was still sharp mentally, and in great physical shape, but he wanted to shift his attention to golf, travel, and his grandkids. He needed assurance his deputy would maintain the vigil over Mrs. Velotti-Costello while spearheading the search for her missing husband.

Vincennes tried to appear sure of himself. He told Robbins, "I'll be there if and when she regains consciousness and can talk."

He would get there, all right. He had to be sure she doesn't blab about their affair. Who knows what she might say in a semi-conscious state after several hours of surgery.

He said, "What I still can't figure out is why Costello didn't call us and wait for us to take over immediately after the shooting. He knocks the shooter blotto and could have held him for us."

Robbins nodded. "Yeah, the shooter most likely sent by someone who wants the former Robert Costello dead. This might be Costello's old boss, Phillip Stanton. But Costello's wife becomes the victim. Why shoot her?"

Both men sipped their coffee. Thinking it out. Beginning with how several months before, Stanton, the Chairman and CEO of Newark, New York's Stanton Corporation, had been tried but found not guilty for corporate income tax evasion.

Robbins said, "The jury chose not to believe Costello's testimony, but the government still made good on its promise of protected witness status. They probably felt Costello had his hand in the till, too, but it would be hard to prove. They wanted the big fish anyway, and were sure Costello would take them there. They would have looked ridiculous going after Costello after using him to try Stanton.

"You were in the basement. Said she looked dead. Costello probably thought so, too, and got out. Why wait around for a possible back-up shooter to pop him? Wherever he is, he has to be wondering if it was his wife who gave him up. And if she took the bullet meant for him.

"I think he has some of Stanton's money stashed. If it's in Chicago, we and the cops have a shot at rounding him up."

Vincennes shook his head. "He didn't bring much money into Chicago. I watched them both unpack in the bungalow. Any cash they had was in their wallets."

"Right. But it still has to be cash. Anything else would be difficult to unload. Costello testified that Stanton wanted the skimmed money kept in safety deposit boxes for easy access. The government found more than three million dollars in them, their basis for the charge of undeclared income. Stanton said that was a lie, that he knew nothing about any boxes. He said Costello gave him reports on sales and anticipated earnings almost daily and that he presumed his trusted financial officer deposited the cash routinely. If he was in on the scheme, he probably didn't want to be seen anywhere near such hiding places. He surely knew how much Costello took to the boxes but he didn't learn how much his trusted employee may have lifted for himself until the government reported its audit.

"We know Costello is a computer nerd, ran the entire Stanton financial operation on Windows software. The only striking anomaly noted by the government inspection team after Stanton's arrest, and it was noted in particular by the businessman's defense, was that Robert Costello handled everything related to company money, from the cash deliveries by fast food and other cash-oriented subs to money orders. I think Costello, at Stanton's direction, rigged it so that only he and his boss knew the day-to-day, week-to-week, income. And Costello handled all income from the company's rapid expansion from corporate purchases of stocks, bonds, real estate and whatever else he negotiated. He also allocated funds for payroll, capital and office expense, state and federal taxes, the works. Assistants did all the employee compensation stuff, health insurance, social security, quarterly and annual reports. He just inserted the phony numbers.

"Costello couldn't have picked the pot piecemeal. He couldn't take the chance that Stanton might make a personal check up on the boxes. He must have pulled off his raid just before he dropped in on the FBI. When the fed troops charged in to confiscate Costello's computer, the hard drive showed the correct relationship between company income and what was reported to the IRS. The adjusted numbers, the phony ones showing what Costello left in the boxes to incriminate his boss, were only on the CDs Costello gave the government. It's the money Costello didn't report is what we're talking about."

Ross didn't interrupt. His boss was on a roll and it was new stuff he hadn't heard.

Robbins said, "My guess is that Costello got away with a lot of money, hence a good motive for tracking the man down. Maybe Mrs. Costello gave him up, but why was she shot?"

Robbins's smile was tight. "There's no way Costello had time to convert the cash to anything else negotiable. Any bank asked to turn a big chunk of cash into any other instrument, would have turned him in as soon as he made the news, and the basement shooting made the news big."

"Maybe he turned it over to someone."

"Yeah? But it doesn't figure. From all reports this guy was a loner, no record of anything anti-social, no gambling or fooling around. He did his work and went home. He had no close friends. Parents dead. No relatives. The feds would have been all over anyone close to him."

Ross butted in, "How about all those New York and Jersey bank contacts?"

"Nope. The government attorneys wrung those people out. They all said they hardly ever saw the man. Clerks took him to the vaults, did their bit with the bank's keys, and bowed out. They barely saw him leave most of the time. As I say he's a loner. The money is buried somewhere. Wherever he is now, the money is damn close."

Ross thought about it. Costello testified that his job was not only to manage assets of the Stanton Corporation, but to keep as much of the income from a wide range of enterprises as free as possible from incorrect taxation by state and federal governments. In that sense Costello's function was comparable to that of any legitimate corporate financial executive.

But why did Costello turn his boss in and end his life as Robert Costello? Why didn't he simply steal all the stashed cash and fly?

Robbins said, "Remember, the government's charge was that Stanton contrived to defraud on behalf of his corporation. This wasn't about his personal tax which apparently wasn't challenged. The government built its case on Costello and Stanton working together. Costello's testimony was supposed to be enough to put Stanton in jail, but it wasn't good enough. The government must have screwed up badly for Stanton to win that verdict. They just couldn't prove their case. The jury didn't believe their only witness who looked much more like a criminal than his boss. Stanton's attorneys threw it back in our government's face. In effect, they said, 'Your key witness is the only crook in this courtroom.' The implication worked.

"For reasons of his own Costello wanted his boss to go to jail. The jury couldn't believe that bright, immaculate, handsome Phillip Stanton was a crook. Hell, he was only recently honored for his business skills and contributions to the community by his local Chamber of Commerce. His dozen or so affiliate businesses were all profitable. Why would he connive to steal even more? Sure, he probably had dreams of even more wealth, but he was a good businessman. He didn't have to steal it.

"And that's all the government had. The Attorney General's office checked Stanton out years before when he allegedly made some illegal political contributions. The check went back at least two generations. He was born Phillip Stanton but there is a Morelli in the mix and before that a small-time hood named Guido Bonaventura. It all led nowhere. There was no basis for RICO charges. Stanton had no sheet loaded with kid malfeasance, and there were no other links to anti-social activity."

"Morelli, huh?"

"Yeah, but the government's case would have been thrown out if they'd even implied any mob background. All of Guido Bonaventura's kin were squeaky clean. The family businesses were all legitimate, all of them successful. Stanton inherited well, then married into more money. He and his wife have a couple of children, live in an unostentatious home in Upper Montclair. He's an on-record contributor to both political parties. His businesses are to all appearances legitimate in every detail. They include none of the old and typical covers such as olive oil importing or other mob bullshit.

"As for communication between Costello and his boss, there was nothing on paper, no office memos or whatever. Stanton said Costello insisted that it was the best way to run the business. The government got mouse trapped on that one. The jury believed Stanton."

"Wow!"

"Yeah, wow. I was impressed, too, that a man like Costello could manage such an operation virtually by himself. He embarrassed a top-five auditing firm, too. They signed off on all the financial reports; you know, that they applied accepted procedures in the Stanton audit and found it fairly presented. The fact is the government miscalculated when they tried to bring Phil Stanton down. His background is spotless, and even if there was a wise guy in the picture several generations ago, the family has covered it beautifully. Phillip Stanton could be a front for the eventual laundering of mob money, but I don't see how."

Vincennes said, "Costello must think there's a connection. He was scared enough to insist on joining our program as part of the deal."

"Sure, Costello may have picked up something that made him think his boss had some criminal background. If so, Costello was sure his defection was a death sentence. Unless someone dropped the so-called dime, maybe Mrs. Costello, Stanton's chances for catching up with his former bookkeeper were about as good as a top payoff in a trifecta. Bob Costello is no dummy. He may have saved his life by making his deal for witness protection if his evidence took Phil Stanton to trial. The government lost the case, but they had to make good on their part of the deal; that is, if they ever expect to get any more snitches."

4

Lou Robbins had it right. Phil Stanton was the end product of an extraordinary plan by his great grandfather, Guido Bonavantura. The plan, expressed carefully on a single piece of paper, was that the $100,000 amassed during Guido's service as bookkeeper-banker for a mob of pre and post World War I hoodlums, would be invested in a manner he had prescribed, and it would ultimately help a son, grandson, or great grandson enter the mainstream of American industry, business, or finance. Guido's document, passed down through the generations, insisted that the ultimate custodian of the family wealth must have an American-sounding name.

Thus it was that the ultimate heir, Guido's great grandson, christened Phillip Stanton, was nearing the status Guido had envisioned. The handsome young man, at just thirty-one years old, was ambitious, resourceful, and adequately educated for the role he would play. Perhaps also qualifying him to head an enterprise devoted to achieving financial profit was a trait his great grandfather might not have approved. It was raw greed.

Phil Stanton had a love for money that paralleled his love for pretty women. He told his parents, friends, and associates, "It's a large black bottom line, I want. Anything I do will make money. Tons of it."

The future scion of wealth had attended one of New England's best prep schools, and then Penn State university where he earned near excellent grades in business management. He also earned three letters in wrestling, and would have tried out for football but his father Renzo, a former athlete and student of the game, begged him not to volunteer.

"You're too small at one-ninety-five to play anywhere in the line, even tight end, and you're too slow for running back and not big enough for line backer."

Rather than have coaches confirm his father's assessment, Phillip found wrestling an ideal outlet for his boundless energy and strength, and when he wasn't flinging himself and opponents around mats, he dated coeds or any other female who showed positive reaction to his dark good looks and penchant to entertain lavishly. An appetite for beautiful women would accompany him into his post-college life.

Upon his graduation he was treated to a two-month vacation in Europe during which a French surgeon converted a nose that would have been unremarkable in Palermo into a shape that would help its owner feel completely at ease in any WASP-dominated board room. Upon his return he was made vice president of the laundry and cleaning business begun many years before by his grandfather Joseph Bologna. Joseph died in WW II, but his widow, Marcella, had enriched the family's fortune by leading the business to success with major hotel and large restaurant accounts. Helping her to this pinnacle was an alliance with a figure she at first considered a menace, but with whom she had ultimately fallen in love.

Marcella had not remarried, partly because no acceptable suitors presented themselves, but also because she enjoyed her role as a business woman. There was only a daughter, Maria, to care for, so she was able to devote most of her time to the expanding the enterprise left by Joseph. She may have been the only woman in a similar role in the city, and she took pride in the fact.

She was relaxing at her desk on a warm and bright June afternoon, tired but satisfied with the day's effort, when secretary-bookkeeper Margaret Walsh opened the door apparently to announce a visitor. Permitting no opportunity for the formality, a tall man in an ill-fitting black suit brushed past Margaret and without preamble, and without removing his ugly black hat, loomed like a threatening cloud over Marcella's desk.

"You run this business. You gotta pay protection."

The visit was not unexpected. Marcella's mother-in-law, Anna, had told her to expect such an intrusion. She had relayed Guido's instructions for dealing with extortion attempts.

"You must remain calm," Anna told her, "but you must insist that you negotiate only with the boss. Tell the hoodlum he is dealing with a business that might need protection for its property and employees, but that you will hire twenty-four hour security for yourself and the business unless you can negotiate a deal with the top man."

Anna said the hood might bluster at the disrespect shown him, but he would relay the message. "If he gets nasty show him the gun Joseph left in the desk drawer."

Marcella was glad it hadn't been necessary. The next afternoon she was again visited, but by quite a different person. This one permitted himself to be announced. Margaret was obviously impressed as she said, "A mister Angelo Brancatto is asking to see you."

The man Margaret stepped aside for was obviously Italian-American, and although Marcella instinctively guessed his mission, his smile could well have been that of a brother she hadn't seen for months but who had hoped to surprise her. Marcella had no brother, but the dazzling smile left her almost defenseless. Almost. She returned the smile, but it was well under control. She only wished she had worn a better dress.

Brancatto's attire was appropriate for a warm early summer afternoon. His perfect fitting linen suit of light gray was complemented by a dark blue tie and white shirt. She couldn't see his shoes but guessed they would be spotless and shined whatever the style. He carried a light-colored fedora. His clean-shaven face was topped by a well-cared-for head of ink-black hair.

He stood before her for a few seconds, then gestured towards the only chair in the office. He said, "May I? Sit?"

"Of course."

The smile was gone, but the look was still engaging, as if he was about to discuss the beginnings of a very nice summer.

He said, "Luigi, that pig of a man who accosted you yesterday, wisely relayed your message. Not to me." He raised his hands in denial of any connection with the threatening visitor.

"I am not in charge of such," he hesitated, "matters, but he said you used the word, 'negotiations.' I am empowered to discuss some of the problems a business faces in this community. How a business person can free themselves to devote his-or her," a brief smile, but not as overpowering as the display of teeth and good fellowship as he entered the office, "time to affairs of business without interruptions from such problems as labor strife, neighborhood hoodlumism, or other negative factors."

Marcella was stunned. This impeccably dressed, handsome man, was using carefully correct language to discuss the rape of her business as if it was plans for a vacation. She forced herself to stay calm,

She said, "How much, Mr. Brancatto? How much is it going to cost for me to continue my business without interruption or harm to my employees. Or me?"

Consternation replaced the partial smile.

"Mrs. Bologna, let me say that it is my, our, desire that your business prosper. In fact, we are in position to help your business expand."

When he described some specific ideas, Marcella was skeptical, but also surprised.

She and her single salesman, Joey Fontino, had already made fruitless proposals to some of the area's larger prospective customers including hotels and restaurants. Brancatto talked as if the deals were fait accompli.

He went away with the promise to call again. He phoned the next day, and the day after that. In the later call he said he had "wonderful news." She agreed to dinner at one of the better local restaurants, and the news was her company now had the laundry and cleaning business for two of Manhattan's major hotels. It would be supplied for one-third of the net profits from that business. Only she, Margaret Walsh, and Brancatto knew of the arrangement, which would not be covered in the company's accounting books.

"And this is just the beginning," he promised.

She was in his bed, or rather a bed in one of the area's better hotels, within the month.

She guessed he was married, which was easily confirmed. He wore a wedding ring, but said nothing about a wife and family. She decided she would never press him to marry her. If it happened, it happened, but it never did. She was satisfied when he said, "I loved you from first sight. I had no idea how I would get that hotel business, but believe me I got creative very quickly after our first meeting."

She never saw Luigi again, nor any other people Angelo only once referred to as "family."

She never pressed him for his obvious involvement in the "protection" racket, but she did overhear a phone call in which he used the euphemism "operational safety."

She never learned of the specifics of his early salesmanship in the hotel and other business he brought in. She had his assurance her company and her employees were safe and there were no costly shut downs over labor contracts. She noted that other area hotels and enterprise comparable to hers were remarkably free of gangland interruptions.

She had done well in maintaining and improving upon Joseph's early efforts. Her contribution to the growing wealth of Bonaventura's descendants was assured. She had done what she needed to do to keep Guido's dream alive. She had been lonely, but had been happy in her secret love.

Daughter Maria was aware of the occasional presence of Angelo Brancatto, and had once presumed to say, "Mamma, why don't you get married again?" Marcella turned the suggestion away. "It's much more important we find a good husband for you, Maria."

She was able to see Maria married, to Renzo Morreli, but breast cancer ended Marcella's life when she was in her late forties. Angelo was not with her in her final agonies. He called her at the hospital, and his final words of love ended with a sentence only she could understand. He said, "The 'protection' is forever.".

5

When Marcella turned the business over to Maria and her husband, Renzo, she followed Guido's counsel to have them adopt an American name. They chose Stanton. The company was then incorporated in the new name, with the family holding all of the stock except for a portion allotted a blind trust simply named "Brando, Inc." Early in the marriage Renzo urged Maria to try to learn the basis for the monthly transfer of a significant share of their company's earnings, but she said, "Absolutely not.

"Somewhere in our family's past, a huge favor was given my mother, It was the promise, a vow really, that our family was under protection by someone. 'Forever,' mother said. I don't know who this is, we may never know, but Marcella had a partnership with someone. The trust was established when our business was small, but its huge growth over the years was due to that unknown help.

"I was at her bedside in those last hours. There was a phone call. She rallied as if she knew who it was. I propped the receiver against her ear. She waved me away from the bed but I heard her whisper, 'My love.'

"That's all she said, but she smiled as she listened. Then, when she let me take the receiver she said, 'You and all of your family will be safe. Forever' And she closed her eyes and died."

Maria and Renzo had only one child, a son Phillip. They hoped he would show the aptitude and desire to take over the business. They needn't have been concerned. It took the confident and ambitious young man only eighteen months after his graduation from college to achieve, in Renzo's eyes, a thorough grounding in the basics of the business. He was named president at barely twenty-three years old. Phillip had, per the durable lyric, the world on a string, and in the next few years he yanked the leash hard and often. Putting to work what he had learned in Penn State business courses, and with some shrewd counsel from Renzo, Phillip saw a string of fast-food restaurants assimilated into the corporate venture. Then came an association of automobile service stations, a printing company, and several computerized car washes. Phillip saw doubling the company's size within five years an easy and certain goal.

Observing the family policy of avoiding anything tainted by mob involvement, he personally interviewed anyone with an Italian name. One of these was Certified Public Accountant Robert Costello. Costello, more than ten years older than Phillip, had applied for the newly created job of Vice President and Chief Financial Officer, shortly after his mid-career addition of a master's degree in business at Columbia. Costello had handled general auditing jobs for a number of clients nation-wide. A placement counselor at Columbia told him a rapidly expanding corporation headquartered in Newark was looking for a financial officer. Costello, who lived with his ailing mother, Estella, in nearby Kearny, was looking for something steady and permanent. He wanted to be near his mother full time, and he also thought the job would offer some stability to his life, including getting married.

He logged onto the internet and checked out the Stanton Corp., learning that the business was headed by Phillip Stanton as Chairman and Chief Executive officer. A Lucia Stanton was listed as Secretary-Treasurer. No other company officers were listed.

Costello told his mother, "This could work out. I'm tired of batting around the U.S. This company is small but owns a nice stable of businesses. The job should be easy enough to handle, and it will bring me home every night."

He updated his resume, addressed a carefully edited copy to Phillip Stanton and sent it to Newark by messenger.

Phillip personally reviewed the resume which described a job history that appeared to cover everything the Stanton Corporation might need in a financial officer. Noting the Italian name he put Costello's application at the top of the stack.

Several days later he smiled over his desk at the overweight, balding Costello.

"So you're hip to all the new methods of handling money?"

"Pretty much. Things are changing all the time, but I try to keep up to date. From what I've learned your corporation is expanding pretty fast.

I think I can help you keep your costs in line, and help with taxes and the like."

"Taxes. We've been doing them with outside help."

"I think I can help save money in that area, keeping the accounting inside. On both corporation and executive income. Sometimes rapidly expanding companies can get behind and then it can cost considerably more playing catch up."

"You mean the IRS can get nasty."

Costello's response to Phillip's smile was cautious. "Well, the IRS can be dealt with, but they can still get rough if they think the rules are being bent."

Phillip asked more questions, some already answered in the resume but he wanted to hear Costello talk about his experience. Was Costello married? No. Family in area? An elderly mother. Where did he grow up and school? Costello listed it all, from Mt. Carmel grade and high school onwards.

"How about computerization? Can you do everything a modern business requires?"

Costello's smile was more open. Phillip thought the man seemed to be breathing a little easier.

"Yes. I'm computer literate, as they say. Particularly in matters related to business and finance. I've been into it for years. I can upgrade your system, if needed. Most of them need constant attention. Things are changing so rapidly."

Phillip sent Costello away with a friendly smile and a handshake. The man could be just what he wanted. Someone experienced, but not too old. Personnel could check out the personal references. The subsequent report showed Costello had done a ton of accounting work before he returned to Columbia. What he picked up in biz school plus the CPA should be helpful for Stanton Corporation's future.

Phillip had some well thought out ideas on the exact role Costello would play. Advanced computerization was helping companies trim accounting staffs. If Costello had the knowledge he bragged about, the man could make a good chunk of his salary from the jobs that could be cut.

Phillip was sure he had sized the man up correctly. The check by Personnel had convinced him the man had no mob background, but Costello might be led to think his boss had. That fear could be the basis for enlisting Costello's help in achieving what he had wanted since joining the company.

He wanted to rig the books.

It was ridiculous paying out all that money to the IRS. Outside financial counsel had helped in getting the best possible tax interpretations in connection with acquiring new subs, but the corporation was making money by the ton and Stanton grieved over every dollar earmarked for government coffers.

We aren't keeping nearly enough of it. There has to be ways to bury some of that cash.

He'd have to be careful. The family would have nothing to do with any funny stuff. Maybe this guy Costello would help, and the first step would be to get him hired. He arranged to have Costello return for another interview which he began as informally as the first.

"Costello, I liked your resume and I think we covered just about everything in our first interview. Now, I have my ideas about what I want in a financial officer. If it fits what you can do well, maybe we can get together. Sound okay?"

Costello showed the cautious smile. "Sure."

"Okay. Let me tell you first what I don't want. It's an executive in a twenty-five by twenty-five foot office behind a glass desk you can see through because there are no papers on it. Sure, you'd be in charge of the usual activities of a financial officer, but what I really need is a hands-on guy who would be accountable for every dollar that comes in and goes out of this business. At the close of each and every business day, I want to know the bottom line within a couple of bucks."

Phillip looked into Costello's eyes to see if they revealed any signs of doubt. So far, the man's face was a blank. Philip liked the idea the man was thinking it out, not just jerking out a quick yes, that he could do the job. Then Costello's head bobbed slightly.

Phillip had more. "Okay. I want a guy who has the energy and drive to personally maintain spreadsheets with all the numbers in place a couple hours after we close shop every working day. Further, I want a boss who can replace with his own skill and effort three of the people we now have working in our accounting department. If you can do that I'll pay you the total of their salaries plus another fifty thousand a year, plus health and the other goodies. There's no profit share yet, but I personally pay a year-end bonus. You would also have the assignment of amending our pension plan which I think is crap. It costs the company too much money."

Costello was nodding slowly as he stared straight into Phillip's eyes. Phillip couldn't tell whether the head movement bob was a sign of approval or something to do with the candidate's nervous system.

"Well?"

Costello raised a hand to rub his chin. He was looking at the figurine of a goddess in Steuben glass Phillips kept on his desk as a paper weight.

He said: "I can do all that, and replace the three accountants." Then he looked back into Phillips face, not quite into his eyes. "But someone else will have to fire them."

Phillip wanted to smile, but he just stared back at the applicant.

Great. The man's a candy ass. He waited a few seconds. Let the guy sweat.

He said, "Okay. Deal. When can you start?"

Costello left Stanton to sign on as a new employee and Phillip allowed himself a few moments of self-congratulation. He was sure he had what he wanted, a very well-qualified financial man who didn't look too strong in the guts department. He would know more about Robert Costello in a couple of weeks. If the man was as malleable as he appeared, he would be an ideal partner to help him hustle the U.S. government out of a lot of money.

7

Estrella had talked with her son about the early days, including the visits by the man in the black hat who came every Friday to take an envelope from Peter.

She sighed, "They didn't take so much, but it was a burden. Our grandparents left Sicily to change their lives, but some things didn't change. Your father wasn't well, but there was no way to avoid it. They said they would help us if Peter couldn't continue working, but when they saw how useful you had become, and an only child, they said we had to pay."

To the kids at school who pretended knowledge they didn't have, it was also "they"—never any names.

Estrella said, "They did say they would help if you would do their bookkeeping, but I told them you would never do that. Now, I can live out my life happy that you will never have to work for those wretches, or give them a dime. You have worked so hard and there will be enough money for you to go to college, then meet a nice girl from a good family and have a family of your own."

A family for Bob Costello appeared unlikely. He had never had a date throughout high school and college years. He had admired several girls, but had accepted his apparent lack of attraction to women philosophically. He had almost no social contact with men, either, but as his accounting business expanded there were clients, some of them women with whom he shared meals. But it was all business. He entertained himself with solitary dining at good restaurants in New York and in many of the nation's large cities. Whether at home or traveling he enjoyed sports events, especially basketball. He also read broadly, but favored crime fiction. He also read anything related to his professional needs.

He entertained clients, and their wives, or husbands, but he was always unaccompanied. It occurred to him he might be thought queer, but he shrugged that off. It didn't concern him that the possible misperception may have thwarted suggestions by business contacts that female company might be found for him.

He bought and used an exercycle, but still added weight. He didn't think he had the time for an exercise regimen at an athletic club. He was Catholic but church and religion laid little claim on his life. He had to admit he hadn't much to confess, unless making an increasingly good living was a sin. There were no sexual peccadillos to report. He was celibate. He needn't admit to a voracious greed for wealth, either. He dutifully sent generous checks to a number of charities, and his church.

Until his mother's death he had managed his lonely life very well, but in the weeks following her death, he felt a growing unease with his totally self-centered existence. It was in a cab after a concert in San Francisco that his preoccupation with what he now perceived as a serious problem was abruptly interrupted by his driver.

"Hey buddy. You wanna get laid."

Several thoughts flooded Bob's mind, including the idea he was being set up for a burglary, and that he probably should try to get out of the cab and report the driver. He glanced at the driver's ident card fastened to the back seat. It was for a Theodore Taliaferro, forty-three years old. It was too dark to get much of an impression of the driver's looks from the small photo, or from a glimpse of his profile.

The driver said, "You're not a cop. Right?"

"No, I'm not a cop."

"And I'll bet you're all alone in this great city. Right. Probably a businessman?"

Bob's silence was taken as a yes.

"Okay, so what's the harm? I can take you to a beautiful place for an experience like you've never had before. It's no whore house. You'll be served any kind of drink you want while you sit around and chat with the hostess and her friends, all fully dressed ladies. There'll be other guys there, too. If and when you get the itch, and it's not at all mandatory—I love that word—you select one of the ladies and adjourn to your own private room. It will cost you only four hundred bucks, and you'll be treated like a prince. If you don't like what you see—and I can't believe you won't see something nice—you pay only for your drinks, by credit card if you like. They'll call me and I'll take you wherever you want to go."

Bob could have interrupted the voluble cabby's spiel, but he let the man ramble. Usually extremely cautious about contact with strangers, and rarely speculative, Bob was always a good listener. Estrella had said, "Listeners make more money unless they are singers or actors." He had already concluded Theodore Taliaferro was probably not a full-time cab driver, but if he was a pimp he was at least entertaining. Somehow, at this time, in this place, in a city noted for inspiring romance, he felt a surge of interest in the cabby's proposal. He had never done anything really daring. He could always back out.

"Okay, I'm game."

The cabby roared, "I knew I had my man. You looked ripe for some adventure in the great city of San Francisco. Hang on. We're going over the bridge."

Bob still had reservations. *God, what if I find one of my clients is in the place!* His concerns were drowned out by several more minutes of chatter from the most unusual cab driver he had ridden behind. The man was a huge improvement over the mostly illiterates back home.

And *what a salesman. I can't believe I would be doing this under any other circumstance.*

Bob had rented cars and crossed the Golden Gate bridge before. He saw they were in Sausalito before they began winding their way upward via an ill-lighted roadway.

"You'll love the view from up here, too. Only house within a hundred yards. One of my fares dubbed it, 'Cloud Nine.' That guy was in a cloud I'll tell you. I poured him out of the cab, but he was delivered to mommy safe and sound. Here we are."

The building was huge, three stories of red brick. Wide white columns supported a porte cochere that would have accommodated a Greyhound bus. Door lamps alongside the large white door threw out a welcome glare. As he let himself out of the cab Bob could hear music from the interior.

He extracted his wallet, ready to pay what might have been a hefty fare.

"Hold it for now, pal. You're off the meter until I pick you up. I'll be nearby. You have fun now." And he was gone.

Bob's unease was something akin to fear as he reached for an ornate door knocker, but the huge portal swung open before his finger made contact. Standing before him was a matronly figure, her short blond hair attractively coifed. She might have been in her late forties. Bob thought the simple black sheath dress looked well-fitted, and expensive.

She smiled and said, "Good evening," and Bob thought it was a genuine sound of welcome. "Come on in. I'm Dorothy. Would you care to tell me your name?"

It was like being welcomed into a new neighbor's cocktail party. Bob heard himself saying, "Sure. I'm Bob."

He never could recall all the words he either heard or said over the next few minutes, especially the rest of Dorothy's greetings. He was ushered into a large softly lighted living room, complete with a flaming log in the fireplace. A party appeared well underway. There were three males in the room along with several strikingly good looking and well-dressed young women. Bob guessed other guests were in adjoining rooms from the murmur of voices through a hallway. The men were dressed very much as he, in light woolen suits for the cool October evening. One of the men was playing a show tune on a grand piano in the corner of the room, a pair of young women at his side. Two other women Bob judged to be in their twenties, or early thirties, were perched on the arms of lounge chairs in which the other men were seated. Everywhere the chatter was amiable, sprinkled with controlled laughter. The sub hostesses were dressed in cocktail garb, mostly black, as if at a party in Manhattan or on Nob Hill. Silken legs gleamed but necklines appeared under restraint. Dorothy made no attempt at introductions to the group at large. Almost at once two more women, a blond and a brunette, were at his side. Dorothy smiled and disappeared "Hi. I'm Bonnie," said the blond with a smile Bob thought showed too much gum. The brunette offered no smile but reached out her hand. The shake was brief, but Bob thought it conveyed sincerity, much as if it was a greeting to a new business client. He thought her eyes were blue under brows that enhanced their large size.

"I'm Frankie."

Bob remembered an old tune. He said, "Frankie and Bonnie. Are you sweethearts?"

The girls eyes went wide. Bob almost blushed at the inference of his joke attempt. They were too young to remember, "Frankie and Johnny," much less its lyrics. Then Bonnie giggled and Frankie smiled. Slowly, not a grin.

She said, "We certainly are, but not for each other."

Bonnie giggled again and asked what they could call him. He said, "Bob would be fine."

He wondered if it would be converted to the childhood, Bobby, but Frankie said,

"What kind of drink would you like, Bob?" Her cultured voice, calm, in no way obsequious, was somehow relaxing. She was paid to put customers at ease, he decided, but could this alluring creature be a prostitute? Not that he had ever met one. He remembered a client who described a call girl he had employed as having "a business degree that went with legs all the way to her ass," but Robert had only seen obvious "hookers," glimpsed through the windows of cabs or rental cars.

The cabbie hadn't prepared him for this, and he wondered if he had been set up for some kind of con, with the investment portfolio guys at the piano waiting for the signal to move in.

He was completely qualified to ward off any kind of pitch, but how did the cabbie spot him for a someone who had influence in money decisions? He would go along with these preliminaries, but there would be no intimacies offered; that is, unless he was confirmed as a viable prospective investor, or whatever.

They were waiting patiently for his answer about a drink.

Wake up dummy. He said, "A cognac would be nice."

He felt moisture on his brow and knew it would be in his eyes if he didn't deal with it. He tugged a handkerchief from a pocket, but his drink was delivered before he could touch it to his forehead. He stuffed the cloth in his sleeve and took the tumbler from a tray delivered by a large black man in a tuxedo. He nodded thanks, then Frankie touched his elbow and led him to a comfortable sofa. The women sat at his flanks. He gave Frankie a grateful look and sipped his drink.

Frankie, who he thought might be the older of the two, in her mid thirties, asked "Is it to your liking?"

"It's excellent, but won't you join me?"

"I suppose I can. I'll have what you're having."

Rising quickly, Bonnie said, "I'll order," and the server was quickly at their side with the drink, but Bonnie didn't return.

Frankie had risen slightly to accept the glass. When she returned to her seated position, her thigh just touched Bob's side.

Bob was having trouble retaining his composure. Where was this was going? The creature gently pressed against him appeared to genuinely like him, and while this seemed improbable in light of his life experience, he was not going to interrupt whatever scenario was unfolding. If this was some kind of scam it was an elaborate one and he might as well enjoy the company of this creature as long as possible. He carefully sipped his drink, using both hands to keep the glass from shaking. Frankie would need to make the next move. He had never invited a woman to his bed, any bed. He hadn't the slightest idea of the correct approach. As it was done here—or anywhere.

Such floundering was spared him. After a series of exchanges about the weather and current events—nothing remotely personal, not even his business interests, Bob, with the aid of a second cognac, felt more and more relaxed. Then Frankie, with a smile that might have accompanied a suggestion she take his arm to dinner said, "Bob, would you like to be more comfortable? I mean, we can talk as long as you like, but we could have more privacy, too."

Bob was sure some red must be bursting through his genetically tinted skin. He tried to remain calm. He said, "That would be nice."

She said, "All right, Bob. I'm going to leave you. Take your time with your drink, then walk up the stairs you may have noted near our front door. I'll meet you up there."

Before he could stand she rose swiftly and was gone, leaving a delicate scent that Bob sniffed, then sucked in a lungful.

He finished the drink with what he hoped wasn't undue haste. He stood up and found an end table for his glass. He glanced across the room at the group around the piano. No one gave him a look. He pulled the handkerchief from his sleeve, gave his brow a pat, and tried to walk as gracefully as possible to the stairway.

He was met by a tiny tastefully-uniformed maid on the second floor landing.

She said, "I am Conchita. Follow me, please."

A few feet down the hall that seemed to have a dozen doors, the young Latin woman taped lightly on one of them.

"Come in," said a voice Bob recognized with a lurch in his chest. Conchita disappeared much as Dorothy and Bonnie had. Bob moved into a room and stood in awe just inside the door. He was in a giant, lavishly decorated bedroom. It made him think of some of the sleeping chambers and boudoirs he had seen in the reruns of old-time black and white movies, the ones with Carole Lombard and other stars of the 40s. This room was in full color, indirect lighting with flowers at bedside, and Frankie was as glamorous as any film star in his memory. Her white silk negligee trimmed in red topped by her pale and serene face left Bob numb. He stood frozen until she stepped forward and kissed him lightly on the lips. Then she led him to her bed.

For the next hour Bob had more attention paid to his sexual needs than he had experienced during his first forty years. Over-anxious, he was rescued from overwhelming embarrassment by Frankie's understanding and skill. Under her murmured guidance he made a recovery that left him both proud of himself and in wonderment. Had he known of places such as this he would have been an active client years before. Gossip around dinner tables had led him to believe whores were out the door as soon as they could arouse an ejaculation.

He lay elated and exhausted in the huge bed. She said, "Was it what you expected, Bob?"

He tried to hedge his response.

"Well, I was assured it was going to be a real treat."

"But you haven't been to such a place before? I mean even one with much fewer basic attributes? As a matter of fact, this was your first visit to any such place. Am I right?"

Bob felt like kissing the lady again. He did so, then said, "Yes, you're right."

She said, "I'll tell you something. Before you walked in the door, Dorothy knew you were a nice person, and that it was probably a first for you."

How did they do this? Oh yeah, the cabbie and radio.

"Yes? Really?"

"That's right. And Dorothy gave me the assignment. You'll remember Bonnie and I were all over you the moment you entered the living room. As you were promised, you could have had any woman not currently busy, but you went along with Bonnie and me. Then just me."

She gently laid a hand on the side of his face. "And Bob, if you had proven to be a nasty or uncouth person, you would have been immediately turned over to one or more of our specialists."

"Specialists?"

"Yes. Girls who can handle the rougher trade and who aren't very discriminating about their partners. I am."

He felt even better about the experience.

"You thought I'd be all right?"

"From the moment I set eyes on you. Bob. Forgive me if I sound preachy, but you have to learn that a woman—I mean a woman, not a child—sees a long way past a handsome face or a nice set of muscles."

He said, "Do all the girls get their choice of, uh, clients?"

Her soft laugh thrilled him.

"No. That has to do with both what they want in joining this special organization and what is expected of them. Dorothy usually decides. Incidentally, she also decided on this room for our meeting and how I would receive you. For you, she prescribed the most romantic setting possible. She guessed you are unmarried. Is that right."

Prescribed, huh? "Yes, I'm single. How did she know?"

"It began with seeing no wedding ring. Nor an untanned space on your finger where one might have been removed".

"Oh, of course. Well obviously, I'm very much impressed. Frankie, you give every impression of being well educated."

"Thank you. I'm still working at it. A well-known pianist-actor named Oscar Levant called his education, 'A Smattering of Ignorance' and wrote a book about it. I think mine is following the same pattern."

"I remember the name. Should I look up the book?"

"You might find it entertaining. There's much better things to read, I think."

Bob said, "I read a lot, but nothing very serious."

"And you are lonely sometimes, hence what happened tonight. I don't think you are going to be as lonely from now on."

"Now that I know you."

She squeezed her eyes shut. Held them that way for several seconds.

She opened them, smiling. "That's very kind, considering who you are talking to, but sweet Bob, this could very well be our last meeting. You are not a San Franciscan, nor even a near neighbor, are you?"

"No."

"And this establishment—something of an experiment in such things—could not last long. It has enemies. There are powerful interests who don't care to see sex made available in this kind of environment. It's much too comfortable—and civilized. These are the interests who want to employ only call girls or see their prostitutes in cribs, ala in Mexico's border cities."

"I'll be back. I'll look for you."

"I'll hope that can happen, Bob, but what you did tonight could very well change your life. You are no longer going to need places like this. I doubt if another place just like this exists. You have learned what you've been missing, and I'm sure your instincts and good sense will help you select a woman with whom you can share love, not furtively nor with someone who serves others." She reached for her dressing gown and gave Bob a gentle push. towards the bathroom and dressing area.

"You shower, or whatever, and we'll say goodnight. It's better than goodbye."

Ten minutes later, he found her still in her negligee, standing by the door.

"A goodbye kiss," she said, and reached for him.

"Frankie. I never dreamed . . . ."

"I know. God bless you, Bob, and I wish you happiness. Go for it."

He stepped into the hallway, then turned to stare at the door as it closed slowly in his face like a curtain closing on a last act. He stood transfixed for a few moments, still in rapture over the magic behind that door. He was suddenly without enough strength to stand, and he sank to his knees, his head against Frankie's door. He was swept by a melancholy that reached into his bones. Frankie had given him a joy he would never forget, but he had now been returned to his mundane life. He felt a wild impulse to burst through the door, crush this woman in his arms, and yell, "Frankie, get out of here. Come with me!"

Instead he stayed in character, turning away in quiet surrender. He could never do anything that unconventional. His mother would have thought him crazy.

He was met at the bottom of the stairs by a smiling Dorothy.

"Your cab is on the way."

"I need to settle up."

"You can do that with your driver, Bob." She patted his arm. "It's been nice having you. I hope you can come again."

His cab pulled up a few seconds after he had stepped through the door. It must have been past midnight, and the cab emerged eerily from a patch of mist. There would be no opportunity to take advantage of the view the driver had mentioned.

"Well, man. How did it go?" The driver may have been buoyed by coffee, or just his innate enthusiasm, but he did not appear in the least tired by the late hour.

Bob would have preferred to be alone with his churning thoughts, but he would have to talk to the man who was obviously involved in larger enterprise than driving a cab.

Bob said, "It was everything you said it was, and more. All I can think of right now is how to get back. I'm scheduled back east tomorrow."

"Well, you won't be able to find me. It would be like pulling a golf ball out of a mound of hay, but I'll know how to find you next time you're in the city. If you stay in a hotel or motel and use the same name."

It occurred to Bob he and Frankie hadn't exchanged full names.

"Oh, I'll do that, all right. What do I owe you?"

"You didn't run up much of a tab. It'll be four hundred plus twenty for drinks and whatever is on the meter. I have to run the meter. It's my cover. Looks like it'll be about fifty bucks."

"Make it a hundred even for the ride."

"Thank you, sir. I think you spent the time with the right lady."

"Yes I did. Where do you find them?"

"They are chosen carefully. Only a few are full-timers. Your bed mate might have been a homemaker, divorced, or a laid off tech worker who needs the cash. It may not last long. The whore mongers who run the more expensive call girls in the city are pissed that our girls can take less and be happy. You noted the atmosphere. Compare that with ordering up a first class hooker to your hotel room."

Bob hadn't ever done that, but he said, "Oh, yeah."

"So we're hoping we can keep it alive, and peaceful. We can bring in guns but then the cops get in the act and everybody loses. We hope it can be worked out."

They pulled up at Bob's hotel. The cabby pulled out his portable credit card register.

He grinned. "I hope we can meet again. You are something special, my friend. I'm not Ted Taliaferro for your information. Probably just as well you don't know my real name. But like I said, I can find you, and it's been a pleasure."

They stretched for each other's hand.

Bob said, "I've never had a night like this, and unless we meet again I can't hope to have another."

He didn't know it would be his last visit to San Francisco for five years. He could have returned at his own expense, but somehow he felt he would not find Frankie and he couldn't imagine finding such happiness with another woman. When he returned on a business assignment he stayed at the same hotel, but there was no call from anyone like a Ted Taliaferro. On his own for an afternoon before his flight home he rented a car and drove across the Golden Gate bridge to Sausalito, then on to Mill Valley, but after a winding search of several hours he gave up trying to find "Cloud Nine."

Bob never sought out another prostitute, but after joining Stanton Corporation he began thinking seriously about finding a woman he could marry, a woman who might demonstrate the basic qualities of the woman who had introduced him to sex. The woman he could never think of as a prostitute.

8

Marti hadn't been sleeping well. Bob, in the other bed in the bungalow's tiny master bedroom, kept her awake with his snores, not loud but persistent, like the rumble of an over-age refrigerator. He had shrugged his shoulders when she said she wanted twin beds to help her sleep better. She couldn't say she didn't want him in the same bed anymore. She could fake it if he did make a move on her, but it had been weeks since he tried. It was as if he sensed her disinterest and was simply trying to be cooperative. They were again polite strangers, retreating to the scene of their first meeting at a party neither of them wanted to attend. It was at someone's home on Staten Island. He had brought her a drink and they chatted, she pretending an animation that might promote more welcome glances from a better looking man. He, no longer bored, was trying for some common ground with his questions. Marti had been civil, making the best of it. Then, braced for refusal, he asked if he could call her sometime.

The marriage ceremony at Newark's City Hall, Marti's third, was perfunctory. Bob was an only child, and his mother, with whom he had lived until he had acquired his MBA, had died. Marti's witness at the wedding was her longtime pal, Rose Benevito, who combined her best wishes with her special brand of vitriol.

"This is the last time I'm putting on heels for one of your weddings, Marti. Next time, do it on a beach in a bikini."

Cora and her father also attended the ceremony. Cora liked Bob, sized him up as a money maker, told her daughter, "You stick it out. Blow this one and it's trampville."

Marti had gone through men as if they were potato chips, beginning in high school. It wasn't about sex then. She was a virgin when she first married. She just enjoyed the excitement of attracting the attention of boys, no effort required, but the calls from persistent swains irritated Cora. Cora wanted every available minute of her daughter's time spent on what Marti considered her mother's almost comic efforts to recreate her in the image of girls described in the self-improvement magazines cluttering their forty-year old clapboard house.

As long as she could remember Marti had been subjected to maternal vigilance and guidance experienced by few children in her social-economic stratum. Her mother was determined her only child would escape the mostly Italian-American neighborhood and marry someone who amounted to something.

Money was somehow found for a "charm" school in Jersey City. A sixty-five year old Miss Parker first checked Marti's posture and walk, "Not bad"—then went to work on an accent that had it been left uncorrected would have resulted in a startling flaw in Marti's rapidly developing persona of beauty and natural poise.

Marti told Rose, "Her name is Parker and she's a female General MacArthur, but she's as Italian as our moms. Her nose is like a banana. She gets me to talk about school and things, but she corrects me before I can get words out of my mouth. Jesus, she gives me vocal exercises to work on and Cora won't let me go to bed until I practice them for an hour."

Cora felt she was getting her money's worth. She thought her daughter, despite some bursts about a "Goddamned Hitler," was accepting the strict regimen that included sessions of table manners and general etiquette for a young woman. Included in Miss Parker's dictates were such speech refinements as dropping "y'know" from her vocabulary and the substitution of more "yeses" for "yeahs." There were also sessions on stretching a young woman's vocabulary.

Cora glowed inwardly one morning when Marti looked up from her coffee and said,

"Mom, I really appreciate what you're trying to do for me."

More of house painter George Lambucci's hard earned dollars went for teaching Marti how to select clothes and how to wear them. She wore one of the outfits on an afternoon with Miss Parker that included lunch at Tavern on the Green and a visit to the Museum of Fine Art. Another cultural event on her instructor's agenda was a concert at Carnegie Hall.

"I could go for more of that Rachmaninoff," she told her parents.

Cora's attention to her daughter's social improvement included rounding up some appropriate suitors. This was a challenge in a neighborhood producing more longshoremen than lawyers. Marti told Rose, "I wonder who mom thinks I'm going to meet at the Italian club, English teachers?"

Marti did meet some teachers, a pair of lawyers, and a few young men embarking on careers in sales. She met some exciting tough guys, too, but Cora successfully squelched overtures from the boys with the glossy hair, tight pants, and built-in swaggers. She managed the tightest control possible while working as a restaurant hostess to help pay for Marti's clothes and special education. When her husband objected to the disrupted domestic routine, she yelled, "Well, paint more houses. Every house in this town needs a couple of coats."

George Lambucci did as well as he could but his efforts didn't bring in enough money to get them into a newly painted home of their own.

Marti later admitted her mother's efforts to help her marry well contributed to her critical judgment of men, and she might have married one of the salesmen, or a teacher, but then she met Billy Dillon, the youthful patrolman.

What a battle she and Cora had about Billy's prospects as a husband.

"You simp," Cora screeched. "I've done everything in my power to make you into something a successful man would go for, and you think you're in love with a cop?

"Sweet Jesus," she wailed. "He isn't even Italian."

And on and on, but to Marti her Billy was beautiful, in and out of his well-cut uniform. More than six feet tall and built like a strong-side safety, they met when he had stopped her car, the family's five-year old Cutlass, on the pretext of spotting a blinking tail light. He issued no ticket, and there was no tail light problem. He had fumbled around in the trunk, then said it was okay, it had been a loose wire. He called her the next evening.

She had only kissed a few of her dates, no power necking, but with Billy the fooling around began on their first date, in the back row of the Starlight theater on 96th avenue. Then, she had whacked him off in his car after he moaned he was going crazy, but he didn't get rough. He just guided her hand, kissing her all the while. From then on it was heavy action several nights a week.

Cora caught her washing her own underwear, a chore her mother always did. Cora screamed, "I know you are going all the way with that cop and you're a damned fool."

Marti never admitted it, but she agreed with her mother that giving it away was dumb. She did want to marry Billy, but she needn't have worried about his intentions. He proposed marriage on Christmas eve, right after mass, and they were married three months later.

It might have been a happily ever after theme, but for the ambitions of Billy's patrol car partner whose turn it was to drive. Siren screaming, roof lights flashing, he chased a teen-age car jacker through a red light, only to be joined in the intersection by another youthful driver whose eyes and ears were only aware of the attentions of his date. At impact with the police car he had only one hand on the wheel. The other was in the hair of the girl whose face was buried in his lap. The car jacker got away clean. Billy and his partner died at the scene. Several months later a fellow officer of Billy's told Marti the only injury to the teen-age couple was the boy's severely lacerated penis.

Marti's reply was, "I wish she had bitten it off."

Marti married Frank Sokol, short for Sokoloski, six months later. Her mother was more approving in this instance. Frank made good money in the used car business. Marti's father thought he knew why.

"He's a thief,"

George Lambucci spent his money carefully, whatever he could squirrel away after Cora paid household expenses and something on the credit cards. He thought he had been taken on the Buick LeSabre Frank sold him. Frank said he gave George the car for exactly what he had in it, but George was dubious. He didn't believe the five-year old car was driven only twenty-four thousand miles, especially when a new water pump was needed after he had driven the car a week. Frank made good, but George still fussed.

Cora said, "George, forget it. Frank makes enough rooking his other customers. He doesn't need to steal from you."

The marriage to Frank ended the attention of several would-be lotharios, none of whom contributed much towards softening the ache left by the loss of Billy. She rebuffed the frustrated dates long before the evenings ended at her door Marti would never have considered trysts in the apartment she and Billy had called their home.

Marti met Frank while accompanying her dad on his search for the used car. The first date with the smooth talking, wavy-haired salesman ended in his frustration. Frank, recently divorced and randy after a dry spell, was openly interested in ending an evening of bar hopping with a final hop into his bed. She declined all his blandishments. She had decided her mother was right. She was not prepared for any career other than creating a home. The next man to get her in a bed would be a husband.

Frank proposed after their second date, but if Marti thought she could revive the rapture of the abruptly curtailed bliss with Billy she was wrong. Frank's smile and physical attributes did approximate those of her first love, but for all his success in the used car business, he fulfilled Marti's early opinion. She found him pretentious and dull. There would be no children, she had determined, and he was obviously in agreement. His pre-sex question, "You ready?" wasn't needed for her to have her diaphragm in place.

There was little to maintain a marriage in which sex was a "raison d'etre," so Marti was ready for another question from Frank about a year into the marriage.

On a crisp October morning over his coffee and Danish, Frank said, "I don't think you're happy, and neither am I. Why don't we no-fault it and go on about our lives?"

Marti had raised her cup. I'll drink to that, but before you trade me in for a new model, I think a separation fee is in order."

Frank pretended shock. "Aw, come on. You're a beautiful woman. You'll meet mister right in no time, without missing a period."

"Maybe so. And so will you. In fact, I think you already have. The new model, I mean. I'll be glad to step aside, but I'll need some living expenses until mister right, as you say, comes along. The bride will need a dowry and you're going to be the donor."

"A dowry? Come on."

Marti wanted out in a hurry and agreed to shortcut the paper work, court appearances, etc., for $75,000. She settled for $60,000, but four weeks after she deposited the check Cora required a hysterectomy and George went down with a heart attack. Most of Marti's new working capital went to back up her parent's pitifully inadequate health insurance.

Enter Bob Costello, who appeared more than willing to offer a very comfortable life. He was too short, much older than she, was going to lose his hair before he was fifty, and in her opinion was about as exciting in bed as a second reading of War and Peace. On the plus side, he delivered her from a series of dreary jobs, the best of which required a fifth grade education. Marti thought she would do better in the job market.

She told her mother, "I don't classify myself as brilliant, but I thought a New Jersey high school diploma would be of more help than keeping me off welfare."

Cora observed wryly, "You wouldn't take high school typing because it meant the trenches of steno pools, but most of those girls have done better than you."

Bob gave her the life Cora had prepared her for, and if she wasn't blissfully happy she was more than comfortable. Old friend Rose helped share her feelings about the new Cliffside Park condo apartment and its surroundings.

"Gorgeous," Rose gasped.

Marti bragged, "Bob let me work with a decorator, but I chose the colors and furnishings. How about those drapes?"

She loved lounging on the glass-domed pool deck and gazing at the scapes of Manhattan across the river. Homemaking was a bore, but a maid did all the housework. Bob worked at making her happy, bringing her things, encouraging her to shop for clothes, and they spent more time in New York's better restaurants than in front of the teevee. The months slipped past, then a year, then two. She admitted to her mother that for the first time in her relationships with men there was more to it than a romp in the hay.

"Bob talks about things. He shows interest in my clothes, has me reading the Times, even the columnists, and he's always complimentary when I make a meal."

Cora knew this wasn't very often. Cooking had never been a priority in Marti's enforced learning experience. Meals in the apartment were rarely something more advanced than microwave heat ups.

She was not blissful, but so at ease in her new life she began to think she might finish her life married to the man. In a phone conversation with pal Rose, she said with histrionic emphasis, "Maybe I'm finally free from further voyages into the seas of sex-inspired passion."

Rose said, "Mama mea, listen to the lady."

Bob's love expressed itself mostly in the form of admiration and almost fawning respect. The sex hadn't been all that good from the start. She decided he just didn't need very much. At first it was all right with her. After losing Billy and the failure with Frank, she thought she could control her appetite, maybe have a child, although Bob hadn't led any of their conversations that way. While not aggressive sexually he tried to accommodate her general unrest. They dined out several nights a month. Their building housed an excellent restaurant, and however tired he might be, he dressed for dinners and sometimes theater in the city.

She told Cora. "I'm bitchy rich, mama."

"Then don't ruin it. This guy is worth ten of those bozos you used to date. And marry."

Bob didn't talk much about how he made his living. He said it was "nuts and bolts" about handling money. "The job won't be nine to five but we'll have lots of cash to play with."

She met Phil Stanton at a party for area business and industrial leaders in Stanton's Upper Montclair home. She met his wife, Lucia, and sized her up as a mouse. After watching Stanton's attentions to the pretty wives of a couple of his guests Marti wondered if the subdued Mrs. Stanton was aware her husband might be a sexual predator. Marti was sure he was a chaser when Stanton brought her a drink. He had somehow learned it was the right drink. Bob was elsewhere in the room at the moment, but Stanton didn't linger. He smiled into her face, and said, "A lovely Chablis for a lovely lady."

She didn't work too hard at shaking thoughts about the good-looking man during the days that followed the party, but she didn't scold herself for the mental infidelity and wasn't in the least surprised by his call. What surprised her was that she made it so easy for him. Any resolve she had about being true to one man for the rest of her life melted in the wake of Phil Stanton's sexy baritone.

He said simply, "I just can't get it out my head that we should meet again."

She said, "What took you so long to decide?"

He came in a chauffeured Lincoln, and they drove around Central Park and down to the battery before lunching at his club atop the Time-Life building. She knew the session was like an elaborate job interview but it amused her to go along. There was the thrill of danger, too, and not only to her marriage. Phil made that clear at the first of their twice-monthly meetings at his Essex house suite on Central Park south. It sounded almost clinical as he described what he hoped would be a lasting "friendship" in the posh living room.

He said, "I'm really impressed with you, Marti. You're beautiful, and smart, and I hope you want to embark on a friendship that will endure, but if it should end we will part as friends. There must be no recriminations or embarrassments caused either of us. Does that sound okay with you?"

She laughed. "Sure. Where do I sign?"

He laughed, too, and the touching began.

Marti was certain Bob was unaware of her perfidy. Then came the evening he used his briefcase to bang open the apartment door, two hours later than usual, pale and silent, brushing past her to the wet bar. She was prepared to needle him for being late. She was dressed for dinner at The Four Seasons. They had discussed the evening's plan by phone that morning.

He poured himself a Jack Daniels, slopping the liquor into a glass, not asking whether she wanted a drink. Usually, he made a small pitcher of Martinis they shared. He took a gulp, then said, "I can't stand it anymore. I'm going to bury that son of a bitch."

She stared at him. He must mean his boss, but it couldn't be because of her. There was no way he could know about her affair with Stanton.

"What happened?"

He paced the large living room, stopping to gulp his drink with his back to her, staring across the Hudson where the sun's last rays blazed off thousands of high rise windows. He again pushed past her to the bar, carelessly pouring more of the liquor.

She said, "Let's eat here." She ducked into the kitchen for a couple of Lean Cuisines.

She called them emergency rations. When the food was in the microwave, she called out:

"Bob, what's up? You trying for boozer of the year? Who are you going to bury?"

He looked at her out of eyes already affected by the unusual dosage of alcohol.

"I'm just exhausted. I was absolutely certain I could handle everything, but we've added three new businesses in the last six months and I simply can't keep up. Now he wants a hurry-up draft of the new pension plan, which will steal a few million from the employees."

"Okay, so quit. You're terrific at your job. People like you are in demand. Didn't you just read me the Times article about the shortage of guys who can do your work? You'd get a bonus and make more money from much bigger outfits than Stanton."

He was silent, looking at the floor. When he looked up she thought she saw the look she had seen in her father's eyes when his business was down.

He said, "You don't understand. Stanton can't let me go with what I know about the business."

"What does that mean?"

"It means I've been holding out on the IRS. Cooking the books. I've shorted the net profit on the quarterlies and annual reports for almost six million since joining the company. And he expects this to go on forever. And it's driving me crazy. I can't stand it."

Wow. Incredible. She shook her head, carrying the food he wouldn't eat into the dinette. His face, always pale from hardly any exposure to sun, was bloodless.

He said, "I'm going to the feds. Make a deal. For protection. I'll need it, too. I'm sure he's old line mob, a Sicilian with a beautiful nose job. He knows how to arrange things. He can simply make me disappear."

Marti didn't sleep that night. She was snapped out of a doze before dawn when a fully dressed Bob nudged her.

"I'll be unavailable for the day. Tell my secretary I'm ill, too sick to talk. Anything."

She tried to reach Phil as soon as the office opened. If Bob went ahead with his crazy scheme Stanton might think it had to do with their nasty quarrel in his Essex House suite the week before. It had begun with his "about time" crack when she arrived twenty minutes late for their meeting. She misread his mood, and said, "Well, I'm worth a little wait. Besides, the waiting makes you hornier."

He exploded, coming out of his chair snarling. "I'm not hanging around here all day to service some over-sexed, under-fucked slut."

She tried to hit him, but he had slapped her face hard before she had her hand back. Then he held one of her hands with one of his, grabbing her hair with the other. He yelled in her face, "No one hits me. Don't you ever forget it."

She ran from the room. He tried to call, several times, but she hung up on him. She thought she might forgive him, but he had to know he could never again pull any rough stuff on her. She would kick his nuts through his tonsils if he ever tried.

Bob's timing couldn't have been worse. If he went to the D.A., whomever, she had to tell Stanton it wasn't because she told Bob of their affair. She had to warn him, convince him Bob wasn't going to the law out of a jealous rage.

Stanton warned her never to call him at his office, but if she had to call she was to be a Mrs. Brown of Hartford Insurance.

His secretary said he wasn't available. Then Marti remembered he had mentioned something about trying to make some points with Lucia, taking her to Atlantic City for a long week end. Jesus, if she couldn't talk to him before the feds picked him up, he would assume she confessed their affair to Bob. Whatever Bob thought he might be in for she would get, too.

Bob returned late that night, actually early the following morning. She stayed awake with the help of coffee so she could try to cool him down, but by then any outward fury had been buried.

He said, "I had to take care of some business. Today, I go to the feds. I'm going to testify against that son of a bitch. I can't tell you much about it. I don't want to get you involved. I'm just filled up to here with that greedy thief and with what I've been doing for him."

She had said, "Bob, you do this and Stanton will assume I know everything. If he would hurt you he'll do the same to me."

He had then grabbed her arm and pulled her into their bedroom and into his side of the his-and-her walk-in closets. He said, "Look," and he pulled out the sleeve of a suit coat. "There's ten thousand dollars sewed into the shoulders and linings, and another twenty thousand in two other suit coats. And that's just a small chunk of what I've stashed. All cash. My deal with the feds will include protection for both of us in their witness protection program. They'll hide us until the time is right, then we'll live wherever we want. Mexico, south of France, you name it."

She still wanted to get to Stanton, but right then it didn't matter as much. Stanton hadn't returned her calls, and his secretary might intercept any other kind of message. She couldn't go to his office. Even if she could somehow intercept him her mouth might be caved in before she could say a word. She had seen the real man at his hotel, the explosive temper and basic meanness. He had been shaking in rage. Maybe Bob was right about mob connections. She had been a damn fool to let herself get in such a pickle. Staying with Bob meant safety, and the idea of living abroad in an exciting locale such as the south of France, would be a thrill.

That's it. She had to take her chances with her husband. Even if she could square things with Stanton there was no future in it. Without a husband she'd be on the down slide. No money, no way to make any. And Stanton would still be after her. She'd been a damn fool. Again. How Cora would pour it on.

She was tossing the Times into a condo waste basket when she found a torn up airline ticket envelope. Minneapolis. She wondered why Bob would go there, but in the excitement of the next few weeks, she forgot about it.

Trying to nab Phil Stanton in an election year, the government was hasty in building its case. Stanton was a highly regarded businessman, a supporter of community do-good projects. All they had was the testimony of Bob Costello, but it appeared decisive. He had convinced them he was in complete control of Stanton Corporation finances with every move approved by Stanton.

Bob said the government was aware of Stanton's name change and the family's vague connection with a small time hood several generations before, but there was no evidence he was criminally connected. Still, they didn't hesitate to approve protection for Bob and Marti immediately after Stanton's arrest and arraignment.

The full meaning of what she was getting into didn't hit Marti until the morning when two men and a woman arrived at the condo and instructed them to pack their clothes and personal belongings into bags they provided.

Bob said, "They're taking us to a safe place, Marti."

She said, "Wait a minute. I have to make some calls."

One of the agents shook his head. "I'm sorry ma'am. No calls."

She exploded, "Bob, what the hell is this? I can't just disappear."

He said, "Marti, that's the idea, but don't worry. It'll be all right."

Anything identifying them was confiscated by the quiet but swift-moving visitors who cleaned out Bob's desk, then emptied their wallets of all credit and charge cards and drivers licenses.

Marti looked around their living room desperately. "Bob, what happens to all our furniture? And the furnishings. Those drapes alone cost a ton."

"The unit will be sold along with everything in it, but we'll be compensated."

Marti was numb as they were led away. Out of the elevator they were directed to the condo's rear door. Waiting there was a van with two more men standing by. They and their bags were loaded and whisked away on an hour's drive which included the Lincoln tunnel. They were on Long Island, but Marti didn't have a clue as to where. The van was in a remote area when it entered a fenced enclosure and drove up to a building Marti thought looked like a small factory.

Ten minutes later they were ushered into a tastefully decorated one-bedroom apartment, except it had no windows. Greeting them inside the door was another agent, a tall partially bald black man in a dark suit. He wore a small mustache and horn-rimmed glasses.

He smiled and said, "Hello. My name is Henry and I'll be looking after you during your stay in this facility."

Marti interrupted. "Where in hell are we?"

Bob had taken her arm, squeezing it softly. "Take it easy, Marti. Let the man explain."

Henry was well rehearsed. He said, "You are in a facility maintained by the U. S. Marshal service. You'll be here about two weeks. During that time you will be helped to determine your new identities and where you will begin you new lives. We call it an orientation course. Now, if you'll make yourselves comfortable I'll take care of a few details in connection with your stay."

Marti heard a click as Henry closed the door after him. He had locked them in. Marti stared at the door, then for the first time in her memory, she cried. Bob patted her shoulder.

"It'll be all right, Marti. We won't be here long."

He was wrong, at least from Marti's point of view. Ten too-long days with much of it alone while Bob spent hours with government attorneys. She was no longer in shock at being deprived of a telephone, but to learn there would be no television, and not even access to daily newspapers or news magazines was infuriating. She wanted to rip into someone, but the realization that whatever she did would be a waste of time somehow eased the frustration. It was then she remembered how as a child her grandfather, Lorenzo, had held her on his lap after a nasty quarrel with Cora. Her mother had been adamant on something and Marti was livid. Lorenzo, then confined to a wheel chair, pulled her to him and said, "I'm going to tell you another war story, different from the others."

Marti, always fascinated by her grandfather's stories of his World War II experience. She put her head on his chest and put her hands in his.

"This story is different than most of my war stories. It's about something that happened on my first day in basic training because it helped change me from a wild kid to a soldier.

"A sergeant named Dimato had us in tow. He was lots older than we were, a strong looking man, regular army, a member of the camp's staff which was called a cadre. He told us to sit down around him and he talked to us like he was a teacher and we were kids. Like you do in school, right? Of course, we really were kids."

54

Dimato said, "You'll be getting a lot of different kinds of orders over the next thirteen weeks. Some of them you probably won't understand. For instance, I or one of the other non-coms or officers might tell you to dig a big hole, four feet by four feet and four feet deep. Then you might be ordered to tour the area for cigarette butts and toss them in the hole. Then you will be ordered to fill up the hole. By that time it might be time for lunch, and you'll be dismissed.

"That afternoon, you might be told you dug the hole in the wrong place, and that it really should be dug a few feet to the left. You'll be sent back to work. About two feet into that new hole, you might feel like slamming down your shovel. You might say, 'Hey, how does this prepare me to fight the Nazis or Japs?'

"That, gentlemen," Dimato said, "is what is known as fighting the problem. It's useless in this man's army, a waste of time, and if you can't learn that, to follow orders no matter how wrong they might seem to you, then it's going to be a helluva rough war for you."

Marti remembered how the story had calmed her or maybe it was because she loved Lorenzo so much. She didn't tell her grandfather she would never argue with Cora again, but she got the message. She remembered Lorenzo and his story when the nuns at school got so bossy she could hardly stand it, or when Miss Parker got snippy, or Cora raged. She had clammed up and got along. She remembered asking Lorenzo if he was ordered to dig any four-by four-foot holes. He said, "No, but when we got to France and heard those eighty-eight shells screaming at us, I dug holes I could climb into without orders from anyone."

Remembering Lorenzo and his story was timely. She knew she had to tough it out, to go along, not "fight the problem."

Tired of feeling sorry for herself she pulled some books down from the apartment shelf full of novels and biographies. There also was a selection of movies for a VCR. It was the apartment's single piece of electronic equipment. The films were several years old, but she thought they might help pass the time. Few of the books, mostly classics, had much appeal for her. Bernard Shaw's St. Joan was familiar. She'd read it in school. The iconic author's Pygmalion was there, too. There were also two of Anne Morrow Lindbergh's diaries, novels by the Bronte sisters, and Katherine Porter's Ship of Fools. She wondered if so many of the works, written by and involving women as major characters, were deliberately chosen for readership by the wives of other federal witnesses, maybe to help them resist fighting the problem.

Henry came in to talk with her several times during Bob's absences. Sitting with cokes at a table adjoining the small kitchenette, he said, "This is hard, I know, getting prepared for your new life, but you have to be separated from old attachments and the time here will help you make the adjustment."

She asked him about the mostly female authorship in the apartment's small library.

He smiled, "You noted that, eh? One of the top people here thinks these books, some of which describe the trials of extraordinary women, will help strengthen the resolve of the ladies to make the program work."

He talked about the importance of selecting a name she and Bob would be comfortable with, and how she and Bob needed to rehearse answers for the inevitable "Where you from?" queries from new acquaintances.

Marti asked, "When can I see my parents?"

"Not here. If everything works out, you will see your folks before you leave the area and begin your new life."

Bob had little to say about his sessions, but explained later that the government had to be sure he wouldn't walk out on his deal.

"They could still find some way to prosecute me. Grand theft, income tax evasion, or whatever, but they don't have to worry. I'll testify, all right."

A few days later they were holed up under guard in a downtown Manhattan hotel where Marti could hardly sit still. She had been permitted to take several of the apartment's supply of novels with her and in her desperation she now buried herself in them. She would have preferred lighter reading but she reread the St. Joan, then got into a couple of Edith Wharton's novels, also finishing the Pygmalion. She and Bob had seen the musical, "My Fair Lady," based on the Shaw story. She also took an anthology of the world's greatest short stories in case she tired of the longer stuff. She read it all and was surprised at how much she enjoyed her first prolonged adventures in reading. It beat crossword puzzles.

When the pre-trial wrangling was finally over and Bob testified, the prosecution led him carefully through the story of his life, emphasizing his achievements as a scholar, and how he had worked in food markets to earn enough for City college, eventually earning his CPA certificate and the master's degree in business at Columbia. Marti sat in a small room adjacent to the main chamber and watched the proceedings on closed-circuit television She found a lot of the procedure dull with lawyers haggling over points she didn't understand, but she was impressed with the long list of clients Bob had served in accounting and financial affairs before joining Stanton. She remembered Phil's brush off of her questions about her husband's contributions to the company.

He said, "He's a very well paid bookkeeper. A bean counter."

Obviously, Bob was much more to the Stanton corporation than that. During his testimony she listened with wonder as he described how he had counseled the scowling defendant on investments and new business acquisitions and how Stanton had instructed him to convert all cash receivables into large bills and place them in safety-deposit boxes in area banks. He also testified that only a portion of this cash was reported as corporate income.

"But the cash seized from the deposit boxes jibed with the numbers only you had access to. Is that correct, Mr. Costello?"

Bob told Marti, "Stanton claimed he would know if the government was going to investigate us, that I would have time to pull the cash from the boxes. 'Just say I have friends in high places,' he said. He was willing to take the chance. His and the company's reputation were good, and I had to agree with him. Corporate and federal tax attorneys are always in argument. We could have worked out a settlement re the short numbers I had on the hard drive. We would have blamed the screw up on the company's rapid growth."

Marti thought it didn't take a lawyer to figure out Stanton's defense strategy.

"They're going to make you the heavy, Bob. They're going to claim Phil didn't know you were juggling the figures and hiding all that cash. He'll say it was all your scheme."

Bob's look held more respect than she had seen for a long time.

"Sure, but the prosecution is going to have to plant more with the jury than the thieving was only for myself. After all, I'm the acknowledged financial whiz. I could have walked away with a ton of money without going to all the trouble of blowing the whistle on my boss."

She thought about that. The bedroom was now dark as they lay in their separate beds. She was glad he couldn't see her face twisted in concentration. She wondered how Phil Stanton had manipulated Bob into stealing from his company. It wasn't hard to imagine her husband knuckling under to Phil. Bob was afraid of the man. She wasn't about to tell Bob that Phil Stanton thought Bob's motive was revenge. Even if she had been able to get through to Phil, he wouldn't believe she hadn't told Bob of their affair.

She said, "But you testified you turned him in because you were sick of working for a crook. I hope the jury will believe that."

Bob's voice was tired, but he tried to placate her. "It may be a little thin. We'll see."

Stanton's defense attacked like hungry wolves. Under cross examination Costello admitted he handled all corporation monies, coming in and going out, and that Phil Stanton had never seen, much less handled, any incoming or outgoing cash.

"It was entirely your responsibility to handle all this money? Isn't that right, Mr.

Costello?"

"Yes."

"Did Mr. Stanton see any of this cash?

"No."

"And the floppy disk you say have the real company income numbers. Aren't you the only person who had access to those disks?"

"Yes."

The defense provided computer specialists who carefully explained basic computer operations to the jury.

"Ah yes, and couldn't the information for the compact disks be changed just as you adjusted the figures for the computer hard drive?"

"Yes."

The confident defense then allowed Phil Stanton to testify, certain their client's poise could not be shaken on the stand. They were right. Stanton, almost affable in his own cause, responded with a smile to his attorney's question, "Do you hold any enmity for Mr. Costello, Mr. Stanton?"

"Well, I can't classify being dragged into federal court a friendly act." (laughter throughout the courtroom), but my main feeling about all this is disappointment in a man I trusted."

Under cross examination that featured sharp questioning as to how Stanton could be unaware of discrepancies amounting to millions of dollars in gross income and subsequent tax filings, Stanton was respectful but alert and precise in his answers.

In their hotel room Bob told Marti, "He's almost perfect in his own defense. His testimony that he was so involved in new biz acquisitions he couldn't be on top of finances, too, might be convincing. It's going to be a coin flip."

It wasn't that close. The jury was out only two hours. Not guilty.

9

Bob had made the choice, overriding her doubts. The Midwest would be the site for their new life. Chicago.

She said, "Hey, why not Florida or California, somewhere it's at least warm?"

"No. A large city in the Midwest is the best place. I hope it won't be for long." They were in a motel room near LaGuardia airport when Marti finally was able to see her parents and say goodbye. Henry warned them, "Remember, if you should slip and mention either your new name or where you are going, it means a lot of extra work and lost time setting up new identities, new credit cards, social security records. The works."

Marti guessed Cora wouldn't be tearful, and she was right. Cora was more concerned about how her daughter would live. In a whispered aside she said, "Marti, how will he make a decent living? He's a snitch. Nobody wants a snitch."

Marti withheld an effort to put her mother straight; that it was either go with Bob or be found floating in the East river. There wasn't much she could say other than to calm Cora's fears.

She said, "That's a minor problem, Mom. He's an expert in his work. We'll be okay." George appeared stunned by the previously unthinkable, saying goodbye to his only child. His arms hung limply at his sides until Marti gave him a hug. She was surprised at the strength of his response and his emotional whisper, "I love you, my little girl."

Marti kissed Cora, whose face was pinched. For a moment Marti thought her tough-as-nails mother might do the unthinkable. Cry. But she didn't.

The new Velottis were led away to board a United Airlines flight. A deputy marshal to whom they weren't introduced sat two rows behind them. He gave no indication he was in their company, but upon arrival at Chicago's O'Hare he identified himself and gave them over to Ross Vincennes as soon as they entered the terminal.

Days later Marti remembered exclaiming as Vincennes drove them away from the airport,

"At least it's near some excitement," meaning the city, but for the entire Chicago experience they hadn't gone farther than suburban Northbrook, where she saw Bob's dinky office. She had a car, but after she met Ross Vincennes, nearly all of her travel was for meeting him.

She hadn't probed the extent of her feelings for Vincennes. If he had been vulnerable to a come-on from a sexy woman whose husband appeared unimpressive, she was as likely to have reacted to a good-looking man who was also unhappily married. It was a "push," a no decision as grandfather Lorenzo had taught her in their card games. The absence of love for her husband was the fundamental problem in her marriage. The situation was made worse by being yanked out of a luxurious waterfront home in the area she loved and dumped in a strange city where she had no friends or family.

The idea of ditching her husband for Vincennes, with a good chunk of Bob's money to bless the union had occurred to her, but she pushed the idea away as unworthy of anyone but a tramp. She didn't think she was a tramp although there were times, day or night, when she'd squeeze her eyes shut, turn her hands into fists and scream, "Jesus, am I a complete air-head whose only thing of value is a galloping libido?"

The self-revilement would come unannounced, like a sudden headache, sometimes as she slept. She would wake up, soaking in sweat, writhing in her hell of self-disgust. Was she just weak, possibly spoiled by an ambitious mother.

The affairs with Phil and Vincennes were piled onto the dung heap of guilt. Her barely existing rationale for the behavior was as flimsy as a cheap cloth coat. So she didn't love her husband. She could see and hear Cora's response to that.

"So what," Cora might have yelled. "Life is made up of deals. Bob offered you ease and comfort. You owed him more than infidelity!"

In the midst of her crisis of guilt, Bob dropped the bomb. After little more than six months he said he was sick of his job with the small public accounting firm.

"It's crap. A kid with high school bookkeeping could do it, and I'm going nowhere. I made a few suggestions for improving the business, and the boss gives me a look. If I wasn't sure he didn't know, I'd say the son of a bitch was thinking, 'Is that the way you did it for the mob?' But I can't risk taking a bigger job. Larger companies are the first place Stanton would check out."

He then stayed home on a work day, then two. She had to get out of the house to call Ross, to cancel a date. She told Bob she had to do some shopping and she called from a small strip mall. He already knew of Bob's absences. "What's the matter with him? Sick?"

"Yeah, sick of his job. He's talking about ditching the program."

Vincennes thought about that for a few seconds, then said calmly, "Hey, we can't hold him. We would report to Washington that he left voluntarily. He has his new identity and can hole up anywhere. How about you? Would you run with him, if invited?"

The question called for her quick assessment on how much real affection there was in her relationship with Ross. They had used a lot of words in their steamy sessions, but they didn't include "love" for each other. In that respect it was the same as with Phil. What they loved was "it,"—"It was great, baby. "How was it for you?"

More of the same with Vincennes. "Let's do it."

They filled motel rooms with all the sounds of mutual approval and satisfaction. Now, over the phone, in the panic of wondering what her options might be if Bob should decide to take off, she had to let Ross know there could be more to their relationship than sex. She would tell him she wanted it to be the real thing the next time she could get her arms around him. She had to declare herself. She had hoped he would say it first, but now she had to put on the pressure. She had to create a back-up approach to continuing her life rather than trail after a husband she didn't love and who, to judge from recent appearances, had lost all interest in her.

Into the mouthpiece she said, "Oh, Ross, you know how I feel. I couldn't stand being away from you."

They made a date for the following week. Vincennes said, "Try to stall him. Maybe we can find him a better job."

Bob returned to work, but to Marti he was clearly miserable. He not only didn't mention leaving the program again, he hardly spoke at all, and barely looked at her. There was no show of affection, not a touch, nor even a friendly look. It wasn't expected, or wanted, but Marti, riding on the edge of indecision about the future, wondered if her husband might have a reason other than indifference to her for the silent treatment.

Hey, could he be thinking about taking off without me?

Which would be all right, except that she couldn't see Ross leaving his wife and kids for the stone-broke wife of a government witness. What in hell could she do out here, marooned, a thousand miles from civilization? She would be toilet paper in a breeze. Not that she had much in the way of choice after Phil's trial. That day she was alone with Henry, the agent told her she didn't have to go into the program with Bob.

He told her, "We want to see wives of witnesses committed to making the situation work. Doubts you might have now will be compounded when you are alone in a strange city. There's no way we can force you to stay in the program, either now or then. If you leave after getting situated it would mean we would have to go through the process all over again with your husband. Also for you. A return to your old life might set you up for a revenge motive."

Any doubts about leaving the area that had been her home for her entire life were swept away when she saw Phil Stanton's look after he had spotted her in the federal courtroom's hallway. The eyes that once peeled off her clothes held nothing but hate. She had managed to sneak a call to him again, after he was in custody, but he wouldn't take it. Whomever she talked with, probably a Stanton lawyer, brought back the message,

"He said he doesn't know anyone named Brown."

Sicilians! She didn't need to know his real name to guess the Italian heritage. Then there was the afternoon at the Essex house when Phil had bragged about his virility.

"It comes from way back, baby. My ancestors were strong."

He used the Italian word for strong. "Forte."

Now she had two other men to deal with, and it was more than a possibility she might be deserted by both of them. The thought of being abandoned by men was both ridiculous and scary. And different. Men didn't dump her. She dumped them. She'd never been alone, either, and the idea of being broke and penned up in a cheap bungalow among strangers left her sweating through every pore in her body. She couldn't let Bob get away with crapping out on her. If he invited her to go with him, she had to convince him that he would do better without her, but that he should leave her some money. Hell, he would have to do that anyway if he'd agree to a divorce, but if he just took off, a strong possibility in view of their current relationship, she had to come up with a plan to get some of that cash, and fast.

Could Bob have somehow guessed she was seeing Vincennes? Until his recent behavior she would have said no way, but there might be more to his current mood than being pissed off about the lousy job the feds had helped him find. It was true enough that she hadn't worked at being much of a companion for him during the entire Chicago experience. She thought he had chalked that up to her dissatisfaction with the house and being away from home.

But hell, the man's mental capacity isn't limited to playing around with numbers.

What would Cora do? Poor Mom. How she wanted a daughter who could escape the neighborhood and become the woman she found in her magazines. Marti shook her head and walked up the narrow stairway to the bungalow's second floor. She had to take a look at Bob's suits, the ones he had shown her in their New Jersey condo, the ones supposedly stuffed with one-hundred dollar bills. If he was going to take off he would have to have more cash than his puny accountant's salary, most of it turned over to her. Bob said the government was taking its time selling the condo and other assets that would beef up their stake considerably. It took her all of ten seconds to rummage through Bob's end of the hanging rod in the tiny enclosure. Oh, no! A suit was missing, the brown wool herringbone. She plunged her hands into the tight mass of clothing, mostly her stuff, spreading the garments as if she was an office worker shopping on lunch break with only minutes to make a choice. Hangers jumped off the rod. She couldn't care less. It wasn't there, nor on the floor. She fought back tears, "The son of a bitch. He's going to do it. Why else would he sneak the suit out of the house?"

She sucked in a breath to steady herself. Take it easy. Two of the suits were still in the closet. If he had taken brownie somewhere to remove some or all of the cash he could try to sneak it back into the closet. Then do the others? Bob said there was another twenty thousand in them.

Right now she felt like ripping them apart and running for it. That kind of money would last a long time in Mexico. She sank backwards onto the small bed.

Who was she kidding? She didn't know enough Spanish to order a taco. She could forget about Ross, and there was no other man to help her find a place to hide. It wasn't enough money anyway. She needed a lot more, especially if she could sell Ross Vincennes on running off with her.

What about he rest of the money?

She scrambled to her feet and plunged her hands back into the over-crowded space, grabbing the gray flannel first. When Bob showed her his handiwork, or that of a skilled tailor rather, there were no tell-tale lumps. She hadn't examined them, but she supposed they would be unusually heavy, even for winter garments. There should be the feel of paper under the cloth, but Bob said the suits would pass casual inspection.

He said, "The government is sure I've stashed some money somewhere, but they wanted Stanton more than me. Besides, there's no way the discrepancy between the IRS shortage and Stanton financial reports can account for all of it. They're sure Phil hid another chunk overseas, on top of the money I banked for him. I'm counting on them to ignore me once we're in the program. This cash will help us in emergencies until it's time to break out the real loot."

Marti wrung the gray flannel suit coat as if it were a dishrag. She couldn't feel a thing. Panicky, she grabbed for the dark-blue worsted and worked it carefully, twisting the arms separately, folding the cloth over her knees, kneading it as if it were bread dough.

Oh shit, there's nothing in there, no paper in either of them!

She tried to remember the largest bill the government printed. A hundred? That would be a lot of bills in each suit. She should be able to feel something, however the damn bills were stitched into the cloth. She wrung the garments again, the suit coats, then the pants. Sweat poured from her face. She dropped exhausted on the bed, not bothering to re-hang the clothing. She knew she would have to do some ironing so Bob wouldn't notice the effects from the rough handling.

She thought of her father sitting in his teevee chair murmuring, "Mama mea," over some news report he regarded as extraordinary. Marti used the same words and a few others to express her feelings now. Her shoulders sagged in the growing certainty of Bob's betrayal. She stared at the mess on the floor, then got to her feet. Maybe the money was somewhere in the house. She snatched up the suits and threw them on the bed, then began her search which would turn the house upside down. It was probably hopeless. Bob wasn't going to leave thousands of dollars in a shoe box.

She gave it a frantic half hour, shoe boxes and all, finishing in the basement by rummaging through a pile of wood shavings left from Bob's wood working. His current project was an end table. He had finished the legs.

Maybe he'd stay long enough to add the top and do the paint work, or whatever. That would be a hoot. He'd clear out and leave her a reminder of his skill as a craftsman!

She was shaking in frustration, furious in the final confirmation of her expectations. He couldn't do this to her. What had been unthinkable only minutes before was now a strategy for saving her life. There was only one thing to do. She had to get through to Phil. Make a deal.

Reach him somehow, make peace, and get his promise for a share of Bob's stash. It should be a lot. Bob implied it would be enough for a lifetime of good living. She could hope Phil had cooled off enough to decide that getting some of his money back might be a good idea. And she could also try to make him believe she had nothing to do with bringing him to trial.

What would happen to Bob? He was scared to death that Phil would hurt him, but Phil wasn't a hood. He was an educated man. He wouldn't do anything crazy, like have Bob killed, or beat up. She could make leaving Bob alone part of the deal. She'd tell Phil she would only give him their address if he promised that neither she nor Bob would be harmed.

Her mind flashed back to Phil's explosion at the Essex house. Bob had told her he thought there was some old-line mob in Phil's background. Then at the hotel where she and Bob were been holed up, a government attorney said there was a bad apple in the Stanton barrel, but he said there's no way any of that, or even Stanton's real last name, could be revealed in court. It would not be admissible, could even get the case thrown out. "Prejudicial," he said.

Also judged out of bounds, for either side, was an admission that Bob Costello would be offered protection under the government's witness protection program.

Bob said, "It's implicit in cases of this type. The defense won't use it because of the implication that I, we, are in danger, presumably from Stanton. The government won't mention it either. It would sound as if they were offering a bribe for my testimony"

Marti concentrated on the option of contacting Phil.

If he wanted the money Bob took badly enough, he could give her some of it. Then, with or without Ross, she could make it. A new start. Alone. Was there a man in the world she could trust? More important. Would she ever be able to trust herself?

She glanced at the kitchen clock. It was a little after noon, New York time. She had to make her call, but it couldn't be from the bungalow phone. Vincennes said they could not use easily-traced cell. She'd go to a big mall on U.S. 41 near Winnetka, a drive of twenty miles.

And Phil had better take the call. He still might hate me, but he would guess I had more on her mind than a makeup kiss.

She had called her mother from the mall despite warnings from Bob that calls could be traced. Vincennes warned both of them, too.

He said, "Caller ID. The people who might want a piece of Bob Costello know who you might call. Family, close friends. They just might go to the trouble of coercing those people into adding the service. Don't take chances."

Risky or not, she had to do it. If the call was somehow traced, the bastards would still have to find a needle in the haystack of greater Chicagoland.

Cora said, "Where are you, Marti? I can't stand it, not knowing whether you're all right."

This from the woman who used to pull her hair for such infractions as leaving a spoon in a soup bowl.

Marti had screamed, "Ma, I won't have a hair in my head if you don't stop."

Cora screamed back, "I paid good money so you wouldn't eat like a pig, so put that goddamned spoon where it belongs."

"I'm okay, Mom," she said in the sneak call, "but you know I can't tell you where we are. Bob thinks Stanton might be mad enough to send someone after him We'll have to lay low for a long time."

Cora said, "I still don't understand why you had to run, too. He made his bed. He could lie in it by himself."

He is lying in bed by himself, momma.

"Momma, what could I do? I'm thirty years old and don't have a way to make a decent living. You want me hanging around with you and dad while I wait for a divorce, then try to scrape up husband number four?"

"Does he have any money?"

"Yes, we'll be okay. He's a good man. He'll take care of me."

But only if I take care of myself first.

She found the iron, and got Bob's suits back into normal shape, then made herself ready for the drive. Unless Phil was out of town he should be back from lunch. She would try the Mrs. Brown code again and leave word, then put an Out of Order note on the phone like they do in the movies. She made it from a piece of thin cardboard and a black marker pen she found in the kitchen. Phil's secretary would recognize her voice, and the name, and wonder about the midwestern area code, but so what. Insurance people travel, too.

She rehearsed her speech and tried to anticipate what he would say as she worked her way across town to interstate I-94. He still might not talk to her. If he was going to be that snotty, she would tell his secretary, "Please tell Mr. Stanton it's about that annuity we've discussed."

Jackpot might be more like it, but she decided no insurance person would use that word. She had to stop at a bank to get a roll of quarters and it was close to two New York time by the time she reached the mall and found an unoccupied phone kiosk. She fumbled for her change, spilling the quarters into her purse after tearing the wrapping paper off the roll. She dropped a couple onto the mall floor in her impatience to get them in the coin slot. She punched out the numbers she had checked before leaving the bungalow.

"Be there," she screamed to herself. "Let's get it done."

If she was being a rat, so was Bob. When they were kids, Rose used to give her chills telling her about how informers were "taken care of" in the mob, and she had seen all the Godfather movies. Marti told herself she wasn't suborning Phil's revenge. She just wanted to follow her first husband's formula for fighting when he was a schoolboy in Brooklyn.

Billy Dillon said, "I tried to hit first. If the other guy didn't quit right then, he might not be as strong or as quick as he was before he took the punch."

When Billy became a cop he had to learn to harness the urge to make the first move.

"I wanted to club some of those smart assholes who had just ditched their stash of dime bags and stood there smirking at me. One time a thirteen or fourteen-year old kid pointed what looked like a real automatic at me. I ripped out my piece. If the kid was going to shoot, I wanted at least a chance to put him down, too, but the kid didn't pull his trigger. By then I figured he was holding plastic. I took a step towards him with the usual order to drop the weapon, but he turned like a scalded cat and ran like hell. He and his Nikes were over two fences before I could get to the first one. I thought I saw a glint of light off the hand carrying the gun when he went over the first fence, but it still could have been phony. No matter, I still couldn't shoot him. Shooting black kids, anyone, especially in the back, means big trouble now."

Hitting before you got hit. Simple. Maybe she was resorting to the way old Italian families took revenge. Rose repeated talk she picked up.

"Do it unto others before they do it unto you," she said. Marti had heard that in a movie, too. If Phil Stanton had some of that old-time blood lust in him, he would want to get even. She had to make him want to help her, too.

The secretary picked up. Surprise, surprise. She said, "Yes, he's in Mrs. Brown. He's been expecting your call and told me to put it right through."

You're kidding. Marti dropped her purse. He was on before she could pick it up.

"Hi. I can't talk from here. Do you want to give me a number or do you want to call later on another number I'll give you?"

She wasn't ready for that one. Maybe he didn't have caller ID on his office phone. He would sure have it on any other phone he gave her.

She said, "Call me back. In an hour."

"One hour. And Mrs. Brown."

"Yes.?"

"I don't have caller ID on this phone."

Oh yeah. "Okay, here's the number."

Oh boy, she had to go to the bathroom after that. His voice was warm and friendly enough, yet she still felt chilled, a little sick to her stomach. She peed, then stood in front of the mirror behind the wash basin and stared at herself.

"Can I do this?" she whispered to the empty room She threw some water in her face and felt better. Then she remembered she had forgotten to put the Out of Order sign on the phone, but it wasn't needed. None of the four kiosk phones was in use. Still she dug out her hand-made sign and taped it to the metal frame above the phone. She sat on a bench a few feet from the kiosk and rehearsed her end of what might be several opening remarks by Phil. Away from his office and unconcerned about possibly being overheard by a nosy secretary, he might start screaming. In that case she would take it. No screaming back. He would have to cool down and when he did she would stay calm and outline her demands.

She was hungry. It was only a short walk to the food court and she had time for a sandwich and a diet coke. She window-shopped as she walked. If things worked out she would add a lot of nice things to her wardrobe, and have a better place to put them than those crummy little bungalow closets.

The food was tasteless. She could only eat half of the sandwich. What if he turned her offer down? He could make her feel like a sneaky rat if he wanted to, send her crawling back to the bungalow with no hope while she gave up the general area of their hideaway. She would have to confront Bob then, ask him point blank. "You clearing out?"

What if he said no, and meant it. What then? She was stuck with him and she might already have tipped off Phil to their hiding place. She couldn't tell Bob what she had done. She had to hope Phil would buy her idea. He was crazy about her once. The spat in his Essex House suite couldn't have happened at a worse time, coming crosswise with Bob's plan to turn Phil in.

She hurried back to the phone even though she still had at least fifteen minutes before his call. He would call on the dot. She didn't have to remember the flap in his Essex House room to know how strict he was about keeping appointments on time.

She tried to force the question from her mind as she stared at the phone.

Can you do this?

Yes, even though she didn't have solid proof Bob was planning to skip she was going to go through with it. She had to. Bob either knew about her affair with Ross or he was so unhappy with his own life that he was going to make her life miserable living with him. He created this mess. He could live with it, or whatever.

She walked toward the phone kiosk on that thought, glancing at her watch. Phil was on time. She picked up on the first ring, but he spoke before she could say hello.

"So how are you?" Sounding as if he cared, emphasis on the are.

"Okay. How about you?" An inane exchange, she thought.

"Well, it's my nickel as we used to say, so I'll tell you. Business is good, but my personal life is lousy. I miss you, lady. I know it didn't look that way in court and when I didn't answer your calls, but I hope you can understand my feelings at the time."

What is there to say to that? Suddenly she's no longer a beggar. She sucked in her first real breath of the day. She took her time, not easy for her. Second husband Frank had called her a conversational "counter-puncher."

She said, "I've missed you, too. It made me sick when you didn't take my calls. I wanted to tell you I had nothing to do with Bob's turning on you. I was sure you thought I told him about us and that he wanted some kind of revenge."

"You're right. I was out of my mind. I thought you were so mad about what happened at the hotel that you told him about us. Whether I was convicted or not, I was going to find you."

She stepped on his line. "Don't tell me what you were going to do then. Just tell me what you would do now if you find us?"

He said, "Look, I know I have a temper. You saw it, and I'm begging you to forgive me. Remember, I tried to call you, but you wouldn't take my calls. As for right now, I'd like to get my money back, sure, but I have to admit your husband did help the company. A lot. I don't forgive him. He humiliated me by taking that phony story to the feds. He was probably stealing from the first day he came to work. I made a serious mistake in turning the entire financial operation over to him. Can you believe it? I had a younger accountant set up to keep an eye on the creep, the basic operation, but the kid said Costello's computer setup was too complicated to understand. The bells should have gone off right then, but we were doing great, adding profitable new subsidiaries. I just let it ride. I couldn't believe he would dare steal from me.

"You have to understand, my great grandfather had a dream. He hoped someone in the family would make it big, like an Astor, or a Carnegie. He specified in a written plan that all male offspring be educated to compete in business. After three generations my number came up and per his wishes I was given an American-sounding name. He thought any Italian who wasn't a musician, scientist or a doctor would never make it in America, especially in business or finance. It's no secret to the government. They checked me out long ago, after they learned my great grandfather, Guido Bonaventura, made his living as a bookkeeper and fence for a mob of punks and thieves. But he saved his money, and invested it, and the cash and his idea became the basis for my upbringing, my education, and my business. When Costello went to the attorney general of the United States and told him I was a thief and tax manipulator, it threatened everything my family and their wives tried to create."

He paused and she could hear his rapid breathing. A hell of a speech, she thought, most of it probably true. He had never talked to her like this. It was all sex. Off with the clothes and into the king-size. He had just helped her understand how he had become successful in business. He was a persuader, a super salesman. He was selling her.

Take care. He may see the time sex with her will again be a priority, but right now he wants his money.

"Hey, Marti, you still there?"

"Yes, I'm here. I was just wondering where I go from here. I'm not a happy camper. I hated leaving New York. I never would have gone into hiding with Bob, but that look of yours in the courthouse scared the hell out of me. What was I supposed to do? I couldn't take off on my own. I didn't have a dime."

"I know. I can see what you were up against. But you're okay now. You have to know that your husband has money. He has what the government thinks I stole. It's a hell of a lot of dough, Marti."

"So help me, if he has that money I have no idea where it is."

"Of course not, but let's talk about how we might get you out of wherever you are holed up. Somewhere around Chicago from the code. Bob probably has a job, probably related to what he knows best, accounting, but not a major operation. The government found a place for you to live, not a very good place, nothing like what you'd become accustomed to back here. Right?"

"Yeah, right." *Keep talking big brother.* She had to admit his voice was coming over her like a warm breeze on a cool day.

"Okay. The situation as I see it calls for helping you get your freedom back, so you can make your own declaration of independence. Ha. How about that? All we have to do is get you a fair share of that money Bob has stashed somewhere."

Do it now, Marti. You've got your opening.

She said, "But I don't know where it is."

God, will he deliver the punch line?

"Right, but you know where he is."

Yes! Like that basketball announcer screams. "Yes!"

He said, "Marti, I can't get you what you need unless we can talk to Bob."

"Talk?"

"Of course, talk. Make a deal. I'm not an old-time hood, like in the movies. You help me get in touch with Bob, not by phone because he's scared and he could run before he'd hear me out. So I'll need an address. I'll make a deal with him for the money and then set you up for life.

How does that strike you, lady?"

"Set me up for life? That would take a lot."

"What do you consider a lot?"

Marti had had the number in mind for a long time.

"A million dollars."

No pause. "Ill go with that. And if you like, I'll help you invest any part of it so that you can live well back here where you belong."

There had been no hesitation. It was if they were talking about small change.

Wow, *how much did Bob steal?*

"What do you say, Marti? Do we have a deal?"

"Sure, but I ought to have some kind of guarantee I'll get the money."

"I can understand that and here's what I'll do. Give me a bank out there and call me with the routing number and whatever and I'll deposit fifty thousand dollars within an hour. Inside. How's that? The government takes an interest in large transfers of money, but we' ll work that out later?"

"Fifty thousand?"

"Hey, Marti, that's fair when you consider there's no guarantee I'm going to get anything from Costello."

Right. And if Bob's gone before you can get to him, then there's nothing for anyone.

Nada. You'll think I tipped Bob and want your money back, and maybe a chunk of my hide. And if I tell you Bob is on the edge of walking out on me you won't give me a dime.

She said, "Make it a hundred thousand. Now, and directly to me. No bank."

She had to wait a few seconds. *How much will he risk to get Bob?*

His voice held a slightly harder edge. "Okay. May I have your address?"

Was he kidding? "As soon as I receive your money order."

"Hey, girl, you are really being cloak and dagger, aren't you?"

"It's as you say, Phil. There isn't any guarantee on what you can work out with Bob. I'll call you tomorrow with instructions for the money order. Okay?"

"Okay, there won't be any delay on my end."

"And when it is deposited, I'll call."

Another pause. "Okay, but let's leave this on a non-commercial note. I really do miss you, and I want you back where you belong."

Back to New York. Wow!

Even Cora and her watchdog attitude would be part of the fun of being back home. And with a hundred thousand dollars and a promise of a lot more, the options for doing anything, going anywhere had suddenly increased, she remembered the word, "exponentially."

She wouldn't be able to avoid seeing Phil again, but would try to break it off if she told him there would be no more Essex House romps. It had to be marriage. Ha! In her wildest dreams she couldn't see him giving up his family and endangering his social position further. He would raise hell about her taking the moral high ground, but she could promise to incriminate him if he had her harmed in any way.

The trial must have stung him badly. His pride was incredible, but she had to admit the description of how great grandfather Guido had provided for the family's future was almost touching. If she didn't remember that at heart he was a mobster. What she wanted, something permanent, was out of the question with Phil, but Ross was as unhappy with his marriage as she was. If he was leaning towards a long-term commitment, the idea of having her and sharing the good life with Phil's million would turn him on.

She had to check out the best place to receive the money order, but first she had to call Ross for a meeting asap. Sound him out. Would he dump job, family, and the windy city to join her and a million dollars? At the same time she had to stall Bob, somehow keep him from taking off for a few more days. Nine hundred thousand bucks could be at stake.

"Negotiation," Phil had said. She needed to learn more about what that meant.

10

Marti almost turned her ankle getting out of the room at the Red Roof Inn.

Good god, was she some kind of fool. Ross was so positive, so certain she had fallen into a trap. Why was she in such a goddamn hurry to call Phil?. He had handled her like she was a stupid fish, going after his bait. Had even given him their new names.

"Down payment," Ross said about her hundred thousand. The words were like a slap in the face. Wake up to reality, per the old lyric. She sold her husband out because she was bored. Sure he might be about to run out on her. She deserved it. Now she had to get to him and get them both out of that house. And she had to get her money out of North Shore City Bank, too. They might not give it all to her at once, but something could be worked out.

She gave Phil the bungalow address and her new name a week ago. Would he come in person? Probably not. Somehow, if Ross was right, Phil would give someone a call and some horrible instructions.

She piled into the Taurus and spun it out of the parking lot. She had to get back to the bungalow. She had stayed too long with Ross. Bob might already be home. Home! She hadn't done much to make it a home. She'd tell Bob she knew he wanted to get away, but that she wanted to get away, too. That admission could help turn him around if he had somehow learned, or guessed she was having an affair with the marshal. She had to turn it on, show him she cared about him. So she would fake it. Better than getting him killed. And Ross said she was in trouble, too. A hundred thousand dollars worth. For him to tell her to get out of town showed he cared more for her than an occasional romp in the sack. But that was probably over. As they said in the old neighborhood, "forget about it."

It was too late for Bob to ask the government for relocation. He must never know she turned him in. She'd need some kind of explanation for her panic, but she had to convince him they had to get out. Now!

A week since her call. Phil had had plenty of time to send whomever he was going to send. She and Bob could be a thousand miles away before anyone in the marshal's office knew they were gone. Ross might even give them more time by stalling his report that they were missing. They could get into Mexico, then take off for anywhere. Bob would know how to make the arrangements. Later, when they were sure they were in the clear, she might be able to convince Bob to give her a good chunk of cash to get rid of her. Then she might get back to Ross, but maybe not. Men rarely divorced wives for the other woman, and with Bob's money and Phil's "down payment" she could start a new life. What she had done to dump Bob was insane, but she had never loved him. He was a bailout. She never dreamed she could stay married to him for nearly four years.

The way Ross looked at her made her sure he knew how she was thinking, but it wasn't disapproval. He didn't give a damn about Bob, had treated him with restrained contempt. She could tell he liked the possibilities, all right, but it would be up to her to clear the way. Now he probably thought her a damned fool. She had sold herself on the sell out—that Bob after all was a squealer. Hating cops and admiring anyone who could beat the law was as basic to her background as pasta. And she married a cop! Dear Billy! She knew what could happen to guys who ratted on their bosses. Rose had filled her up with that crap, so she had conned herself into believing Bob deserved his showdown with Phil, but also that Phil was not a thug and would handle the matter as described in their telephone deal. It was right that she should be free to start over, rather than spend the rest of her life in hiding, but Ross had scared the hell out of her. Her freedom couldn't come at the price of Bob's torture, or having murder on her conscience for the rest of her life.

His Mercury Marquis was in the single-lane driveway. She wouldn't block it. His big trunk would be the best car for a long drive. She pulled up in front of the dreary house she had hated at first sight, made a quick check for any personal belongings in the seats and glove compartment and ran for the door. She used her key, and yelled, "Bob." She was supposed to use "Lee," even in the privacy of their home, but there was no time to worry about that now.

There was no sound at all for several seconds, then she heard his voice, muffled because it was coming from the basement.

"Down here."

Right, working with his tools. She had neither encouraged it nor discouraged it. It contributed to what she wanted, a growing dissolution of common interests with the man.

The door to the basement stairway was closed. She swung it open and stepped down without hesitation. There were only three or four steps remaining when she saw her husband wasn't alone. A man in a black overcoat with black hat to match, seeming almost as wide as he was tall, was holding a long gun pointed at her husband who was standing next to his work bench. She froze, gripping the handrail. No explanation was needed. He was an executioner, about to kill Bob. And her? The hood swung dark expressionless eyes from Bob to her. No one had ever looked at her like that. Without seeming to move his lips, he said, "Yeah, join the party." It was horrible. She couldn't let this happen

Wait a sec. Phil wouldn't send someone to shoot his betrayer. He had to know where Bob had stashed his loot. This would involve the "negotiation" he had described.

She glanced at Bob. He was standing with one hand resting on the workbench as if he needed it to hold him up.

Why didn't he yell at her to run when she first called out? Did he know she had sold him out? Had he lost any interest in protecting her? He was looking at her as if she was a stranger intruding upon a private conversation.

Then, when she stepped down the remaining steps and turned towards the gunman, he said "Hey." Not loud, but as if surprised.

In fact he was surprised to see her. The moment he opened the bungalow's cheap front door and backed away from the stocky intruder he was sure he had guessed it right. Marti had turned him in. What lay ahead was as easy to guess. The squat ugly man and his ugly gun would use whatever methods he had found successful in extracting information from people who were loath to give it. He should have guessed that taking Marti into hiding with him wouldn't work. When she appeared willing to go into the program, not just resigned, he felt the years of living in fear, the lonely hours at the computer, sneaking cash into bank safe boxes, then stealing from them, had been worth it. Her agreement confirmed what he had thought was part of her persona, the character to honor a commitment. She had been the only woman he had ever pursued, but his surprise at her agreement to marry him was accompanied by the awareness he was probably regarded as a good catch. He could see that assessment in the eyes of Cora Lambucci, too.

Her beauty had been an overwhelming lure, and he thought he was in love, but he learned almost immediately the emotion was bound to an event of years before, an experience he could never forget. An extraordinary woman, discovered on a rare night of adventure, had led him into paradise. He thought Marti might have helped him relive those precious moments, but his basic intelligence quickly brought him to understand the reality of marriage as opposed to living a fantasy. Marti was a beautiful partner with wit and style but with an edge he thought might have hidden some needs he couldn't fulfill. That she would betray him for money should not have come as such a shock, but once he realized her unfaithfulness he confirmed his decision to run away. Obviously, he hadn't moved quickly enough. For Marti to be here to witness his humiliation, and certain death was terrible. He felt sick to his stomach. He would not be able to withstand any torture. He would tell the fat man that more than three million dollars was resting in a public storage facility in Minneapolis. They would take his locker key, check out the locker's contents somehow, then he would die.

The chunky man with the gun was a contract assassin. His base was Detroit, but he rented apartments in New York and Miami. Business was that good. His usual contact had spelled it out by phone only a couple of days before. He was to gather Leland and Karen Velotti and pen them up somewhere until he got further word. They were not to be harmed, especially the woman. The point about leaving her alone was reemphasized. Not hard to figure. She was a knockout. She came down those stairs like a movie star. A star in a hurry, but maybe he could learn more about his assignment Whoever ordered the kidnapping and whatever he was to do next involved some special plans for the lady, and it wasn't to kill her.

Marti had no plan, not the slightest idea what she would tell Bob if she was able to stop this thing. She thrust herself forward, not really afraid, sure she was in no danger. Phil said she would not be harmed in any way. Neither would Bob if she could somehow stop this ape. She had to get Bob out of there. Now! Telling herself the gunman wasn't going to shoot, she walked straight at him.

Bob said, "Marti!" and she could see the intruder's forehead wrinkle under the black hat.

Making a sideways swipe with her hand, she said, "Bob, get out of here." In two quick strides she was in front of the gunman, between him and Bob. She reached out for the gun. To turn it away from Bob and give the intruder a hard push.

The gunman hesitated. *Who's Bob? And Marti?* He came to pick up a Leland and Karen. He lowered his gun slightly, but swung it back in reaction to movement from the workbench.

Marti heard the quick footsteps behind her. She felt a slight tug as the gun's long snout snagged in her blouse. Then her belly was on fire.

11

Marti was awake and hurting. Not alert, but scared. The pain was everywhere. In her stomach and arms, then down through her legs to her toes. She groaned. They had to give her something, but she wanted to stay conscious. She tried to raise an arm, but it hurt too much. She could say that she didn't remember a thing. Bull shit. Statements like that from gunshot victims in teevee and the movies was a lot of crap. Or it was in her case. She didn't remember any pain, that was right, but she would never forget how the blow to her stomach had knocked all the air out of her, how some powerful force tried to smash her face into her knees.

The husky nurse with the Irish face and nice smile announced another visitor.

"It's your brother. I told him to wait a few minutes. If you like I'll give your hair a brush."

Brother, what brother? It has to be Ross, doing the cloak and dagger routine. Good, she had to tell him what happened, get his ideas on what she should tell the cops.

Marti managed a woozy smile. Even it hurt. "How long have I been here?"

The nurse said, "You're into your third day. You were pretty well out of it the first two, and doing a lot of snoozing since then. The bullet did a lot of damage, but you are on the road to recovery. How's the pain? We'd like to ease off on the heavy dope. We don't want you to get a liking for the stuff."

Marti grimaced. "It hurts. Everywhere. But I'd like to stay awake from here on out."

The nurse had found a brush and comb but first used her fingers to untangle Marti's hair.

"Okay, you look much better. Your brother looks anxious. Shall I let him in?"

Marti nodded. "What's your name?"

"Margaret Delaney, but friends and patients call me Peg. Marion Harris and I have been on your case since you came in. You've been through some kind of hell, but you're going to be okay. I heard Doctor Morgan talking to therapy. We'll get you on your feet as soon as possible and have you working out in no time."

Marti wanted to ask how soon she would she be up, and what kind of therapy. She had hated exercise since the enforced jumping, bending, running, and stupid games in grade school. Ross strode in. Her first thought was how beautiful he looked, then how awful she must look. She had to get some makeup stuff in here.

"Hey." She wanted to needle him for coming in unannounced, but it came out as a croak. "I'm trying to look like a human being. What's your hurry?"

Delaney stepped aside, and Ross, looking all business, stepped close to the bed but made no move to kiss her. Like a brother, but how could he with a tube sticking out of her nose.

"I can't stay long. I talked with a Doctor Morgan. He said I can't stay long."

Marti tried to see around Ross for nurse Delaney, but the door was closing on the RN's broad back. Hearing the door close, Ross bent over the bed quickly, brushing his lips against her face.

She tried to grin. "Thanks. I needed that."

He smiled, not as tense. "I couldn't tell them I was a marshal. How do you feel?"

"I feel pain, that's what." She hoped she didn't smell like an operating room She gazed up at the man whose face showed concern. He was probably the best looking man she had ever known—since Billy. Not pretty, like a Tom Cruise or other Hollywood studs, but all the elements of his face and body had good proportion. The brown eyes were well spaced. The nose fit the tanned face, and the chin was good, no cleft like Cary Grant, but strong. Remembering the pledge she had made just hours before, she had to face the reality that she didn't love him, but it would be good to press herself against all that strength.

He was back to business. "Tell me how you got shot"

He nodded as she described the scene in the basement and pursed his lips when she told him of the last few seconds. "I remember getting hit so hard it folded me into a horseshoe."

"Costello must have hit him. I found the hammer."

"I hope he knocked his head off. What happened to the son of a bitch?"

"He's back in his hole, wherever it is." He held his forefinger across his lips. The door to the private room was closed, but he still lowered his voice.

"Marti, listen. I don't want to know anymore about that asshole than his description. I don't want or need to know how he got in your basement, or why he was there. Understand."

She understood. He was covering his ass. He had put it all together after she shot off her mouth in the motel about how she was coming into money. Did he think she would admit turning Bob in to Phil Stanton? No way. He needn't worry. She could hope he thought she ran out of the motel room to warn her husband. But she wouldn't admit that, either.

He was sitting in a chair he had pulled up close to the bed. He reached for her hand.

"My job now is to protect you. The hood messed up his assignment. He won't be back, but whoever ordered the visit might be. Do you understand?"

Marti tried to look puzzled. "What do you mean?"

"I don't think the hood was supposed to kill anyone, and my guess is he's in deep doodoo for harming you."

Not bad thinking, but I'm still not telling the whole story. Not yet, anyway.

She said, "Bob ran because someone is after him. He probably thinks I'm dead, but he knows, or should know, I tried to get him out of that basement. My only worry is about whoever thought I helped Bob get away."

She stared at the face she once thought she could eat like cereal, no milk or sweetener necessary. She felt a stab of pain and closed her eyes for a second.

Ross said, "Hey, you okay?"

It pleased her that he looked concerned. She said, "What am I going to tell this cop I see hanging over my face every time I come to?"

Ross's grin was appreciative. "I told my boss you wouldn't give the program away. You just tell anyone who questions you that the guy with the gun found you both in the basement, that you didn't know what he wanted, maybe robbery, maybe he was a loony and followed you home with rape in mind. Anyway, you got in the way somehow when Bob went for him, with a hammer. You don't remember anything else."

"So how do I explain why Bob took off?"

"You don't know. And no one can make you speculate. The cops have all they need to know. There was a stranger in your home who shot you. Your husband took off for his own reasons. That's it. You just don't know."

She said, "Hey, who found me? In the basement?"

"I did. I wondered what yanked you out of the motel so fast. I called the house from my car, but there was no pickup. I drove over, saw your car, but not Bob's. The front door was unlocked. It took a minute or so to find you, then I called 911 and got out. I couldn't wait around and have to identify myself."

Right. He had to cover her protected witness status.

He said, "Can you describe the shooter?"

She did pretty well, she thought. A short, very-wide man. Fleshy face, dark eyes under bushy brows, a somewhat bulbous nose, red at the end as if sunburned or from too much booze. She couldn't be sure of hair color because of the hat, but she judged his age in the middle forties.

He listened without interruption, making notes on a pad. Then reached for her hand and leaned over to kiss her cheek.

"I'm out of here. I could be spotted by someone who knows me. Questions would be asked. I can't claim you as a relative again."

She wondered, would he ever have a claim on her again?

"When can you come again?"

"When I'm sure the cops have lost all interest in you."

He gave her a finger wave and was gone.

12

The unsmiling doctor, about forty-five, tall with strong cool hands, a nose like a parrot's beak, and bushy eye brows, said his name was Morgan. He played feely with her feet, asked her if she could move her toes. He seemed satisfied, said she could be moved from critical care that day and that she was "a tough little lady." He said it would help her recovery if she could withstand some of the pain but that she could have something to make it easier whenever she wanted it. "She said, "Right now!"

Nurse Delaney was ready with the needle.

"Last shot. I don't have to puncture you anymore. "Aren't you glad? Doctor ordered a PSA pump for you so that you can administer your own morphine."

"Was that the doctor who operated on me? I ought to thank him."

"Yes, Morgan was the main guy. Your treatment began with the crew in the ambulance that picked you up. Then in ER they had to get you stabilized. There was lots of blood to replace, four units in the OR and a couple more later, lots of other work for Morgan and a vascular surgeon, Gene Bennett. The internal exploration and patchwork took them eight hours. The bullet missed your spine, but nicked your iliac artery. You just satisfied Morgan you can use your legs.

"They had to sew up your large intestine, too. The NG tube in your nose will have to stay there until your bowels can start working again, and you're wearing a catheter for urine. The other tube under your shoulder blade will furnish nourishment until you can take real food. Morgan could have told you all this but he doesn't talk much. He's one of the cutters with a nice, even disposition. He always looks grim."

She saw Marti didn't get her little joke. She said, "I could tell he was pleased."

Marti was moving her hands across her stomach.

"Lots of bandages."

"Oh yeah. On your back, too. The slug went all the way through."

Marti didn't hear her. Whatever Peg punctured her with had done its job.

Peg Delaney thought her patient's face was more relaxed in slumber than it had been to that point.

A really beautiful woman, but she might not want to wear bikinis anymore.

Peg had heard that Morgan and the other surgeons had to make a huge hole to check out all the internal damage. *Ah well. Karen Velotti could join her and the great mass of women who would never be invited to pose for one of those Sports Illustrated special swim suit issues her husband, Mike, looked forward to each year.*

She shook her head. *Get going girl. While Velotti snoozed it was a good time to find an orderly and move her to her new room. The detective said it should be private, and an officer would be sitting outside the door twenty four hours. What had the beautiful lady done to have someone trying to kill her?*

13

To be, and how and where to be was the question, as it had been for the five-hour drive. Exhausted, more from an endless review of the scene in the bungalow basement than from the trip, Bob Costello ramped off I-94 for a Western Inn near Eau Claire, Wisconsin. He paid cash, then on the registration card he wrote Samuel E. Balestri of 46 Lawton Ave., Cliffside Park, New Jersey, 07010 and a number totally different from the one on his new Delaware license plate. He drove to his room and crapped out, exhausted.

He was alive, but Marti was surely dead. The fat son of a bitch who shot her might be dead, too. He had given him a hell of a smack with the hammer, a tool he was about to return to its place above the workbench when he was interrupted by the jolly caller. When the thug went down, the instinct to run took over. He wanted to kill Marti's killer. He had stood over the son of a bitch for several seconds, willing himself to use the hammer again, to smash the life out of the bastard. But he couldn't do it.

He hadn't panicked, but he almost threw up when he saw Marti folded over like that, and all the blood. He was sure she was dead. He called 911, but not until he was a couple of miles from the bungalow and on his way out of town. He couldn't wait there in the basement. He had already decided to leave. It was just one day earlier than he had intended.

The 911 message was as brief as he could make it. He was sure they had caller ID. He jumped all over the voice of the female dispatcher. He said, "A woman has been shot in the basement at 2435 West Lawndale," and hung up. The dispatcher would use her play back to give the cops the address, and trace the source of the call. She did what she was supposed to do, trying for the caller's identity instead of just listening. Bob didn't care if his voice could be identified. By whom? Vincennes? So what.

He had thought about taking the hood's gun on the chance he'd need it before he could get to his car. The fat man might have had some backup waiting outside. While grabbing his stuff in the bedroom he peeked out on the street for anything suspicious but he saw only Marti's car and the same cars at the curb that were there when he returned to the bungalow.

Taking the gun would have been a sure way to be accused of shooting his wife and giving the fat man an alibi, if the son of a bitch was still lying there when the cops arrived. He hoped so. Maybe he should have found some rope and tied him up. But that would have told the cops he might have been there, might have been in on the shooting. Of course his prints were all over the hammer. But who else's would be on it? Jesus. What a mess! Let the cops sort it out. Let Vincennes tell his boss how his protected witness disappeared.

He had no thought of calling Vincennes. He was convinced the marshal, or Marti, or both of them, had conspired to get him killed or kidnapped and tortured. He might still be a protected witness, but he wasn't going to be protected any longer by that son of a bitch.

Who called Stanton? Who else? Maybe Marti had guessed he was taking off without her. Maybe she had poked around the bedroom closet and couldn't feel anything like money in the suits. But then why did she come to the rescue, walk right up to the hood and say, "Bob, get out of here?" *Maybe she knew she wasn't to be harmed, but why the attempt to help him get away? If Stanton had set the thing up, the idea would be to force his enemy to cough up the money, then kill him. The hood seemed in no hurry. He may have been waiting for Marti to show up, but if she had called Stanton, or whomever, why did she come back to the bungalow? And she yelled his name when she came into the house.*

He was certain of her betrayal, but it sounded like a warning. He instinctively wanted to yell for her to get out, but the fat man jerked his gun and said, "Get her down here."

Maybe she wasn't in on it but had somehow learned what was going to happen. From Vincennes? Whatever, she saved his life.

He had everything ready to take her with him, and was about to tell her his plan. Then came that morning, when he normally would have been at Northbrook. The deputy dropped in and he saw the look she and Vincennes give each other, the look that could mean only one thing. That cut it. He left some cash in their checking account, might have sent her more, and he had stuffed $10,000 in one hundred dollar bills in an envelope with the intent of leaving it on the bed. With Marti lying dead in the basement he threw the envelope into his suitcase on top of his underwear. After making his decision he hadn't done much to camouflage his feelings. Marti might have guessed he was taking off alone, but not exactly when. He had planned his departure over the past two weeks, removing the cash from the suits. The car was ready. All he had to do was pack some clothes and take off.

He hid the cash from the suits and the checking account in the car's upholstery. He mustn't forget it when he sold the Mercury. He had already checked out the Eau Claire dealer by phone as he drove. He would see him tomorrow and with any luck at all he would be in the clear and in Minneapolis early in the afternoon. The new car he would buy in Minneapolis would be part of his new identity, along with the Delaware stuff.

The shooting could have been an accident. The look on the fat man's face was like, "What the hell are you trying to do, lady?" but the gun still fired. Maybe the fat man was stalling until Marti arrived, then he was going to conduct the question-and-answer session. Possible, but that scenario didn't fit with Marti barging in that way

Marti dead. Oh my god. Sure, marrying her was probably a mistake. She didn't love him. She loved the comfort and luxury he bought her. She was never unkind, but never really affectionate. She had had two other husbands, but that didn't matter. What he thought he saw in her was the embodiment of a memory. He had foolishly thought he might recreate or build upon the experience of that wondrous night in San Francisco. He had been inspired by a lovely interlude with another woman. He had hoped Marti might help him recapture love he had paid for. Well, he paid for Marti's love, too, but it wasn't an apples to apples comparison.

He was just a well-educated bean counter, making a good living but housekeeping out of a suitcase until he met Phil Stanton. Stanton, the whitewashed crook, the man who fronted profitable legitimate enterprise, but who still wanted more. The greedy prick thought a well-trained financial specialist would easily agree to help him steal it.

He should have known. From the start. Stanton's idea for dumping those accountants and running the entire financial end through a single station smelled like something sitting too long in Fulton's fish market. He should have gotten out of there, but the job was a challenge he enjoyed, and spending money on Marti was more than just satisfying. Maybe he had grown to like the idea of having money too much, and when Stanton dropped his bomb instead of walking out he listened. Maybe it had been too easy to sell himself on the notion Stanton would have done harm to him if he had told the son of a bitch to shove it.

Stanton had taken his required accounting and bookkeeping in college, but he was a babe in the woods with computers. He showed no interest in the upgraded equipment I brought in. There were no were no compliments on the surprisingly low costs, either

The Dell professional model was capable of meeting Stanton's demand for day-by-day report on receipts and profit forecasting. Bob had some other ideas for the late model Dell. He thought his previously limited work on studies in derivatives—options and futures—could help the company. He had the time, at least in the first year. All the ancillary responsibilities fell into line with the help of three accountants who survived Stanton's purge, and from their computers he picked up all he needed for quarterly and annual reports as well as the day-to-day numbers Stanton insisted upon. On his computer everything was encrypted, too.

Getting things set up the first several months was the easiest job time he had spent since getting his CPA. With accountability to no one but Stanton he was able to enjoy some long lunches with the usual crowd of bond and security peddlers that descend upon all financial officers like bears to honey. He kept Stanton appraised of all such sessions, and his recommendations for investments and acquisitions were invariably approved, often with a wave of the hand. Stanton kept his distance. Meetings were brief with no relaxed chats about how thingswere going. It would have been obvious to anyone with a smidgeon of financial training they were going very well. The idea of siphoning off some of the flood of cash he was personally shepherding into purchases, investments, and bank deposits was coincidental with Stanton's invitation to meet him at the office on a Saturday morning when no other employees were in the building.

Stanton hadn't wasted any time on chit chat. He said, "Look, re the IRS, we want to pay our fair share, right?" It was as if he were talking to a bug hidden somewhere on his desk, maybe in the glass goddess paperweight. He didn't wait for Bob's obvious answer, but what he said then eliminated the possibility he was covering his ass on tape.

"You're a smart guy, Costello. You say we are on target to earn nine per cent after taxes and practically no debt load. So we are liable for some hefty taxes. What I'd like to see is the corporation earn between six and a half and seven. I'm the major shareholder. I'll live with that, but if we pay tax on the lower earning there should be something left over for the good guys, shouldn't there? I mean you and me."

He had hoped the stunned look on his face passed as calm, but his heart was trying to jump out of his chest. Any number of clients had admonished him, "If you make any mistakes, make them in our favor," and he had always answered with a smile, "Of course." But there were no mistakes. He was an accounting machine. Had been since keeping the books for his parents. There had been one occasion he had deliberately "cooked" some books. It was to help keep boyhood friend Billy Lichtenstein's legs from being broken. His only close friend had run up gambling debts with some impatient people, and Bob had helped him pay off with cash owed the IRS. Bob had never stolen a penny's worth of candy in his life, and he didn't take a dime from Billy, either. Now his boss, as if remarking that they might be due for some rain that day, hits him with this brick. Here this reputedly squeaky-clean businessman, only recently cited as "Newark Entrepreneur of the Year," was inviting him to steal from the U.S. government.

He remembered thinking, "Jesus, how can this guy suggest such a thing? Doesn't he know I'm as square as a baseball diamond? That I might go straight to the FBI?"

Stanton sat without movement behind his all-glass desk. He smiled slightly.

"What's the matter, Costello. Have I offended you?"

He hadn't offended him. Stanton had simply scared the shit out of him. The business golden boy was suborning a key executive to steal from a powerful and unforgiving source. Phillip Stanton had just announced he was a crook and the implication was clear. "If you're on my team you play the game my way."

Lying on the motel bed, Bob felt the same chill grip his heart that he felt as he stared across the desk at the handsome, smiling, impeccably groomed young man who exhibited his self-confidence—*arrogance?*—in the way he leaned back in his expensive swivel chair. Bob hadn't seen this smile since his second visit to Stanton Corporation when he and Stanton shook hands on his employment deal. It wasn't the good guy grin doled out to other employees, or at Rotary meetings. In Stanton's eyes was a look of assessment. When Bob first saw it he wondered, "What am I getting into here?"

Scaring him even more was the realization that Stanton was certain his financial officer would not pull the plug. If Costello went crazy and tried to blow the whistle, he was fully prepared to protect himself.

Bob remembered thinking, "He isn't afraid I'll go to the authorities, and if I did he would say, 'There was no such meeting,' or words to that effect. Then I would later die in an accident, my car eventually found in a lake or river. Not right after getting canned at Stanton, but later, maybe years later. Phil Stanton would never forget."

He was right about Stanton's readiness to cover his ass. Stanton was as ready to shuck any charges off his back at that moment as he was later in federal court.

Bob had heard himself say, "Sure, I can handle that. I'll prepare two reports for your daily review, beginning right now."

Then Stanton laughed. "The hell you will, bookkeeper. You do your financial mischief in our reports to shareholders, with our auditors, and the government. What we clear will be strictly between you and me. All cash, and I touch none of it. No memoranda. Nothing on paper or in a laptop."

What Bob Costello's share of the ultimate take would be was never mentioned by his boss, but as he later told Marti, it was right then he decided he would take care of that matter himself. A few seconds after that meeting he switched on the computer in his brain for planning how a good chunk of the money he stole for Stanton would ultimately become his money. A collateral idea was also hatched—how he could fuck up Phil Stanton with the government.

Bob's fear of Stanton ballooned into hatred as he walked out Stanton's office.

How could he have gone self righteous and turned the man down? It was either okay the scheme or get lost. Stanton couldn't let him keep his job if he had offered any response other than approval. The man couldn't have a former financial officer running around loose, possibly going to the FBI or IRS. There was no way out. Go along or Stanton would make him disappear. Was he over-dramatizing the matter? What other way was there to look at it?

He was convinced he had hopelessly compromised himself; but that wasn't the only basis for his hatred for his boss. The rage almost boiled over at a party in Stanton's home when he saw Stanton give Marti a look that could only be interpreted as a pass. He had never before wanted to injure another human being, but he could have killed Phillip Stanton that night.

In the car on their way home he told Marti he thought Stanton was a womanizer. She had said, "Bobby, you may be right, but he is doing no eyezing with this woman."

He had believed her, and during those early years of marriage his happiness in having this beautiful woman as his wife almost negated the pressure and guilt of what he was doing at Stanton.

But it wasn't until she agreed to go with him into witness protection that he was satisfied he could confide in her. Later, when things cooled down, they would leave, adopt new identities and live well on Stanton money for the rest of their lives.

He told Marti the overwork at Stanton and the knowledge his boss was a crook motivated him to report Stanton to the FBI. Actually, he would have continued the accumulation of illicit cash but for another meeting Stanton had called.

For most of their brief sessions, Stanton had not even invited him to sit down, but for this one he waved at a chair.

"How are we doing with our little fund?"

The question was asked only a few times each year. To Bob it was as if the man may have enjoyed learning how the secret accumulation had grown. Stanton had Bob's daily update which included the amount of cash from the company's subsidiaries deposited in money market accounts. This report did not include what Bob was skimming for deposit in the safety boxes.

Bob always gave Stanton exact numbers. Stanton could have accompanied him to the vaults in the half dozen banks used for the secret fund, but Bob was almost certain Stanton would never risk being seen grubbing around bank boxes. Or he could have sent someone with Bob to ascertain the amount, also highly unlikely. Bob was certain Stanton wanted this to be a two-person arrangement only. Still, he took no chances.

He said, "It's pushing six million. I was wondering. Would you like any of it shifted off shore?"

"Hell no. You've heard as well as I have the government is starting to snoop on such holdings. Leave it where it is."

Then Stanton had stared at his CFO. "Six million, huh?"

Bob had thought he had anticipated further questions such as, "You wouldn't be holding out, etcetera?" but Stanton had just stared at him for several long seconds, then said, "I realize you are carrying a hell of a load. I'm going to keep an eye out for an assistant for you. Only for the basics, of course, nothing about our arrangement."

Minutes after the meeting Bob was glad he had been sitting. He hoped his face hadn't shown the shock that nearly choked him. All his fears that Stanton was more evil than only consumed by greed were true.

He wants to dump me. Somewhere they won't even find my body. He might as well have said, "I want you to prep your replacement because you know too much."

The addition of an assistant, someone chosen carefully, not a bump up for one of the current staffers, would be the first step. Soon after the new aide acquired what Stanton called the "basics," Stanton would call an end to the "fund," perhaps using the pretext of giving me my share. But I wouldn't see a dim. I would then disappear. Stanton would have it all. The son of a bitch.

Paranoid he might be, but Bob remembered the old joke; that it isn't paranoia when you know it's going to happen? He was been convinced that if he had refused Stanton's scheme and walked out, he wouldn't have made it back to the condo. Whatever, Bob was convinced he was enmeshed in an inescapable web, with Stanton the hungry spider.

It had become time to exercise his escape plan.

14

Stanton's acquittal was a surprise, a shock really, but to Bob Costello whether Stanton was found guilty or not guilty his former boss wanted revenge. He and Marti would have to go into deep hiding.

Bob had told an anxious Marti, "Even from prison Stanton could send goons after me. Stanton knows there was a lot more money in the bank boxes than the feds found. Besides wanting a piece of my hide he'll want the money he knows I skimmed before I blew the whistle on him."

The motel bed was comfortable. He propped himself up against the headboard with a couple of pillows and a fifth of Jack Daniels unwrapped from some underwear. He sipped his drink and tried to force his thoughts away from the bungalow scene, but he could not help but think about Marti and Vincennes. He wondered if Vincennes had seen Marti on the basement floor. If they were lovers it must have been a shock for him, too. The bastard.

As the sour mash did its job he gave thanks to Billy Lichtenstein who involved him in the only time he ever broke the law; that is, before Stanton. Billy, a high school classmate, owned several profitable discount auto parts stores but was in trouble for gambling away the profits, and then some.

"Bob," he said, "I'm squeezed between the IRS and some very nasty people. I've gotta siphon some cash from my company's gross."

Bob worked until two in the morning to convert Billy's modestly profitable year into a net loss, thus freeing up some cash to pay off Billy's debt and keep both the thugs and the IRS at bay.

Billy was fulsome in his thanks. "Bobby, you saved my ass. If you ever. You know?"

Billy was given his chance. Bob called him from a public phone near his Northbrook office, telling him just enough to convey his needs.

Billy said, "I read the trial coverage. Man, I thought how did my boyhood buddy get himself into such a mess. I'm glad to have a chance to help you now. I owe you, man. That business loss I took helped me kick the gambling habit."

Billy said he wasn't personally into the kind of items Bob needed, but he knew someone who might be, and Bob had his package in three days, sent to general delivery in Chicago's suburban Evanston. He called Billy to thank him and ask him what it all had cost.

Billy said, "Hey, forget about it. We're square. Will I ever see you again?"

"I don't know, Billy. I hope it's on this earth."

The Delaware driver's license, no picture required, was for a Frank C. Librioni, the address somewhere in Paterson, New Jersey. The packet also included a forged title for the Mercury. It was made out to George A. Scarpetti, a Dover, Delaware address. Also in the packet were two Delaware license plates, one of which Bob switched with his Illinois plate before getting on the interstate.

He also had a new social security number, for Mr. Librioni. A note from Billy in the package said, "A Librioni is reborn. Good luck, Frank!"

15

Bob drove into Eau Claire the next morning to find a newsstand with Chicago and Minneapolis papers as well as the local daily. He took them back to the motel's coffee shop and when he read that Marti was alive he almost slopped his coffee. The Associated Press report, Chicago dateline, was brief, only a few paragraphs, no pictures, beginning, "A thirty-one year old housewife, Karen Velotti was today found critically wounded in the basement of her north side Chicago home."

There was no mention of the shooter, but the article said a neighbor told police two men, one identified as Velotti's husband, Leland, were seen leaving the Velotti bungalow about thirty minutes apart.

The son of a bitch got away, but Marti is alive.

Bob sucked in a couple of deep breaths. His compulsion to hurt Stanton, then his jealousy, had wrecked their chances for a lasting marriage. Marti may have betrayed him, but now she had to live with the guilt and pain.

He had to get going. Sell the car, take the bus into the twin cities, reclaim his money, buy another car, find a temporary place to live, and plan for the future.

He again drove the Mercury into Eau Claire and found Empire Motors on the north edge of town on state route 12. Dealer Ed Harvey was waiting, his smile suggesting he expected to make out all right on this one. Per the call from Mr. Scarpetti, Harvey had amassed the cash he expected to pay for a two-year old Mercury Marquis LS. The car was out of Delaware.

Stolen? He didn't think so, especially after meeting the owner who would fit no profile as a car thief. The guy was clearly a business type who for his own reasons needed some cash. Why Scarpetti hadn't taken the car to a local Ford or Mercury-Lincoln dealer Harvey told himself he didn't need to know. Harvey walked around the car, took a look at the odometer, and invited Bob into his office. He said, "I'm ready to deal, Mr. Scarpetti," and fifteen minutes later Bob was in a cab to the local Greyhound station. He guessed he had just made Harvey richer by at least a couple thousand dollars, and the dealer would brag about it, but the car and its former owner would be damn difficult to trace. Bob Costello's objective now was to make himself impossible to find.

The bus was cool enough but sweat was soaking into Bob's shirt about twenty minutes before the Greyhound eased into its Minneapolis terminal. Would the suitcases be where he left them? For months, ever since his one-day visit to the city during the Stanton trial, and all the time in Chicago, the worry about the bags and the more than three millions dollars in them had hovered at the edge of his thoughts every minute of every day. He couldn't do a thing but sweat it out. Another trip to check on the money was next to impossible, and for what purpose? He was stuck with the cash until he got into Mexico.

Rounding up the cash before the first Minneapolis trip was a scramble. He had to raid six banks the afternoon before the flight from Newark. He had time in the terminal to call ahead for the storage place he found in his computer. Twin-City Storage promised twenty-four hour security. They had the small locker he wanted and the transfer of the two suitcases to the mid-town facility had gone smoothly enough. He had to bring his own padlock, and he bought the best he could find, the one in the teevee commercial where they put a high power rifle bullet through it to prove it can't be opened without a key.

The padlock and the steel-door locker stared back at him just as it had several months before. His key was at work seconds after the thirty-minute cab ride from the bus depot. Seconds after that a Samsonite was open and he had his hands on all those bills. Wooey! What was all the worry about? No problems. He had his big stake again, plus the other cash including that from the Mercury sale. He relocked the bin after stuffing a big block of hundreds into his briefcase. Two hours later he had another car, a four-year old Buick LeSabre. The papers were made out to Frank C. Librioni, with the address in Paterson, New Jersey, exactly as shown on the second driver's license sent from Billy L. The Italian names were a good idea, no need to raise questions by trying to pass as a WASP. Once, during the years he used to moan to Billy about the prejudice against Italians in business, he said, "All I have to do is admit I live across the river, and they think I'm in the mob."

Billy said, "Change your name to Smith and dye your hair and wear contacts. Hell, Bobby, you could pass for the first male off the Mayflower."

Maybe he'd do that. In Mexico.

He had again bypassed factory-connected dealers and settled on Best Deal Motors north of downtown Minneapolis. Dealer Howard Carlson wasn't a smiler. There was no meaningless chatter. He didn't ask if there would be a trade in, and didn't bat an eye when the deal was closed and Bob counted out the total price, all in hundred dollar bills. As was the case with Harvey in Eau Claire, the dealer was all business. Few words were exchanged. Bob thought the man might have had a headache, or some other problem. A hangover? Carlson didn't fit the mold of a car salesman, but Bob appreciated the no-nonsense approach to business. The dealer's eyebrows didn't move upward when he saw the pack of bills, either.

He might think I robbed a bank, but so long as these hundreds are good, he doesn't give a damn."

Bob needed shelter. On his last hurried visit he thought the neighborhood of older but well-maintained homes and three and four-story apartment buildings around east 38th street would be right for his brief stay, and also was convenient to Twin Cities Storage.

He parked the Buick in front of the four-flat apartment building and introduced himself to the only employee he could see in the small office, a tall and slender older man who stepped from behind a wooden desk with a wary smile. Bob was sure the man thought he was a salesman for something he surely didn't want.

"Can I help you? I'm Albert Capshaw."

Bob reached for the man's hand. His need, he said was for an efficiency apartment he could use for occasional visits to the area.

"I sell computer software. I'm looking for something for a month, if possible. If it works out, I'll renew."

He got lucky, no long lease required. Capshaw showed him a plan for a unit and volunteered to walk him through it. Bob declined. He said he was in a hurry because he was. He paid for a month, and for another month as a deposit. He nodded as the manager explained there would be other deposit fees for electricity and a telephone. Bob told him his schedule was unpredictable.

"I'll be in and out, sometimes between long stretches on the road."

Capshaw, more expansive than either of the car dealers, smiled.

"I'm sure you will find the unit to your liking, Mr. Librioni."

Bob found a Holiday Inn Express for his first night back in the city. He chose it because he thought he could get lost in it as easily as anywhere in the midwest. Capshaw said he could move in that day, but Bob said he wanted to make the place livable first. The next morning he shopped for some bed linens, pillows, towels, soap, and other supplies. It was late in the morning when he arrived at the second-floor unit where he found everything in working order beginning with the light switch inside the door.

It would be a tight fit but workable. The single-room unit was designed for occupants who weren't troubled by claustrophobia. Dominating the small apartment was a queen-size bed. A recliner chair faced a nineteen-inch teevee sitting on a wall shelf. There were additional shelves below. A set of drawers was also built into the wall. The kitchenette, a tiny alcove barely wide enough to hold a two-burner stove, had a small adjoining counter over which hung a microwave unit. A mini-refrigerator and freezer was built into the wall below cabinetry for dishes and utensils. A small table with two chairs and a reading lamp completed the furnishings.

He hung his suits in the room's only closet and glanced out the apartment's sole window which looked onto a courtyard. He thought he would bring in some food later after eating something at a small neighborhood restaurant directly across the street from the building's entrance. Now hungry, he washed up in the tiny shower-equipped bath room and slipped out.

He ate his soup and sandwich and then picked up some basic groceries including coffee, milk, juice, bread, and cereal at a neighborhood delicatessen. He walked back to the apartment building with the single bag of food, remembering that the activity of the past hour was pretty much what he did while living with his mother. He thought how horrified she would be to learn what had happened to her son over the past several months. He could still remember the slight trace of old-world accent when she admonished him often to "be a good boy."

I tried, momma.

16

Marti woke up in her new room. The tubes were still sticking out of her body, but the surroundings were a lot different from critical care. There were some nice pictures on the blue-tinted walls, and there wasn't as much medical equipment standing around. Nurse Delaney came in as if on cue to announce another visitor. It was the cop, Carey, who came in with a smile after exchanging a couple of words with the nurse at the door.

He pulled a chair up to the bed. He said, "I told nurse Delaney I knew her husband, Mike. He was a sergeant in a south side precinct where I once worked."

"I could care less," she thought, but she managed a small smile.

Carey started with the basics, asking for a more detailed description of Bob than furnished by his neighbors. He wanted to know how long they had lived in the bungalow. She gave him the background furnished by Mr. Henry in New York, wondering if it would hold up. Then he segued into what took place in the bungalow basement, beginning with how she had walked onto the scene of the shooting after doing some shopping. She thought she was being pretty smart when Carey asked her what she had bought.

"Just a couple of personal items. Women's things."

He smiled slightly, then said, "From the powder burns we could tell the gun was held very close to your body. I would think if the man intended to kill you he would have given himself more room. Can you help account for this?"

Careful. The cop for all his friendliness was no dummy. He wasn't taking notes but he might have been wearing a recorder to help him remember exactly what she said and how she said it.

She gave him the full benefit of a direct stare. Billy Dillon called it her power look.

She said, "I hoped he wouldn't shoot me. It was the way he looked, as if he was confused. I wanted to distract him so Leland could get away. I just walked up to him. Obviously, I got too close."

The cop wrinkled his forehead. She thought it might be an act, the way Peter Falk played detective Columbo, who always had one more question.

"But you never heard him announce his purpose?"

"No." *Try to stick to yes and no answers.*

"And you have no idea why he came into your home?"

"No"

"Did you husband say anything? Did he appear frightened, like a man about to be shot?"

"No, and not particularly."

Another quick smile. "Then why do you suppose he ran away, leaving you like that?"

She put on a puzzled look, as if she was really trying to figure it all out herself.

"I don't know. Maybe he have thought I was dead."

She had to make the cop think she was cooperative, but she remembered Vincennes's warning, "Avoid speculation about Velotti's actions."

Carey thought that over, not taking his eyes from her face, then said, "When you are able I hope you can review our file of known criminals."

"Sure."

He asked her to go over the scene in the basement once more. She repeated what she had told Vincennes, adding, "I noticed his other hand, the one not holding the gun. His nails were polished as if he might go to manicurists. He also wore dark brown loafers that looked expensive."

Carey smiled at that effort, too, and said he would send in someone to do a sketch based on what she could remember.

"Tell me about your husband's job?"

She told him what she knew, which wasn't much. Obviously he could get more from Bob's former boss. She purposely she raised her eyebrows when Carey asked her whether she was aware of any enemies her husband might have, and whether he gambled, or owed anyone money.

"Not that I know of."

He said, "Does your husband like to go to bars. Do you eat out often?"

How in hell would this help the cop find Bob?

She tried to make her answers sound sincere. "Leland wasn't a drinker."

She couldn't talk about that night he came into the condo and slopped up all that bourbon. She had to be careful. She was tiring and would tell him so. Carey might be counting on her to drop her guard. This cop wasn't like the idiot sheriffs portrayed in the Angela Lansbury show. Somewhere in her answers he might pick up a clue to what was behind a home invasion and shooting, if he hadn't figured it out already. If he really started to dig she would have to remember all the fictitious stuff drilled into Bob and her about their lives before they came to Chicago. She needed some rehearsal time if he got into that.

She made a little moan. "I'm awfully tired."

He stood up and pulled his chair away from the bed.

"Sure. You need your rest. I'm glad you are going to be all right."

He smiled again and headed for the door.

Twenty minutes later Carey was sitting across the desk from his boss, the sometimes querulous but usually attentive Lieutenant Gerry Phelan. Carey liked Phelan, not only because the lieutenant had approved his request for permanent night duty Carey was a man without a family. A few months after the death of his wife by cancer almost two years ago, a son stationed with the army in Germany died in a vehicular accident. Phelan had assisted Carey with funeral arrangements after each tragic incident and had tried to spend as much time with Carey as possible, including numerous invitations to Phelan's Beverly Hills home. Carey had responded by becoming the top detective under Phelan's supervision.

A strong department rumor had it that Phelan was moving up. Carey was the most likely successor, but Carey wasn't bucking for the job. He enjoyed working with Phelan, hoped things would stay as they were indefinitely. Carey told rookies and department newcomers, "He's fair and a good collaborator in sorting out facts and suggesting possible leads. He's a good listener, too. Just have your facts in good shape and spill your story fast and in the order of the way things happened. He likes hearing good reports, reminds him of his good days and nights on the street, but keep an eye on the color of his skin around his collar. If it turns red and the red moves up toward his ears, try to get away from him in a hurry."

Carey knew he had a case Phelan would find interesting so he took his time with the Velotti report, not concerned about testing his boss's impatience thermometer.

"I have all I'm going to get for right now, and we can pull the uniform off her door. She's in no danger from hired killers. Her husband was the intended victim, and I have no doubt that she was shot accidentally.

"I asked her why he took off. She said, direct quote, 'He may have thought I was dead.' May have? Wouldn't she expect a husband who gave a crap about her to try to make sure?"

Phelan said, "He did call 911."

"Yeah, but even then. It looks like she tried to play hero, but maybe she was sure she wouldn't get shot. She helped him get away, but whether he was to be killed there or elsewhere is one of the questions. There's a possibility she and Mr. Velotti are in protection. If so, someone gave them up. Maybe Mrs. V.?".

Carey said, "She's very pretty. No air head, either. She's much younger than her husband. She could have set him up, maybe with someone else, like a boyfriend. But I hope it didn't go down that way."

Phelan smiled. *Ah Leo. Always the sentimentalist.*

He said, "You'll find out. Soon as we find the husband."

Carey said, "She's taking care to avoid any implication she caused the mess. She told me she thought her husband ran because he thought she was dead. He left her lying there, but he did nine one one which might mean he cares about her. We can play the tape for her if it matters. On the other hand, if he's convinced she dropped the traditional dime, he might come back to exact some revenge."

Phelan grimaced. "Exact revenge? Sounds like something from one of those English mysteries on public teevee."

"They're very good, and I know you like 'em, too."

"Who told you that?"

"Your wife."

Phelan sighed. "Yeah. You're the detective. Now do some detecting. Find Velotti."

17

Ross Vincennes was in Lou Robbins's office to request some vacation time twenty minutes after Marti Costello told him of her dream.

He hadn't returned to the hospital to see her since his only bedside visit more than a week before, but they had talked several times by phone. She said she was okay and into her therapy regimen. They had never done much talking on phones before. Really there wasn't much emotion they could convey except missing each other. That was about it.

Then during their last conversation Marti told him she thought she might have an idea where her husband might be. "Minneapolis."

He said, "Why Minneapolis?"

She said, "I was dozing after therapy and thinking about our old condo in New York. Somehow my mind turned to Bob's one-day trip before he went to the FBI about Stanton. I was dumping a newspaper in his desk waste basket. There was a torn up boarding pass in it."

Vincennes stared. *Yeah, He found a place in the twin cities to hide his loot and get back in only a day.*

Robbins approved the time off, but Jody had questions. about his "assignment."

"Where? How long?"

"Can't tell you that. You know I can't discuss witness protection matters, and I don't know for how long."

The woman, not in Marti's class for looks, had stared at him across the breakfast table.

She wasn't happy, but he couldn't help that. Or maybe he could, by giving her more attention, try to get along better with her girls. He had never considered himself their father, a construction equipment salesman they still saw several times a year. They adored the man, who called regularly and sent gifts. Vincennes was sure the man could buy and sell him. He wasn't going to compete with that, anymore than Jody could compete with Marti. Even if she knew there was competition. Arranging dates with Marti had been easy enough. He was certain they aroused no suspicion with Jody, or at the office. He wasn't desk bound, often spending time on routine errands and checkups on such witness-clients as the Velotti-Costellos. Besides, the meetings covered little more than a long lunch. Which might have helped account for his hunger for the woman. He wanted more of her. She had become more than a convenient lay. If she hadn't suggested running away together, he might have brought up the idea, whether there was enough money to do it right or not. Now her brainstorm might save the situation. Bob Costello might be in Minneapolis-St. Paul. Marti had saved her husband's worthless ass, but if Costello could be found just a few hours away by car he wouldn't have either his money, or his life, much longer. There had been precedents to help explain Vincennes's sudden need to travel. Less than a year ago he had to escort a witness from New York to the coast. It involved four days, but he couldn't guess how long the Costello search might take. He had to get lucky, but the luck had already kicked in with Marti's surprise clue to Costello's whereabouts. Finding that ticket jacket had been a break, especially as Marti admitted to her dislike for house cleaning.

He had the vacation time coming and then some, but Robbins had been querulous.

"What the hell? You've picked a weird time, and on really short notice. Don't you want to monitor the cops progress on finding Costello, I mean Velotti?"

"Frankly, Lou, I couldn't give a crap. We're almost certain he skipped town. If he has some of Stanton's money, probably all cash as you said, he's going to have to launder it somehow, and my guess he'll do it in Mexico."

Lou bought it. "You're probably right, but we have to remember Velotti-Costello took off on short notice. He had no time to arrange another change of identity. He's going to need a new car, too."

Vincennes remembered how he had stayed calm in the chair in front of Lou's desk. Robbins was talking himself into a scenario he wanted to believe, something that would play in Washington. The district chief wanted to retire on an up note. He wouldn't want his record tainted with a lost witness.

Robbins had locked a pair of big hands behind his head and tilted back in his chair. His look was speculative.

"What I can't understand is his ditching his wife, unless he thought she had given him up."

Vincennes interrupted. Robbins was getting too close. "Yeah, she might have, but why did she take a slug in the belly at close range. As for Costello taking off, remember, she told me she thought she was dead."

"Yeah, but why didn't he call us? You?"

Vincennes was ready for that theory.

"Lou, what if Costello wanted her out of the picture so he could get out of the program, run with the cash he stole from Stanton. I could see from the start they weren't getting on all that well. The first day, when I took them to the bungalow, she was griping about the house, said it was a dump. And she wasn't too happy with him, either. What if he just got tired of her bitching and brought in someone to take her out? If he has some money, and I agree with you he surely has some of Phillip Stanton's cash, he could start a new life, without the extra baggage of an unhappy wife."

"How about the chunky guy? The shooter Costello slugged in the basement?"

Vincennes twisted his mouth and raised his eyebrows.

He said, "According to Mrs. Velotti, her husband made a move on the shooter. The cop, Carey, told her it was with a hammer, but she didn't see contact. She heard Velotti's footsteps and saw the hood's gun swing across her body. She said the gun had a long snout, so it was silenced. Probably had a hair trigger, too. It went boom when it snagged in her blouse.

"Remember the witness, the neighbor who said a second man left the bungalow after Velotti-Costello left. She thought he was holding his head. We're supposed to think Costello tried to defend his wife, that he thought she was dead, even though he later called nine one one. Then he ran because he thought the shooter had come to kill him, or both of them. What if Costello rigged the whole thing and the shooter faked the injury as part of the package? In any event, if he is ever found, he has an alibi for running."

Robbins look had become appreciative. "Go on. Take your vacation."

Still impressed with his fairy tale, Vincennes was in his Chrysler and on the interstate for Minneapolis-St. Paul an hour after the meeting. The trail could be cold after a week, and he had told Robbins that Mexico could be Costello's ultimate destination. He could be there now, but he had to give it a shot. Why not?

Vincennes decided his boss had it right about Costello's need to change cars, so the first stop in the hunt would be Wisconsin's state capitol in Madison to try to trace Costello's Mercury. If Costello was using his head he would sell his car in Wisconsin and buy another in another state, presumably Minnesota.

It had been unbelievably easy. Vincennes had the identification number for Costello's Mercury. It was routine to have it for protected witnesses. In a state department called Vehicle Registration, an attractive brunette with a slight teutonic sound in her voice was impressed with Vincennes's credentials. She said she would be glad to make the checkup for a U. S. marshal. And she hit! Gone for only a few minutes, she returned with a smile, handing Ross a slip of paper upon which she had written:

"Vehicle sold to Hermann J. Rohrig by Empire Motors, Eau Claire, on September 20."

A few hours later auto dealer Ed Harvey wasn't all that happy when Vincennes drove into his dealership and identified himself. Vincennes assured him it was routine.

"I don't have any interest in the car, Mr. Harvey. Just tell me about the guy who sold it to you."

The dealer, an overweight struggler whose good humor disappeared when Vincennes flashed his ident, glanced at the Costello head-and-shoulders shot, and nodded. Bingo.

The phony name and Delaware address in Harvey's records was no surprise. Vincennes made note of them, probably non-existent. In Minnesota Costello would probably change them again. For as long as he was in that state, anyway. It was an all-cash deal for the car, of course.

Just to twit the guy, Vincennes asked him if he wasn't a little suspicious by the all-cash transaction with a stranger from out East.

Harvey didn't bat an eye. He said, "Oh, I do a lot of all cash deals."

Vincennes gave him a look. Of course. He decided Eau Claire's car dealers were probably as sharp as anywhere, especially when Harvey added, "He gave me a phony Delaware title. Its number didn't match the cars. I had to do some extra paper work for the Rohrig sale."

Why not. Had the phony ident number found its way into state computers, Costello would never have been traced to the city French fur trappers named for its clear waters.

Harvey's revelation confirmed that Costello had help in his getaway scheme. Which meant he had time to plan.

He must have guessed about Marti and me. God, the weird story he'd concocted for Robbins could almost fly for real.

A final question for Harvey. "Did he take anything out of the car?"

"All I saw was an over-the-shoulder suit bag, and a small suitcase." Vincennes sat in his St. Paul Travel Lodge room, wondering how he could speed up the process of finding his quarry. If he could find him. Things had stalled since the major break in Eau Claire. The trip to Minnesota's equivalent of Wisconsin's motor vehicle department was a bust. In the St. Paul office he was given a printout of all driver's licenses issued since Costello's presumed arrival in the state. They had photographs of applicants, too. Vincennes had first confined the paper search to Minneapolis-St. Paul. This took only a few minutes. He expanded the coverage to include applicants within a fifty-mile circle around the Twin-Cities. No luck.

Costello had to have wheels. Maybe he was driving without a license. Taking a chance, but if he wasn't going to stay in the area for long, he might try it. He could have found someone to sell him a car, no questions asked. Someone like Eau Claire's Ed Harvey. Costello had the cash to pay for more than a car if some sort of payoff was needed.

Vincennes had hoped to get the job done in a couple of days, sure the trail left by automobiles, sold and bought, would turn up gold. Now, he was at a dead end, at least with area hotels and motels. A couple of room clerks thought the photo Ross showed them looked familiar, but a check of their records over the past several days didn't furnish a clue. Vincennes knew his quarry wouldn't stay in a motel room for very long. The man could be living in a trailer in the woods. He wouldn't make himself easy to find by booking himself into easy-to-check lodging.

Vincennes had given a lot of thought to what to do with Costello-Velotti. He had no hesitancy about putting a couple of slugs in him. The single hitch he had spent in the Marines had proven he could kill another human being. During the mop-up after the Panama invasion he was alone for a couple of minutes when other members of his squad were checking out buildings along a street behind the government center. Armed with a carbine he was about to follow a couple of the guys into a four-story tenement when a young male in civilian dress came out of an adjoining building armed with an automatic weapon of some sort.

Ross had yelled, "Drop the gun," in Spanish as instructed, but the kid either misunderstood or was going to put up a fight. Ross hadn't waited for him to make up his mind. He fired, putting three rounds into the boy's torso before the body hit the ground. He knew there would have been ample time to react if the kid had made a real move with his weapon. He'd never tell anyone why he hadn't given the kid a chance, but he had no feelings of guilt. There were no questions asked.

He told his sergeant, "For all I knew the kid might have killed some of our guys."

All the troopers in his platoon had sprayed shots at invisible targets when their unit was first deployed, but he had wanted to fire for effect sometime during that fucking exercise. This guy he knew he had hit. Later, in government service, he was sure he wouldn't hesitate to shoot if the occasion presented itself. If pressed to admit his feelings on the matter, he might have admitted to looking forward to another opportunity.

After a coffee-and-sweet-roll breakfast, he returned to the hunt armed with the section of Yellow pages headed Automobiles, Pre-owned. He didn't think he would need much time at each location, and fortunately as in most cities, the businesses were confined to areas traditional for dumping used cars.

His routine began with showing Costello's photo. He watched for the slightest reaction. He thought he could tell if they were lying. When one guy hesitated he jumped all over him. "Well?"

It had nothing to do with selling a car. The lot owner thought he had seen someone looking like Costello downtown. Jesus, a million Italian-Americans might look like Costello. He tried to be methodical, dividing the huge metropolis into a grid and covering each area thoroughly before moving on. At the end of the day he had covered most of Minneapolis, but it was dis-couraging to review the city map and see all the suburban areas still to be covered. He reviewed his effort in the motel that evening. He had by-passed most of the smaller lots which didn't appear to have a car that would appeal to Costello. The man liked his large Mercury. He wasn't going to settle for a junker, or something too old. It could be a clue that he liked products made by Ford. He bought a Taurus for his wife.

The next morning he decided to work north and west of the city's hub and after veering off Lakeland avenue onto route 100 near Brooklyn Center he spotted a lot with several recent model Fords. The dealer, untypical in that he offered no smile of greeting when Vincennes entered the fifteen-by-fifteen foot building fronting the lot, stared at Costello's photo for a second, then said, "Yeah, guy named Frank Librioni. Sold him a navy blue ninety eight Buick LeSabre three days go All cash. Took awhile to get it counted, then checked out. It might have been counterfeit."

Holy shit! Vincennes's mind exploded with self congratulations and relief. He couldn't help smiling at the dealer, Howard Carlson. "Did he give you a local address?"

"Nope, said he was a salesman. Said he totaled his previous car, wanted to get back on the road."

New Jersey address. Carlson said he didn't ask to see a driver's license. "No need."

Right, thought Ross. An all-cash deal, the universal pacifier.

Carlson added, "He drove the car away. He has to pay the state tax and registration fee before he gets a title and plate."

Of course. Vincennes thanked Carlson, and got the dealer's promise to call him at his motel should Librioni call the dealer or return to the lot for any reason.

"There's a hundred bucks in it for you if he happens to mention where he's living."

Still no smile from Carlson. The dealer simply nodded.

Vincennes thought, "For all he knows, the price on his customer's head might be ten thousand. It might occur to him that federal officers don't or shouldn't offer cash inducements for private citizens to do their duty, but I doubt if he will call the local office of the FBI."

The next stop was back to the state's motor vehicles department. This time he was looking for a Frank C. Librioni who purchased a Buick from Best Motors within the past several days. He stood at the desk of a male flunky, ignoring the clerk's invitation to sit down "and take a load off."

The clerk returned in a couple of minutes, gave a classic shrug of his shoulders.

"We have nothing on a Frank C. Librioni."

Vincennes stared at the man for a several seconds.

Shit! Costello was taking no chances on a trace through the state vehicle registration. The son of a bitch was driving without a title or owner's registration. What kind of plate would he have on the car? Costello must have had outside help. Would he have a driver's license for Librioni, too? It was looking more and more as if Costello had the kind of connections, and or mind set, he tried to tag on his former boss, Phillip Stanton.

Back in his own car he sat staring straight ahead, trying to put himself in the head of the financial whiz turned fugitive. He thought it out.

Costello had reason to be confident enough he had covered his tracks. He had to be long gone from the area. Why would he take a chance on being stopped for a minor traffic violation, and get nailed when he couldn't show he owned the car? He had the dealer's receipt, but that wouldn't be enough for a cop following the book. Yeah, the man had to be gone. A careful accountant wouldn't take a chance on getting involved in some kind of local scrape before getting out of town.

He broke into a sweat at the thought of losing Costello after getting this close. He started the car so he could get some cool air into his face. He had to think it out.

What in hell would Costello do now? Mexico still had to be Costello's best bet. He could hide somewhere in the states as Frank Librioni or still another also known as, but Mexico was far safer. No extradition and tons of Americans down there, living on social security and retirement checks, hoarding cash they were determined wouldn't be surrendered in taxes.

And, no one stateside wants him, except me. Oh yeah, and Phillip Stanton.

He drove back to the motel and his key was in the door when he heard the phone. He grabbed it on the second ring. It was Carlson.

"Librioni just called. We made the deal so fast I didn't check the trunk. I shorted him a spare tire. He said he would pick it up later today. I told him I'm out of here at five, my wife's birthday. Taking her to dinner. If that deal with you for the hundred bucks is still good, we can have some wine with the meal."

"I'll be right over. If he beats me there, try to stall him somehow. You still get the hundred. You get it if I beat Librioni to your place. Later, if I can't stop and have to follow him."

He was out of the motel parking lot ninety seconds later, and at his watching place across the street from Carlson's lot ten minutes after that. Carlson, standing at his office door, left hand resting on a spare tire, saw him pull up. No wave. Vincennes sat still and ordered the dealer to his car with a quick gesture. Jesus, he didn't want Costello arriving while he was in Carlson's office.

He had enough cash to pay Carlson off, hastily handing twenties, tens, and singles out of the window.

"Thanks Carlson. You did a good job. It isn't the policy of the federal government to tip civilians for doing their duty, but you deserve a break today. Just don't mention our little deal to any federal employees you may know. I have a boss who will not only make me eat the hundred but give me a rap on the knuckles, too."

He was still trying to get some kind of rise out of the dealer. "So you just keep cool. I'm sure Mr. Librioni won't take much of your time."

He needn't have instructed the laconic Carlson on remaining calm. The dead-pan dealer pocketed the bills, nodded thanks and turned away.

Vincennes slumped down in his seat, hoping the wait wouldn't be long, sure that nothing would keep Costello from picking up his tire. It was a break that the accountant wanted to extract full value for his money. That or not wanting to make a long drive without having the security of a spare.

Wow! Another break.

He had just raised his head to look up and down the four-lane commercial street when a sedan loomed in his rear view mirror. It had to be Costello. He ducked his head as the blue Buick turned into the drive alongside Carlson's office. He peeked over the sill of his open window to see an unhurried Costello swing open his door and step onto the lot. It gave him a chance to memorize the numbers on the license plate. New Jersey, how about that?

Carlson had left the tire leaning against the building. He came out of his office to meet his smiling customer. Vincennes, raising his head cautiously, saw Costello, apparently not censuring the dealer, accepting Carlson's apology for the oversight,. The transaction took only a few seconds, ending with a quick hand shake after the tire went into the Buick's trunk. Costello had learned, as had his pursuer, that the dealer wasn't much for small talk.

Costello drove onto the highway confidently swinging into the right lane toward downtown Minneapolis. He was close enough for Vincennes to recheck the letters and numbers on the license. Could be useful, but Ross was certain he could follow without fear of being spotted. *The man can't be so paranoid that he thinks someone is on his tail.*

"But someone is."

18

Marti had lots of time to think about things other than herself. At the moment, she was contemplating the broad bosom of nurse Delaney, who was fussing with what she called a Hyper Al tube that had been was inserted somewhere near Marti's shoulder blade.

"It's how we're feeding you right now. We're using the subclavian vein which is large enough to handle the nutrients that go into your blood. Your tummy can't take any real food for awhile."

Marti decided the strong and competent woman had too much bulk to go with a pretty face. She thought the combination was like a bowl of fruit sitting on a refrigerator. The nurse's broad shoulders stretched the nylon uniform and the roll as she walked suggested an effort to protect sore feet. A lot of miles on rock-hard hospital floors, Marti guessed. The woman had to be in her early fifties, and after the years of hospital service her feet must feel like balls of fire at the end of her shifts.

Marti was no expert on feet, or their care. Her size sixes had been spared some of the punishment young girls wanting to be women inflict upon themselves. Cora and Marti's teachers, Caremlite nuns, had both insisted on "sensible" shoes. Cora because they make sense for kids. "You'll have all the years you want in heels."

Cora's private thought was that the nuns might have had a moral schtick against anything that might improve the looks of a woman's legs, but she saluted them for sharing her views on the matter of shoes, and also for their insistence on good posture.

Marti wanted to get into heels, but she went along with the edicts on keeping her back straight. She told her mother, "Those brides of Christ are fanatics about it. I'll go along with whatever they want. I'll walk like a goddamn marine if I have to. So long as they don't hit me with those hard-edge rulers."

Marti remembered seeing Cora soak her feet after her long hours on heels.

Her mother preached, "You'll be doing this, too, if you wind up behind a counter." Marti wanted to call Cora, Rose, too. When she was stronger. Even flat on her back and with the tubes making her look like something in a horror movie, the relief of knowing she could again communicate with family and friends was like a lilac-scented breeze.

She was growing to like Delaney. A lot. The nurse with the nice eyes always seemed to be smiling, and her regular presence and attention were as comforting as a kid's teddy bear.

Marti guessed the nurse could be tough enough. She looked grim during Carey's first visit. Marti didn't remember much about the first interview except that Delaney was protective. She didn't want the cop to stay too long or make her talk against her will. How about that? Marti wondered if she'd said anything revealing during the hours she was unconscious or sleeping? Would Delaney somehow protect her if she had said something incriminating?

"So, how did it go?" The nurse meant the most recent interview with Carey. She was beaming as if her patient was a subject of pride.

"Okay, I guess. How long will I be lying here?"

"It's kind of up to you. Morgan thinks it will be a couple more days."

"Oh?"

"You surprised it could be that soon? It would be sooner except when the bullet nicked your iliac artery. It cost you a lot of blood. Units we call 'em. Morgan also repaired a couple of holes in your large intestine. That's it, but that's a lot.

"If it's okay with you, I'll stall the newspaper and teevee people. They keep calling. Want to know when you will be available for an interview. I know Doctor Morgan doesn't want you worn out from more questioning."

"Oh yeah. Stall those reporters. I don't want to talk to any of those people. Especially while this tube is in my nose." Delaney had explained the nose tube was keeping her stomach cleaned out, so that nothing would leak into the intestine.

And no pictures. Good god, what if a shot ran in the Ledger or News. If Cora or Rose, or anyone who knew her saw it, they would go bananas. Even though she might not be recognizable.

She grimaced. She must look like death warmed over. And about as strong as a wet noodle.

Delaney was patient in describing how the tubes did their jobs, including the catheter, "because you won't be able to pee normally for awhile. Later we'll bring in a commode.

"Morgan said you look like a fast healer and that we'll be able to take them out soon. You'll get your strength back in a hurry then, especially after you can take some real food. Hey, would you like me to read the newspaper accounts of what happened to you?"

"No thanks, I was there. I know what happened."

Marti hadn't intended to sound like a smart ass. Delaney's smile stayed in place.

"Sure. How's the pain? Just squeeze that pump in your hand when it gets bad, It'll turn off automatically if you are getting too much."

"Pain's not too bad right now, but why am I so weak?"

"Because your system took a hell of a hit. And you can't have any real food until your sewed up intestine heals."

"Oh? How will you know?"

The nurse chuckled. "Oh, we'll know. You will, too, when you start passing gas."

Marti had heard how hospitals were trying to trim costs, getting by with low-level help, but she heard no complaints from Peg Delaney. Marti noted that Delaney often did some of the tasks her rank called for her to supervise. Such as changing bed linen, juggling a bed pan, or shifting Marti to get her off her back for awhile.

God, she'd be glad when they got these tubes out of her. The morphine reduced the pain, but lying here like this would make for some dreary hours.

She dozed a lot, but passed some of the time watching the day-time soaps. They reminded her of how she had screwed up her life. And she could sleep, "perchance to dream." Who wrote that? Maybe Shakespeare. What play? High school stuff. Forget it. She nodded off. The escape into sleep was welcome.

She often awoke thinking about Ross. He hadn't returned after his visit of several days ago. He might have tried the brother ident again, but he might be seen by someone who knew him and questions would be raised. Obviously, he couldn't make himself known if it was important she maintain the Velotti identity.

Now that Phil Stanton knew where she was, did it matter? Bob knew where she was, too, or he'd have no trouble finding her. Did he go to Minneapolis? He had the money from his suits, and maybe he had the rest of Stanton's money up there. Did anyone give a damn? Except Phil. Why would the marshal service work hard at finding a protected witness who no longer wanted to be protected? The Chicago cops would like to question him, the marshals, too, but he wasn't guilty of anything more than running away from his former boss. Stanton is the guy they should be questioning. And that would be a waste of time.

She dozed off on that thought, then awakened from a dream in which Phil Stanton was screaming at her, each word smacking into her like bullets, "Where's my money?"

She shivered. Phil's goon might be sitting in the lobby, waiting for his turn for a chat. Wow, wouldn't it be fun to slug that guy with a bed pan. She almost chuckled but the sudden intake of breath hurt. She gave the pump another pinch.

19

Phil Stanton snatched up the phone.

"Is she going to make it?" He squeezed his eyes shut while Joeseph Brancatto made his report.

He said, "She's in intensive care, but going to be okay. We got it from a hospital orderly who got if from a nurse."

Stanton half heard Brancatto. *Marti was alive, that was all that mattered. Whomever Brancatto had assigned to find and hold her and her son of a bitch husband had nearly killed Marti and nearly got killed himself. And Costello had disappeared. It was a fucking disaster!"*

Now he had to continue his reliance on Brancatto, an ally he wanted as little to do with as possible. He had made contact with the man after thinking out all the possibilities of incriminating himself or setting himself up for extortion. He had to take the chance. He might have to hedge that move later. Right now, he was out twenty thousand and it surely cost more.

It didn't matter. The itch for revenge against Costello had become a hunger. The millions Costello had stolen from didn't matter as much as the need to get his hands on the son of a bitch. He would convert the basement of Costello's cheap Chicago bungalow into a slaughterhouse. Costello would cough up the cash, all right, and it wouldn't require any outside muscle for the beating he would give the bean counter. He'd use the rental car to dump the bloody mess outside an emergency room after reminding the rat how and when he would die if the cops were called in. Then he would bring Marti back home. Costello could live out his miserable life, and if he did go to the law, highly unlikely, there would be a dozen witnesses to vow that Phillip Stanton had never left the New York area at the time of the alleged torture.

Who in hell would Costello have complained to, and about what—losing the fortune he had stolen? He'd keep his mouth shut unless he wanted to face charges of tax evasion and a few other charges the government could bring against a witness who deliberately deceived them.

20

To Joseph Brancatto, the agreement to find and hold a fellow Italian-American named Leland Velotti fell into the parameters of the vow grandfather Angelo made many years before. Angelo's pledge of "protection forever" to his beloved Marcella Bologna had been accepted by following generations of Brancatto's as unbreakable law.

A blind trust created for the Brancattos by the Angelo-Maria union helped maintain Bracatto diligence for their task as well as lots of cash for the support of family enterprise. Joseph's financial consulting firm had been backed by some of this cash although his gratitude had little to do with his decision to help Phil Stanton.

Whatever Stanton might think about him, Joseph had no idea how to go about finding a kidnapper. He needed an underworld contact and he hoped his older brother, David, might help him. Every adult in the Brancatto family was aware that Dave, a prominent Manhattan defense attorney, "knew such people."

David was surprised with his brother's commitment. "Joey, how in hell is helping Phil Stanton going to help maintain granddad Angelo's vow to protect this mutt or his family? Aren't you really mostly interested in getting his business? I know you threw that bash to get acquainted with the guy."

David was right. Joseph had organized the lavish party for the sole purpose of introducing himself and his nephew, Carmine Ambrosia. He told Carmine's parents. "We need someone inside the Stanton business. Carmine would be a perfect fit If it would help set up a client relationship for my company with Stanton, all the better."

At the party, attended by many of the area's civic, business, and political leaders Brancatto was able to hold Philip in conversation about sports for several minutes. He waggled a finger to bring his nephew into the conversation.

He said, "Carmine has just earned his master's degree in business at Fordham."

Philip liked the looks of the young man, but someone came to lead him to another group so there was no conversation with the scholar.

Carmine wished to return to his date, but his uncle held his sleeve for a moment.

He said, "I want to get you employed by Mr. Stanton. He would make a great client for me."

A few days later a dutiful Carmine Ambrosia visited the Stanton personnel department with a resume. The market was good for people with his training, but he was still surprised when after he filled out an application for employment he was kept for an interview with a Personnel Director. He thought the question and answer session went well after which he was told the company was fast growing and was keeping an eye out for promising people.

He called his uncle. "They said I was promising, uncle Joe."

A few days later a surprised but delighted new Stanton employee called uncle again.

"Mr. Stanton remembered me from your party, uncle Joe. He asked a few questions then took me into the office of his financial V. P., Robert Costello. I'll be working directly under Costello who apparently is a one-man gang corporate financial officer."

Joseph was pleased his nephew had landed an important job with Stanton, but he was not as elated when Stanton presumed he had underworld connections and asked him to break the law.

Now, he too was a Stanton employee. He was certain Stanton would not fire him for the Chicago mess up, but now he had to follow up on the matter. He had no idea who had done the actual kidnapping. David told him nothing, would not discuss the matter again, even after he learned of the fuck up in the Velotti basement.

Philip Stanton remembered Joe Brancatto only as the host a very nice party. He knew nothing of any pledge to protect him and his family. Brancatto's nephew came to mind when he decided to find a watchdog for Bob Costello.

A friend in the district attorney's office who had attended the same gathering told Philip that Joe Brancatto was a "financial consultant with strictly above board clients. Or so they said."

Philip snorted, "You guys checked him out because he was a money-making Italian operating in New Jersey."

Philip's need and the list of candidates furnished by personnel met head on. Carmine was well qualified. That he was also Italian helped assure Philip's interest. The coincidence he was the nephew of Joseph Brancatto cemented the deal.

A week later Carmine Ambrosia was shepherded into Costello's office by Stanton.

"I have a nice surprise for you here, Robert. Meet Carmine Ambrosia, just graduated with an MA from Fordham."

Costello smiled, stood up, and came around his desk to shake hands.

Stanton said. "I'm sure Carmine can help you as a personal aide. You don't have any people with advanced degrees in finance so Carmine here should help share the load; that is, after you introduce him to how you accomplish your magic with all the numbers from our growing family."

"Nicely put," Bob thought as he trailed Stanton back to the much larger office at the end of the hall.

Stanton closed the door and turned to Costello but didn't invite him to sit.

"As we discussed, Costello. Just the basics. I interviewed him personally. He's a good kid, good family, and he did well in school. He should be able to take some of the load off. Obviously, he's to know nothing about our arrangement. Will that pose a problem?"

Costello decided not to smile, or respond with a quick, "No problem," It might be a problem depending on how bright or inquisitive Carmine Ambrosia was.

He looked thoughtful. "Let's give it a couple of weeks and see how it's working out.

The young man will be well schooled but we have to maintain a helluva pace to keep up with all we have going on."

Stanton smiled and moved behind his desk. "Yeah, we're doing very well, aren't we. And we're going to get bigger."

Bob quickly decided Ambrosia was bright and well-educated, but the kid was light years away from the skills needed to understand the computer and financial legerdemain Bob brought to the Stanton Corporation. It was like asking someone to run General Motors finances with an abacus. Phillip Stanton was aware but not the extent of his financial officer's work in derivatives and other financial manipulations. Bob's new assistant would work with the portion of those earnings that matched the reports on his computer's hard drive. Those correct numbers were the basis for tax and other filings. The rest, the millions siphoned off for the "fund," were on a single floppy disk Bob recorded the day he left on his first trip to Minneapolis. It contained information on the transfer of just one-half of the secret fund Bob had accumulated and transferred to the bank boxes.

So he had done exactly as ordered. He invited the bright, ambitious, and grateful young man to sit at his computer and learn the company's basic accounting system. He would work with the numbers that would correctly report Stanton Corporation's to the government. Carmine Ambrosia would get a world class education in modern finance, but learn nothing about the number shuffling maintained by his teacher.

21

The current generation of Brancattos, as was the case with the matching generations of Bonaventuras was not identified with hoodlumism. Marcella Bologna's lover, Angelo Brancatto, used the business he created for Marcella to create a new square world. Inspired by his love for Marcella and her endeavors to succeed in a world dominated by corporate power he used his share of profits from her business to invest in legitimate enterprise.

I le told her, "I'm a lawyer. My father used mob money for my education so I could help keep him out of jail. But I couldn't prevent his murder. Now I have a lot of dirty money, but I never had a stomach for the business. I'm getting out."

He proclaimed a bravado he didn't completely feel. His moves to free himself from direct involvement took many months of cautious negotiation with lieutenants who could assure he would not be assassinated for his departure.

"I am not a so-called made man," he told his love. "I did not have to kill anyone. My dad said they didn't want to lose me to a prison sentence, but I know how everything works, including who killed who. I did authorize the killing of my father's killer. And several others as a matter of fact. I would have ordered the death of that scum Luigi, the one who first approached you, but I needed the help from his two powerful brothers."

Marcella longed for Angelo's presence and attention, but her desire to have him as a husband subsided as her business interests grew. The management of the growing enterprise consumed her. Angelos's initial contributions and the addition of still more enterprise projected her into a prominence she enjoyed. Socially as well as in business. Prominent friends tried to interest her in adding political responsibility to her role, but her final illness precluded any serious moves in that direction.

Angelo's decision to combine his careful transition from legal counsel-mob leader to upright citizen involved his roll as a father He saw two sons become lawyers and one of them fathered David and a younger son, Joseph.

Joseph was educated in business at Columbia. Then, after several years with a Merrill Lynch office in the area he used some of his generous inheritance to found a counseling and small business financing company bearing his name. He was successful and his clientele was universally legitimate although he sometimes suspected the funds backing some of their enterprise was not.

About the pledge, he told his wife, "Something very important must have been done for the family to cause granddad Angelo to start this thing and to provide funds for its maintenance. Our kids will know about it before I die. All we can tell them is the family's good fortune is directly related to the vow."

He was surprised with Stanton's invitation they lunch at a little known restaurant in Jersey City. He was on time for the date, but Stanton was already seated in a booth well away from the main traffic area.

Stanton stood to greet him. They shook hands, sat down, and urged each other to use first names. The chitchat wound down with Joseph's remark-question, "My nephew Carmine Ambrosia is very happy with your fine company. Did you want to talk about some problem involving him?"

"Oh, no, Joseph. He's doing a fine job. He has a good future with us."

Brancatto's relief was obvious. "Hey, I'm glad to hear that. So will his mother, my sister. What can I do for you?"

Stanton smiled. It was a good start. It would be tricky to discuss his need for the man to perform an illegal service, but Brancatto's pleasure in hearing his nephew was doing well may have guaranteed the man would go along.

Stanton thought he had worked out his presentation as well as for any dog-and-pony pitch for adding another business. He was moderately sure Brancatto wasn't mob connected, at least directly, but his research had produced the background of Brancatto's lawyer brother.

He has to be!

Brancatto listened without interruption as Stanton explained the reason for his call, the need to reach and detain an elusive Leland Velotti.

"I can't break away myself, and I can't use private detectives. Let's face it, I'm skirting the law by detaining a person against his will, but anything other than direct contact won't work. He must not be harmed, just detained. He is an obstinate man for whom I've worked out a great business deal. He'll turn it down out of hand unless I can have a couple of hours to persuade him I can make him richer than that guy in Omaha."

I'll take care of the harming after I send Brancotto's hoodlum on his way. If Marti is in the house, I'll send her to a hotel and then kick the shit out of Costello and get my money back.

As Stanton had calculated Joseph sought out his brother for help. David had his doubts but within forty eight hours he called Joseph with the price.

"Even hoods, or at least this one, work by the hour, Joey. The man found for me, and I have no idea who he is, where from, etcetera, wants a thousand for the round trip to Chicago, two hundred an hour for the fourteen-hour search between the hours of ten a.m. and two a.m., and five hundred an hour for billeting and holding the wanted man. Ten thousand guaranteed, with half up front to a dead drop."

Both Joseph and the client with whom he hoped to ultimately have a more normal business relationship found the drop uncomplicated. Half of the $10,000 was delivered to a bar in Jersey City two days later.

The bomb drop of Joseph's report on Marti's disaster made things a great deal more complicated.

22

Phil Stanton was unhappy. The big hurt was losing Marti. He had been so certain she had told Costello of their affair and brought about the whole mess. Now she might die from a bullet that should not have been fired.

He hadn't realized the extent of his feelings for her. Hitting on women had been a game since high school. He took none of the conquests seriously. After college he thought life would be all fun, business interwoven with a succession of pliable and beautiful women, none of whom would demand more than an evening's devoted attention. The loose lifestyle had distressed his parents who had pushed his marriage to Lucia. The hookup between the families meant another step in the growth of the Stanton corporation. Packaged with Lucia was her family's profitable substitute sugar business. He had been swept along, possibly because Lucia may have been the first woman to deny him his pleasure. There was nothing more than hand holding and chaste goodnight kisses until they took their vows. He loved the kids that came with the dull marriage, but his initial lust for Lucia settled into marital boredom. He became as active as ever in his pursuit of women.

When he first saw Marti, and then called her, he was a little disappointed at how easy it had been to get her to agree to a meeting. Then she made that funny crack, "Where do I sign?" and after a couple of their sessions he wondered who was playing whom. He had always been in control, but he didn't feel that way with her. She enjoyed the sex, or appeared to. There was very little foreplay. A kiss at the door, some nuzzling. She'd take a drink, but drank it as if it was a dose of cough syrup. She basically entered the suite and headed for the bedroom.

She had always returned to a condition of calm after each sessions in the big bed. There were no seconds and she didn't care to lie there with him. She would duck into the bathroom for a shower, and soon be on her way, leaving behind a quick smile and a promise. Till next time. It was like a regular appointment with an expensive call girl, but for free. Except there was a cost. She had gotten under his skin, something no other woman had ever done. No woman had caused him a moment's concern, either, unless it was about where they would dine. Marti's face was burned into his brain, her voice sweeter than any music. How could she have married a man he considered a spineless bean counter. His fury after Costello went to the law was multiplied by his misjudgment of the man who had the balls to hustle him for several million dollars. His first reaction, that Marti must have known of her husband's chicanery, made him feel like a fool.

Marti was certainly the first woman he had ever admired for her style. The models he had dated, the beautiful people, were so absorbed in their looks it was like going out with self enchanted robots. Marti wouldn't leave the suite with him for as much as a cup of coffee, but he knew how she would handle herself. On one of her early visits to the hotel, he had been in the lobby florist shop picking up some flowers. Through the glass he saw her walking to the hotel's elevators. A half dozen male heads turned to watch her confident, heads-erect stride, a tiny smile on her lips. He knew her watchers were attracted to more than just good looks. He asked her later if she had had any training as a model.

She said, "No, but I have a mother who will still kick me in the ass if I don't keep my shoulders back."

Marti could talk tough, but he quickly learned of her numerous social refinements. He knew she was old neighborhood, but she had somehow lost the joisy sound. And he never heard her use the kid expression, y'know, which had hastened the end of his relations with at least one playmate.

Another cause for his respect was her good grip on grammar. Phil had gone off to prep school with strict orders from his father to get the most from his education, particularly in the use of the English language.

Renzo said, "It's the number one way to distinguish yourself as having class. Impress people with your grammar and use of words and you can get away with drinking the finger bowl."

Renzo, whose table manners were right out of the book on etiquette his mother made him read while he was still in his teens, and then practice what he learned, was horrified at the picture he had just created. He had

127

giggled, then burst into laughter when he saw that his son thought his dad had said something funny.

Renzo (Stanton) Morelli did not make jokes. He was as serious as his father before him. He was proud of his Italian heritage and privately hated the name Stanton. Neither he nor his wife ever visited their son at prep school or college.

Renzo told his son, "Your friends would know we are Italian Americans, and may ask questions. Or worse, not ask. Your great grandfather, Guido, was probably right. He lived at a time when he thought an Italian, even if born in America, could never be regarded as American by the white anglo saxons who got here first and took the land from the indians.

"Guido stole, sure, or more correctly he was an agent of thieves, but he was a thinker, and he saw the time in the future when his savings could help his descendants take a normal place in American society, even become leaders. He sent word to me, and now to you, that achieving respect was a lifelong goal regardless of whatever else has been achieved."

Obviously, the family had done well. Guido's dream was being realized, but Renzo said obeying Guido's final edict, to surrender the family's Italian identity, was very difficult.

"Guido thought any wealth we might accumulate would be attributed to illegal effort so we have made every effort to appear educated. This and our new name are two major steps towards success in the white anglo saxon world, to becoming WASPs."

Stanton thought Marti might have been a good student, at whatever educational level she had reached before beginning her string of marriages. He imagined that if he complimented her on her management of the language she might credit her mother for that social skill, too. There was no questioning her spirit. She wasn't one to be pushed around. If she'd had a gun when he slapped her during that spat in the suite she might have shot him. He had tried to apologize, but then Costello brought the roof down, leading to the ruinous misunderstanding. It was a fucking mess, but now it had to be fixed.

He had to face the problem, try to assess it as a business situation, think of Marti as a much-wanted but hard-to-corral customer. He had to come up with the motivational key, words used by his company's marketing people. Obviously, Marti wanted security, the reason she married Costello. It had to be the only reason. But she was no whore. There was a core of softness. The femininity that charmed him originally was still there. He heard it in her voice during their recent conversation. What troubled him, and it probably added to his desire for her, was her complete self-control, the absence of any demonstration of affection, even during their love making. He had not said he loved her, either. He would if he could get her in his arms again. Many of the women he had bedded told him they loved him, which he only found embarrassing. He couldn't tell them any more than that they had been a good lay. If that. Maybe if he had told Marti he loved her he might have penetrated her reserve, and she would be his, full-time, or almost. The family would go crazy if he divorced Lucia, presuming she would go along.

Probably not, and if she did he'd be lucky if he ever saw the kids again. And the business would be wrecked. It would never work He had to keep Marti in his life. With Costello out of the picture she might want another husband, but dealing with that had to be part of his selling job. He had to convince her he would spend so much time with her and give her so much he would be better than a husband. She was a woman who enjoyed doing things on her own, too. She didn't have to be waited upon. He liked that, but he could maintain her interest, keep her under control. It could work.

Marti had bargained well for the $100,000. He had followed her instructions on shipping the money. She would surely bank the money, and the deposit would have to be reported. It could be disguised as an insurance settlement, but any follow up would be unlikely in a first transaction. Smaller banks hated such bookkeeping. They hoped to have uninterrupted access to such large deposits for their own pursuits.

Marti had delivered on her part of the bargain, but the botched scene in her basement home would prevent her from sharing any recovered cash from her husband. At least until they could catch up with the son of a bitch. Brancatto owed him for the fuck up. He would have Brancatto get someone to keep watch on Marti, keep her room in flowers, too. Costello might turn up. He would be certain his wife snitched on him, and might try for revenge. That would be totally out of character, but no use taking any chances. Later, depending on her recovery, he would call her and plan his trip to Chicago. Key to everything was finding Costello. If the bastard was on his way to Mexico he could kiss the three million goodbye.

23

Vincennes decided Costello was in no hurry, or else he was being particularly careful not to get picked up for speeding. Whatever, it should be was easy to trail him on the four-lane highway back into the city.

Marshals did little surveillance by automobile. Vincennes knew he had to depend on Costello's complete unawareness of being followed. He glanced into the opposing lanes. Traffic was building up outbound. If Costello drove into a snarl of commuters in the downtown area, it could be a lot more difficult to keep him in sight.

Good. Costello was swinging into the right lane and signaling a turn. The street he selected would take him away from the downtown area. Okay, the traffic was lighter, but a couple of other cars had wedged in behind Costello. No problem. Costello might spot a single car on his tail.

Where in hell was he going? Hopefully to his hideout. He couldn't be on his way out of town. If so he would already be on an interstate. Vincennes was prepared for that. He was traveling light. All his stuff was in his car, including a pair of cheap drugstore glasses and a mustache he found in a novelty shop. If he had to flash his badge to get past a doorman, landlady, or building manager, whomever, he would need to alter his appearance somewhat. Possible witnesses would never be able to recall what his badge looked like. Or tell the difference between it and one shown them by a traffic cop. The glasses and a mustache would screw up any ident, especially if he was seen briefly.

He wasn't sure Costello had ever had a good look at his car, a Chrysler Intrepid. His few visits to check on the Velottis had been made after dark, and he was using a government car when he picked them up at the airport months before. It still wouldn't matter. He had no intention of getting close to Costello's car, and there was no way the fugitive could think he was the subject of a tail.

Ten minutes of forty-mile an hour driving, and several stoplights later, Costello made another turn, this time towards the heart of the city. The traffic was more congested, and Vincennes's grip on the wheel tightened. He couldn't lose Costello now. Oops, another right turn. Costello was slow with flashing his signal, moving into the right lane quickly, almost as if he sensed he was being followed. Vincennes glanced into his right hand mirror. He couldn't get over in time. A van was on top of him. Shit. He had to go through the intersection, looking wildly to his right as Costello's car disappeared.

Blasting his horn, he cut in front of a Ford and screeched around the next corner, nearly hitting a pedestrian who had just stepped off the curb. Jesus, he hoped no cop saw that. The next quick turn a block later was made without incident, and there was no traffic on the side street that took him back to the four-lane artery. He cursed the traffic that prevented him from making his left, then jammed his foot on the gas to cut in front of a UPS delivery truck. He was sweating and furious. Had he screwed it up? He sped down the lightly traveled street a half mile or so, then almost slammed on the brakes. He saw Costello's car a block ahead. It had slowed. Now it was turning into some kind of business. A sign came into view. Holy shit. A storage outfit, Twin Cities Storage.

What the hell.

There was a space behind a string of parked cars and Vincennes maneuvered into it. He was barely a hundred feet from the Twin Cities entrance.

He didn't have to wait long. In less than ten minutes Costello's Buick was nosing back into traffic. Turn right, Vincennes pleaded, and he got another break. Costello swung into the right lane. Vincennes would not have to make a U-turn to follow his quarry.

Keep cool. Was Costello storing something, or taking something out? It was too bad he couldn't have driven into the storage company's parking space. That would have been too risky. Chances are good that Costello would be returning to his hideout. He would want to be close to his stash. It had to be money Costello was storing. It was chancy. Such places could be broken into, but where else would he hide a huge pile of hundred-dollar bills? Trying to hide that kind of money in bank deposit boxes presented special problems. He wouldn't want to go through the routine of signing in every time he visited his loot. And the

formality of boxes meant he intended to stay in the area for an extended period.
That didn't make sense. The man must want to get as far away as possible.
Costello had proven he could handle money. A storage locker was as about as
good as he could do short term, unless he buried the loot.

There were several cars between Vincennes and the Buick when
Costello made a right turn and reduced speed. They were on a street lined
by residential dwellings that gave way to a row of four-story apartment
buildings father along on the right. A string of neighborhood businesses
lined the other side of the street. Vincennes slowed, looking for a parking
place should Costello be close to his home. Watch it! He had nearly missed
Costello's quick right turn. The Buick had disappeared just past the last
apartment building. Vincennes guessed it wasn't another street. There
was no crossing traffic. It had to be a drive of some sort, but he had to
get closer. He couldn't lose him now. He eased forward until he could look
down the drive, ready to turn in pursuit, but all he could see at the end of
the two-lane roadway was a line of bushes. It was a dead end. Costello's car
had disappeared. It had to be in a parking lot back there.

He made the right turn and drove alongside the building's blank brick
wall. Then stopped. He couldn't take the chance of being seen if Costello
was still in the lot. His quarry might have been parked by then, and in the
building, but if he was wrestling with a load such as suitcases crammed
with cash, he might still be in the lot.

He had to get a look without driving any farther. Anyone driving
in behind him would wonder what the hell he was doing, but he wasn't
blocking the entire roadway. He left the transmission in park and was out
of the car and alongside the wall in seconds. There was a short wall of
shrubbery to step over, but in a few moments he was able to cautiously
poke his head around the end of the building.

Another good break. From about the length of a couple of basketball
courts he saw his man. Costello was carrying two Samsonite suitcases
into a back entrance. He had managed to get the door ajar and was using
his butt to work himself into the building. Suddenly it was pushed open
from within and Costello nearly stumbled, then stepped back holding onto
his suitcases. A woman was coming out and she then held the door for
Costello.

Vincennes had seen enough. He was certain Costello had picked up
his loot at the storage place. Back in his Chrysler he slipped into gear
and moved forward at a speed used by any regular tenant. He made a

right and was in an open-air parking area about half-filled with cars. He spotted Costello's Buick in a few seconds. He cruised past it, noting the 2B stamped in black on a concrete stopper beneath the Buick's bumper. Good. There would be no need to rouse a building super for Costello's apartment number. If needed.

A few second later he was parked in a Guest Only slot, congratulating himself on his luck to that point. The next move was to check Costello's car. He had no break-in tools, but he had to see if Costello had left anything in the front or back seats that would indicate he was ready to leave the city. He could see no one in the lot so he edged out of his car and walked confidently to the Buick. Making another quick look around the lot, he leaned over to peer into the car's windows.

Hey, it's unlocked. What's with the dumb asshole?

Hooking a finger around the handle he swung the door open. A few seconds later he found the truck lock release button and pressed it, careful to smudge the finger print. Closing the door with his hip, he took three quick steps to the trunk and raised the lid. Nothing. Okay, the money is definitely in his apartment. He closed the trunk. The search had taken less than a minute. He glanced around again. The parking area was still empty of people.

Back in his car he reviewed his options. His next move depended on whether Costello was in for the night or was planning to leave on some errand, possibly for something to eat. Or he might take off permanently, too. It would depend on how he left the building. If he was lugging the Samsonites and his other gear the bookkeeper was a dead man. Face it. He couldn't let Costello drive off into the sunset. Following him would be a bitch of a problem. He had the plate number, but it wouldn't be much help. He couldn't use it to let cops get into the act.

What if the man wanted to drive all night and then some? Vincennes tried to remember how much gas he had in the Chrysler. The very real possibility of trailing his man for hours and then running out of gas was ridiculous. He couldn't go for a fill-up now. He had to wait the man out.

Costello had to die. And he had to disappear. He and his Buick would find the bottom of one of Minnesota's ten thousand lakes. How else could it be done? Shooting Costello as part of a stick-up wouldn't work. Costello's prints would be found in the files of protected witnesses, and the Chicago office would be alerted. Robbins would call him in to talk about it. He could play the conversation in his mind. "How was the vacation, Ross. Where did you go?"

Vincennes knew his boss was a demon for seeing things through. The case was an embarrassment to him. Going into his retirement with a lost witness on his watch would make him very unhappy. He couldn't chalk up the Costello case as one of those things, and he would stew over the report of a stick-up murder. He would remember their chat about Costello and their speculations about how much loot Costello had skimmed and where it might be hidden. Then he would close the circle with the supposition that whoever dropped the dime on Costello might have known where he was going. Further questions to his deputy about his "vacation" would follow.

The trail I left in Minnesota is as wide as the state itself. It would all come apart. They wouldn't be able to convict him. Even if Marti could be made to admit she tipped him about Costello's possible hiding place. He would deny ever finding the man. If they found Carlson, the laconic car dealer, he would insist he lost Costello in Minneapolis drive-time traffic.

He would blame Phillip Stanton, say Costello's old boss had somehow found Costello and arranged the murder with the goal of retrieving the cash Costello had stolen from him. Stanton would have an iron clad alibi, of course. End of story. End of career as a marshal. End of the Marti dream. He would have Costello's cash. but he might as well bury it in a six foot hole. He would have pretty much the same alibi for Marti. She would accuse, too. He would simply tell her he had no luck finding her husband. Let her rant, "Where's the money?" He would stick to his story, and she would have to shut up. She could admit to telling him where she thought her husband has gone. She could say he had deserted her and she wanted to find him, but not to kill him or steal from him. She would have to settle for her hundred thousand. And her freedom.

Every law enforcement officer asks himself whether he could kill another human being if he was forced to. Vincennes had dealt with the question and the answer was yes. He learned he was capable of killing a man during his stint in the marines. In the deeper recesses of conscience he had to confess he had cut that Panamanian kid down without hesitation. If Robert Costello left the building with his loot, he would have to die. No sweat about it.

He would wear his disguise, not to fool Costello, but to foil any potential witnesses. If any apartment dwellers entered the parking area, he would hold Costello in his car until they left.

God he was hungry. He hadn't eaten since breakfast. There just hadn't been time, and he couldn't leave now. No, even if he had to wait all night.

He could only make his move when he was certain Costello had the money with him.

The late afternoon sun had slipped behind the row of apartment buildings. Lights bordering the parking lot, presumably on a timer, flooded the area. He instinctively ducked, then ducked again when a black Chevy sedan drove into the lot. A middle-age woman left the car with what looked like a bag of groceries. Vincennes expected her to produce a key to open the back door, but she just tugged at the handle and it swung open easily. Ten seconds later the door swung open again.

Holy shit!

He threw his body to the right on the seat. It was Costello. He came into the light carrying nothing and walked briskly to his car. His parking space was close enough for Vincennes to hear the Buick's engine rev. Vincennes raised his head to see the fugitive's tail lights as the Buick left the parking area.

24

Costello thought he would take off the next morning. He had pushed the Samsonites under the bed and sat in the tiny apartment's reclining chair checking the Atlas he had picked up in Eau Claire. He had used his computer to chart his route, too, but he liked the Atlas for detail. The route was clear enough. Interstate 35 all the way to Laredo, Texas, and then into Mexico. Or he might veer slightly eastward into another border city, McAllen, crossing the Rio Grande into Reynoso. A fellow CPA who had attended a convention in McAllen said the city across the river was called Boy's Town, that it was filled with whore houses.

The friend said border patrol is practically non existent after six o'clock in the evening, but he wasn't interested in catching the clap. He just needed the easiest possible passage into the country that would be his home for the indefinite future. He didn't think anyone would step out from a patrol shack and lead him away from the border. He was wanted for questioning by the Chicago cops, and the marshal's office would be curious about what had happened to him, but he couldn't see why they would pull all stops to bring him back to Chicago. The purpose of the witness program was to help maintain his anonymity. He was taking care of that himself.

Again he tried to reason it all out.

Stanton must have sent the chunky man, but probably not to kill him. At least not until he made him give up the money. It was clear Vincennes and Marti gave him up for a chunk of the cash. Marti knew it had to be a lot because he had told her they would be independent forever. It was a hell of a temptation for them. She had become infatuated with the handsome marshal and he might well have told her he would run away with her if their elopement could be properly financed.

So why did Marti butt in in the basement? It was pretty late in the game for her to show conscience. Stanton must be fuming. Now, even thinking about a meeting with the man made him shiver. If he ever heard that Stanton was vacationing in Mexico, he would immediately head for South America. As for Marti, she would have Vincennes for protection.

He had chided himself for going back to Carlson for the spare tire, and wouldn't have except it was the wheel holding the spare that might be needed. The trip back to the car dealer gave him a chance to put more miles on the Buick, too. If anything was going to go wrong he wanted it to be here, and now. He knew damn little about cars, but U. S. car makers in general were producing better products since the Japanese led the way, lifting billions in profits from Detroit. The slam-bang build it and get it to the dealers days were over. During his freelance CPA days he had told a couple of clients their bottom lines over a five-year period would look better if they put more money in quality control. He wasn't invited back by either of them, nor by another client after he told their chief operating officer that foreign producers deserved their American business if they could make a better product.

"I mean not just cheaper. Better," he said.

His mother helped instill the attitude about not taking things too fast. He had surely waited long enough to get married. He pushed the Atlas aside and leaned forward to hold his head in his hands. He had fallen hard for Marti. She had reminded him so much of Francie and the night in San Franciso. He could never convince himself that Marti held any real affection him, but being her partner and seeing the admiration for her in the eyes of other men was fun at first. He enjoyed the flurries of her preparations before they left the condo for dinner at a good restaurant. She loved the shows, too, but often had to keep him awake for third acts. She was no dummy. As soon as he met Cora Lambucci, he realized how his wife's sharp intelligence and good looks had been the basic ingredients with which Marti's ambitious mother created an exceptional woman. It troubled him that he hadn't been all Marti would have wanted as a sexual partner. She had shown no impatience with him, but he knew he didn't perform normally for a male pushing fifty.

He was simply too tired to keep pace with a youthful, dynamic young woman. He fought fatigue from the moment the alarm jolted him into wakefulness until he gratefully slid into bed, barely whispering a "Good night, dear" unless she was still in the den watching a late movie.

He would think about Marti during the day, even get an erection, but more often than not when he arrived at the condo he was ready for a drink, a quick dinner and dreamland. She was understandably impatient with that routine. She was a beautiful young woman wanting to smell all the roses. He tried to conserve his energy to help her enjoy the post work-day excitement of the city that never slept, but fatigue became as much a part of his persona as his conservative suits.

At first he had worried about his health. A doctor told him he was okay in general but said he should make an effort to improve physically, drop some pounds. The doctor said a Viagra-like product was a possibility but his relatively high blood pressure made such usage risky. They discussed strength exercises and doing some jogging to strengthen his heart.

God, how could he find time for that? He was doing ten-hour work days, sometimes twelve, also driving to the office on Saturdays.

Marti hadn't seemed to mind his poor performance in the sex department. Her basic personality didn't change. She wasn't as quick to laugh, or always in her best humor, but she was never a grouch. Until Chicago, when Ross Vincennes came into their lives.

So much for the soliloquy.

He sucked on a beer while consulting the Atlas, also deciding whether to go out for some groceries or try the Perkins restaurant he saw about a mile from Twin Cities storage.

He opted for the restaurant.

25

Vincennes stared after Costello's taillights.

How long would he be gone? The money had to be in the apartment. The question was, could he get it before Costello returned? What a fantastic break it would be. He could be on the road back to Chicago in a few minutes. There would be no need to kill Costello. What could the asshole do, call the cops!

He grinned thinking of Costello's reaction to the missing suitcases. He would go bananas, then try to think it out, finally guessing his wife had tipped her lover the loot might be in Minneapolis-St. Paul, but what could he do about it?

Get going! There was no way to guess how long Costello would be gone. He wouldn't want to leave his money unprotected for long. It was time to go into his act. He reached for the new glasses and mustache lying alongside him. He needed only a few seconds to get the disguise in place with the help of the rear view mirror. His handgun, a .45 automatic souvenir from his tour with the marines, was in its holster under his left arm. No way was he going to risk a trace back to his regular piece, a .375 Magnum. He reached for his hat on the back seat. A hat made it difficult for anyone to describe hair color.

He sat for a few seconds, working out a plan. If he was challenged inside the building for any reason, by a manager for instance, he would say he was looking for an Adam Goldsmith, and after being told there was no one by that name in the building, he would say, Oops, that he had a wrong address and bow out. He would find a place to hole up for a couple of minutes, returning after making sure he didn't run into that person again.

He pulled the car door handle. He had to go for it. The cash had to be in the suit cases. If Costello showed up, he would get his a one-way trip to one of the state's ten thousand lakes.

26

For Marti, it was five days in bed and she was going crazy, but she must be making some kind of progress. Delaney said today would be UAA day.

"Up and attem," the big nurse grinned.

About time. The tubes were gone, the catheter last, and Marti had been taking some broth, but God she was weak. A commode had been placed alongside her bed.

Marti said, "No, I'm okay, but why am I so weak?"

"Hey, you've gotta expect that, all the dope and no solid food or exercise, but as soon as we can get you on your feet and walking, your strength will start to come back. Morgan and our physical therapist, Julius Warshawsky will be here in a few minutes to help you get started."

"Julius Warshawsky?"

"Yeah, a great guy in spite of the handle. We call him Julie, and he's good at his job."

"I have to look human. Where's that comb?"

Delaney reached into a pocket. "I have it. Let me help." In a few seconds she handed Marti a mirror.

"How's that?"

"Superb. You're a pro. Marti pinched some color back into her cheeks. She had to get some cosmetics in here.

Delaney said, "Julie's gym is on this floor, right down the hall. That's part of the reason for shifting you into this room."

Marti thought, "What am I in for?"

Marti could never stand pain and she was sure any rehabilitation exercise would hurt. Before the slapping incident with Phil Stanton she had never been struck by anyone. Her father never touched her in anger.

She couldn't remember many hugs, either. Cora was a hair puller, not a hitter. She remembered yelling, "Mom, you want me bald? That's what's going to happen."

Delaney had heard lots of patients express fears about rehab. Some of the more heroic said, "Hey, it can't be all that bad. Whatever it takes, it will be worth it."

The door swung open or Delaney might have described what she was in for. Dr. Morgan strode in followed by a much younger man who had to be Warshawsky. The rehab specialist was carrying an aluminum walker.

Morgan wasted no time asking about the feelings of his patient. He said, "Mrs. Velotti, this is Julius Warshawsky. He directs the hospital's rehabilitation program. He will have you up and about in no time."

With that introduction, Morgan headed for the door. Peg told Marti later that a quick exit was Morgan's technique for avoiding patient's questions. She said, "An old OR nurse told me Morgan was a talker as an intern, used to chat with patients, and was very solicitous. Wanted to know their names, et cetera, but when he got into heavy surgery and lost some of them on his workbench he lost his early style. It happens."

Marti noted Morgan called Warshawsky mister, so he wasn't a doctor. But he was no shrinking violet. He immediately took over. His voice was strong, medium range, not bad.

"Hi, Mrs. Velotti. Call me Julius, or Julie if you like. Nurse Delaney and I are going to help you stand up. Then we'll get started with your therapy. Okay? Now, if you will let nurse help swing your legs to the edge of the bed, we'll get the show on the road."

Oh boy! Marti already hated the air of boundless energy and good cheer. She examined the young man as Delaney fussed with the bedclothes. He had a good head of hair, she decided, a slight wave to it. The haircut was barbershop, not styled, and trimmed short around the ears and on the neck, as if he didn't care to spend much time with it.

The face was reminiscent of Frank, husband two, not bad, probably third or fourth generation Polish-American. There was a tint to the skin on his face and hands, sun or maybe sun lamp. The eyes were brown, as near as she could tell, and alert as he watched Delaney, but not impatient. His first look at her was right in the eyes. Frank's eyes, his best feature, always flicked away after making initial contact, as if he was up to something, like hustling a few extra bucks out of a sale.

She felt the strength in the therapist's hands as he gripped a knee and helped swing her legs over the side of the bed. Delaney, from experience, helped Marti maintain her modesty by grabbing the hospital gown to keep it from flying like a slack sail caught in an unexpected puff of wind. There was a flood of pain with the movement, and Warshawsky said quickly, "We hope you can do without the pump for this exercise. It will help us assess your rehab needs, Mrs. Velotti. I hope you can ride it out for this first session."

For some reason she wanted this guy to see she could take the pain. She nodded. Then Delaney was putting something on her feet, and she was up, although far from erect. The rehab man guided her hands to the walker handles. Delaney's big arms were around her shoulders to hold her up.

"There we go, he said, his voice level down and more solicitous than before. "Now, tell me where it hurts the most."

She wanted to scream, "Everywhere," but she gritted, "Stomach. Hips and legs, too, I think." She knew she must look awful. Delaney was dabbing her brow with a moistened towel while adjusting another gown over her shoulders to cover her backside.

Warshawsky was moving his hands across her shoulders and back and down her arms.

"How about here? And here? Can you take a step?"

Marti felt his touch, but it was no balm to the pain. She groaned and tried to move a leg forward, but she couldn't get any response from the order she sent to her brain.

"I don't think so. It hurts like hell all over."

Morgan was back. Without speaking he watched the therapist's moves, alert to Marti's reactions. Both men looked thoughtful. Morgan said, "Pain can be a good sign for the healers, but awfully hard on the healees."

Delaney's eyes opened wide. Morgan speaks. Warshawsky said, "Doctor, I'd like to start with Mrs. Velotti right away."

The therapist had his arms around her shoulders, gently, but she could feel his strength as his muscles tensed from holding her up. He eased her back to the edge of the bed, then Delaney helped him hoist her back onto the bed and swing her legs up so that she was again horizontal. Delaney adjusted the bed clothes. She said, "That was your first workout, kiddo." Marti knew she must be the color of the ceiling. She heaved in some air and almost grabbed the pills Delaney offered. She was given her pump back, too.

Morgan stayed for all this, then said, "Yes. Get started tomorrow. Mrs. Velotti, what happened to you calls for a bunch of your body's nerve systems to return to normal. Your rehabilitation is going to require extensive therapy, so you should be prepared to stay with us for awhile."

"How long?"

"We really can't tell, right now. A lot depends on you."

With that the doctor, as if he had made his contribution to that point, again turned for the door.

Warshawsky was smiling. He said, "We won't beat you up, Mrs. Velotti. We try to set realistic goals for each day, and suggest to our patients they try to treat it as a game, or contest, to see how well they can overcome the obstacles. I hope you can take it in that spirit."

Marti thought, "The guy sounds like one of those teevee evangelists." She saw Delaney smiling in the background.

She must like the earnest young man.

Marti said, "Hey, I just want to get out of here. I'll do what I have to do."

Both Warshawsky and the nurse looked relieved. Warshawsky said, "Okay, we'll see you tomorrow."

The nurse gave a little wave and walked out with the therapist. Marti watched the door close, then blew air through her lips. Her brave statement about wanting to get out of here was baloney. Out of here was nothing but trouble. The simple exercise of getting out of bed was excruciating and exhausting. She was slipping into a doze, but the faces of the three men in her life accompanied her to dreamland. First was Bob, just plain scared; then Vincennes, unsmiling, interested in her guess about Bob's whereabouts; and finally Phil Stanton, contorted in anger as in their fight in his Essex house suite. He would know by now that she had screwed up the fat man's assignment. He would want his money back. And her. Or both.

27

She felt a little better the next morning, strong enough to sit up and eat the hospital food. She had never been much for breakfast, but keeping her weight down was the last of her worries now. She'd finished scarfing the eggs and toast, and was sipping the last of the coffee when Delaney came in with the walker and a bundle of clothing under her arm.

"Good," she said. "You cleaned it all up. Are you ready for Warshawsky and his machines of torture?"

Delaney immediately looked apologetic when she saw Marti's grimace.

"Hey, it isn't going to be easy, but look at the bright side. Every stab of pain is a step toward full recovery."

You're kidding?

"Julie will be right in. This morning you are going to walk down to the gym. That will be your first exercise. First, though, I'm going to get you into a robe. Then I'll help you get your hair in shape. I don't think you need any help with your face. Your natural color is coming back but I can get you some makeup if you want it."

"Just a mirror and a compact, please."

"Be right back."

Marti found the strength to push the food tray away and had begun to untangle the bed clothes from her legs when Delaney returned with the compact and mirror. Also a lipstick She said, "Give me your hands," and Marti was surprised at how quickly the big nurse had her sitting o the edge of the bed.

"Now for your new outfit," and she unrolled the cotton robe she had brought in with the walker.

"The idea is to wear something you can get into right now, while you are still wearing the compression stockings. Later, we'll use some loose clothing, shorts and T-shirts that will be easy to get in and out of. Warshawky calls it utility wear He wants the sweat to run freely. And there will be a lot of massage."

Marti didn't expect to wear Dior, but she thought the outfits might look like the body-hugging outfits worn for the Jane Fonda workouts. She had some of the outfits in her own wardrobe, but she could see Warshawsky's point. Patients as weak as she was would never be able to get into any kind of normal wear.

In all the pushing and pulling, the nurse never made an improper move, but Marti still wondered about Delaney's sexuality. She was married but was she a dyke? There had to be a lot of nurses that were lesbians.

She remembered that a couple of girls she had schooled with at St. Agnes were queer and went into nursing. One of them, Myrtle something or other, a pale blond, had made a move on her in the shower after swimming. She should have been alerted when the girl volunteered to soap her back. The offer seemed innocent enough. She had forgotten Cora's warning about girls that get over-friendly.

They were the last pair in the shower room. She closed her eyes as the warm water and the smooth feel of Myrtle's hands made her feel almost sleepy. It was when Myrtle let her soaping extend under her left arm pit and over her breast that she came out of it.

"Hey, what are you doing?"

Marti remembered spinning around to face the girl who looked startled, as if awakened from a nap. She was taking short quick breaths as if recovering from a run. Then she looked as if she would break into tears. She said, "Oh, I'm sorry."

That's all there was to it, no big scene. Marti didn't tell her mother, or anyone, not even Rose, but she later heard a couple of other girls talking about Myrtle making out with a girl they called Pooch, maybe because she was considered the ugliest girl in the class. Myrtle didn't return to St. Agnes after summer break, and Marti never heard anything more about her except that she had gone into nursing.

She examined the compact Delaney had brought her. Good guess for shade. She dabbed at her face.

Delaney nodded. "You look fine."

"Thanks. I'll pass on the lipstick. Too hot against my pasty skin. I guess you will put this stuff on my bill."

"Don't worry about it."

She wouldn't. A husband who skipped with her financial future, and a former lover who might want her dead, these were worries. As for the present, she presumed her medical and rehab expenses would be covered. She knew Bob had hospitalization coverage. Chances are the government would step in, too, if costs got out of hand.

Delaney left the room again, returning with Warshawsky. The therapist was all smiles, showing some good teeth, Marti thought, but old-time executioners probably wore smiles, too, under their black hoods. She gave a little shiver, but if the therapist noticed he gave no sign.

He said. "First day of a brand new life."

She gave him the are you kidding look.

"You guys are in a hell of a hurry to get me out of here."

She knew she should try to improve on her usual early morning disposition, but she just didn't give a damn. Warshawsky might be Mr. Personality to his victims, but she wasn't going to pretend to be grateful.

Maybe he was used to the flack. He didn't miss a beat with his comeback. The smile even widened a little. He said, "You are absolutely right about that. We have a contest, with a pool, on which of our rehab patients is discharged first."

It was an innocent remark, but to Marti it sounded as if she was about to undergo some kind of assembly-line cure. He had said in their first meeting she wouldn't be beat up, but what did that mean?

"You said, we?"

"Yes, I have two aides. Both of them do most of their work with non-trauma patients, so I'll be your main therapist."

Oh goody.

The torturous move from the bed to the walker took all of three minutes.

"No hurry," said Warshawsky, and Marti gritted, "You guys must be paid by the hour."

Both the therapist and Delaney laughed, but Marti wasn't trying to be funny. It was worse than the day before. Her head was spinning, and she was suddenly sick to her stomach. Delaney was holding a wet towel, and she dabbed at Marti's brow. They had her on her feet again, her hands on the walker handles. It hurt but not as much as the day before. She stifled a groan. Warshawsky must have heard, but he ignored it.

"Okay, let's go," he said. He had an arm around Marti's shoulders. Delaney walked ahead as if running interference. Marti, head down, watched the nurse's broad backside, and broke into a slight grin as she thought how Delaney might furnish blocking for a Notre Dame running back.

The therapist saw the smile. It prompted more encouragement as she inched down the corridor.

"Great, you're doing fine."

She didn't mind the help, which made her feel that only about half her weight was supported by her feet. The guy was strong, all right, and with that thought came self-rebuke.

Jesus, are you nuts? You've gone through three husbands and you were in the sack with your current boy friend only a few days ago. Now you're sizing up a hospital worker. Come on, get wise.

The recrimination made her wriggle her shoulders in disgust with herself. The therapist misinterpreted the movement.

"Oh, too much pain?"

"No, I'm okay." *Okay my ass.*

They had walked about fifty feet. Delaney pushed the door open to the rehab department, then watched as Warshawsky maneuvered Marti to a set of parallel bars within a few feet of the entrance. To Marti the equipment, not new, looked much like the ones in her high school gym. She could see that these had already been adjusted so that she could just fit her arm over the bars with the bars fitting snugly in her arm pits.

She was gasping. Delaney had the cool towel on her forehead in a flash. Warshawsky's right arm went back around her shoulders, his hand close to her breast.

"You okay?" Marti remembered a nun who said that question was one of the most over-used cliches in human communication.

"How in hell can I be okay. I feel as if one of those umpty-ton waste haulers just ran over me."

Delaney said, "Let's get her back to bed. I'll get a gurney."

Warshawsky nodded, looking at Marti. "We can do that. Try again tomorrow."

He had a little smile on his lips, but she was looking into his eyes which were about a foot from hers because his arm was still around her shoulders. The eyes weren't approving. It was a new look for Marti from an attractive man. The expression was clinical, like Doctor Morgan's in his first visit. The man was sizing her up, not as an attractive woman he might like to get into his bed, but as a sick hunk of female flesh who may or may not respond to his special area of treatment.

Marti couldn't remember anyone looking at her like that, not even the nuns before they reached for a ruler. She knew she didn't like the look, and she instinctively wanted to change it. How? By reacting in her usual way? Either turning on, or off, for a man she was sure wanted to get to bed with her. Not this time. This guy was all business. Of course she could collapse in his arms and force him to do the male-rescues-helpless-female act, but for all she knew about this guy's methods he might let her bounce on the floor. She turned her head away from the therapist. He hadn't let her sag, but her feet were barely touching the floor. Neither they nor the parallel bars were supporting much weight.

Delaney looked anxious, and again used the age-old query, "You okay, honey?"

Marti said, "I'll stay. You can let go of me."

Warhawsky's grip immediately relaxed. He said, "You're sure. Do you feel any nausea?"

Delaney had found a cup of ice water somewhere, and held it to Marti's lips as she sipped a little. The cold liquid scalded her throat, but she felt better; at least she wouldn't throw up the only food she'd had in weeks.

She said, "What do you want me to do on this thing?"

Both helpers looked relieved.

Warshawsky said, "Grip the bars with your fingers, then use your hands to pull your shoulders forward. First the right one, then the left. Then try to move your feet to follow. I want you to get used to feeling your weight on your feet again."

Okay, boss man, here we go.

Marti tried to do as she was told, and got one of the biggest surprises of her life, beginning with the attempt to grip the bars. Her fingers felt lifeless. The metal seemed to repel her grasp. She couldn't move an inch. She told Delaney later, "With that grip I couldn't have squashed a ten-week old banana."

To Warshawsky, she said, "The bars are slippery."

He produced a small bag of powder from somewhere. Wordlessly, he dusted her hands liberally, one at a time. Then he said, "How about giving it another shot?"

Delaney, standing alongside Warshawsy, gave a little groan. Marti glanced at her.

She thought, "She's hurting, too, just watching this."

Warshawsky said, "Peg, don't you have something you should be doing?"

Marti thought the nurse would be offended. Delaney just grinned.

"Okay, I'll get out." She put a hand on Marti's wrist. "Julius thinks I take his therapy harder than his patients. I'll see you later."

She dropped her wet towel over one of the parallel bars, gave Marti another light pat on the wrist along with a reassuring smile and turned for the door. Marti thought. Jesus, I'm alone with Doctor Frankenstein in his laboratory. Then she fainted.

28

Vincennes was out of his car and pulling at the building's back door in a few seconds. A hallway, poorly lighted by low wattage bulbs set too far apart to do a decent job, ran straight through the building. He could see a small lobby and a glass entranceway at the other end of the hall. Immediately to the left of the doorway he had just entered was a flight of stairs. The building's back stairs. He was tempted for a moment to run up them and check Costello's door. A waste of time. This job had to be a theft, not a break in. He had to hope the superintendent, or building manager, was available, and right now.

He moved quickly down the hallway. If his luck held up, the building would have a live-in manager. Yes! Another break for the good guys. The first doorway to the left of the main entrance had a name on it. Orlando Ordonez, Apartment Manager was imprinted at eye level. There was no buzzer, so he gave the door a couple of hard raps. He could hear sounds from a radio or television behind the door. Someone had to be home.

He heard movement behind the door, then the query, "Who is it?"

"It's the police, Mr. Ordonez."

The door opened before Vincennes finished saying the man's name.

Not a stereotype super. No suspenders over a T-shirt. No spray of week-old whiskers. The man peering at him through thick glasses was of moderate height, about fifty five, chunky but not flabby, and neatly dressed in a light tan sports shirt and matching slacks.

More like a super's wife was the woman peering around Ordonez's broad back, obviously Mrs. Ordonez. She didn't have the looks to be anything else.

"Police. What police? What's going on?"

Good. His visit wasn't a day-to-day occurrence. He flipped open his wallet and gave Ordonez a brief look at his badge, and mumbled "Sergeant

Smith," prepared to bully the man into cooperating if he got huffy, or wanted to examine his credentials.

Ordonez smiled nervously. "Yes, officer, what's up?"

"You have a tenant, Frank Librioni. In two B, and I want to pick him up. He didn't answer his door and I'm not going to stand in the hallway indefinitely, so I want you to let me in."

A question flitted across the man's face, but it vanished almost immediately. The officer's request was reasonable. All he knew about police work he saw on television. It was like the old country. The cops did what they wanted.

Ross added a touch of urgency. "He could be back any minute. I need your help right now."

"Oh sure." Ordonez turned his head to order, "Get my keys in the kitchen."

The woman scurried away. Ordonez said, "I hope there won't be any trouble. I've never seen whoever lives in the apartment."

Mrs. Ordonez returned with the keys. Ordonez snatched them as Vincennes said, "Okay, let's go."

Ordonez stepped toward the elevator, but Vincennes said, "Let's walk up." Then as they stood on the second floor landing in front of a door to the inner hall, Vincennes tugged his automatic out and said, "Just in case."

Ordonez's eyes were wide and staring. He didn't need any reminders to pay attention to his task. Vincennes led the way down the narrow, empty hallway, moving quick-step, Ordonez on his heels. At the door Ordonez was ready to insert a key, but Ross shoved the man aside and used his gun to rap on the paneling.

No answer. Good. It was unlikely anyone was in there, such as a woman. That wouldn't fit Costello's profile at all. He nodded to Ordonez, who turned the key and gave the door a shove, almost jumping away from it. Vincennes gave the man a sideways look. The light in the hallway was even worse than on the main floor. There was no way Ordonez would be able to swear it was Vincennes. If it ever came to that.

Vincennes said, "Mr. Ordonez, please assure me you or your wife will not mention this matter to anyone. We don't want a panic here, or curiosity seekers. I have no idea when Librioni will return. When he does I'll call for backup and take him to headquarters. Thanks for your help. Oh, and don't look for anything about this arrest in your newspaper or on television. Nothing will be released to the media on this matter. At least right now. Now please go back to your apartment and stay there."

Ordonez received all this with the wide-eyed innocence of a child.

"Yes sir. He hurried back down the hallway, not looking back. Vincennes slipped into the room thinking that Ordonez might never have talked to a cop before. Or perhaps he came from a place where an appearance of anyone who said he was a cop, flashed a badge and showed a gun was enough authority to command instant obedience.

It took only a glance around the tiny apartment to see a search wouldn't take long. He took two quick steps to the apartment's only closet. Nothing, other than Costello's suits. He glanced around the tiny room for any other possible hiding place. The Samsonites had to be here. Oh shit, would he have stuck them in the building's storage lockers. That would mean another step in the process, shepherding him out of the building, et cetera. No way he would shoot him here. He didn't have a suppressor on the forty-five. Silencers didn't work on army forty-fives.

Costello could live and probably do well enough somewhere; that is, if Stanton didn't catch up with him. Who would he complain to? He could come back to Chicago, his tail between his legs and risk another visit from Stanton's goon. Or he could just disappear, get a job keeping books for one of the Indian tribes now in the casino business. But if he stole from them, he might get scalped.

Smiling at the idea of city-bred Costello on a reservation, Vincennes dropped to his knees to check under the bed. He was already half convinced Costello had left the loot at Twin Cities storage and he would have to wait for him.

He almost yelped in delight. Suitcases, two of them. He yanked them from their cover so fast he felt pain in his shoulder. They weren't locked. He threw one of them on the bed and flipped the latches. Jesus God almighty. The packs of hundred dollar bills was a stunning sight, some packed in rubber bands, some loose.

He had to move fast. He'd check the other suitcase later. It's weight was identical with its twin. Not as much cash, but some clothing. He moved to the door, opened it, and cautiously peered down the hall. Empty. Good. He pulled out a handkerchief and took a few seconds to smear possible finger prints on door knobs. It didn't matter. Costello had no resources to check them out.

The Samsonites weren't heavy and he was down the hallway and on the back stairs in a few seconds. He needed one more break. No one to see him. He had thrust his gun into his belt. If he ran into Costello in the parking lot he would kill him on the spot, dump him in the Chrysler's trunk and make him disappear forever.

He was sweating by the time he hit the ground level. He shoved the door with his shoulder, not a soul in the parking lot. He was at the side of his car in several seconds. He pulled open the back door and shoved the suitcases inside. He'd transfer them to the trunk as soon as he could get away from here.

Oh God, I've done it.

He revved the Chrysler's engine and eased into reverse. He had to get back to Chicago. Fast. He'd stash the cash, make up some kind of story for Robbins, maybe even admit that he had tried go find Costello, but failed.

What could Costello do? Call a cop?

29

Peggy Delaney watched Karen Velotti finish her coffee. The young woman looked great, good color, her eyes alive. She was doing well in rehab since first getting on her feet several days ago. She was off the parallel bars and using a walker for unaided tours around Warshawsky's gym. She and the therapist appeared to be getting along okay after the rocky start. No open displays of friendship. But no apparent enmity, either.

That first day, the walk down the hall, and the feeble struggles to move on the bars had been a disaster. Delaney was at her station when she saw Warshawsky pushing a gurney carrying an inert Karen Velotti back to her room. The patient was conscious but deathly pale. The nurse rushed into her room to apply some cool towels. Velotti looked up and whispered, "Get that guy away from me."

Delaney chided, "I didn't think she looked too good in the gym." Warshawsky conceded. "Yeah, I pushed her too hard. I thought from her general appearance, good weight and all, she would be in better shape physically, but I think the limit of her exercise before she was shot was pushing an elevator button."

"Come on."

"I mean it. I should have guessed on the walk to the gym, holding her around the shoulders. There was no muscle tone. It was like holding onto a pillow."

"Yeah, a very nice looking pillow."

"Cut it out, Peggy. The woman is a patient. And she's married."

"Okay, I'm sorry," but she noted a touch of pink penetrating his tan. What man wouldn't be impressed with this patient? Warshawsky was single and subject to a lot of kidding. Delaney knew he had dated a couple of obstetrics nurses, but there was little or no gossip about him. She had sized him up long ago as an exceptional young man, dedicated to his job. He would marry when it suited him. She didn't have any idea what the hospital paid him. Maybe he couldn't afford to get married.

Karen Velotti had her version of that first day.

"I could have killed the man. I was dying on that thing."

She meant the parallel bars. Delaney couldn't help insert a mild needle.

"So why didn't you tell us, or him." She remembered Julius had asked her to get on about her business.

"I don't know. Maybe it was some sort of challenge. But you know I didn't get out of this bed again until I was good and ready."

She was repeating a stand she made several hours after Warshawsky wheeled her back into her room. Delaney had said to herself, oh, oh. She knew the costs for Karen's care had gone to the moon. Even though her care was paid for, Administration was already asking for a forecast on her recovery. They wanted someone in the bed who needed lots of service, not just a sleeper.

Julius Warshawsky had his priorities, too. The hospital's affiliated rehab service, situated in a building just across the street, normally took over therapy cases after Warshawsky and his assistants, Jane Doerman and Cindy Mathers, got them ambulatory. Getting trauma and any other assigned patients, including fire, stroke victims, and children, over to the outside service as quickly as possible was the goal. He had been able to show hospital administrators and trustees that it made sense to maintain his facility, that his small gym requiring no expensive equipment and convenient for patients confined to the hospital, was ideal for the basic rehab work. He often reminded Jane and Cindy, "We can't waste time. We must take all the time we need, but we can't waste it."

Warshawsky was not a believer in the no pain, no gain school.

He told his small staff, "I'll leave that to the football coaches."

But he didn't believe in letting patients dictate the terms of their rehab schedules, either. He was only thirty six, but he had read deeply into nerve and muscles function during recovery from accidents and other critical injuries, such as Velotti's. He combined his own training and research with experimental work that was surprisingly positive. Proof in the pudding was in the sharp reduction in recovery time for patients sent across the street.

"We have to set the pace. We have to be able to make our patients not only cooperate but share our challenge in making them well, or as well as possible."

He found some of them were more ready to take punishment than others, but revolt against therapy was not unheard of. If his assessment of Karen Velotti was in the ball park, that she was a hothouse flower, it was going to be a more difficult task to get her involved in her therapy, but he had to get her started. New cases that would eventually require his department's services were being admitted daily. Confessing to administrators he needed more help would permit detractors to beef up their arguments for combining his operation with the unit cross the street.

Delaney was interested in how Julius would go about motivating Karen, and she didn't have to wait long. She was in Karen's room the morning after the aborted session when the therapist gave the door a sharp rap, then entered with a smile and a single rose in an upraised his hand. The women stared at him as he stepped toward the bed with the flower held in front of him. Then he stopped, right foot advanced, so his move could be interpreted either as a gesture of peace or as preparation for war.

Delaney got the humor, or attempt at it, and laughed. "Hey. Are you Galahad, or the bad guy?" Her patient continued her unblinking stare.

Julius moved forward and Delaney guessed he had decided to be gallant. She quickly swung the food table away from Karen permitting the therapist to place the rose midway between Karen's breast and her lap.

Stepping back, he said, "Mrs. Velotti, I want to apologize for not adequately understanding your weakened condition. I told Peggy that I had improperly rushed you into your first session." He glanced at Delaney, "Which she may have told you, but I hope you will forgive me and that we can begin again on a fresh note."

Karen wasn't giving an inch, thought Delaney, but her face muscles had relaxed.

"When? How?"

"Whenever you think you are ready. And walking will be the basic therapy."

"Oh yeah?"

"Yes. But I have an idea for you that I believe will help make you ready for the more strenuous stuff."

Delaney thought most men would go into remission to their teen-age years from the power of Velotti's eyes. Warshawsky stood there motionless. It was like he was fending off some powerful force.

Delaney later told her husband, Mike.

"He looked as if he had a steel shield in front of his face, and his own power look was not bad."

Velotti said, "So?"

The therapist took the one-syllable response as acceptance.

Smiling, he said, "All I'd like you to do is to try some exercises without leaving your bed.

"Like this," and he reached forward so quickly he had Karen's hands in his before she could react. Standing close to the bed he raised her arms over her head. Slowly, gently. Karen winced but offered no resistance. Warshawsky lowered her arms.

"Okay, he said. "Will you do that while taking a deep breath, then releasing it as you lower your arms. Nice and slow."

Still looking dubious, but not as defiant, she raised her arms and took the breath. Then she dropped her arms to her side. "Okay?"

Julius was smiling. "Yes. Good, but it will work ever better if you lower your arms slowly rather than let them drop as you exhale. See if you can do it five times."

Karen patient did as requested, Warshawsky watching closely. Finished and breathing as if from a more strenuous exercise, she granted them both a smile, mostly aimed at Delaney.

"Hey, can I do all my therapy in bed?"

"You wish," said Delaney, grinning.

Warshawsky said, "We have patients who can't move anything other than their arms, but the exercise forces more oxygen into the blood stream. It also helps activate the thyroid gland. I'll have a couple of two-pound weights brought in. If you like, put one in each hand as you raise your arms. But," and Delaney saw the smile that made the hearts of most female patients flip, "don't drop the weights on your head.

"Tell you what. Do the arm thing several times today. Then, when you feel stronger, try swinging your legs out of bed and standing up. Delaney, you should be here for the first try, and use a belt. Then, when Mrs. Velotti feels like moving about, to the bathroom, for instance, we'll get the walker in the act."

Delaney had been watching her patient's face throughout Warshawsky's speech. The nurse knew the therapist was a student of psychology. Hospital gossip among staff females was that when he wasn't active with patients, or into his athletic mode, he was in his office, head crammed in books with multi-word titles. It looked to Delaney as if Julius had done it again, won over another stubborn patient. The look of mulish denial had left Velotti's face. There was a hint of a smile.

30

Costello slept well, then took his time over a large breakfast at the neighborhood restaurant across the street. He scanned the Minneapolis Tribune, looking for anything more on the Karen Velotti shooting. No coverage. It was old news. All news is local, is the journalistic axiom, and the Twin Cities had its own share of mayhem.

He chided himself for staying in Minneapolis this long, but he was certain he had covered his tracks as well as possible. There was no particular reason for hanging around. It may have been the weather which had been absolutely gorgeous, and he had to level with himself. He really didn't look forward to the long drive and getting situated in Mexico. But today, he was taking off. He checked the closet for the suits and wrestled them into their carryall. He smiled. He mustn't forget the most important part of his baggage. He dropped to his knees to reach under the bed.

The shock of grasping only air almost deprived him of his ability to breathe. He collapsed on his belly to stare at the void. He wanted to scream, to cry. He pounded the carpet with his fists. Then he just lay there, trying to grasp the impact of what had happened to him. How? Who? It wasn't possible.

He struggled to his feet and lurched to the door. It took only a glance to see entry to the apartment was not forced. Someone just walked in. And out. With his life.

Who had a key? The building manager. He remembered seeing the door with a name on it just off the lobby. Maybe the enterprising son of a bitch saw him come in the back door with the Samsonites, and decided to check them out. *Surprise, surprise.*

That's it. He looked around the room for something with which he could threaten the man, smash him. There was nothing. He would throttle the man with his bare hands.

Gasping, he was out the door and running for the front stairs in a few seconds. He nearly ran into an older woman standing by the elevator.

"Excuse me," she said in subdued outrage.

Running, nearly falling down the stairs, he tried to think. The thief probably had allies, and the suitcases were probably already gone.

Oh shit, why didn't he leave last night?

He had just reached the door when it swung open. The manager, or whatever he was, a middle aged Latin male, stepped into the hallway. When he saw the breathless, wild-eyed man before him he instinctively reached back for the door knob, but Bob grabbed his arm.

"Where are they?" he yelled. "What did you do with my suitcases?"

Ordonez, who had not entirely recovered from the episode with the policeman the previous evening, sputtered, "Hey, who are you? What are you are talking about?"

The man's answer was what a thief would be expected to say, but his look of complete surprise combined with outrage was like a slap in the face to a hysteric. Costello froze, still fighting for breath. The man didn't know.

He stared into Ordonez's face. He said, "I'm Librioni in apartment two B. I was robbed last night. Somehow they had a key. Did you let anyone in my apartment?"

Ordonez's face betrayed him. It was a picture of fright and confusion. The excited man before him must be the man the cop said he was going to take in last night. What happened?

Ordonez was not unintelligent. The realization of what he might have done almost made him gag. Had he been duped by a thief? As he looked into Librioni's outraged face, he saw the good life he had enjoyed since earning this job was gone. He was a janitor, promoted when the building owner couldn't get anyone else because of the city's tight labor market. Now he would be fired and labeled a fool. He might even go to jail.

Bob relaxed his grip on Ordonez's arm. The man's terror was obvious.

"Just tell me. Who did you let into my apartment?"

Ordonez tried to look over Librioni's shoulder, anywhere but at the distraught tenant.

Could he lie, deny letting anyone in, then stand on the company policy that guests are entirely responsible for their belongings?

It didn't matter. He sighed, then looked into Bob's face.

"He said he was a cop. Come to arrest you."

Bob wailed, "Oh no, what did he look like?"

Ordonez felt a faint breath of hope. If only the thief could be caught.

He said, "I couldn't see him too well. Our hallways. Too dark. The boss says they don't need larger bulbs."

Bob, still holding the man's arm, increased the tension.

"Tell me all you saw."

"He was tall."

"White or black?"

"Oh, white. He spoke well.".

A possible clue. "How do you mean?"

"I mean your language, American. He sounded educated."

It couldn't be. How could they have traced him that soon?

"Anything else?"

"He wore glasses."

Bob's fleeting picture of a possible thief faded.

"And there was a beard. I mean what is the word, on his upper lip."

"A mustache?"

"Yes, that's it, but it looked funny."

"What do you mean?"

"It was a little . . ." Ordonez used his fingers to describe what he had noted.

Bob took it from there. "It was off center, cockeyed?".

Ordonez nodded vigorously. Eager to please, more so when a look of comprehension crossed his interrogator's face.

Bob thrust the possibility away. It was at once an answer and a disaster, but who else would have taken the trouble to camouflage his face unless he could have foreseen the desperate session between his victim and the building manager?

He stared at the man he somehow pitied for falling for Ross Vincennes's ploy. It had to be Vincennes, the son of a bitch. Who else could have traced him here, somehow getting on his trail, probably through the car sale and the Buick buy? Now he was certain Marti was in on it. She was the only person in the world who could have somehow learned his destination might be Minneapolis.

How could she have guessed? It had to something related to his first trip to hide the Samsonites. Did he talk in his sleep? He'd never done that in his life.

Bob Costello was an orderly thinker, with a brain capable of a great deal more than understanding and manipulating huge quantities of numbers. In the few seconds that lapsed before asking his next question he retraced every step he had taken on that first trip to the Twin Cities.

And his return. He remembered throwing away the ticket receipts, but what about the ticket envelope?. He may have dropped it in another suit coat pocket, then tossed it at the condo. That's what Marti must have seen.

Back to the manager. "Did he show you a badge?"

Eagerly. "It was in his wallet. Very official. Gold."

"But you didn't read anything, I mean proof of his identity. Next to the badge."

Ordonez couldn't keep his head up. "No."

Bob's head sagged, too. His money, more than three million dollars, was now in the hands of a man who was not only ravishing his wife but who could now make him dead with another call to Phil Stanton.

31

Julius Warshawsky wasn't as optimistic about winning over Delaney's patient as the nurse. He told her, "I may have made a point or two, but this lady is going to take her own sweet time about letting us prescribe a program after that bad start."

Delaney said, "I don't think so. She wanted to get on her feet an hour after you got her started on the arm exercises. She called me in, said, "Enough of this arm swinging bull. Give me a hand and I'll try to get out of this bed."

Delaney chuckled, "It may have been because she wanted to use the portable commode.

She said it was good to sit down again. On anything."

The next morning Karen Velotti was not only on her feet, but standing behind the walker when Delaney answered her call.

Delaney said, "Hey, you shouldn't get up without help, and a belt"

Karen shrugged. "Lady, I'd like to take another shot at getting to the Polish prince's gym."

Delaney picked up Karen's phone to call Julius. "She's asking for a Polish prince."

He said, "I'll be there inside thirty minutes."

He arrived, pleased to see Velotti on her feet, and clothed in exercise gear.

"Good morning, and good going."

Peg's grin of greeting was by far the most generous, but Julius thought Velotti's half-smile was a promising start. He stepped to her side as if to help her, but she waved his hands away.

"Someone grab the door."

She made it in stages, stopping every six feet or so to heave in some air. She was laboring and Warshawsky, his eyes intent on her face, said, "That's right. Set your own pace."

That counsel brought forth a look both he and Delaney interpreted as, "You bet your sweet ass I'm setting my own pace."

Marti's actual thought was, "Wow, this is murder. Why doesn't he just grab me to keep me from falling on my puss."

At about the half-way point Delaney said, "I have to get back. Call me if I'm needed for the return trip."

Marti gave her nurse a do you have to go? look, but said, "Thanks, Peg."

Warshawsky wanted Velotti to finish what she had started, but he didn't want a repeat of their first session.

"We can try this again tomorrow," he said, but she shook her head slightly, like a fighter clearing his head after taking a punch. She moved forward, not stopping until they entered the gym and reached the parallel bars.

She didn't resist his efforts to get her arms over the bars. She took a couple of deep breaths, not looking at him. He had the feeling she didn't at all like being in a position where she needed another person's help.

With a smile, he said, "You did very well, Mrs. Velotti."

She showed no reaction to the compliment. She was still taking long breaths and her look was aimed at the floor. He wondered if it might be a good time to describe his training facility. She beat him to the punch.

"Okay, Mr. Warshawsky. What are you going to do with me? Dumb question, I guess, but what else do you do in here?"

Surprise, surprise. Julius had been entertained by women who knew the way to a man's heart was through his stomach, but he thought here was one who would never cook him a meal but who knew another way to earn a man's attention.

He said, "I'll be glad to tell you all about us, but why don't you ease yourself forward to the end of the bars, then try to shift your arms so that you can turn around and come back. Just so your muscles won't tighten up while you stand there."

She didn't answer but slowly began the movement he had hoped to see during her first disastrous visit to his rehab gym. He watched her, hoping he might inspire her to combine the walking exercise with building up her arm and upper-body strength, too. He hadn't discounted the debilitating effect of his patient's wound, but he still thought her muscular tone was only average for a woman of her age. He had decided he would give her extra attention, not because she was beautiful, as Delaney had teased. It had to do with learning more about the woman with the blue eyes that could throw a chill into a sauna.

He hadn't been surprised with her testiness in their first meetings, not at all unusual in such cases. It was the therapist's experience that the word rehabilitation, to most patients was synonymous with pain. From his first day on the job he had learned that seriously injured men and women, having survived grueling operations and the grind of bedtime recovery, weren't apt to rejoice at the prospect of further pain and discomfort, no matter how therapeutic. Velotti was showing him a crisp outer shell, and there was a tension, too, as if she was on the verge of exploding. It could be related to the condition Julius saw in most trauma patients. He called it the "How did this happen to me?" outrage.

He expected some anger to be directed at him, particularly after their first session together, but he hoped whatever else was burning inside her would surface. He was convinced she was intelligent, and there was a basic femininity she couldn't bury in tough talk. And she was gutty. Morgan told him what happened to the woman. Taking a bullet to save another person was as gutty as it gets. If he handled her properly, and himself, maybe she would open up to him.

She had managed the turn-around at the end of the bars.

He said, "That's great. While you work I'll give you our story. You can see we have a small staff and not much equipment, such as fancy exercycles and treadmills, et cetera. Most of your work, at least over the next few days, will be directed towards getting you walking without support, along with some massage. You, we, will only need your legs for that. Ha. The real machines of torture for advanced rehab are across the street in the hospital's affiliate, Memorial Physical Therapy. Over there they have a pool and specialists who do a lot of joint work, knees, hips, and shoulders, and tons of rotator cuffs.

"Either I or one of my two assistants, Jane Doerman, over there with the little girl, or Cindy Mathers, you can see her in her office, will be with you. They are both career therapists. Jane is especially good with children while Cindy specializes in helping stroke patients. We will be watching you walk, not just to catch you if you should stumble, but we can tell from your action how you are progressing. Seeing our patients maintain balance and walk well is a major part of our program. When we, and you, feel that you can walk adequately, you can finish your rehab work on an out-patient basis. I can anticipate your question as to when that will be, but I'll have to say I honestly don't know. It's partly up to you and partly a matter of what your repaired body can be expected to do for you."

He realized he was babbling and took a breath. She raised her head and smiled. Her first real smile at him, he thought.

"Is this a speech you give to all your patients?" She knew she was asking for it.

"Well, actually, I was hoping we might follow the basic walking with some strength and aerobic work, Maybe some agility exercises, too."

"Oh, is all that necessary?" The cool blue stare was back.

It was basic to what he expected during whatever time they would have with her, but he couldn't tell her so and run the risk of more rebellion.

Why in hell was he working so hard at it anyway? If she turns it down, she turns it down.

He looked directly into her eyes and she stopped moving along the bars to gaze right back. "No. It isn't absolutely necessary, but in my opinion it would be very helpful to you health-wise, I mean over the rest of your life after you leave here."

"Oh yeah?" She appeared to be thinking it over. She gave a little toss of her head, and said, "Well, let's get on with the basics. What should I do now?"

She was a little paler than when she entered the room. She had gone up and back on the bars twice during his speech.

He said, "Let's get you back to your room. You've done well and enough for today."

Cindy called from her office. "Phone for you, Julie."

He would have seen Velotti back to her room, but he called Cindy who was alone.

"Cindy, will you get a chair and help Mrs. Velotti back to her room?"

Velotti didn't object to the idea of sitting down for the trip back to her bed, he noted, and her look might have held a hint of gratitude.

When Cindy returned, Julius invited her and Jane into his office.

"You guys," he began, "can help Mrs. Velotti rebuild her self confidence. She, as you probably heard, took a slug in the gut, something that would remind most victims of the tenuous nature of existence."

The young women, both of whom had long ago assessed Warshawsy as an unlikely candidate for marriage because he had obviously limited his approval of them to that of co-workers, enjoyed their youthful leader and often teased him about his sometimes weighty pronouncements. Jane had raised her eyebrows at the word tenuous, and Cindy punched her boss on the arm.

"Okay, Boss, we'll get right to work and try to convert tenuous to strenuous."

Jane added. "Yeah, about existence, we'll try not to kill her."

Later, while discussing their new patient, the female therapists agreed she must have been shocked when she saw her scars, front and back.

Jane said, "Morgan is good, but a tummy torn up by a heavy caliber slug will never look the same in a full length mirror."

Cindy said, "Give me a face like that and they can puncture me with hot pokers for all I care."

32

Julius had accepted his mother's invitation to dinner for that evening. Adeline agreed to make it fairly late, about seven thirty because the drive north was brutal. All routes would be jammed, with each car estimated by traffic officials as carrying slightly more than one person. Julius thought he might tell his folks about Karen Velotti, but they might tease him, too, so as the conversation turned to his work he chose to generalize about some things. He knew they enjoyed hearing about his experiences and his views about his craft.

Father Al said, "You told us a couple of weeks ago you talked to the trustees. How'd it go?"

"Okay, actually. I was worried about a couple of people, one man, one woman who wanted to move all rehab across the street, but I calmed them down when I showed them some numbers on how our staff and equipment needs on a cost-per-patient basis are practically nil compared with over there. And they can't beat us for patient convenience. Also, the gym takes care of some important basics besides getting them moving. We earn the patient's trust and help them regain their self-confidence."

He sipped his mother's excellent coffee and said, "It's still challenging. More than ever, really. I think I'm getting better at assessing how to work with patients one on one. You know, we get them in all sorts of mental shape as well as banged up physically. From some of the patients about the best I can expect is resignation. Some are openly rebellious. Some are in severe depression.

"I'm talking about people recovering from really awful accidents, car smashups mainly. Sometimes members of their families are also in intensive care, or dead. All of them hurt something awful and the pain runs deep. The drugs can only do so much.

"I see my job as getting them to a point where they can see it's going to work out and that they'll be themselves again, better than their original selves in some of cases. If I and my minimal staff can do that, it's worth maintaining the program."

His parents nodded vigorous agreement. "You bet," said Al.

Julie thought of Karen Velotti when he said, "Most of the people we get were not in very good condition before their injuries. I think only a few among the hundreds of recoveries I've supervised involved patients who were in top physical shape before the car smashups, falls down stairs, et cetera. Those few were easiest to deal with. They had to overcome the usual shock and depression over what happened to their bodies, but they had already pushed themselves hard to achieve personal fitness goals. I see my job with these people as a part-time cheerleader, assuring them they can get back what they've lost."

He couldn't help himself. "There's a woman we are trying to help now who is in the less-than-top-condition category. She was shot in the stomach. There was a lot of nerve damage and there was considerable bed time before we could get her started on a program."

Al said, "Is this the north side woman whose husband left her lying in a pool of blood in their basement?"

"Yeah, dad. The nine one one people probably saved her life. Doc Morgan, you met him at the open house, did a great job on the operating table. There had to be a lot of shock both physical and mental, and I think there are some things on her mind that might impede her recovery. I'm used to resistance from patients, but I think there's more than the usual problems bugging this lady."

Adeline said, "Is she pretty?"

Julius managed not to blush. "Yes, mom, she is, but she is also married."

"But her husband disappeared."

"Mom, come on. I'm not interested in the woman except as a patient."

Al and Adeline Warshawsky knew this was probably true. They worried that their son would never find a marriage partner, thus derailing their dream of combining old age with the joys of spoiling some grandchildren.

Julius said, "I also told the board we perform the important initial job of outlining programs to patients that don't scare hell out of them, but at the same time we have to help them realize their recoveries can take time.

This includes situations in which a victim of a car accident who hopes to be back on his job in two weeks can be led to understand that rehab could take eighteen months. These people are scared. Some may never make it back into regular society or have a job again. With all of them there's huge anger. Every one of them has the question most of them will rarely ask aloud, 'How did this happen to me?'"

Back to Velotti in spite of himself. "This woman I told you about. She was a hot house flower, I'm convinced. I'll bet she never pushed herself physically beyond a hard day's shopping."

Adeline said, "So you are interested in her?

"Mom!"

"Well?"

Al had enough, too. "Hey Addie, back off. Julius is just telling us about a special problem. The fact it involves a young woman is coincidental, right Julie?"

"Right, dad. I really shouldn't bring my problems home."

The parents chorused, "Oh, we like to hear everything."

Adeline said, "Who else can you talk to? You don't have a nice wife to hear your troubles."

"Mom!"

Al said, "Oh boy, and pushed back his chair. "Anything good on the tube?"

33

Mentioning Karen Velotti to his parents wasn't too smart, but somehow he wasn't sorry. It opened the subject and he let himself think more about her as he drove home.

That quick smile. She threw it like a blind pass in basketball. Zip. Be ready to catch it or it was gone.

The next morning Marti again used the walker to navigate the trip to the gym with Peg Delaney riding shotgun. She moved directly to the parallel bars, where without Peg's help she maneuvered her arms into a support position. Jane and Cindy were already at work, Jane supervising a somersaulting child on a mat, Cindy in a cubicle with a stroke victim. Julius, alerted by Delaney that Velotti was coming in, had shifted a couple of other appointments so he could watch her on the bars. If she was doing as well as reported, she might be ready to try some steps without the walker.

Julius met her at the bars with a pair of two-pound weights.

She eyed the objects with suspicion.

"Hey, I'm having enough trouble carrying my own weight."

He smiled. "Okay, but how about leaving the bars and making a tour around the gym without the walker?"

She looked into his face, probing it for any sign of insincerity.

She said, "You're kidding," but she cautiously extricated her arms from over the bars, backed off, carefully turned around and took a cautious step forward. And fell forward into his arms.

Embarrassed and furious, she struggled to free herself. "How in hell did that happen?"

Julius helped her regain her balance. "That happened because that small tentative step you took caused you to lose your balance. You have

170

been taking larger steps with the walker, and the walker has helped you keep your balance. Try it again, but take a larger step. Here, use this cane."

He looked across the room. Jane was momentarily unoccupied. "Jane," he called. "Would you accompany Mrs. Velotti. She is going to do some walking on her own."

Marti smiled grimly. "You getting tired of propping me up?"

He grinned at her. "Not at all, but I have a couple of things I have to attend to. Good luck and I'll see you tomorrow."

Later that afternoon, Jane told her boss, "She got about half-way around before she needed a chair. Not bad. She is determined enough, but something seems to be troubling her. She doesn't have a mad on that I can tell, and she's decent enough, but she can't seem to relax."

The next morning, Marti arrived in the gym on the walker. She said to Cindy, the first staff person she saw, "Where are those weights? She then did a full turn around the gym, She flushed with pride when Cindy clapped her hands in approval. She couldn't remember the last time anyone had openly approved anything she had done. She grimaced.

Other than in a man's bed, that is.

Warshawsky noted Velotti's s pleasure with her progress and might have been surprised at her desire to push herself. He could see her as a kid in school gym classes, hanging around the ends of lines, hoping if an exercise such as a somersault was to be repeated, another exercise would be ordered before her next turn. Visualizing the scene made him grin, and Velotti caught him at it.

She was breathing hard after trying a new exercise he had suggested, some push-offs against the gym walls.

"What's so funny?" she demanded.

He fibbed, telling her he had just thought of a joke he'd heard at breakfast, but the incredible eyes weren't believing.

Those blues could burn through three-inch steel plate.

"Hey, Julius," she called a few minutes later. "What kind of exercise do you do?" He stared at her. Her blues fired right back.

Jane and Cindy overheard the challenge. Cindy said, "Yeah boss. Show us something you've picked up from all those visits to the Y".

He gave the challenge a few seconds thought. He had been working on some back flips, but he didn't want to do something he couldn't handle.

"Okay, ladies," He waved them back, then sucked in a breath, took a step forward and flung himself into a full three-sixty back flip. A perfect landing set off a hand stand and a back flip to his original position.

All three of the women laughed and clapped, but he mostly enjoyed Velotti's low register chortle. Then she said, "You're a real triple threat boy," and she turned to begin a walk around the gym. He wondered, why was he grinning after her? And what was a triple threat? He let his eyes linger on her backside. In condition or not, and even in the shapeless workout clothes, she had a very nice ass.

Julius was only thirty-six years old, but he'd been in therapy work for more than twelve years after a stint with the county's emergency service. He told his parents, who had helped put him through Lake Forest college in Social Science that he didn't think he was cut out for the 911-related work.

"We try to help so many people who aren't going to make it. They might survive, but in so many cases the living habits that led to the breakdown, heart attack, alcoholism, what have you, will cause a repeat. I'd like to get into something that will not only help people get back on their feet, but keep them there."

His older brother, Ted, came up with the therapy idea. Julius borrowed some money to pay for the training, and had his first job with a hospital in Rockford. Ted, a hospital-supply salesman who had dated nurses, told him of the opening at Memorial's therapy affiliate. Julius was invited across the street to the hospital after three years. A couple of guys were ahead of him in seniority, but both turned it down. One said, "You will have a lot of heavy trauma and stroke people to work with. It's a downer."

Julius didn't find it so. He had little more than basic training in working with stroke victims, but he often pitched in to help Jane and Cindy. He was surprised with his patience in the work, and enjoyed seeing progress, however slow in many of the cases.

He had lived with his parents in North Chicago when he first returned to the big city, but he finally found a one-bedroom apartment he could afford a few blocks from the hospital. He was comfortable, and somehow he didn't begin the kind of relationship with a woman that led to marriage. For one thing, it took money to set up housekeeping in the city where he was sure he wanted to spend the rest of his life. Also, though Julius thought he was paid fairly, he was not a saver. Almost every spare dollar he came up with went for tickets in support of Chicago teams, amateur or pro. There was football, baseball, hockey, and of course basketball during the reign of Michael Jordan. And when he wasn't watching the games, he was playing them. The hospital had teams in touch football, basketball, volley ball, and softball, with Julius an enthusiastic participant. If not the team's best player, he could always be counted upon to show up.

His desire not to miss a minute of athletic action was discouraging to a number of young women who campaigned for some consistency in their dates with him. Julius had to admit he favored spontaneous dating, and he wasn't averse to an occasional one-night stand. Brother Ted, safely married, with three beautiful kids, told him at a family dinner, "I don't think they can make a net that can trap you, much less hold you, buddy."

Julius found the remark more disconcerting than complimentary. He wanted to be netted. Sometime. Right now he loved his work, spending far more time at the hospital than required by the most demanding administration. Then there was his allegiance to his pro teams and his own sports activities, including a recently acquired enthusiasm for gymnastics. This he could do in the YMCA gym with no interruptions by patient needs, then swim to maintain a far better than average aerobic level. Another enthusiasm was pool, especially eight ball, the only game he would permit himself to gamble for modest stakes. Julius was not consciously seeking to sublimate his basic sexual needs, but most of his days ended with a pleasant exhaustion, his body ready for eight hours of sleep. If he wasn't too tired, he read, professional stuff and crime novels. The days slipped past, also the years.

Ambitious ladies, who pretended to share his enthusiasm for sports, were quickly found out, which usually ending the relationship. There was one fellow Memorial employee who tried one of the most honest and effective ploys for earning lasting interest. A dietitian and home economist, she cooked expertly, but Julius, initially attracted to her lovely bosom, couldn't care less about a meal that took three hours to prepare. He thanked the lady fulsomely for the evening, which ended after a tumble in her bed, but if she thought she had made an investment in earning more of Julius's time she was in error. Julius didn't care all that much about food. He ate to live, nutritious staples in small quantities, which helped account for his more or less permanent physical status of one hundred and eighty pounds on a spare six-foot frame.

Peggy Delaney's hope that her favorite charge and the therapist were going to get along was clinched when Karen remarked to her, "That guy is conning me into stuff I thought I'd never do. Do you know I made it three times around the gym today carrying five pounds in each hand."

34

To Marti Costello, the name Karen Velotti was beginning to feel as cumbersome as Warshawsky's weights, and she decided to do something about it. She worked on her plan as she stood in her shower, directly under the head, letting the hot water cascade down over her body, its smooth descent only diverted by the ugly slash alongside her belly button. The surgical staples had been removed before she began serious therapy, but the area around the wound was still tender. She hadn't given much thought to the eventual scar. She had enjoyed lounging beside the pool at the riverfront condo, but she had never been much for bathing beaches. Wearing up-to-date bathing suits might never again be a part of her lifestyle. The thought of those easy days and nights made her shake her head in denial, but she couldn't fight off one of the last looks Bob had given her at the bungalow. It was like that of a dog, kicked unfairly. He knew about her and Ross, but at the time she didn't give a damn. Now, thinking about what she had done made her sick.

What in hell had happened to her since she took that slug in the gut? She could live okay until she had to go to find a job. Phil's hundred thousand blood money lay untouched, but she would need some of it right away, to get a place to live outside the hospital.

A man from Memorial administration explained that she would be discharged as soon as rehab decided she could walk well enough to leave their care. Right now, Marti's feelings were mixed on whether to stretch out her therapy. Warshawsky was a pusher behind his easy manner, but as Delaney said, he knew what he was doing. He had suggested a couple of exercises that would improve her strength. The wall push-offs was one, and she had to admit to herself, though not to him, that it was probably a good idea. She had spent her life avoiding exercise, probably because she never had to work at maintaining her figure. She'd never heard of an exercise program she didn't dislike, including the group workouts Rose tried to get her to join. She hated the bodies of those muscle broads, probably lesbians, who stretched themselves out of shape on teevee. If Warshawsky's ideas made sense, she would give then a try.

For someone who had almost been given up for dead she was feeling better than anytime in her memory. The hospital food tasted decent, and she slept well, without dreams, and without drug help. The horniness that seemed to be a part of her living, breathing apparatus had toned down, too. Why not? She didn't have the strength to service the best looking man in the world, and the only men she'd seen in the hospital that were on their feet were either orderlies, no thank you, or duplicates of Doc Morgan.

Warshawsky? Are you kidding? He was a kid, always laughing it up with his two aides, probably taking them both into the sack. At the same time? The idea made her laugh, and nearly choke when a mouthful of shower water slipped into her windpipe.

Tomorrow morning, first thing after breakfast, she would make her call, get this show organized so that at least some of the pretending could be put behind her.

She had decided to stay with her married name. She would continue to be Marti Costello.

Bob might have disappeared forever and she would need a divorce so she could start over but Costello it would be for now.

But the change in deportment would be permanent. No complications, no more fooling around, which had been so dumb. It was time to grow up. The past was done. There would never be another Billy, but she was still young and had her looks. Who knows? She had Phil's money as a stake. He would want it back, but he couldn't have it. She would tell him it was the cost of doing business. She would have to protect herself, as they do in the movies. She would tell him she had left a letter, to be opened in the event of any kind of harm to her. It would name him as an attempted murderer. It might not be enough to implicate him, but it could make him leave her alone.

35

Marshal Lou Robbins was wondering why he hadn't heard from Ross Vincennes when his secretary announced a call from Mrs. Velotti. He punched the lighted button on his desk. He would tape this one. It might not be useful, but at least he could review it.

"Hello there. How are you doing, Mrs. Velotti? Heard anything from your husband?"

"Doing fine, thanks. Re my husband, no. I've called because I don't want to be Karen Velotti any longer. I want to go back to being Marti Costello."

"Oh. Have you thought it all out? I mean, leaving the protection of the program and all? You know you are still entitled to all the benefits given your husband, which include your hospital and rehabilitation expense."

"I'm glad to hear that officially, but I don't think I'm in any danger. My husband is gone. I don't ever expect to hear from him again, and I can't help anyone who wants to find him."

"I guess you know who that is."

She hesitated. "Sure, but if it's Phil Stanton he has no issues with me, and I can't help him find Bob, I mean Leland."

He remembered Vincennes's theory, and said, "You were being very heroic in stepping in front of the bullet, but is it possible your husband set up the whole thing? That he meant for you to be killed. But deliberately, not by accident."

A shocked response. "That's crazy. Why would he do that?"

Robbins shifted in his chair. Why should he feel uncomfortable? At least the question had tested the legitimacy of Ross's ideas on the shooting.

"Well, might he have been trying to take off on his own? Did he invite you to leave with him?"

There was silence at the woman's end for at least five seconds, then, "No."

"Okay, then by bringing someone in to make it appear he was in danger, and after you tried to stop what appeared an attempt on his life, he could be implicated somehow. Else, why doesn't he come forward? After all, he did leave you, perhaps for dead, on that basement floor."

More silence, then her voice, less strong and less confident. "I don't think Bob wanted to injure me. I think it was strictly a revenge situation. Phil Stanton probably wants to square things with Bob for trying to put him in jail."

"Stanton might come after you, thinking you could lead him to your husband."

"As I said, Mr. Robbins, I can't help him. I wouldn't help him. I'm sorry, Mr. Robbins, but getting a little tired with all this talk. I'm still weak as a kitten. Could we continue this at another time?"

Robbins hesitated. He had her on the ropes. She may have contradicted herself in some of this, but he would check it out on the tape.

"Of course, but one more question. Can you tell me when you'll be all through with the therapy and rehab work? I'll hold up the cancellation of your enrollment until then so all your expenses will be covered. How about the bungalow? Can we dispose of the property?"

"That would be great. I'll get my stuff out as soon as I can drive my car. I'll get back to you regarding the windup of my rehab, and thanks for everything to date, Mr. Robbins."

36

After disconnecting, Marti fished around the drawer next to her bed and found the card left by detective Leo Carey. As she punched out the phone number she decided she wouldn't let the conversation drag on as it did with Robbins. She wondered why the marshal didn't remind her that by giving up her alias she was canceling any use her husband might have for either name, Velotti or Costello. Obviously, Bob had other names for such uses as passports. He must have had that all worked out when he thought she was still his loyal wife.

Carey was on the late shift, but they must have found him because he returned her call within a few ten minutes.

His greeting was friendly. "Hey. How're you doing?"

"Fine thank you. I wanted to call you because I have some news.

But not the news you'd really like, big boy.

"I and my husband have been under the protection of the federal witness program. He is Robert Costello and I am Marti Costello and I am leaving the program."

"Okay. Nice to meet you, Mrs. Costello. Does this mean your husband has also left the program. Has he contacted you with another brand new name?"

"No. He hasn't called, but I wanted to tell you. Also, I'll have a new address just as soon as I can find an apartment near the hospital."

"Hey, good for you. I want to thank you for your cooperation to date, and I hope you will be back to normal soon. One question. Who was the male visitor to your bedside?"

"That was Ross Vincennes of the U. S. marshal's office. He came to make sure I wouldn't spill the beans about my phony ident. Now I've got that load off my back."

"Well thank you and good luck, Mrs. Costello. Call me if I can help in any way."

Marti was now doing two gym sessions a day. After her afternoon workout, she was seated on a chair by her room window reading a morning paper when Delaney, who was on the late shift, came in with her usual smile.

"So how did it go today?"

Marti said, "The second go-round was murder. The Polish prince makes me walk till I want to drop. He had me on the push-aways this afternoon, making me put my feet farther from the wall. It's torture. I'm supposed to keep my body straight, my butt in. I could only do two of them, and he was disappointed. Stood there looking at me like I was some candy ass weakling."

Delaney looked sympathetic. "But you won't be for long."

Delaney was sure Karen was putting on a show. She guessed there would be a distinct difference in what Karen told her and what actually happened. She was right. Warshawsky later told her his look after the push-away effort was not disapproving. His vocal reaction, he said, was "Not bad, but you'll do better." Why, the nurse wondered, was Karen trying to make the therapist into a sadist? Maybe it was Karen who was disappointed in her own wall-bending performance? "She'll do better," Delaney told fellow RN Marion Harris, "She'll try to show Julie there is nothing he can put her through that she can't handle."

Delaney heard her patient say she had some special news.

"But I also have a favor to ask, Peggy."

The nurse raised her eyebrows. "The answer is yes to the favor, if possible, but quick with the news."

"Okay. From now on call me Marti Costello. That's my real name. My husband is, or was, a protected witness because of some trouble he got into in New York."

Delaney made no effort to conceal her surprise. "Wow! That's why you got shot. The news people guessed right. Someone was after your husband and you came to the rescue. He thought you were dead, so he ran, but why doesn't he come back for you now? Or at least call?"

"He's afraid, Peg. He's sure I'm being watched. Anyway, my identity doesn't make any difference. No one's after me. Now, can I ask that favor?"

"Fire away."

"I need a new place to live as soon as I can get out of here. Close to the hospital, maybe within walking distance of Warshawsky's gym, or the rehab across the street if Warshawsky sends me there."

Peggy grinned. "You may be in luck. I have a cousin in the real estate business with an office in the neighborhood. She helped Mike and me find a new place so I could be closer to the job. I'll bet she can help you."

37

Ross Vincennes had swapped Bob Costello's problem for a similar one; that is finding a hiding place for so much cash. He had been away from Chicago for five days, then in Elmhurst, a Chicago suburb, for another day. Thus far he had handled Costello's two suitcases exactly as the former owner had. They were in the trunk of the car when he was in it, and under his motel beds when he slept. Chances are, he would follow Costello's lead and choose a commercial storage place. It needed to be near at hand for the time being, readily accessible, but safe.

He wasn't home completely free. While driving back from the Twin Cities he had played out a number of scenarios, beginning with reviewing his decision to run with the loot, rather than wait for and kill Costello. He reviewed favorably his option to run. Why risk a murder charge, and the link with Marti made this very possible. There was still the risk that Costello would come after him. He would still have to watch his back. Marti would need to watch hers, too.

His first idea for stashing the cash was a bank box, more than one, but that could be dangerous. What if Costello went bananas, risked a ton of federal charges, and tried to implicate him? Or Costello might make an anonymous call. Costello would have given up all hope for seeing his money again in either case, but a call to Lou Robbins could mean special trouble. He wasn't sure how he could protect the boxes from a government raid. He'd have to use different names for each location, at least. It would take a lot of time he didn't have.

If Costello tried to turn him in, it would be no use denying he had gone after him. He'd say he hadn't been able to find the missing witness, and Robbins would probably call him a liar.

Robbins might be pissed off enough to start an investigation and it would surely turn up Carlson, the car dealer. End of story. He might claim he had tried to follow Costello, but lost him, but Robbins wouldn't buy it. Neither would a board of inquiry. End of career. End of everything.

But there was no way Robbins, or anyone, could break down his denial that he had Costello's money. Costello couldn't prove he was the thief, and if the money couldn't be produced, Costello had no basis for his charge.

Costello might be desperate enough to come after him, even try to kill him. Not likely. It would be completely out of character. Costello finagled for money, he didn't kill for it. He was an intelligent man. He'd figure the percentages and choose for trying to get his money back. He would surrender to the Chicago cops for questioning on why he left the scene in the basement, and reenter the witness program, probably with a new identity.

From that base he might try to come after me. How? He'd need contacts he probably doesn't have. Someone helped him change his ident, but chances are they won't be available for setting up assassinations or any kind of squeeze play. Maybe I should have waited for the bastard and killed him. I was just too impatient to wind it up, to get back to Chicago with the money.

And to see Marti, although the idea of taking off with her was now out of the question. Such a move would be a clear tip he had Costello's money—to Jody, too.

He had to see Marti, but he didn't need to promise he would marry her. Why mess things up? Now, with all that cash, he had the world by the ass. He could get along with Jody so long as he had Marti on the side.

He still had come up with a way to have easier access to the cash than a storage locker, Bury it? Like a goddamned pirate. But where? He sipped on a scotch and water in his Elmhurst hotel room while he considered his options. Costello took a chance using that storage company, but the guy was desperate, giving himself only a day for gathering the cash and hot footing it to Minneapolis. How about getting the cash out of the country? He'd have to get on his computer and read up on the legalities of shipping money. He had never encountered any situations like it in his career, but he'd heard other agents discussing how the drug people did it. It might work for him.

One thing for sure. He had to go into the office, tell Robbins he was rested after the week off and ready to get back to work. He had to arrange for a tap on Marti's phone, too. Robbins would buy the idea because

Costello might call his wife, and hopefully reveal his whereabouts. Maybe he should just tell Robbins what he had been up to. Except for the swiping Costello's cash, of course.

He needed to intercept any Costello calls to Marti. Costello might call her for several reasons including a threat to kill her. It was out of character, but Costello must be crazy with rage. The man must be sure she tipped Stanton to their Chicago address. He could visualize Costello on the phone, his anguished scream, "You told Vincennes where he could find me."

How would that play with her? If Costello had already called her, she would know Costello had lost his money. To whom? Who else? He had to check that out.

38

Marti was getting organized in her new one-bedroom apartment when Vincennes called. He said he tried to reach her at the hospital but learned she had been discharged.

She said, "Yes, and I've decided to leave the witness program."

"I guess you figure the name doesn't make much difference anymore."

"Right, I'm tired of hiding. I don't think I'll ever see or hear from Bob again.

"He hasn't called, huh?"

"No. I guess you didn't find him?"

Vincennes sucked in a breath. "No. He's long gone. He was there, all right. I found a dealer who sold him a Buick, but it was quite a while ago. It's too bad you had your dream a little late. I thought he might have called you. He must know you're alive."

He said, "I've missed you. When can I come over?"

Marti was ready for the request.

"I'm still very weak and I'm spending most of the days in the hospital's therapy department. Let's put if off for a few more days."

"Hey, it's been too long. Can't I just see you?"

Marti wasn't sure that was all he had on his mind, but she said,

"All right, come on over, but don't figure on staying long. I'm used to the hospital hours. They've been dragging me out of bed at hours I used to call the middle of the night."

She needed to see him, but not for love-making. She wanted to test her new resolve, to see if the new Marti Costello, the one who needed a bullet in the gut to wake her up to reality, was ready to reenter the real world. The self-loathing she had felt about swapping Bob for some of the money he had stolen had subsided as she regained her strength, but she still associated the shame with Ross Vincennes and their affair. She had acted like a silly bored bitch in heat, dangling the bait before the marshal who had made no real commitment. If there was anything like love between them they would have discussed how they could make a life together without her promise of a lot of money. God, she certainly knew men. Why had she thought this one was going to leave his wife, however bored he might be with his job or how much he disliked the step-daughters? And giving up his job. A U.S. marshal would have to be insane to take off with the wife of a protected witness. How ridiculous it all seemed now.

He must have called from somewhere nearby. She barely had time to remove the slacks she had been working in, arranging books and some CDs, and get into a skirt and blouse. Nothing to turn him on, at least nothing more provocative than what she wore at their old meetings.

Then he was there, stepping through the door and taking her in his arms. Marti was at first glad to have the support. Her knees had weakened despite her resolve to keep cool. God, he was a beautiful man. His long and hungry kiss was accompanied by much groping of the hands, one of which slipped down to her knees, the other around her shoulders. Jesus, he was going to pick her up. She twisted her mouth away from his.

"Ross. What are you doing? Cut it out."

She was hurting, too. There was still pain in her legs and torso. Warshawsky said it would be with her for another few weeks. She tried to regain her feet, but Ross, laughing, swept her into his arms.

He said, "I guess the bedroom is this way," and he carried her struggling through the short hallway into the room she never intended for him to see, on this visit or any visit.

She didn't want to scream and create a scene for her new neighbors, but this had to stop.

"Godddammit, Ross, put me down."

He did, but not gently. She bounced off the queen-size bed. Hard. And that hurt, too. She winced, but he gave no sign of being aware of her distress. She looked up at him, shocked. He was starting to peel off his suit coat. She summoned the strength to throw her legs over the opposite side of the bed. She was furious as she struggled to her feet, almost yelling. To hell with the neighbors.

"Ross, I didn't invite you here to be manhandled. Now get the hell out."

Surprised, one eyebrow up, he said, "Hey. Take it easy. How did you expect me to react to seeing you. It's been a hell of a dry spell. I've missed you baby. I can't help it the way you turn me on."

All the old bullshit. Baby. Turn me on. All the sincerity of husband Frank in his car salesman role. As real as Ken the Barbie doll. She could never love this man.

She stared at him as if she had never seen him before. It was good that he came on like a cave man, home from the hunt. It made it all the easier to throw him out of her life. She was breathless. And scared. She had never before seen this look on his face.

"Ross. It was a mistake. I was wrong. We were both wrong. I was bitchy about leaving my home town. Unhappy with Bob, too, I guess, but we've had our fling. Now it's over." He couldn't believe it. He had thought about this reunion for weeks, and she just stood there staring at him. What in hell had happened to her? Did the goon's slug knock her into menopause? It was the money. She was pissed about not getting the money

He said, "Wait a minute. We had a great thing going. Just a few weeks ago you wanted to run away. So I didn't find your husband, or get the money you thought you were going to get. So what? I'm still the same. You're going to be the same."

She knew that he knew she had caused the scene in the basement, but it was still a shock to hear the accusation, and the sneer in his voice.

"Ross, I'm not the same. All the hours in that hospital bed, and now the therapy. It hurts like hell, but it gives me a lot of time to think, too, and what we had wasn't real, it couldn't last."

He could see she meant it. At least right now. He had to back off. He wouldn't give her up. He couldn't, but the bitch was really upset. He had to give her more time to get back to normal. She'd come around. He took a side step toward the bedroom door, then turned his back on her and walked into the hall toward the front door. He thought she would follow him, but as he let himself out of the apartment he could see she was still in the bedroom.

39

Marti lay on her bed for an hour. The son of a bitch had hurt her. He just walks in, grabs his hands full and expects her to drop her pants. Sure she had felt something when he came in the door, but after this, it was really over. Any possibility she would have succumbed to the old itch for Ross Vincennes was gone. And thank God!.

He had never acted like this before. No man had. She had always been in control, even with Phil Stanton. It was part of her persona, the deep-down certainty she was in charge. Who she had sex with, and when, were basic to that part of her. Ross Vincennes, who looked at her as if he would take her by force, had stripped her of her belief in her ultimate respectability, her feeling of self-worth. What was left of it.

She knew what she did to men, most men. But it was her decision if she was to respond, not theirs. The complete gall of this guy. Her fury made her burst into tears.

Most men. After Billy she had gone berserk, dating guys who never dreamed they would get lucky with her. Dinner with some drinks, a Broadway show, gambling in Atlantic City. It ate up the hours of the long nights, helped assure her she was still a desirable woman, helped her forget how Billy had been taken away.

But then it was goodbye Charley to those guys, that's all for you. She wasn't a whore, and she had never felt like a whore.

She knew she had shorted herself on education. Poor Cora hated her job, standing in the restaurant for hours, but she had poured every extra dime into converting her daughter from a street kid into the beginnings of a lady. It was a shell. She could walk, she could talk, she had learned value in clothing and how to wear it. Cora had even insisted on formal instruction in table etiquette. A good college was the next step. Cora would have mortgaged her soul for the tuition, but when Billy came into Marti's life, an ambitious mother's creativity came to an end. Marti, barely out of high school, became a homemaker. Any hopes Cora had for seeing her daughter mature into a multi-dimensional woman with ambitions that matched her mother's dreams went the way of button shoes. Marti's advanced education would be turned over to The Young and Restless and the other soaps.

The year with Billy had been a sexual sleigh ride. She loved him in his uniform or without a stitch. She was convinced she would love him forever. She did, but his forever came too soon.

Frank was a return to the real world. She learned how to balance a check book, and how to tell a decent car from a clunker, but he also introduced her to false values and several sides of maleness she would despise for the rest of her life. Super vanity was the least of Frank's undesirable traits.

Bob, poor Bob, had simply tried to give her anything she wanted. He was oriented around his profession, but he tried to lead her into thinking about something more than what's on teevee tonight? He was a kind man, too. She would always remember how she had sounded off about some laborers who had whistled at her from a truck as she walked into the condo.

"Those dumb apes," she fumed. "Why don't they get decent jobs?"

Bob said, "They may have all they can get, Marti. I can never knock a man for honest work, whatever it is."

She had stepped over the line with Ross Vincennes. She had been the aggressor. She couldn't blame him for his surprise at her reaction, but now she knew, and she hoped he knew. It was over. With Bob, too. He could never trust her again, even if he did return. He knew he had been betrayed, but he couldn't have known what to make of her move in the basement. Carey said there were two calls to 911. One of them could have been Bob's. He had committed himself to running, perhaps not right then, but he had guessed she or Vincennes had called Stanton. He might have felt she deserved that slug in the tummy, but Bob probably wasn't vindictive, just scared. She couldn't blame him for that. He couldn't have been sure the fat man hadn't come to kill them both, and that Phil only wanted revenge. He must know the shooting was premature, accident or not, but one thing was for sure. He wasn't coming back. She would get a divorce and reorganize her life with the help of Phil's hundred thousand. If he would let her keep it.

Right now, she had to get strong again. Julius Warshawsky and his enthusiastic young aides, Jane and Cindy, were taking her there. Julius told her she would be a new woman, with new strength, stronger than ever. He had clenched and shaken his fist when he delivered the forecast, like some athletes when they have made a successful play, or golfers after sinking a winning putt. She could tell he was strong. Jane and Cindy, both with tendencies to giggle, said he was the hospital's star athlete. Marti asked no questions about him, but the girls seemed to want to brag about him. Marti had decided Warshawsky wasn't involved with either of them. Both in their late twenties with bodies that may have been nourished by farm food, they behaved like virgins. Way to go girls. Marti remembered Cora's admonitions about giving it away.

Marti was happy with her post hospital regimen. Muscles no, but strength yes. The idea, once repugnant, was now a goal. She didn't want to look like those bulging women she hated, but it would be nice to know she was among the women who could take care of themselves. She had asked the girls about the self-defense programs for women. They promised to help her enroll if she was still interested after her therapy.

She found herself watching Warshawky as he worked with other patients. Not openly but with side glances. That was the key to effectiveness, patience with patients. He used it to inspire trust. There were lots of smiles, friendly touches on arms and shoulders, encouragement. He moved himself and his patients purposefully, but no one was rushed. He kidded with the men, even those in stroke recovery. Marti guessed he hoped to promote reactions. Cindy, massaging Marti's legs after her walk, saw her watching the head therapist, and said, "He's a con artist, all right, but he believes in his own con."

Not a bad way to put it.

The girls insisted that Warshawsky played no favorites, but he certainly was a favorite with women patients, who practically came unglued when he came into the room. He joked as much with women patients, Marti noted, but he was usually on the serious side with her. She thought it probably went back to the first day when she snapped at him. Was he that sensitive? She had been careful to watch her mouth since, even when the rehab hurt the most.

The day she was officially leaving the hospital, Warshawsky followed her to her room after her workout.

He said, "Doctor Morgan has approved extended therapy, Mrs. Velotti, I mean Mrs. Costello. You can have as much of our time as you need to get back to full strength."

She would have told him of her name change, but Peggy Delaney had beaten her to it. Peggy was there to help her check out and Marti smiled at them both.

"Good. How could I go on without you guys?"

Peggy had delivered on a good place to live near the hospital. It was a one-bedroom apartment just three blocks from the hospital. The availability of the partially furnished unit coincided with her checkout. Marshal Robbins had arranged to deliver her car to the hospital, and Peg, off duty, had done the driving, first to the bank for some cash and a new credit card. Then Peg did some basic shopping for food, towels and linens, etc., while Marti sat in the car.

Peg said, "Julie hopes you'll be able to walk to and from the hospital soon. He may keep you company."

Oh yeah. Probably a good idea. He wouldn't want her falling on her face, but Marti wondered if Peggy was trying to promote something between her and Warshawsky? Delaney knew Marti was still married, but she also knew her husband had ditched her. It was a weird thought, and she urged herself to forget about it. Julius Warshawsky, for all his attention and care for his patients, had reached his middle thirties unattached, and she was sure he wanted it that way.

Addressing her as Mrs. Velotti, until Delaney told him to switch to Costello, was in Marti's view not a way to promote a closer relationship. If she saw any signs on his part to move in, it would be she who put up the screen. She was still married and part of the new woman she was beginning to see in herself didn't include any more affairs. She still had too many men in her life. Bob was surely gone, but there was still Vincennes to unload. And Phil Stanton who sounded amorous in their telephone talk. He would follow up for sure, probably for more than his money. Now that he didn't blame her for letting Bob get away he'd be sniffing around again. Peggy had helped her move in, which involved transferring some clothes and belongings from the bungalow. A lot of the stuff she had bought wouldn't fit in the apartment, but with Peggy's help she saved some of the pictures, a brand new area lamp, some bedroom and bathroom stuff including a scale, clothes hamper, some nice lotions and soaps, more bed linens and towels, and a couple of clocks. There was no way she and Peggy could haul the TV and a recliner chair from the bungalow, but Robbins came to the rescue again. When she called him to report her discharge from the hospital and her move into the apartment, he said he would arrange for the delivery of any heavy stuff she wanted. She read him a list, and the day she moved in a delivery truck showed up.

She decided he was a nice man, and she sent him a note to that effect after she picked up some stationery. She reminded him in the note that there were still several things in the bungalow that could go to Good Will or the Salvation Army. He could handle that with a phone call, she thought. She wondered if Robbins would let Ross read her note. She and Ross had never corresponded, but she hadn't written many notes in her lifetime to any other man, and very few women.

The phone pulled her out of her reverie, and off the bed. It was Ross, she was sure. He should apologize. But it wasn't Ross.

"Marti, it's Bob. How are you?"

"Oh Bob." She had never felt such relief. "How are you? Where are you? Check that. I don't want to know."

"Well, it can't be avoided because I'm in the city, and I want to see you. The hospital gave me your number. Have you completely recovered? Seeing you on the basement floor that way, I thought you were dead. It drove me crazy until I read you were okay, or I should say, recovering."

"I'm doing all right, but still in therapy. It could take awhile. I have an apartment near Memorial hospital. I want to see you. Could you come here?"

"No, I think not."

How could she blame him?

He said, "Can you drive?"

"Yes, for the past couple of days."

"Okay. There's a McDonald's at the corner of Pulaski and Devon. Could you get there tomorrow evening?"

"What time?"

"About eight?"

"I'll be there."

"Okay. And Marti, am I taking any chances?"

The question was like a slap in the face, but she knew he had to ask it.

"No certainly not. And Bob."

"Yes?"

"I'm very sorry. And ashamed for what I did."

"Marti, it took a while to figure it out, but I thought you were sorry when you came into the basement and stepped into that bullet."

40

Phil Stanton eased the receiver back into its cradle. after hearing Brancatto's report.

Brancatto said, "She's out of the hospital but still goes in for therapy. She's living in an apartment near the hospital."

He told Brancatto he appreciated the call, which was true enough. After all he was paying enough to maintain the surveillance in Chicago. He now had Marti's address and phone number. He wanted to call, but what if her phone was tapped? Not too wild a thought considering how the law would be hoping her husband might try to make contact. He told Brancatto to have his Chicago man send her flowers.

"Anonymously, of course. Better yet, from an admirer."

He had to clear some time and get out there. There had been no sign of Costello. Chances are there wouldn't be. The bastard was long gone, and so was more than three million bucks. In cash. Which could be a problem for the son of a bitch. He remembered one conversation with the glorified bookkeeper about converting the unreported cash to bearer bonds. Costello had argued for them, said they'd be easier to handle, but he had thought, yeah, for you maybe. He had told Costello to leave the unreported cash in bank boxes. At the time he thought it was six of one a half dozen of the other, but now the decision looked good. Hauling all that cash must have taken a couple of suitcases.

Per their plan, Costello used a bunch of banks to hide the cash. There was no hanky panky in that part. Costello gave Stanton the list of banks and how much went into each box. Stanton held the keys, the only keys, and he personally handed them to Costello on the morning of the days they were needed. Costello returned them the following mornings, except for THAT morning, the morning Costello didn't come in. The keys were delivered to the office by a courier. Costello was ill. Stanton's secretary told him by phone because he and Lucia were en route to Las Vegas. He might have smelled a rat. Costello might have known he'd be gone that day, but Stanton hadn't even told his secretary about the plan to treat his wife to some gambling and night life. He had mentioned it to Marti and it had fired his certainty she had conspired with her husband.

He had to admit he had been lax about keeping tabs on Costello. He could, should have accompanied him to the banks at any time, but he couldn't believe such a mild-mannered, highly educated man was a thief, not that kind of thief anyway. He was wrong. The son of bitch must have moved with the speed of light to scoop up all that cash and stash it somewhere, all in a single day away from the office.

It wasn't the Bahamas. No way he would have chanced lugging all that cash into the islands on one trip. In one day!

Forget about it. He still had the best of the deal. Marti was rid of the guy, and he would ride into Chicago on a big white horse to make her days, and nights, more bearable.

41

Vincennes hadn't missed much at the office. Routine. Robbins had built an empire. More employees than work. Any other way wouldn't be governmental. Or bureaucratical!

He was braced for the worst when Robbins called him in, but the boss had nothing more than news he had heard the afternoon before—from its source. Karen Velotti. She was back to being Martina Costello.

He had clearly made a mistake with Marti. The lady was in a rage, and he had never been more frustrated. He had to settle for a sexual homecoming with his wife. Jody accepted him gratefully, but wondered why he came home so late in the evening. It was after nine. Ross made up a tale about driving a lot of miles to get home before bedtime.

He thought he knew how to bring Marti back into the fold. Good old fashioned cash. That's what motivated her to begin this thing. It had been a mistake to rush her like that. She had gone through a hell of an ordeal in the hospital. She obviously had a way to go with the therapy. He'd call her, apologize, and suggest a meeting, any time, any place, her choice. He'd call today, before the tap on her phone was in place. As he had guessed, Robbins agreed to his suggestion It would take a couple of days to clear approvals.

He was sure the money was safe. He had some ideas for moving it off shore from his stints on the computer, but that might come later. Right now it was in a locker at a security outfit called Super Safe on Fullerton. He declined their insurance protection. He wasn't about to itemize three million dollars, but they did have twenty-four hour security.

42

Marti was on time for the meeting, first to arrive. There wasn't much street traffic on the cool early October evening. She wore a dark sweater over a skirt and blouse, nothing to attract any attention. Her new pixie cut, showing her unadorned ears, was provided by a salon she discovered on her first walk to the apartment. It would take care of her hair for awhile.

She thought Bob might have been waiting nearby, possibly across Kedzie, until he could be sure she wasn't followed, or had company. She couldn't blame him for being careful. She might have been followed but she though she had been careful. Despite his last remark in their phone conversation, in which he seemed to forgive her complicity in giving him up, he had to have doubts. She said she was sorry, but how could he know the depth of her regrets and self-loathing? She still had a long way to go in achieving her avowed new approach to living out the rest of her life. It was heavy stuff for a girl-woman who had never taken anything very seriously, but for the past several days, before the intrusion by Vincennes, anyway, she had never been happier. She was walking with less pain and gaining strength daily. She never dreamed she'd actually enjoy pushing iron. The weights were only a few pounds, but she could feel the surge of new strength as the sweat poured.

Today, Warshawsky had walked the five blocks with her to the apartment, and he was openly approving which pleased her. Approvals from males outside a bed were rare, and she liked it. She was back behind the wheel of her car, too, regaining confidence as a driver while performing short errands in the neighborhood. All in all, things were in pretty good shape except for having too many men in her life. At least Bob was alive, and he would move on without her. Vincennes could be a problem, but all she had to do was say no. Eventually he would go away. She could hope so, anyway.

Phil Stanton, too, would have to take a hike. If push came to shove, she would send him his money. Well, maybe not all of it. She had kept her end of the deal, although her apparent misunderstanding of the basement scene messed up his party for Bob, and her.

Bob feared Phil had connections with bad people. She hadn't thought so, but Phil had somehow arranged for the fat man to come after Bob. At the trial, Phil's attorneys had described an outstanding citizen and business and family man. They were stretching it about the family part. Marti was sure he loved his children, but in the loyalty department he was about as true blue as Benedict Arnold. At least to his wife.

She grimaced. *Look who's talking.* If Bob was in a forgiving mood she was grateful, but she didn't want to go away with him if that was what was on his mind. The best way would be to end their marriage as part of beginning her new life. She was anxious to hear what he had to say, hoped she could help him somehow. She glanced at the door. If he showed up.

She took her coffee to a booth well away from the counter. The only other customers in the restaurant were a couple of teen-agers and a pair of older men.

She had been nursing the coffee for several minutes when Bob slipped in. He saw her and gave a little wave before he walked up to the counter. In a minute he slipped into the booth across from her. He was careful in putting his coffee down before he reached for her hand.

She gave it gratefully. "How are you, Bob?"

She didn't think he looked all that well, especially under the eyes. He was dressed in slacks, tan woolen shirt with open collar, and a leather jacket, informal wear for him, and she could see he had lost a few pounds, which for him was gaunt. His gaze across the table wasn't that of a man seeing his wife for the first time in weeks. It was a look of exhaustion, as a man might look when something bad has happened to him that seems unfixable.

He said, "Several days ago Ross Vincennes came to Minneapolis. God knows how he found me, but he stripped me of two suitcases holding more than three million dollars"

Oh no! Marti looked at the table. She didn't know how she could look up, but she did when she felt him squeeze her hand.

How could she tell him the truth? She could start with it.

"Bob, I thought you were taking off without me. In the hospital, lying there with a bunch of tubes running out of my body, I remembered seeing the ticket jacket for your one-day trip. I told Vincennes."

She cringed as she uttered the words. She couldn't look at his face.

What had the man done to deserve such a greedy unfaithful bitch? No more lying. She could have claimed she only told Vincennes because it was the duty of his office to try to find Bob, but Vincennes made his mission clear, as well as her complicity, when he took Bob's money.

Bob was looking down at the table, too.

He said, "Yeah, I was feeling pretty sorry for myself about losing you to Vincennes. You were right. I was about to take off. Who called Stanton, you or Vincennes?"

"I did."

"For the same reason?"

He was trying to make it easier for her.

"Yes. But he said he only wanted the money. He said he wouldn't hurt you and I would get some of the money."

She saw the corners of his mouth turn up.

Of course it sounded dumb. How did she think Stanton would get Bob to cough up the money unless he was threatened with excruciating pain? It was incredible, really, that this man so outrageously betrayed, could just sit there and listen to this garbage and not grab her by the hair and smash her face into the Formica-covered table.

She had to help him. She had to say something to make up for the last dumb remark, something that would somehow convey her hope he could forgive her, as hopeless as it might sound.

"Bob, maybe I can do something to help you get it back. I've ended the affair with Vincennes. Somehow, over the past several days, maybe with the help of my therapy, I've seen what a selfish bitch I'd become. I didn't marry you in good faith, but I was desperate. Two marriages and I was high and dry. I didn't know how to support myself, and I wanted to live the life my poor mother had tried to create for me. I thought being married to you would settle me down, and I did enjoy the home you made for us and the fun we had together.

"It's all an alibi, I know, but somehow the move to Chicago brought out the absolute worst in me, even when you told me we would be able to get out of the program and live well somewhere. I thought Vincennes

197

represented a means of regaining the good life you gave me in New York, and that I might somehow be able to go home."

Bob was staring into her face. "How could you help me?"

Think, lady. What can you possibly do to help this poor man?

She pressed her fingers to her mouth. "Maybe I can make Vincennes give up the money. I don't think he could stand it if I told his boss of our affair."

"Marti, that could be dangerous. Any hint of a threat and the guy could kill you and blame it on whoever shot you at the bungalow. You already are in danger. If you tell him you know he has the money, he might assume you would go to the same people who sent the fat man. I consider myself lucky in one respect. He could have waited for me in my apartment in Minneapolis, taken me somewhere and dumped me."

Marti could believe it. Now. The look Ross gave her when she ordered him out of her apartment was mean, a lot more vicious than that of a guy who had a bucket of ice water thrown in his crotch.

Hoping it would add to her believability now, she told Bob of Vincennes's visit the previous evening.

"Bob, it's hard to believe, I know, but I have changed. When he grabbed me I screamed at him. Ordered him to get the hell out. Hell yes, I think he might be capable of murder, but I'm damn sure he'll call again. I'm ashamed to say it to you, my husband, but this guy still has the hots for me. I think he will tell me he has the money. He'll tell me because he thinks it will bring me around, make me renew the relationship."

Get her back in his bed, she might have said, but not now.

Costello wrinkled his forehead and ran his hand across his chin. She thought he needed a shave, but what he really needed was a major break. Some feeling of hope.

"Marti, remember, neither you nor I have any proof he has the money, and he's had enough time to bury it so deep Captain Kidd couldn't dig it up. If you could somehow get him to concede he has the money, then maybe you could say, okay, show me the money and let's get out of here. Then it's put up or shut up time and there might be a chance we could somehow reverse the hijack job he did on me."

They stared at each other across the table, both straining for some additional point that would move Bob's idea from guesswork to a plausible plan.

She spoke first. "Okay, I can try to do that. What then?'

For Bob, his idea had none of the dimensions of the money matters he had dealt with throughout his career. He had stolen the cash, now wanted it back, but he hesitated to put his wife at risk. She had betrayed him, but their was no doubt about her sincerity now. She wanted to make good.

He said, "Look, if Vincennes calls again . . ."

"He will, he will. I know he will."

"Okay. Why not tell him you see no future in resuming the affair, that you don't see him leaving his wife and job, especially with no money, and that the whole idea was based on having a lot of money with which you could take off together. I hope he won't let you get that far. I hope he will butt in to say he has the money."

Marti leaned forward, excited. "What then?"

"Once he admits to having the money you can say you want a share and you could challenge him to go ahead with your original idea, to take off with it. If he agrees we could somehow set a trap. He could buy into this. After all, you got the whole thing rolling. He never would have had the Minneapolis lead without you. I know we can't expect the thief to play it fair and square, but you have a hold over him."

He wasn't accusatory, but each word was like the thrust of a knife. All she could say was, "That sounds good."

But Ross will want a show of affection before he would believe I would run away with him. How can I do it? Bob thinks I can. How can I blame him for thinking I'm a tramp.

He said, "You could still be doubtful and insist on seeing the money. At this point I think he would want you to see it."

Marti digested that and nodded.

She said, "I don't believe he wants to run, now that he has the money. A couple of weeks ago, I might have thought so, but he wasn't as desperate as I felt. He griped about his wife and a couple of air-head stepdaughters, but he has a good job. No, he won't suggest taking off. I'll put it to him. If he waffles, I'll insist on getting my half."

"Okay, but suppose he does want to run. With you and the money. Can you handle that?"

What he can't say is can I show Vincennes some proof of my affection.

"Bob, you leave that to me. I'll suggest a meeting in a restaurant. He can't get amorous there, but if he admits to having the money I'll think of something to get out of anything later. Hell, I'll tell him it's the wrong time of the month."

"But it still could be very dangerous."

"Bob, I've crapped up my life, and ruined your chance to get away. If we can get your money, any of it, I'll feel a hell of a lot better about myself."

He sucked in a breath. He had come back to Chicago without hope, but Marti was showing a side of herself he had never seen, never thought existed. He had never thought of her as beautiful but dumb. He had respected her obvious intelligence, but her life, the life she had led with him, was built completely around her needs. Now, she might have a chance to help him, and a share of whatever they could retrieve from Vincennes was better than nothing.

She read his mind. "About the money, I don't get a dime, whatever happens."

She reached for her purse. "If that's it, I have to get home and get some rest. My therapist is working the tail off me."

He struggled out of the booth. "How's it going?"

"The pain is easing up, and I'm getting stronger" She laughed, "Would you believe it. My therapist has me lifting weights."

Bob walked her to her car in the McDonald's lot. He had parked on a side street. She gave his arm a squeeze and brushed a kiss against his cheek.

"We'll make it work, Bob. You call me tomorrow night."

"Okay, Marti. Good luck."

43

The flowers came with an unsigned card. From an admirer. She guessed they'd come from Ross, and that they guaranteed he would follow up with a call. Of course he wouldn't take the chance of signing the card.

It had been an active day, beginning with a call from Warshawsky. He wanted her to step up activities for both morning and afternoon sessions.

"Walk over at ten and we'll have you do some weights and work on the bars, then do a longer walk in the hospital corridors. Lunch here, then rest. At two we'll do some arm and leg exercises and a massage, then finish up with the walk home. Okay?"

"Okay." He had her agreeing to everything.

She had walked back into therapy after walking what seemed like miles throughout the hospital, stopping only to chat with Peggy for a couple of minutes. Back in rehab Warshawsky popped out of his office.

"How about some lunch?"

"Sure." Surprised. This was a first. Marti had lunched a couple of times with Jane and Cindy, but Warshawsky usually disappeared. He explained as they walked to the cafeteria.

"I usually take the time to get in some gymnastic stuff and a swim over at the Y, but today I thought we could grab a bite and review your progress."

Marti shrugged. *Why not? It wasn't like a date.*

They filled their trays, Marti with a salad and tea. Warshawsky went for a tuna salad sandwich. He led the way to a table for two. Seated, he didn't waste any time with his pronouncements.

"I told Doc Morgan how well you are doing. He was impressed, too. As far as we are concerned, you can set your own pace from here on out.

Frankly, I hope you'll continue with the strength stuff, and later on, when you can move without any pain, I hope you will get into some aerobics, too. That's where you jog or walk fast to make your heart work harder and thereby make it stronger."

She thought he looked very intense. The dedicated teacher. She looked at his forehead rather than into his eyes.

He said, "You are welcome to come here, but if you wanted to try some of the other equipment across the street, that's okay, too. Or, if you are tired of the hospital atmosphere, you might consider joining the Y's division for women. It's right up the street They have a track for the aerobic stuff and a couple of pools."

This guy was a big brother, Marti decided. Wouldn't it have been nice to know such a young man in the old neighborhood?

She said, "You've sold me on the workout stuff. I'm still hurting a little, but I intend to continue. I feel better for it. Frankly, I feel better about myself."

He was not smiling. He said, "You've had a tough time, not only recovering from that bullet wound." Then, "Have you heard from your husband?"

"No. Hey, you want to do me a favor?"

"Name it."

"Call me Marti."

She thought she wasn't promoting undue familiarity. She had heard the therapist call other patients by their first names.

He grinned. She thought the smile made his face appear very youthful.

"Okay, Marti. I have no problem with that. And you should call me Julie. Now, why don't you find a workout table and take a snooze until time for your afternoon session."

He walked her home again that afternoon, picking up the pace so that she was puffing slightly when they arrived at her apartment building. They stood for a few seconds before the three steps in front of the entrance.

She said, "Come on in. See what Peggy and I have done with the place."

He hesitated. Then, "Sure."

There was more to be done, but she wasn't unhappy with what had been accomplished in a few days. The apartment was on the first floor in an older brick building, built after WW II, but it had been maintained well. She and Peggy had found a couple of throw rugs for the living room's hardwood floors and some pillows to give the beige couch a splash of color. There wasn't time to plan a treatment for the windows facing the street, but she did find some ready-made sheer curtains. There were pictures for the walls, brought over from the north side bungalow, and a bookcase with a few books she had picked up during the months with Bob. It looked livable. Warshawsky nodded approval and when he spotted the flowers Marti had placed in a vase on the dinette table he said, "From an admirer?"

Marti grinned, "Yes, that's what the card said." She thought she would kid him. "I thought they might have been from you. For all the good work I've been doing."

The man blushed.

"Hey, when I send flowers, I'll own up to it. I want all the credit I can get. Tell you what, though. You are right about your rehab to date. How about letting me buy dinner?"

Marti thought that sounded okay.

"I'd like that Julie, but I'm too tired to go out. What say we call for a pizza?"

"Sounds great."

Marti showed him the phone and the Yellow Pages, but Warshawsky already knew the number. She hurried into her bedroom to ditch the workout clothes. There wasn't time for a shower, but she sponged herself off and came back into the living room in blue jeans and a light sweater.

Warshawsky said, "They said fifteen minutes."

She said, "Hey, I'm ready. What'll you have to drink? I have some Zinfandel dragged over from my old place, and some soft drinks."

"Thanks, but I'm not much into wine. A coke, diet or regular, will be fine."

They had talked about exercises and body building over their brief luncheon, and Marti. easily picked up where they left off.

"You mentioned aerobics. I've heard of it, but how does it work?.

"Yeah. The concept has to do with pushing the heart in exercises that flush more oxygen into the cardiovascular system, helping the heart to work more efficiently, hence better health, longer life. Such exercises as jogging, swimming, and cycling work best. I have some pamphlets at home that will spell it all out for you. I'll bring them tomorrow."

"It'll help me?"

"Oh yes. It will help almost anyone. I told Peggy after that first bad day with you that I was surprised with your lack of strength. I knew what you had gone through, but you have a good body and I miscalculated your muscle tone."

Marti had never been complimented on her body in quite this way.

"I already feel good. I'll feel better?"

He said, "Right. You'll even . . . ."

Marti reacted to the hesitation. She smiled and said, "Look better?"

A touch of pink came through Warshawsky's facial tan, but he was saved by the bell, the doorbell, and he gratefully hopped to his feet. "I'll get it."

The arrival of the food interrupted his dissertation. He closed the subject by repeating his promise to bring her reading material.

"It's easy stuff to understand, and it will tell you how you can get started. Once you get into it you might find yourself liking it. A lot of marathon runners started with basic aerobic exercise."

Marti said, "I've seen a lot of people jogging around the old neighborhood."

He said, "I wouldn't recommend it in this neighborhood, but the Y has a good track."

"Do you use it?"

"Yeah, I do some jogging, several miles a week. Why don't you drop in over there, see what they have to offer. It doesn't cost a heck of a lot."

"I will. Tomorrow. Hey. We can't let this good food go cold."

Julius attacked the pizza with good appetite. He had a good set of teeth, she noted.

He caught her looking. He said, "My uppers are phony. Got the teeth I was born with knocked out in high school football."

Marti was embarrassed. "I'm sorry. Actually, I wanted to compliment you on a great set."

He grinned, "Maybe I was lucky. The originals weren't all that good, and the school paid for the replacements. Incidentally, you have a good set. Are they the originals?"

She pretended indignation. "Heck yes," They laughed together.

Marti asked about his background and training in rehab work.

"Chicago's my home town. Or North Chicago, really, but I can't imagine ever leaving the area. How about you? Are you homesick? Want to get out of here?"

Marti thought about it. "I was, but not so much anymore. I'll probably go back east after getting my full strength back, but I'm in no big hurry. Why? You want to get rid of me?"

He took a sip of his coke, put the glass down, and said, "No. I'd like to see you at full strength, and then some."

He stood up. "This has been fun, Marti, but I've gotta go. I promised my old high school coach I'd scout a game for him tonight. You're welcome to join me. The game's in Austin, several miles west of here. Probably get you home about ten."

She was tempted, but she was too tired to sit in a grandstand for a couple of hours. She also wanted to be available for another call from Ross.

"I'm really tired, so I'll take a pass, but I hope you'll invite me again."

"I sure will, Marti, and thanks for the hospitality."

"I should thank you, Julie You bought the dinner."

She saw him out. He was in a hurry and there were no words at the door except his, "See you manana."

Marti rested her head against the door for a few seconds, smiling.

Just like the girls in the movies.

Was that a date? If it was, she'd never had one like it. She'd never had more fun in a one-on-one with a man, in or out of bed. The guy was like fresh air. He came on like an inexperienced sixteen-year old, but he obviously knew how to get along with women. Peg Delaney adored him, and Jane and Cindy would run through the hospital's concrete walls if he snapped his fingers.

What if he made a pass? How would she handle it? She'd convinced herself her invitation for him to see the apartment was innocent enough, but she'd known men who would have interpreted the gesture as a come-on. If Julie was in that category he certainly had his chance a few minutes ago. Instead, he invited her to join him on his football errand. Maybe he would have made his move later. She hoped not. That would spoil it.

Could she be interested in him? It would be like falling in love with a kid brother. How could it ever work, even if he stopped treating her like an older woman? The exchange about the teeth was funny. And he had almost blurted out, 'better looking' when he listed the benefits of aerobics.

Maybe he didn't consider her very pretty. She had never had trouble in the looks department, but she was pushing thirty-one. Maybe Julie preferred body-building Brunhildas. Forget it. Was he trying to promote company for his Y workouts? It could be worth the trouble to check out a membership. He mentioned a women's division. She'd check it out. Was it possible to build a friendship with a man?

She once asked her mother. Cora said, "Sure. If he's a fairy."

44

Julie wouldn't be able to use the therapy excuse to continue walking her home much longer. She was doing as well as he could have expected. He had stepped up the pace for the walk today, and she had matched his strides, so it might be sayonara to that companionship. He was pushing her, but that's what he was supposed to do. Get 'em up and get 'em out. Still, it might be nice if he considered her a special case.

Come on, stop the day dreaming. The man is helping you to get in the best physical shape of your life, maybe mental, too, but that's it, period, end of story.

The telephone snapped her back to current problems. It was Vincennes. Crunch time. She had to go into her act, get it right, as rehearsed with Bob.

He said, "Hi, baby. You okay. I hope you've cooled off since the other night."

As if he hadn't acted like a complete jerk.

Her voice was cool enough. "Oh yes, I'm okay. It hurt to be tossed around like a sack of flour. But I'm all right now."

He chuckled. "You felt like a sack of sugar to me. I sure want to see you?"

"Ross, you tell me if it's worth the trouble. Our relationship is going nowhere. It was a mistake, mostly my fault. I was homesick and unhappy. Now I may be available, but you aren't."

"Wait a minute. I'm a big boy. I knew what I was getting into. I was ready to take off with you. You were going to supply the money, remember?"

"Yes, I remember, but all that blew up and I have a big scar in my belly to prove it. And there was no money."

He hesitated. "What if I said we could have the money?"

"What's that mean?"

"It means we can do whatever we want."

This is it. Don't blow it now.

"You found Bob. You got his money. You didn't hurt him?"

"Of course not. What do you think I am? He's all right."

Okay, Mr. Vincennes. Put up or shut up. How badly do you want me?

"So if you have the money, seems to me we should consider our original plan."

Pause. "Hell yes."

"How much was there?"

"Didn't Costello tell you?"

"Yes he did, Ross, but you will know, too, if you really have it."

"Well, I can't be sure how much he stole, but I recovered more than three million."

"Wow. He told me the truth. Can I see it? Touch it?"

"Not practical. It's in a safe place."

"Look, Ross. Let's cut the crap. That bullet did more to me than tear up my insides. It forced me to look at the whole picture. As I see it now, I'm going to go it alone from here on out. Right now I'm trying to get into the best physical and mental shape of my life. Then I'll either go back home, or get a job and start over here.

"What I could use is some money, my share of Bob's money. If you aren't going to give it to me, then I'll have to consider some alternatives."

"What does that mean?"

Oops, careful. Bob warned that threats, even implied, could be dangerous.

"As I just said. I'll have to get a job, make a living."

"How about that hundred thousand you have in the bank. That cash should keep you going for a long time."

"Ross, as you said on that scary afternoon at the Red Roof Inn, that money was a down payment for something that never happened. If I use that money I'll have to run for it, and I'm not in condition to do that. A much better deal for me would be to return the hundred thousand and have my share of Bob's money, which would be half of what you stole from him. Then I'm as free as the breeze to take off when I'm ready."

"Marti, what is this? Is this a turnoff? You dumping me?"

This is it. Put up or shut up.

"Who's turning off whom? Will you divorce your wife and marry me?"

Hesitation. That's it. From now on it's bullshit.

"Sure, but Marti, what's the hurry? You have to get well. I'll need time to tie up a lot of things. Let's get together and plan our next moves."

What crap. How could she have thought she might be in love with this guy. That bullet did her a favor. It might have been the best thing that had ever happened to her.

She said, "Okay, let's do that, but you bring me my money. Check that. Pick a restaurant, a big noisy one, and bring all the money and we'll split it up in the parking lot."

"Marti, the money is in a safe place, but hard to get at on short notice."

"Okay, then take me to it. We'll split it there. I'm not kidding, Ross. I want my share."

"I don't like the idea of a parking lot. Sounds like a setup. I'll bring the money to your place When?"

She had to concede he was good at protecting his rear end. Of course she had a setup in mind. With a chance for Bob to hijack his money back.

She said. "Okay. My place. Tomorrow night, eight thirty."

"I'll be there."

45

Julie Warshawsky showered and yelled and snapped towels with his teammates after the game won by his last-second three pointer, but he turned down a beer stop. He wanted to be alone, to think about something that hadn't been a presence in his life for a many months. Ever since Pam Billows. When she dumped him, or rather when they came to an agreement to stop seeing each other, he had just about decided marriage might not be for him. Not that he was immune to loving someone, and he certainly wasn't immune to sex. What was scary was the idea of interacting with someone else's emotional needs.

Pam had never thrown the word commitment at him. She was as unselfish as anyone he had ever met. Perhaps that's why the relationship lasted as long as it did. She was no dummy, either. She scorned the word "relationship," said it was the overused phrase for safe, convenient and comfortable sex, sharing a bed and sometimes living quarters with someone who you may or may not share love. So they agreed they wouldn't live together. She based her decision on moral reasons, but he just didn't want to get that close to permanency.

They hadn't quarreled, but she stung him with her calm judgment:

"You're a boy for all seasons, Julie. You're into games, and I'm resigned to that. It's your life. You play them, watch them. Your life is built around athletic schedules, who will play whom and where and when, or what's on teevee."

He said, "Hey, I don't play golf, and I hate fishing, or bowling. Those things really eat up the time."

Her smile was weary. "I know. My mother married a golfer so I know that story, but there is no way you could work golf into your current schedule, and I'm resigned to the fact you are having a tough time working me in."

Actually he was relieved. It hurt for awhile, not seeing her, because she was bright, decent, and companionable. Their sexual relationship wasn't all that hot, but it was steady, and he didn't have to go on the prowl for it. Pam never really got the hang of good sex. He did all the work to get her aroused, and when they did spend an entire night together she seemed strangely tense, even upset with him the morning after. He chalked it up to not enough rest, or she may not have been a morning person. He had rarely seen her before nine a.m., so he didn't know. In any event it was over, and he was usually successful in making himself tired enough from his personal athletic endeavors to sublimate his normal sexual appetite. To a degree.

Now he was facing another dilemma in the person or rather the shape and face of patient Marti Costello. He had never had a patient who worked harder. Once she decided she was going to cooperate with the program, she followed every suggestion without questions or hard looks out of those gorgeous eyes. She just went about business, and she didn't quit. She was making wonderful progress, pushing through her pain threshold like an ice breaker, not very fast but steady. She had earned the unqualified approval of Peg Delaney and his assistants, too. He didn't see a three-for-three approval rating from those ladies all that often.

But her special aura of privacy was still intact. In a gym with its forced intimacy of rancid sweat clothes, grunts of frustration, groans, and cries of pain, the lady's real name was her only concession to opening up about herself. At least they were now on a first-name basis.

The invitation to see her apartment and the impromptu dinner had been fun and may have been a breakthrough. He had never been very good at initiating friendships, making the first move, but Marti Costello had made it easy. She made it seem so natural, loose and relaxed, as innocent as kids seeking new playmates, but there was a gracefulness to it, too, as if they had been friends for years.

She could kid and take a kidding. The tensions he had noted had disappeared for that pleasant hour. Hey, he forgot to ask her what she meant by triple threat man, her crack after his gymnastics demo. Maybe next time.

Why wouldn't she be at ease with men? Maybe, to judge from the shooting, with at least one of the wrong kind. She had survived a bullet in the gut, and was working hard towards complete recovery, but he wanted to understand what had happened. Why was she shot? And what was the story behind her husband, the protected witness? Is he still in the picture?

He wanted to know more, but if he ever expected her to open up he'd have to come up with something to keep her around for another chapter. He could continue to walk her home, but only for a couple more days. He couldn't offer her much help in aerobics, other than to monitor her progress. She could do that, and she was pretty much on her own for the strength stuff. She seemed interested in the Y. He'd follow through on that, take her some promo materials. If she joined, meetings there would be natural enough. That might be the way. He would pick up the literature tomorrow morning at coffee break.

46

Ross Vincennes sat at his office desk after a poor night's rest.

What happened to Marti? Did she expect him to commit himself to undying love? That wasn't going to happen, but he could give her some of Costello's money. He shouldn't have admitted he had it, but it seemed the only way to bring her around. Instead, she jumps him with the question about marriage. No way. He needed going through a divorce about as much as he needed another pain-in-the-ass step-daughter.

The blackmail threat was bitchy, too. It was in her crack about considering alternatives. She backtracked fast but it was there. She could call Robbins, but that would be unbelievably dumb. Kill her chances of getting any of the cash, and she would take all the heat for causing Costello to run for it. Robbins would fire him, but he could still hide Costello's hoard until he could carry out one of the money laundering schemes he had checked out. Get it out of the country.

What else could she do? What if she called the same people she called to snitch on her husband? No. I convinced her at the Red Roof how dangerous that would be. They'd come after me, but she wouldn't get a dime, and they'd take that hundred thousand back, too. Then kill her.

I scared hell out of her.

He should be able to calm her down, make her see the sense of continuing the relationship while living like a queen. She'd come around.

Women! Jody was all over him about his absence, and both of the step-daughters were steering clear of him. Their whines for money came through their mother. God, he hated those kids!

"What's all the secrecy about?" Jody said. "I'll bet if I called your office they would tell me?"

He risked a bluff. "The hell they would. They'd tell you I'd been on vacation."

"Vacation?"

"That's what they'd say. Go ahead, try 'em."

She fussed, but she didn't call. There was no way she was going to know about that Twin Cities trip.

His meeting with Marti tonight would probably define the future of their relationship, if there was to be one. She had changed, but her new attitude had somehow made her more desirable. He could deal with her on the cash if it could bring her around, but if he couldn't talk some sense into her tonight, he would have to consider what would have once been unthinkable.

His willing bed mate of a few days ago dead? Jesus, it wouldn't be easy, but now he was rich. Beautiful women came with the package. He couldn't throw a bountiful future away on a woman who might get in a snit over something dumb and get him fired, or worse yet, tortured and killed. She made the call that brought in the fat man. She could make another. Could it ever come to that? It would be her decision, actually. He had to be certain the money would bring her around.

What was once unthinkable might now be the best way. Her death could be blamed on the hood who botched the job in the basement, and whoever sent him. He had to give some thought on how to make it happen. It would be too bad. She was such a sweet piece of tail.

47

Bob called just after Julie walked her home again. She and her therapist chatted briefly on the apartment's stoop. Before the walk he said he was on call for a major touch football game that afternoon. She wondered why he mentioned the game before their walk. Was he afraid she was going to invite him in again? He needn't have worried. She needed every minute to rehearse the meeting with Vincennes. And with Bob.

Bob and she made it brief. "It's on for tonight. Vincennes admitted he has your money and I told him I wanted half."

"Did you threaten him?"

She was prepared to fib. Bob might call the whole thing off if she described the "other alternatives" slip in the conversation with Ross.

She said, "I told him if he didn't share with me it was goodbye. He doesn't want that."

"What time is the meeting? Where?"

"Eight-thirty. My apartment. I suggested a restaurant, and splitting the cash in the parking lot, but he said it sounded like a setup."

She heard a sharp intake of Bob's breath. He said, "Nice try. It would have been. I have a gun and if I have to, I'll kill the son of a bitch."

"Hey, take it easy. I'm counting on both of you guys to keep your cool. He has to realize it makes sense to split the cash with me. We each have reasons to keep our mouths shut about how this thing developed. Remember, he could decide to eliminate me from the picture, but if he gets nasty you can step in."

He thought that over. "Okay, I hate the idea of the son of a bitch having a dime, but I've decided half a loaf is better than none. He's a snake, but he could have killed me and gotten away with it. Now you'd better tell me how to get to your place. I'll be there at least an hour before he shows up."

"Good, but park away from the building and come in the back entrance."

She furnished the address and some directions, and they hung up. She felt exhausted. Would it work out? She headed toward her bedroom and a shower and decided to call both Cora and Rose. They would help her forget her problems. Trouble was she couldn't tell them a goddamned thing.

Julie made her work hard on the last walk, but she felt hardly any pain, and was breathing easily when they reached her building. She thought she would invite him to dinner but not then. It could be in a few days when she could plan and prepare a real meal. Cora had never taught her much about cooking. She had tried some things for Bob, basic stuff, but for him and two other husbands she mostly relied on frozen dinners. There had been a class in school, but she had paid little attention, forgotten most of it. She would have to pick up a couple of books, test a few recipes.

Julie might turn her down. He might think she was coming on to him, and he had a thing about getting involved with patients. Could he be queer? Not according to Cindy and Jane.

What was she thinking about? She had three other men on her case, and the ones coming over tonight were the top priority. Bob possibly pitted against a trained policeman? That could be risky but he said he had a gun, and it could be an equalizer. Hell, what did she know? She had to hope Ross would be reasonable. If she could just help Bob get half of his cash back she could go on with her life. Her new life. Now she had to get a shower, make herself something to eat, and call Cora and Rose.

48

The office was pretty well cleared out when Vincennes found the note left by a technician. Marti's phone had been tapped. He dialed the code and squeezed the receiver when he heard Costello's voice. He smiled as he listened to the conversation.

Now he knew. Costello had guessed he had hijacked the Samsonites, and he came running back to town hoping his wife could help get it back. *How did he alibi running out on her, leaving her in a puddle of blood. He must have done a helluva sales job, or is Marti on a guilt kick and wants to square things with him.*

He slammed his fist on his desk. What had happened to the woman? From lover to a goddamned Judas in a few days!

So Costello has a gun. I should have killed him. Shit, he wants it all. He might even try to kill us both. Well, wouldn't that be a hoot. Swapping salvos with a fucking accountant. Jesus Christ!

She wants a nice sit-down, how-the-hell-are-you-doing meeting, thinking Costello will be satisfied with whatever she would give him from some kind of split. Shit. Costello knows I won't give her a dime if any of it is going back to him. She still might blow the whistle, too, ruin everything, wash him out of his job, disgrace him, ruin his marriage. Fuck that. He could see himself standing in front of Robbins's desk, giving up his gun and badge. Shit. No way. He'd kill them both before he would go through that.

He erased all the messages, then ran the tape forward to cover the time lapse. If Robbins asked he'd tell him there was nothing yet.

Actually, having them both together was a break. It should be a fairly simple scene.

Costello would be hiding somewhere while Marti and I discuss the money thing. She would have me sit so that he could come at me from behind, or at an angle. How was the apartment laid out? She could have me in the dinette, and he would come out of the bedroom hallway and through the living room. I don't have to rush things at that point. He isn't going to kill me without learning where I've stashed his cash. I'll simply take over from there. Costello probably has never held a gun in his life. It would be child's play.

He thought it out, the basic plan and all the what-ifs. The story he would tell Robbins was simple. After fleeing from their bungalow, Costello had returned to kill his wife for revealing their hiding place.

I'll say I was visiting the apartment with view to offering Mrs. Costello any counsel or assistance re her decision to leave the protective witness program. I was hoping she might hold off her decision until it could be learned who had shot her, and why. I had just parked my car when I saw her husband enter her building.

It was my idea then to apprehend him, as he was wanted for questioning in connection with the shooting. I rushed into the building, the inner door was still ajar. I arrived in time to interrupt the murder, but Costello aimed his automatic. I shot him before he could shoot. It was self defense.

He wouldn't have to kill Marti. She would have to back him up or she wouldn't get a dime of Costello's money. Then he would call the cops and tell his story. It would work. Robbins could well question his luck in calling upon Mrs. Costello on the same night Costello showed up—he might want to review the tape of her calls—but there was nothing on the tape. Nothing else could be proved.

Robbins could think a lot of things, but if he, or anyone else, wants to tie me to the killings they have to come up with a motive.

He'd better call Jody. He'd miss dinner. Eat out. Better food, actually. Tell her it was night work. She'd bitch about it. So what else was new?

49

The city was back on standard time. Street lights were already on when Vincennes drove into a pitch-dark alley two buildings down and across the street from Marti's place. His watch showed just past eight. Costello would already be in the apartment, having entered by the building's back entrance. He would be wait a little longer, be on time. He again adjusted the Magnum 9 mm in its shoulder holster and reviewed his memory of the apartment.

Eight-thirty. Let's go.

He picked up the small valise stuffed with newspapers and took a long step out of the mouth of the alley.

Hold it! There was the flare of a match, or lighter, in the car parked across the street almost in front of the apartment door. He retreated into the darkness as the car's occupant, a white blocky male, pushed open the door and got out holding a cigarette.

What the hell was this? The guy's a perfect fit for the shooter Marti described.

The smoker, dressed in a dark suit, even the hat Marti described, took a drag from his cigarette as he leaned against his car, his eyes concentrated on the entranceway to Marti's building.

This had to be the guy! What was he doing here? He couldn't know Costello was in Marti's apartment. What was he waiting for? Costello?

The watcher flipped his finished cigarette toward the gutter and lighted another, his eyes not leaving the entranceway. He was motionless, the smoke from the cigarette curling upwards into the windless night. A couple of cars ambled quietly through the neighborhood street but there were no pedestrians. Light streamed from nearly all of the windows in nearby buildings. The area was about as quiet as a Chicago residential neighborhood gets.

Vincennes leaned against the building abutting the alley, his mind juggling a scenario that seemed to fit the situation perfectly. He'd been given a helluva break. He spelled it out to himself as he would to a cop with a notepad. It would work.

Neat. He again reviewed the plan. Marti, Costello, the gunman, all would die but his alibi would be perfect. More than three million bucks was at stake. He couldn't risk having Marti or Costello in position to blackmail him, or to try other schemes for stealing the cash.

Jesus. Now I'm treating the cash as if I had it all along. But why not?

He wouldn't need the bag of fake cash so he returned it to his car. Checking for any movement of traffic or pedestrians, he again slipped out of the alley and crossed the black asphalt street silently, drawing his Magnum just two steps away from the squat figure.

He hadn't made a sound until he shoved the gun into the man's broad back.

"Freeze," he said. He had never used the word before, identifying it with movie drama, but the big man's body stiffened.

"What the fuck you want, man? Money, I'll give you money."

"Shut up," Vincennes ordered. "Where's your gun? Don't move, just tell me."

"Left shoulder."

Vincennes confirmed the answer by reaching and pressing against the hard outline. It had an extended snout. A silencer. Good.

"Okay, we'll leave it there, but keep your hands at your side. Now, I want you to walk into the foyer of that apartment building. The one you were watching. Okay, go. I'm taking my gun out of your back, but it will only be inches away. Don't make any moves other than what I order."

"Okay, okay, but what the hell's up?"

"Shut up, and move."

They were in luck: no pedestrians, no kids. He could thank TV and probably computer games for the absence of kids. He and his pals in the old Milwaukee neighborhood used to frolic under the street lights on beautiful fall nights like this one.

In the foyer the hood again wanted to make conversation.

"Hey," but that was all before Vincennes gave him a hard jab with his gun.

"I said shut up. Now buzz the button opposite the name Costello."

"Hey, wait a minute."

Another jab with his automatic. "Talk again and I'll hurt you bad."

Vincennes glanced at his wrist watch. It was eight forty five. Marti wouldn't mind if he was a little late. He told her he was anxious to see her. She didn't know he had come to end their relationship. Forever.

The buzzer opened the foyer's inner door. Vincennes shoved the fat man into the corridor. He counted on Marti not opening her door in advance of his knock. That would be a gesture of welcome, and on the basis of their last talk he would be about as welcome as the measles. Her first look wouldn't be at him but at what was in front of him. What she would see was the man who nearly killed her in her bungalow home.

He sucked in a deep breath and again visualized the apartment layout. Costello would be out of sight, in the kitchen or bedroom. Either way he could handle it. It would have been much easier if he had killed Costello in Minneapolis, but he never dreamed Marti would do a one-eighty in their relationship. He hadn't counted on finding an ally in the fat man either so it was a wash. The thug shifted uncomfortably. The move got him another dig from the Magnum.

They were about ten feet from Marti's door in the poorly lit hallway when the fat man learned what he was there for.

Vincennes whispered, "Here's what's going to happen, and you can get out alive if you do exactly as you're told. We're going into this apartment and you are going to kill a man and a woman in there. You will remember them both, especially the woman. You shot her several weeks ago."

"Hey, they ain't supposed to die. I'm supposed to hold them. That's all."

What he hell was this?

"Who said so?"

"I dunno. I get orders over the phone."

It didn't take a huge imagination to guess who was paying the fat man's fee. He would have to work out how to deal with that later.

"Okay, it's a new game. Now put your right hand on your gun. Keep it there. Pull it out when the door opens and shoot whoever you see. If you or your gun swings toward me at any time, you die. Now let's go."

Vincennes wanted the fat man to believe he would somehow survive the crazy scenario laid out for him.

It's his only hope. He has to think he can somehow get a shot off at me when I let him get his hand on his gun. I'll have to kill him if he tries, then go to the original plan.

Vincennes reached around the fat man with his right hand and gave two sharp raps on the door, still keeping the point of his Magnum firmly into the man's back. He felt a momentary pang of regret. Jesus, he didn't want Marti looking at him when she took the slugs. Those meetings were so sweet, but she made this mess for herself.

The door opened immediately. But cautiously. Marti in blue jeans and sweater stood backlit, framed by light from the apartment. It took her only a second to recognize the intruder. Surprise and fear filled her eyes and she tried to slam the door, but the fat man, pulling his gun, used his foot and shoulder to prevent that effort. Marti still hadn't seen Vincennnes. Her eyes were glued on the fat man. When she saw his gun she spun away from him, into the living room and yelled, "Bob."

She had taken two quick steps when she stumbled and fell. The fat man, thinking more about how he could possibly shoot the son of a bitch who forced him into this situation than kill the woman he was only supposed to watch, got off a single deliberately missed shot toward the scrambling target. He didn't get off another. He was sure the man with the gun at his back intended to kill him, either in the apartment or elsewhere. He would probably die trying but he wanted to go down blasting. He used an old stunt that had once saved his life. He thrust his gun under his left arm pit. He would spray as many slugs as possible toward the man somewhere behind him.

Too late. The fat man's silenced gun was barely on its mission when Bob Costello came out of the kitchenette firing a Glock automatic. He fired three times, as fast as he could pull the trigger, hitting the fat man just once, in the left shoulder. The fat man went down on one knee, dropping his gun. A moment later Vincennes, moving into the room, glanced at the fallen thug, but then swung his gun at the stunned Costello who was staring at his victim as if in shock over what he had done. He made no move to cover Vincennes, but Ross didn't hesitate. He fired his Magnum twice, centering two slugs in Bob Costello's chest.

The six shots took all of a few seconds. Marti, cowering with her face to the floor, sure she would die, didn't see Vincennes calmly shoot her husband. Then, when Bob's body crashed to the floor, she twisted to look and screamed. She crawled to the man who was lying on his face.

She looked up at Vincennes, stunned. "You killed him, you son of a bitch."

She scrambled to her feet, and ran at Vincennes. He stopped her by pointing the Magnum between her eyes, but he couldn't shoot her now. He didn't need to, actually. He had fired in self defense. If he did shoot her now it would have to be with the fat man's gun.

But the fat man was gone. With his gun. While Vincennes was firing at Costello and holding off the enraged Marti the fat man had slipped behind Vincennes and out the still open door.

"Shit." Vincennes started for the door, then closed it. He might be able to run the man down, but the son of a bitch might anticipate his move and be waiting for him. He swung his attention back to Marti who was on her knees beside her husband. She was in tears, holding the dead man's hand.

She sobbed, "Oh, Bob, I'm so sorry."

Vincennes had holstered his Magnum. "Calm down, Marti. I was coming to the rescue. The fat slob was going to kill you and Costello was trying to kill me."

"No way," she yelled. "He tried to protect me. I'm to blame for this."

Vincennes stepped away from the small blotch of blood where the fat man went down. His original plan was in the toilet. He had to think. Fast. Someone would call 911. He should get in a call first. Any delay on his part would add suspicion to a story he had to make work. And he needed Marti's backup, not accusations.

He could still kill her but there were complications. Witnesses would remember the cadence in the shots, hard to explain if he added another now, a few minutes after the initial gunfire. He felt a little queasy. What a mess. It already looked like something out of the gunfight at the O.K. Corral. He could still bring her around, but when she made her deal for ratting on Costello she knew the shooting in her house basement was accidental. The fat man's plea just moments ago that he was assigned to hold Marti and her husband, not kill either of them, was a surprise. It further backed up the idea that Costello's boss, Phil Stanton, put the scheme together. He wanted Costello alive, hoping to get his money back. Revenge, too. The fat man was waiting outside Marti's apartment, hoping Costello would show up, not knowing his quarry was already in there.

Now Marti had to see this and how he could protect her. One quick step and he grabbed her shoulder, forcing her to look up at him.

"Listen up, Marti, this is how we say it happened. I learned Costello was here because we have a tap on your phone. I came here to pick him up, but I saw the fat man enter the building. He fit the description of the guy who shot you and I was a few steps behind as he entered your door. Luckily the foyer door hadn't closed all the way to lock.

"The fat man got off a shot at you before I could stop him, but your husband hit him with one of his shots. Then he turned his gun on me. I fired instinctively. It was self defense."

"That's crazy. Bob didn't want to shoot you. He just wanted his money. How would he get the money if he killed you?"

"I thought he was, and that's how it's going down. Remember, you're already going to be blamed for telling someone how to find Costello. And that's a scenario I'll back if I'm forced to. I'll toss in my two cents worth that the fat guy came to finish the job you interrupted at the bungalow. And don't forget I know where you stashed the money you got for tipping off who ever wanted revenge against your husband."

Marti blanched as she saw how it might play out.

Vincennes grin was sour. "Yeah, Marti, you didn't get all the money you wanted but you got some. There was a time you wanted me more than Bob Costello. Maybe that's over, but what's done is done. If you start raving about my involvement with you and the money, you only put more heat on yourself. Do it my way, and you get a chunk of Costello's money and we get past this mess. And I'll protect you from the people who want Costello's three million. Now I can't wait any longer to call. What's it going to be?"

Marti stared at him. She had actually made love to this slime. Now, everything she had worked for since taking that bullet in the guy was ruined.

Oh God, what had she done? This bastard was going to get away with shooting Bob because he's right. It all comes back to my greed and silly boredom

Vincennes was holding his cell phone staring at her, willing her to agree.

She nodded. "Okay. Your way."

Vincennes stabbed out the numbers. Then he was talking fast. She didn't listen. She forced herself to the new recliner and sank on its edge, putting her face into her shaking hands. Bob had tried to protect her and was dead. She was safe from the fat man, but Phil could send others. And now she had Ross to fear. She shuddered. He had shot Bob down as if was a rabid dog. And now she was his captive. A man she once thought she could love.

Vincennes came to her side. He said, "We got a break. I beat any other 911 calls, and asked for Carey, the cop who first interviewed you at Memorial. The basement shooting and Costello's disappearance are still his case and we can hope he's on duty. This saves each of us a lot of time and inconvenience. We only have to tell our story once, for now anyway." He touched her shoulder. "Everything fits, Marti. Let me do the explaining to the cops. All you say is yes or no to any questions. Volunteer nothing."

He gave her shoulder a firm squeeze, enough to make her wince. "Got it?"

He brought his head down to look into her face. "You aren't going to pass out or get hysterical, are you?"

She shook her head, as if to clear it. "No. I'm okay. I'd like a glass of water, I think."

Vincennes was bringing the water with a water-moistened towel when the flashing lights filled the windows. Seconds later the apartment rocked from the hammering on the door. It was Sergeant Leo Carey and several uniforms.

The detective didn't seem surprised to see Marti again. He said, "Hello there. You okay?" He didn't wait for a response. He glanced at Costello's body, then turned to Vincennes.

"What the hell happened here?"

Marti had to admit Vincennes was up to the situation. He first identified himself, then described what took place, cool and concise with his story and answers to Carey's terse questions. She wondered at Vincennes's ability to act with such composure after killing another human being. She sat in the recliner shivering, forcing herself not to look at the man lying in his blood on her floor, the man who had loved her and whom she had betrayed.

Vincennes said, "I saw the man Mrs. Costello described as the basement shooter enter the building. The foyer door was ajar and I was yanking out my gun when I saw the man push himself into the apartment. I couldn't see whether he was armed from my position behind him. He got off a shot at Mrs. Costello. I would have shot him in the back but Costello came charging in from the kitchenette firing. The fat man went down from Costello's first of three shots. When he swung his gun toward, I put him down. I've no idea why the man would try to shoot me. Unless he thought I was here to pick him up on behalf of the Chicago police. And he didn't want to be turned in."

An officer standing at Carey's elbow was making notes on a small pad as Vincennes described the path of the bullets. Another officer who had confirmed that Costello was dead tapped Carey on the shoulder and held out a shell casing.

Vincennes said, "See. Just one shot. From a silenced revolver. Then, while I was facing Costello, the son of a bitch slipped out from behind me and ran for it. Two of the slugs from Costello's automatic should be buried in the wall somewhere."

Together he and Carey ran their hands over the plaster and wood work.

"Here," said Vincennes. "And here."

Carey was apparently satisfied, He said, "Okay, we'll want you and Mrs. Costello to come downtown and make formal statements. We'll get investigation and forensic units here to do their thing and clean up the mess."

Vincennes said, "I'm going to call my boss. I can bring Mrs. Costello downtown."

Carey said, "No, I'll do that. You come along as soon as you can."

Vincennes hesitated. Marti thought he was going to object, but he said, "Sure."

He stared hard at Marti for a couple of seconds, then said, "I'll see you later." She got the message, hoping Carey hadn't noticed.

Somehow the media had been alerted. Cameras and microphones were shoved in Marti's face as she was led from the building. Shouted questions. There was a lull for a moment as Carey yelled something to the news people and helped her into his car. He was driving a large Ford. Marti remembered there was some traffic during the swift drive downtown, but for most of the drive it was all patches of light and dark. Carey had to remind her to fasten her safety belt. She didn't remember him saying anything else before the car was parked.

50

There was a door, and an elevator. Then she was seated across a steel table from Carey in a small room made ugly by the absence of anything related to a normal living space. She'd seen hundreds of such rooms on television cop dramas, two-way mirror included, but the fact she was the person in the picture made her feel the situation was absolutely unique.

Carey dropped into his chair and went into a routine she half heard. It sounded like something about interviewing her, and concluded by asking if she had any reason she might want a lawyer present.

"You don't have to answer any questions. We just want to get your picture of what took place in your apartment tonight. Is that okay with you?"

She nodded.

"Fine. That's fine, but you will need answer my questions orally. The recorder can't pick up nods." He smiled. "It's a dumb machine."

The word recorder snapped Marti out of the semi shock she had been in since the shooting. She said, "Could I use the lady's room?"

Carey escorted her to the door of the women's toilet and waited outside. Marti sat on the toilet cover, her face in her hands, writhing in the flashback of those horrible seconds in the apartment. The terrifying sound of the shots followed by the thud of Bob's body as it hit the floor brought a flood of nausea. She stood quickly and started to turn, but the surge to throw up subsided.

She sat again. She had to reassemble everything Vincennes told Carey along with his instructions to her. She tried to anticipate the questions Carey would ask. The first, she knew. What was Bob Costello was doing in her apartment? Number two had to be why did he leave their bungalow in the first place? There had to be a ton of others?

She again saw Vincennes's face as he held her at bay with his gun. She had wanted to scratch the eyes out of the face that had once melted her on sight. She had never before hated anyone, but now she knew the emotion. How sneaky clever of the bastard to ask for Carey in his call from the apartment. He knew Carey had been sympathetic with her at both hospital interviews. Also, Carey had enough background on the case so that Vincennes explanation wouldn't be like going over everything from the start.

God, she had to be careful. The cops on TV seemed to trap witnesses into lies so easily. The closer she could stay to the truth the better.

She shuddered as she visualized Carey's reaction to the whole story, especially when she told him how she had called Phil Stanton and taken his blood money.

She couldn't do it now, maybe never. She had to see Ross Vincennes punished somehow, but it might have to be outside the law. The hell with the money. She wouldn't take a dime from the son of a bitch. She could get a job. Maybe therapy, a career in what Jane and Cindy were doing. The training might be expensive, but maybe she could make some kind of deal with Phil Stanton, so she could keep his money without fear that he would come after her.

What a confusing mess. Phil Stanton told her he didn't want to hurt her. Did he change his mind? Was Ross telling the truth? Was the fat man coming to kill her, then torture Bob into giving up the money? If so, he could have had her killed long before tonight. Phil was pretty convincing about wanting her back. Should she tell him that Vincennes had the money?

She shuddered again, remembering that Vincennes knew she had that option. Would he try to kill her after she went on record that he was blameless in Bob's death? Maybe he had come to kill her and Bob at the apartment, but how could he have known about the intrusion of the fat man? And why did the fat man come in shooting? The situation was exactly as it had been when she found him with Bob in the bungalow basement. Phil didn't want her killed. Or Bob either.

At least, not until he got his money back.

Should she follow Billy Dillon's old counsel of getting them before they got you? Vincennes didn't want her to report the deal they had made any more than she did, but what if she told him she had prepared a letter describing how she had betrayed her husband at his suggestion? She hadn't but the lie might be her only protection.

Five minutes later, after splashing cool water in her face she felt a little better as she looked across the table at Carey and heard him ask the anticipated question. She was ready.

"Bob called to ask how I was. He said he wanted to see me. That's about it. We had a few minutes to talk before that man, the man who shot me at the bungalow, barged in."

Carey said, "You weren't expecting anyone?"

"No."

Take your time. Speak slowly and think before you answer.

Carey said, "I was wondering how the intruder got through the foyer door, and why you opened to a unexpected knock."

No problem with this one. "I thought it might be a neighbor. I don't know how he got into the hallway. He probably buzzed one of the other apartments. Someone must have let him in."

The detective thought about that for a beat, then combined a statement with a question. "Mr. Costello didn't blame you for the original visit by the unidentified killer, or the would-be killer in your basement?"

"No, why should he? He said he was sorry I got shot, and that he ran because he thought I was dead and that whoever sent the goon would come after him again."

Carey's face was bland, as if they were just chatting.

He said, "Yeah, we talked about that at the hospital. I asked you why you got shot. It was at such close range, as if the hood walked right up to you. Or did you walk up to him?"

Marti knew she was talking too much. She hadn't said anything that would contradict Ross's statement, but she remembered his counsel during his hospital visit, that she didn't have to speculate on her actions or those of anyone else.

She said, "I'm sorry, I just can't remember."

She expected Carey to scoff at the lie, but his broad face remained calm and thoughtful.

He said, "It's interesting that the intruder, the same guy who shot you in your home, would show up at your apartment on the night of your meeting with your husband. He had been missing for some time now. Did he tell you where he had been during your time in the hospital?"

Marti tried to keep her face as expressionless as Carey's.

What's he getting at? He knows the thug shot at me.

She said, "No."

He was studying her face. "Well, I'm glad you escaped this time and that you are getting back to normal. Now I'm going to leave you alone with this yellow pad so you can write down what happened, right from when you opened your apartment door. Take your time. When you are satisfied you have included everything, just sign the statement, and give the door a rap. I'll be nearby."

She wanted to get out of there so she wrote swiftly, echoing Ross's statement in the apartment. She was finished in fifteen minutes. After rereading her words, she signed at the bottom of the second page and carried it with her to the door. Carey, waiting outside, glanced at her effort.

He said, "Thanks for coming in. I'm going to give you my card. If you think of anything you want to tell me, please call."

"Sure. Thanks."

"I'll have you driven back to your apartment or wherever you want to go. Maybe you'd prefer to stay somewhere else."

He held a portable phone in one of his huge hands.

"Is there anyone you'd like to call?"

Marti had thought of Peg Delaney as a haven before Carey's question. The nurse was on days and would probably be at home. She said, "There is someone."

"Go to it." He held the phone out to her, and with a smile he heaved his big body out of his chair and left the room. She fumbled in her purse. Peg had given her the number several days ago. Peg answered on the first ring.

"Oh my God, Marti, It's on the news. Are you okay? Where are you?"

Marti told her. Peg said, "Have the cops bring you here. You stay with us tonight."

She gave her address. "Do it right now."

"Thanks Peggy. I'd appreciate that."

The front door of the south Loomis street bungalow swung open before Marti could ring the door bell. The officer in the black-and-white waited until she was inside the house before he drove away.

51

Marti unloaded the full story of the shooting after Mike Delaney made her a stiff drink. It made her woozy, but it did the job for which it was intended. She sank into a soft chair in the comfortable living room and just let the story, Vincennes's version, flow. She needed no prompting. She was surprised at how easily she relayed the big lie, repeating the supposition that Bob thought she had been killed, and adding that Bob had returned because he thought he and she could be made safe again, that the government would find another safe environment for them.

Mike was interested in how Carey handled matters at the apartment.

She said, "He looked very professional to me, both in the apartment, and later when I gave my statement downtown. I was really shaken up, but he was very kind."

"He has a reputation as an excellent homicide cop," Mike said. "He'd be a lieutenant right now if he was more political."

Peg said, "What now?" Then seeing the blank look on her friend's face, she reached down to pull Marti out of her chair.

"That's a dumb question, Marti, and I'm sorry. Let's get you to bed. You have to be exhausted. Everything will look better after a good night's rest."

Marti let her friend lead her from the living room, thinking how often Peg must have said that during her nursing career. In the guest bedroom, Peg poked around a drawer and came up with a granny gown. They both roared when it nearly wrapped around Marti twice.

"Girl, you've gotta beef yourself up a little."

Peg glanced around the tastefully decorated room. "It's finally getting some use, but the. bed may not be as good as your bed at Memorial."

It was better to judge from the speed with which Marti dropped off. She lay awake only a few seconds, reviewing the horror of the events in the apartment and the jam she might be in, but the drink did its job. She dropped into unconsciousness, eight hours of dreamless rest.

Peggy made a breakfast Marti tried to turn down, but she had to admit the coffee tasted great with the scrambled eggs and cinnamon toast.

"My favorite," said Mike, who ambled into the kitchen with the morning paper.

"First page, wanna look?"

She didn't, but she managed a smile as she turned down the offer.

Peg said, "Save it, Mike. Marti knows too much about what happened."

Marti gave a weaker smile in agreement with Peg's assessment. The good sleep would help her deal with the horror of the slaughter in her apartment, but not with herself. She had made a pact with the devil in backing Ross's explanation of the shooting. Now she had to find some way to incriminate him while getting herself off his hook. She didn't see Bob shoot the fat man or any of Ross's shots. She was flat on her face through all of the gunfire, but she knew Ross lied about shooting Bob in self defense. He stole Bob's money, then took advantage of the opportunity to kill him. And she had backed his story. She didn't see how she could live with that, but she had to be careful with Ross. If he thought she might make another call to the same people who sent the fat man, she was as good as dead. He would kill her, then not wait around for Phil's goon. He had no love or allegiance for his family. He would take off, buy himself the good life in any of a hundred places.

To hell with the money. To hell with Phil's money, too. Phil would show up sooner or later and want an accounting. What if she told him Ross had Bob's money, Phil's money? What could he do about it? Would he dare risk taking on the cops by sending another goon after Ross? She would never let Ross touch her again, but she had to convince him he had her under control. If he had any doubts about whether she might turn him in, he would surely kill her or arrange for someone else to do the job.

Peg dropped her off at her apartment on the way to the hospital. The nurse was obviously interested in coming in to see the scene of the shooting, but Marti said she would be all right, deliberately ignoring the nurse's curiosity.

Peg said, "Okay, then. See you later at Warshawsky's chamber of horrors. How you getting along with the man?"

Peg knew Julie was walking her home, but she didn't know Marti had invited him into the apartment.

"Okay, we're doing fine. He's making me into a new woman. A better model."

Peg rolled her eyes and drove off.

Marti didn't know what to expect, but the living room was as neat as if she had just returned from a day at the hospital. Not a chamber of horror. The morning sun, as if acting as a cleaning agent, poured across the living room floor. The cops, or whomever, had made an effort to return her home to normalcy. Carey may have had something to do with that. She'd have to remember to thank him. Perhaps a note. She might never see him again.

"Home." She lived in a home with her parents, unappreciated then but how she missed it now. She had a home with Billy, too. The expensive condo with Bob was just a temp, a layover, a jumping off place for pleasure or mischief. Promiscuous mischief in the case of both the condo and bungalow. What a jerk she had been. She remembered the pledge she made while coming to in her hospital room. To remake her life.

She stared at the hardwood floor. In the movies they drew chalk around the bodies, but there was no evidence of the fallen men. If used it had been erased. She put her face in her hands as she stood over the area where Bob lay sprawled only a few hours ago. Somehow she had to avenge his murder. She had worked hard to bring herself back physically, and her goals for the future were honest and wholesome, but she had betrayed her husband and caused his death. She could never forgive herself for that, but somehow she had to help punish his killer.

Going to Carey and telling the whole story would wreck her life. Her comeback would have been futile, and Ross might still go unpunished. In a trial she would be made to admit she had not seen Bob aim his gun at Vincennes. He would be thrown out of his job if she admitted her affair with him, but he would deny he had told her about the money. Even if they found it they wouldn't be able to prove he killed Bob. Somehow she had to avenge Bob's murder. Saving herself appeared impossible. There was no way she could see that happening now.

What did they do with Bob's body? She would have to arrange for burial. No. Cremation would be better. She didn't know of a single family member or friend that would mourn for him. She would try. He did try to protect her.

She fished Carey's card out of her purse and dialed the number. He wasn't on duty, but when she explained her needs, the officer who took the call told her Bob's body would be released to any funeral company she chose. He said his name was Barker. "And Mrs. Costello. We are trying to learn the final address of your husband. There will be personal effects you will want to examine. And we've impounded his car, the Buick he used to reach your apartment. It will be safe until you give instructions on what to do with it."

She had forgotten Bob's car. She thanked the officer. Later, she wondered what Bob had done with his Mercury. Probably dumped it somewhere in Minnesota.

The arrangements were a lot easier than she thought they would be. She picked out a nearby company, Lodar Funerals. "We Care," was the headline in the Yellow Pages, and the arrangements were completed in fifteen minutes. She said she would pay cash and would drive by later that day. That meant a trip to the bank.

Ross had stunned her with his reminder about the hundred thousand in North Shore bank. She'd forgotten how she had shown him her bank book at the motel. She couldn't do anything about that, but she had to do something about him.

52

Julie hadn't seen the late news after coming home from a Bulls pre-season game, but he almost choked on his morning coffee over the Tribune's report of the shooting. He ran all the way to the hospital and found Peggy, expecting her to know.

"Have you seen her? Is she okay?"

Peg said, "We had her at our place overnight. Yeah, she's okay. I think she'll come in as usual, too."

Marti proved her friend right. She walked into the gym at the usual time, and there were no dramatics. Julie's girls came over and gave her hugs, but asked no questions. Their boss had told them to treat the matter as none of their business. Julie was not on the floor and Marti gave no impression of looking for him. She began her warm up routine with stretching and moved into the now unsupervised routines.

When Julie came in he did nothing more than smile her way. Later in the morning she saw him chatting with an elderly female patient who was working out under Cindy's supervision. He walked over. When she turned to him with one of her quick smiles, he said, "Lunch?"

"Sure," she said, "Right after my shower."

As she washed and changed into a plain lightweight black wool skirt and pink cotton blouse Marti thought about what she would tell Julius. A few minutes later in the hospital's cafeteria they took their trays to a corner table. They placed their food on the Formica surface without speaking, but as soon as they were seated, Julius said, "Hey, it must have been terrible. You could have been killed."

She had arrived at the hospital with a slight headache, but it disappeared somewhere during the workout. Looking across the table at

Julius she again decided it was good to be alive and to have a good-looking man interested in her well being.

"He missed me, Julie. You might have had to start all over again."

He may have appreciated her light touch, but it didn't show.

He said, "This guy. Vincennes. He was the marshal on your case. I mean when you were a protected witness?"

"Yes." Julius waited for more, but she took a forkful of salad and chewed, just looking into his well-shaven anxious face. She would not do or say nothing to ease his discomfort. What could she tell him about herself that wouldn't horrify him? He was the most innocent man she had ever met. What kind of life had he led? Had he ever told a lie? She'd bet he had never sassed his parents, or teachers, or had a traffic ticket. How shocked would he be to learn she had had two other husbands before Bob, that Vincennes had been a bed partner more than a protector, and that she had sold Bob out and probably caused his death?

She felt sorry for Julie's discomfort. He was fooling with his food, struggling to come up with a question that would give him what he was beginning to crave, more dimension to his portrait of a patient who had become transformed into a desirable woman.

She took pity on him. "You were going to get some information for me, from the Y?"

He brightened. "Oh yeah, I picked up some stuff. Got it in my office. Let me walk home with you and I'll bring it."

"Fine. I'll ditch my afternoon workout. Be ready when you are."

Julius returned to his office to finish some reports. He found Marti in Cindy's office. Cindy said, "Marti is asking me about careers in therapy."

Marti gave Cindy a look. She had only been passing the time, asking the therapist a few questions about her work and how she had trained for it.

Marti grinned. "Yes, I think if you guys can do it, anyone can."

Julie chose to come back with a serious answer. "All you need, really, is the ability to persuade people to put up a fight against pain. Look what we did with you?"

Marti said, "Touche."

Julie told Cindy he would be back in an hour.

"Take your time, boss. We'll keep 'em limping."

Julie set a brisk pace as he and Marti left the hospital. He had the Y materials in an envelope. Marti carried her bag of sweat clothes

He waved a hand at the still mostly-green trees lining the street. "Another gorgeous fall afternoon in Chicago."

Marti nodded, sucked in a breath, and worked to match the therapist stride for stride.

53

Phil Stanton was on a United Airlines Chicago flight two hours after he got Brancatto's telephone report. Brancatto insisted there was no way the unknown intruder wounded in Marti's apartment could be traced back to them.

"He probably has a record. The cops might find his prints, but he had no direct contact with me. Don't worry about it."

Stanton decided he would worry. He sat motionless in the first class seat, but his mind was more active than it had been for any recent business problem.

He had to get out there and see Marti. Costello may have told her where he hid the money. Why in hell had he suddenly turned up? With a gun! Why did Brancatto's man go in shooting? It was all nuts.

This marshal. Vincennes? He claimed Costello shot at him, but why would Costello do that? Costello must have been trying to protect Marti. The newspaper report said his first shot wounded Brancatto's man but the thug got away.

Stanton was traveling light, a carry-on bag with clothing for a couple of days, a cellular phone, and his computer. Off the plane he went directly to the Hertz counter and was in the reserved Lincoln town car a few minutes later. Brancatto had given him Marti's address and phone, but he wanted to surprise her. She was still in rehab, Brancatto said, and walking between the hospital and her apartment.

Mid-afternoon traffic into the city was terrible. He didn't think anything was as bad as New York, but this was. Finally off the expressway, he worked his way southward into the city. He saw the hospital zone signs before he hit the cross street that carried him past the massive eight-story building. Brancatto said Marti lived only a few blocks away.

Jesus, is that her? Walking fast with a guy, early autumn leaves swirling around her feet. Looking great, hair much shorter than how she used to wear it. A traffic light stopped him, but she and the guy stayed in view until they entered a side street. Moving again, he reached the corner where they had turned. He swung the wheel to follow them, barely moving the big car, no hurry to catch up.

They stopped. Her apartment, he guessed. His car was barely a hundred feet from the them, but he was shielded by other cars parked on the side street. They were talking, she smiling and accepting an envelope from the guy. Suddenly Marti moved her head forward quickly and gave the guy a quick kiss on the cheek. What the hell?

Holy shit! She steps away, as if to go into the building, but the guy grabs her, spins her around, and plants a real smacker on her lips. And he doesn't let go.

When he did, she just stood there looking at him. She should have slapped the shit out of the son of a bitch. But she's smiling and saying something. The bastard touches her shoulder, then turns away and trots back up the street. Not a bad looking guy, but dressed in blue jeans.

Someone from the hospital. He'd find out soon enough.

Marti had disappeared as he drove past her building. He swung around the block and headed for downtown. If the steering wheel had been made of wood, his grip would have squeezed it into sawdust.

54

What Marti said to Julius after his resounding rejoinder to her light kiss was, "Hey. Was it something I said?" Julius grinned at her and then said, "No. It was something you did." Then he turned away and ran.

Obviously, she had turned him on. It wasn't deliberate, she insisted to herself. She just did it, possibly caused by some compulsion left over from the past. She certainly hadn't expected such an enthusiastic response. Now she might have another man to worry about, although with Bob gone it was still three.

Ross would call again, or more likely just show up rather than risk being recorded if her phone was still tapped. He would want to know how the interview with Carey went. As far as his sharing Bob's money with her she was sure she could forget it. Giving her anything would solidify his admission he had robbed Bob and thus had a motive for killing him. He wasn't going to suggest running away with her, either, unless he had a scheme for taking her somewhere and murdering her.

Had his obsession for Bob's money turned him into a vicious killer? Getting rid of her and blaming it on the same people who wanted Bob dead would be no big problem He was a trusted U.S. marshal. Who would challenge his explanation? They bought his story of last night's episode, didn't they?

What in the world could she do?

The phone. Careful, whoever it is. My God, it was Phil.

"Hi, Baby. Are you okay? All the excitement made the New York papers, too."

"Phil, where are you?"

I've got to get him off the line. If I'm still being taped this call could furnish Vincennes even more proof I set Bob up.

"I'm here, I mean in Chicago, at the Drake."

She jumped on his line. "I was just going out the door. I can't talk, even for a second. Give me a room number. I'll call you back in fifteen minutes."

"Okay, Baby. It's eight oh two. I'll be waiting. Bye."

She would have to look up the hotel's phone number but she had stopped him from saying any more. Greeting him by name was a mistake. She hoped Ross canceled the phone tap so that she could make unrecorded calls. Oh god, she didn't want to see Phil. He might want his hundred thousand, and he could have it, but he might also want to resume the relationship they had before Bob went to the feds. She had no more feeling for him than she had for Ross. Nothing. The only man in her life right then was Julius Warshawsky and the relationship hadn't even reached the hand-holding stage. He had kissed her, sure, but it was no more a declaration of love than a hearty handshake. Or was it?

God, it was crazy to think of him at this time. He was a boy. Two other men controlled her fate. Fate, that was the word. She was doomed. If Julie got involved it would be his bar bells versus their guns and she would be responsible for the death of another man. She shuddered.

She was out of the apartment in ten minutes, grabbing a sweater, but making no effort to fix her face or improve on the basic outfit she had worn to and from the hospital. It would really screw things up if Ross, or even Julie, showed up before she could get away.

She headed for the loop in the Taurus, a twenty to twenty-five minute drive at this time of afternoon. She would call Phil from the hotel's lobby. Might as well. He would insist on seeing her in his room, rather than meeting some place. She would have to convince him to get out of town. Now. Tell him what Ross had done, how Ross was probably calculating at this minute how he could ensnare Phil. What a triumph that would be for the agent. To arrest Phil, and her, on charges they plotted to kill Bob Costello. Who would believe her story that Vincennes murdered Bob? Would detective Carey make an effort to untangle the mess?

The traffic was awful, but she finally reached Michigan boulevard and drove south to the hotel. She turned her car over to the doorman and found a lobby phone.

"Hey, you said fifteen minutes," but he was obviously pleased she was in the building.

"Come on up."

She was prepared for him to grab her, and tried to look pleased as he pulled her into the suite and wrapped her in his powerful arms before running his huge hands from her rump to the bare skin under her blouse.

He tried to hold their kiss until he could work his tongue into her mouth but she broke free.

"Hey, take it easy. I just got here."

He frowned. "Okay, Okay, but you can't blame me for being excited. It's been a long time, way too long."

She hoped her smile looked genuine. "Right. Hey, got anything to drink up here."

Surprise. She wasn't that interested in drinking with him in New York He waved at a table and a bottle of rye he had ordered from room service.

"I only have the basic New York stuff. You'd think Chicago would be aware of a favorite New York drink, but they always seem surprised out here when I order rye. How'd you like it?"

"Lots of water."

He brought her the drink and then made one for himself. She found a chair but he pulled her out of it and made her sit next to him on the sofa. He reached out with his glass to click it against hers.

"Here's to a new chapter in our lives, baby. It's too bad Bobby had to go down so drastically, shall we say, but he was leading a dangerous life. Tell me about what happened at your place?"

He sipped on his drink as she reconstructed the scene, still following the scenario created by Ross. Stanton looked thoughtful, holding her eyes with his."

He said, "And the marshal was right behind the hood."

"Not really. When I opened the door I only saw the fat man. He filled up the door."

"And you went down on the floor? You didn't really see the rest of it? I mean Costello's attempt to kill the cop?"

Marti thought the question was one that Carey might have asked. "No."

Stanton finished his drink and got up to make another. While dropping fresh ice into his glass he said, "It's screwy, Marti. Right from the start, when you took the slug in the belly. The hood wasn't supposed to shoot you then, and he had explicit orders against harming you since.

"He was just supposed to keep an eye on you until I could get out here. From the beginning, all I wanted was to interview Costello, get my money back, and bring you back to New York. I think the fat man was a patsy in the shooting. I think the was set up, and I think your U.S. marshal over-extended his prerogatives. Why would I think that, Marti?"

She had taken only a sip from her drink. Her mind was spinning out explanations as fast as a sitcom writer on deadline might be trying to mend a script that wasn't working. The shrewd and intelligent man now looking down on her wanted some answers. And right now. Could she tell him the truth? Up to a point.

Phil's eyebrows were raised. "Well?"

She took a good sip from the drink and then took her time setting the glass on the coffee table in front of the sofa.

Okay, let's see if he will buy some real cock and bull. Buy it and get back to New York and out of my life.

"I'm sure Vincennes thinks I called you. Who else would have a revenge motive against Bob? I think he must have a tap on my phone. I don't know how else he could have known Bob was coming to my apartment. I just hope he doesn't know you're in town."

"So what's his game?"

"I think he's after Bob's money. Your money, rather."

"So why'd he kill him? Now, he'll never know where it's stashed."

"I guess he told the cops the truth. Bob was going to shoot at him. It was self defense."

Stanton took another pull at his drink. "But why in hell would Costello want to kill a marshal who was sworn to protect him?"

"I don't know and I may never know. Bob may have thought it was Vincennes who gave him up, and he was sure of it when I stepped into that bullet in our basement. Bob said he ran away because he thought I was dead. He said I had saved his life and he wanted to get back together. We would ditch the program and run for it. We could live well on his money for the rest of our lives."

"And how did you react to all this?"

Marti tried to look uncomfortable, shifting in her seat.

"I didn't want to go anywhere with Bob. And after making peace with you and banking your money, I was trying to stall him. I was going to call the Chicago police on some kind of pretext. If I could get him picked up, even though he would be released almost immediately, I might have been able to fulfill my deal with you. You could have gotten to him before he ran off somewhere."

Stanton smiled.

Was he buying it?

He said, "My man was waiting outside your building. His orders were to observe only, but if he saw Costello go in he thought he was to finish the original job, to hold you and that rat husband of yours till I could get there. He had a cell phone and should have gotten through to me about what to do, but it would have taken time he didn't think he had. Vincennes told the cops he followed my man into the building but arrived too late to prevent the hood from getting off a shot. At you. It doesn't play. My man wasn't there to shoot anybody. He was there to protect you"

Stanton took another sip of his drink.

He said, "Vincennes heard you make your date with Costello. I'm thinking he came to force Costello to cough up at least a chunk of my money. I should be getting my guy's report on what happened, but he has to hide out, get his wound taken care of."

Stanton's look wasn't quite as intense as before the first part of her big lie. Now she needed another. She looked into her drink and shifted her position again.

She said, "I'm trying to remember the scene. I don't know where your man was looking when he fired. I was terrified. I started to turn away from him as soon as I saw him in the doorway. I yelled for Bob, then tripped and fell when I tried to run. I didn't see him try to shoot me. And as you say he didn't want to shoot Bob, but Vincennes's story that Bob turned his gun on him may be true. As far I know now there's no evidence to prove that either."

Not bad. Please buy it, Phillip.

Stanton's look of inquisition eased. He took another pull at his drink, then smiled.

You may have it right, Marti. I happen to know the fat man's gun had a hair trigger, a major reason why the gun exploded into your gut, but why did Vincennes say my man was shooting at you?"

"I don't know. Maybe it seemed reasonable to him after the guy barged in that way."

Stanton shook his head. He had had enough of this.

"Marti, I'm starving. Let's order something up."

There was a menu on the suite's desk. Marti was hungry enough but she wanted her story to hold up more than food She also wondered when Stanton would ask about his other money, the hundred thousand.

He didn't. The conversation turned to New York, which Marti couldn't help but find interesting, and the condition of Stanton Corporation,

"Damn good. I was lucky to get a kid Costello trained for the financial end before he took off. He's doing a great job."

The food arrived and Stanton devoted his attention to the service. Marti had ordered a club sandwich, but Phil was working on a medium rare sirloin steak. Marti couldn't help but wonder at Phil's super white teeth as he tore into the food.

"When will you be going home, Phil?"

"Just as soon as I can convince you to go with me."

"Phil, we've been there, done that. You aren't going to divorce your wife, and I'm not going to live a life where I see you once every couple of weeks."

"Hey, we can work that out. I'll see you a lot more often than that. We'll go on trips. Have a ball. And remember, you are going to be a very wealthy woman."

"Oh, how so?"

He looked up from his food, as if surprised she had overlooked the obvious.

"Hey, you're the heir to Bob's money. Or a million of it per our deal."

"Phil, I haven't a clue as to where Bob put that money. It may never turn up."

"Oh, it'll turn up, all right. There'll be clues wherever he was holed up. Keys to lockers, banks, or something. It has to be within easy reach if he said you could run off together."

He believes that, but I know that if Carey and his people find Bob's Chicago hideout and possible belongings, including keys to a locker in Minneapolis, they would find nothing.

Stanton waited for her response as he sipped his coffee.

She said, "Okay, will you stay in Chicago till the money turns up?"

"Probably not. I don't like the idea that this Vincennes guy might be after me. I don't even want to have to answer any questions about why I'm in town. However, if things get complicated for you, legal stuff, I'll get you some help. In the meantime you have some money to live on, and to judge from the way you walked from the hospital to your apartment today you are getting in first class shape again."

It was like a blow to the stomach. He had seen her with Julie.

"Yeah, I followed you home." He laughed. "I'd never seen you move as fast, other than the time you ran out of my suite at the Essex House."

He must have expected her to laugh with him, but all she could do was stare at him.

"Who was the young guy with you?"

Oh no. She had to keep Julie out of this.

"He's my therapist. He walked me home from the hospital as part of the aerobic exercise I'm doing. He set a tough pace."

"Is that why he got a kiss?"

"That was nothing. He's just a kid."

"He didn't kiss you back like he was a kid."

"Phil, you have no right to spy on me."

It was Stanton's turn to look uncomfortable.

"I wasn't spying. Seeing you was an accident. I had your address and drove to your place from O'Hare. I wanted to surprise you."

She wanted to maintain the offensive. "So you would have. Why didn't you stop? I would have shown you my new apartment. We could have had our meal there."

She thought she had him on the run, but not for long. He didn't run a string of businesses by being a simpleton.

"Goddammit. Seeing you kissing that kid pissed me off."

"I wasn't kissing him. He was kissing me."

"You should have slapped him silly."

"Oh come on, Phil. He's just a kid. Over-enthusiastic about his work."

Stanton slammed his wadded-up napkin on the table. "Yeah. Maybe I'll have a talk with him. About his manners."

Oh no. That's all she needed. If Julie meets Phil it will add another question to what has to be a growing list about her and her history.

"Just forget it, will you please?"

Stanton retrieved the napkin and was dabbing the last juices of steak from his lips when Marti saw another look, one she recognized from their trysts at the Essex House. She was resigned to his invitation, demand really. It meant having sex with a man who no longer had the slightest appeal to her, but to turn him down would bring more inquisition. Damn. Being seen with Julie was a disaster. She couldn't do anything to further Phil's interest in that direction.

In New York, Phil Stanton had been a substitute for a husband whose interest in sex was so perfunctory it made her feel unwanted, but Marti had resolved that sex would no longer be an exercise to replace a void in her life. Now it would be part of loving a man, a permanent thing. There would be no more casual arrangements. Especially not an affair with its furtive planning and hotel and motel rooms. She never had loved Phil Stanton, and anything she felt for Ross Vincennes had been completely wiped out by the events of the past few days.

God, she wanted out of that suite, but if Phil was to accept the story she had fabricated so plausibly, a trip to his bed would have to be included. She felt ill and apparently looked it.

He said, "What's the matter. You okay?"

She needed another lie. "I need to use your bathroom."

She sat on the toilet's cover and rehearsed her alibi. She would tell him it was the wrong time of the month, that she was a mess. And look as if she was really sorry, promising a super party next time. At her new apartment.

Back in his living room he wasn't the least bit sympathetic. "Oh shit. You know how I feel about that. To hell with it. I'm using a pro."

She had used the excuse once before. By telephone, with the tryst postponed. Now he was prepared and horny, probably because he might have to get out of town before they could meet again.

He said, "Let's go. I have some etchings I want to show you. Something else, too."

She forced a smile, and pushed her chair back. She had to put on a show. Turn him down now, and his rage might not be controllable. He would remember her kisses with Julie and attach even more significance to them. The thought of another fat man stalking her or harming Julie made her squeeze her eyes shut. She couldn't show Phil how he had scared her. She ducked her head, digging in her purse. Taking longer than necessary to find the diaphragm. Taking no chances. To be impregnated by this beast was unthinkable.

She didn't want him to help her with her clothes, and she didn't watch him tear at his shirt. She thought she would be revolted by the sight of his hairy body. How could she have enjoyed those romps with this ape? She must have been desperate. She slipped into the king-size bed first and actually gritted her teeth. It was going to be like a trip to the dentist

Oh God, if you are out there, help me now.

It was a hell of a time to ask for help from a God she hadn't acknowledged since she was a young woman. Almost to the day Billy died. An appeal for divine help in this situation seemed ridiculous.

Phil was as active as ever, kissing, pawing, sucking, squeezing, not awkwardly, it was familiar territory. Marti didn't have to do much to appear a willing partner. She moaned and grabbed at his hair, something to hang onto, and ride it out. He murmured his usual lustful litany. "Oh baby, oh baby. This is so good." No words of real affection. She would have hated that. At least he was fast. It had been a long time since the Essex House meetings. Now, it was a pathetic charade.

She had thought of Julie as a boy? Why? He's more of a man than this ape, or Ross Vincennes. Billy was her only love. But now she wanted to believe she could rediscover love, with Julie. Forever.

She was doing what a whore must do. Thinking about anything until it was over. What did they think about? What they would do with their money, what they would have for dinner, how they might redo their hair? It was time to fake an orgasm, and then it was finally over.

Phil made a mighty thrust, literally bouncing her on the mattress. He heaved a great sigh and rolled over on his back laying quietly, but she could hear the sounds of air pulsing into and out of his giant lungs, a human bellows.

God, she felt dirty. With Ross she always hopped out of bed and ducked into the john for a shower. But Phil usually wanted seconds. She murmured something appreciative of his efforts and awaited his usual words of approval. She silently mouthed them for him, "Jesus, baby, that was great. I hope it was that good for you."

Only he didn't use those words. Instead, with his face, now hovering over hers, he said,

"Did you ever hear the gag, when sex is good it's very good, but when it's bad it's not bad?"

"No." And she knew he wasn't trying to make her laugh. His tone frightened her.

"Well, it's a perfect description of what just happened. After all these months I thought you would be as eager as I was, but I might as well have been jerking off. You just weren't there, baby. What's the story?"

She had to calm him down.

"I didn't think I was all that bad. Hell, it's been a long time. I'm still recovering from a bullet in the gut, you know."

Why hadn't she used that alibi while they were still in the suite's living room? Before she agreed to come? Oh yeah, she thought the phone was still bugged.

He thought that over. "Yeah, but even then."

She said, "Maybe you've been enjoying some special sex lately."

"Don't be a smart ass, Marti. You know you weren't putting out. I can understand the alibi about recovering from that slug in the gut, but maybe you're saving it for the pretty boy I saw you with today."

No, no, no. Don't let him get into that.

"You saw nothing that means a thing. As for tonight, I'm sorry if you thought I didn't give full value for my dinner. I worked hard in my therapy today. I'm just tired."

She moved to get out of the bed but he had a hand on her upper arm that was viselike. The full value crack must have stung him. The meanness went out of his voice, but he would have the last word.

"Hey, maybe I'm tired, too, after rushing to catch the plane after a lousy night's sleep. Forget what I said, but remember this. I'm not letting anyone move in on you now that you are free from that asshole bookkeeper. You are bought and paid for lady, and don't you forget it."

He's insane. I'm supposed to be a loving bed mate after that crack. I don't care if he kills me, I'll never let him touch me again.

He interpreted her silence as submission. He was wrong. She was seething. If he said another word she would explode. He released his grip on her arm and left the bed. She waited until she heard the shower before she scrambled into her clothes. She had to put a stop to this. Maybe she would go to jail, but she would be free of this brute. She ran from the bedroom and grabbed her purse from the sofa. She was out of the suite and into an elevator in a few seconds.

55

In the lobby she pawed in her purse for Sergeant Carey's card, then found an alcove for making the call on her cell. She hoped he was still on the evening shift. He was. As soon as she recognized his voice, she said, "Sergeant, I want to talk to you. Right now."

A surprised Carey said, "Sure," and gave her directions to his office.

She sat in the Taurus, ignition key in hand.

Do I want to do this? Hell no. Do I need to unload a story that will make me appear a selfish airhead pig and possibly send me to jail? What other choice do I have? I can't juggle these two bastards while trying to begin a new life. I can't even look at either of them again much less let them into my bed. I could get poor Julie in the middle. If Phil harmed him I would somehow kill him. As for Ross I'm a sex object he hardly needs now that he has the money and an alibi for Bob's murder. There's no happy ending here. I have to unload my mess.

Carey, smiling, met her at the elevator door and ushered her into the same room used for her interview. Marti was much more aware of her surroundings on this visit. Carey had instructed her where to park and how to enter the Michigan avenue building, a side entrance. It would have been like stepping into the offices of any other large Chicagoland business if she hadn't been greeted by a uniformed officer who ushered her into an elevator.

The scene on Carey's floor reminded her of a rerun from the old Barney Miller TV series, but the scope was much larger befitting one of the nation's largest police organizations. She walked into a huge, brightly lit, wide open bull pen, a sea of desks rimmed by offices, presumably for supervisors. Uniformed and plain clothes officers, men and women, sat before computers, or talked on telephones or in groups. The room easily absorbed the hum of vocal exchange, spiked by bursts of outrage, denial, even laughter. Seated in chairs alongside some of the desks were civilians, some seemingly at ease, some hunched towards their interrogators, their supply of facts or lies recorded on hard drives. A pretty young black woman, explaining her situation with gestures, looked up at Marti as she passed. She made a slight grin which may have been intended as sisterly. Marti was too engrossed in how she would launch her meeting with Carey to respond.

Carey closed the door, chopping off the drone from the huge room.

She said, "Where are all the criminals?"

The large man chuckled as he pointed to a chair.

"Not up here, unless they are in those uniforms out there. We don't have many suspects or what the TV cops call perps on this floor."

He looked her over. I'm glad to see you. I've worried about you all day. Tried to reach you by phone a couple of hours ago, right after I came on duty."

"Oh. What about?"

"Well, I'll be glad to tell you, but you called this meeting. Why don't you get the ball rolling? We're not going to tape anything right now. If it looks like we should go on record, and if you want to, we can do it then."

She had thought how she would tell her story as she drove south on the city's famed "Boul Mich." Carey's remark about worrying about her cemented the deal. She would tell it all, from the top. No fumbling, or slipping and sliding. He would get it all, or nearly all, right from the sordid beginning. She wouldn't need a just-in-case letter to Ross's boss, either. She was barely seated opposite the officer before she began.

"I was married to Bob Costello when I had an affair with his boss, Phillip Stanton of Stanton Industries, Newark, New Jersey. After Bob testified against his boss on charges of tax evasion, I went into the witness protection program with him because I was afraid Stanton would take out his revenge on me if I didn't run. I was sure he thought I told Bob of the affair, and that Bob betrayed him for that reason.

"Bob didn't know of my affair with Stanton, but he hated Stanton because Stanton forced him to use his accounting and computer know-how to hide company assets and to underpay taxes.

"Bob was not a criminal, but he thought Stanton had connections with mob people. He was deathly afraid Stanton would have him killed if he tried to back out.

"I was enjoying the best time of my life, living well in a beautiful condo apartment. Didn't know a thing, I swear it, about Bob's plan. But then after he tried to send Stanton to prison he told me he stole enough cash to set us up for the future. Stanton beat the case but the government honored its deal. We went into hiding. Here in Chicago."

She looked at her hands, hesitating. Carey said, "How about a cup of coffee?"

She shook her head. She hated the idea of Carey thinking she was a tramp. She liked this man, but he had his duty. She kept her eyes locked on his.

"Bob and I lived very well. He was my third husband. My first was a policeman. He was killed in a car crash."

Carey saw her eyes squeeze shut for a beat at the word "crash." She gave no other sign of losing her composure except to suck in a deep breath. Then she added, "I was divorced from the second. A bounce-back marriage."

Carey could see she was ashamed. He didn't move a muscle, just returned her look with a steady gaze. He knew the story. Cop widows, especially young ones, sometimes move too quickly into another marriage, hoping it will bring new happiness while sustaining the best memories of the past. He knew why she married the third time. Couldn't blame her for trying to live as well as she could. Maybe he was facing a promiscuous woman, but he thought not.

She said, "I hated leaving my family and friends in New York. I was at loose ends in the bungalow. You saw the place. Then I made a big mistake." She sucked in a huge breath. "I began an affair. With Ross Vincennes, the marshal assigned to our case."

Carey couldn't dead pan this revelation. His eyebrows raised a fraction and he blew a soundless whistle.

She made a sad little smile as if to say, See what a horrible woman I am.

"Bob was acting strangely. Our sex life was non-existent. We hardly spoke to one another. He complained about the job the government had found for him. I guessed he suspected my affair with Vincennes, and I wondered if he was going to take off without me. He said he hid some of Stanton's money in several of his suits, but I checked and it was gone. That made me sure I was going to be ditched. I just panicked.

"I was scared of being left alone so I told Vincennes I was about to get a lot of money, and we could run away together. I didn't name the source

251

of the money, but I think Vincennes knew. Then he warned me that what I was doing could be dangerous. I'll say that for him. He also said that if I wasn't named in a will, or had specific instructions on the whereabouts of the money, it might never be found. He was right. In my panic I hadn't thought it out. Then he said whoever held the money wouldn't give it up short of torture. That did it. I drove as fast as I could back to the bungalow. I was going to warn Bob, get him out of there. I would have gone with him."

Carey interrupted by holding up a large hand.

"You knew Bob was in danger. Why?"

She didn't intend to break down, to blubber, to extract sympathy with one of a woman's oldest ploys, but her eyes still moistened.

"I had called Stanton. He said he had no intention of harming Bob, that they would negotiate a settlement on the money and I would get a share. He said he mostly wanted to get me back to New York. But I thought Vincennes might be right. Bob could be tortured, even killed."

Carey was nodding. "So you found your husband in the basement with the man we can guess was sent by Mr. Stanton? The same man wounded in your apartment."

"Yes, and I walked up to him because I didn't believe he intended to shoot Bob, or me. How would the money be recovered then?"

"What's your theory on why you were shot?"

"I think the man was trying to wave me away. I just got too close. Then I heard Bob coming from behind me. That's when the gun went off."

"And Bob left you for dead?"

"Yes, he told me he was sure I was dead. He said he had to get away because Phil Stanton would surely send someone else."

"But he came back. Why?"

"Because of a lucky, or unlucky guess I made as to where he might be found. The day before he went to the FBI about Phil he disappeared. I later found a ticket envelope marked Minneapolis in our apartment waste basket. I told Ross during his visit at the hospital. Then he somehow found Bob up there and somehow stole the money."

"So what was he doing in your apartment when the bad guys came?"

She didn't smile. *Bad guys. Right.*

"We, Bob and I, hoped we could somehow get Vincennes to share the money. Possibly scare him into thinking I would tell his boss of our affair."

Carey jumped on that admission.

He said, "But Vincennes heard you on the tape and knew what he was walking into. He knew your husband. was armed. His first idea may have been to lure your husband into a shoot out. That would have been no contest. The arrival of Stanton's thug was both a complication that became an opportunity. I'm beginning to think Vincennes used him to kill you. Then he was going to use his gun to kill your husband.

"I may be wrong. It's a weird scenario, but it does make sense because of one flaw in Vincennes's story. He told me he was able to catch up with the gunman because the foyer door failed to close after someone buzzed the man into your hallway. Then this morning, after one of your neighbors admitted me, I worked with that door for several minutes, pulling it open and letting it swing shut. You know, I couldn't make that door stay ajar. I must have swung it open fifty times. It closed and locked every time. Then I checked with all the other building residents. None of them buzzed that door. I believe Vincennes had the thug under control and may have promised him freedom if he charged into the apartment and shot both you and your husband."

Marti's hand was covering her mouth. "But he missed me."

"Probably deliberately. The miss may have looked legitimate when you fell down, but Vincennes thought the shooter was badly wounded by Costello. He had to turn his attention to your husband. The wounded man got away. Vincennes could be in the cat bird seat. It looks like his position of self defense in shooting Costello will hold up. What's your relationship with him now?"

"I hate the son of a bitch. He shot Bob while Bob was trying to protect me. Then before you arrived at the apartment he said I had to back the story he told you."

"How does that play out?"

"Stanton wants me back in New York. He has no idea Ross Vincennes has Bob's money. He thinks it will be found and eventually turned over to me. I don't give a damn about the money. I just want those two men out of my life. I'm scared to death of both of them."

She thought of Julie. "And anyone I'm close to could be in danger. Vincennes promised to give me some of the money if I keep my trap shut. I think he'd rather drop me in the Chicago river."

Leo Carey had never seen anything close to this one. He had been given city-wide assignments ever since his collaboration with Journal reporter Sid Coffin on solving what became known as The Byline Murders.

A major politician fell from grace and Leo's elevation to lieutenancy was assured. He begged to be left on special assignments for a few more years. A widower, and childless with no great itch for more income, Chicago crime was his life, the new Michigan avenue headquarters his home.

He was able to give himself assignments and the case of a Karen Velotti, seriously wounded in her bungalow basement, definitely turned him on. The case then revolved around the whereabouts of Leland Velotti, now known as the late protected witness, Robert Costello This after Karen Velotti, that is Marti Costello, admitted to being his wife.

The shooting in Mrs. Costello's apartment brought him back on the case, and now, with the remorseful lady describing something out of Law and Order, he might even have a murder to spice up the stew. He had long ago swapped sympathy for objectivity in his investigations, but the lady's story was beginning to fit into his own idea of what took place in the apartment.

As of right now, he didn't think Mrs. Costello was a black widow. It was a sure thing her life had been sent into a tailspin by the loss of her first husband, the cop. Wives of cops who lost their lives on the job are always tragic figures, but this beauty had been sought out and exploited by a number of men. Carey never expected to learn how many, but if she had been unwise in some of her associations she was surely trying to rid herself of the entanglements now.

He wanted to help her, and perhaps he could. Thus far he couldn't see her involvement in any crime. She admitted she had dropped a dime on her husband, but he wanted to believe it was not for the purpose of his murder. Anyway, Costello was no longer in danger of whatever Phillip Stanton had in mind for him.

Her relationship with Vincennes and Stanton was cloudy, but he thought he would not press for any more than he had. One thing for sure. She could be in serious trouble with either man.

Carey smiled and Marti thought the detective's look of pleasure did a lot for the man's rugged face. Carey's fellow cops would have had a different play on the situation. They would have interpreted Carey's grin as the look of a veteran crime fighter for whom all the pieces were fitting together.

Rarely did the veteran policeman confide his preliminary thinking on a case with anyone involved except other officers, and not very often to them, but he decided the troubled young woman, who apparently had spilled her guts, deserved something in return. He tried to dismiss another reason for his decision to help her. That she was beautiful.

Marti felt chilled. Her confession and the detective's summation of what very well could be accurate, was overwhelming. Tears were running down her face.

"How could I ever think I could make a life with that man?"

Carey reached for his handkerchief, grateful it was clean.

He said, "He may have wanted to, but he loved your late husband's money even more. Right now, he's a very dangerous man. To you. He might get away with the murder of your husband, but you still represent a threat to him. As for Stanton, he's in the clear unless you announce you collaborated with him to find your husband. You didn't do that to have him killed and I'm sure he has covered his tracks well in connection with hiring the hood. As you describe the situation, his current role in your life is that of a pest."

Marti dabbed her nose while nodding. She wouldn't tell Carey that Phil was more than a pest. He was a danger to the man she loved. She left out one other thing that might cost her Carey's sympathy. The hundred thousand dollars Phil sent her. She'd gladly give the money back if Carey could help her get out from under the thumbs of those two bastards. Carey said, "I want you to repeat what you told me on tape. Don't be frightened. It will never be used against you. It will be for your protection. Then you can tell both Stanton and Vincennes to get out of your life."

"Sergeant, they'll flip a coin to decide which one of them will strangle me."

Carey answered the crack was a tight grin. "I think not."

56

Julius chugged up to Peg Delaney's station. Breathless.

"Hey, Mrs. Costello didn't show today. What's the story?"

It was another opportunity for Peggy to twit the young man. She was now convinced Julius was very much smitten by Marti Costello.

"Hey, I'm not her keeper. I don't know, but isn't she making her own schedule now?"

"Sure, but she still comes in every day."

"So give her a call. You have her number."

Julius looked dubious. Peg thought, "Ah, another young man torn by the doubts of giving his heart away."

She wanted to help him. "She called. She has some errands today, but she's coming to my place for dinner. Want to come?"

She took his look for, "Oh yeah, hell yes," but what he said was, "Sorry, I have a conflict." He hesitated. "Could I check with you later?"

"Any time up 'till cocktails. We start our drinking at five-thirty sharp."

He sped away and Peggy smiled after him. He'd be there, but it would be a tough call. The hospital touch football team had a game that night.

She had invited Marti for dinner a couple of days before the shooting in Marti's apartment. She was serving pork loin, a favorite recipe, and it would be a great opportunity to quiz Marti about her future.

What was the girl going to do? The news media had no luck getting anything from her, but it was still a major story. High drama. They played the old story of a woman in trouble, possibly caught between the law and the forces of revenge. Coming to the rescue was marshal Ross Vincennes who says he defended himself in killing Marti's husband, Robert. But, Peg wondered, why would Costello want to shoot Vincennes? And who was the intruder shot by Costello? What was his mission? Sergeant Leo Carey would not be quoted other than to say, "We are still trying to sort this thing out, beginning with an identification of the stranger. He apparently is the same man who shot Mrs. Costello in her bungalow basement."

Marshal Ross Vincennes would not be quoted. Nor would his boss, Lou Robbins, other than to say, "The matter is in the hands of the Chicago police department."

The Chicago Journal had dug all the way back to Robert Costello's testimony in New York against businessman Phillip Stanton. Stanton was not available for comment. His secretary told callers he was out of town and nothing else

Peggy was about to quit for the day when Julie called.

"If the invite is still there, I can come"

"You got it. Don't dress up."

"Me dress up. You've gotta be kidding."

Julie was famous for ignoring conventional attire. Peggy remembered his outfit at the hospital Christmas party. Jeans and a sweat shirt labeled "Xmas is party time." Somehow Peg guessed he wouldn't repeat that performance tonight.

She guessed right. He showed up two minutes after six with a bottle of wine and some flowers. He had walked the several blocks from his place dressed in light gray wool slacks and a blue sport coat and what appeared new tasseled loafers.

Mike, who knew the therapist only as a decidedly casual dresser, answered the door and called, "It's the Polish prince. I think."

The men shook hands. Mike said, "Nice threads," then, "What are you drinking? Can you handle a good beer or should I bring out the stuff you buy?"

"Mike, my palate craves the best. Am I not dressed for it?"

Julie was sipping a Michelob when Marti arrived a few minutes later. It had been a busy day and she hadn't had much time to think about what she would wear. She grabbed the first thing she saw in the closet. It was a black crepe sheath to which she added a string of pearls. A little formal for the occasion but it would do. She was grateful for the short hair which trimmed getting-ready time to a few brushes.

"Sorry I'm late" were her first words to Mike. Then she saw Julie and saluted the surprise of his presence with a big smile.

"Hey, Julie. How nice. I didn't know."

Julie knew, but he was ill prepared for the woman he had only seen in sweat clothes, skirts, and jeans. He smiled back at the vision, but had trouble responding to her simple greeting. He managed a "Hi" just as Peg came in from the kitchen and dragged Marti over to a two-person love seat. She gestured for Julie to sit next to Marti. From another chair she said, "And what kind of a day did you have? We missed you."

Marti had prepared her fib, and it came out smoothly enough. She described a day of driving and a visit to a giant mall in Gurnee.

"It was a lot of driving and you know how bad it is in this town, but I enjoyed the break from the routine."

Julie emerged briefly from his fog. "I like long drives."

Peg smiled, "That's very profound, Julie."

She accepted her husband's delivery of a drink, and said,. "Any news from the crime front? Papers are full of it, mostly speculation. The news people, and the cops, too, would like to chat with your husband's old boss, Phillip Stanton."

Marti said, "I don't think they'll get much from him."

Mike Delaney cut in. "They'll never link him with the gunman who died in your apartment. Unless he's very stupid."

Marti said, "Oh, he's not stupid, Mr. Delaney."

"That's Mike, please."

The group moved to the dining room. Julie came to life and contributed to conversation about politics, movies, and sports. Especially sports. Peg thought her dinner was well accepted by the guests as well as her voracious husband. Mike and Julie engaged in some good-natured banter that made the everyone laugh. Later in the kitchen Mike said to his wife,

"Julie's a great young man. Do you think he likes Marti?"

"Mike, does a cat like tuna? He's crazy about her."

At goodbye time, Marti learned Julie had walked so she volunteered to drive him home. As she put the Taurus in gear, she said, "I'm going to have to miss tomorrow, too, Julie. Some matters I have to take care of."

He tried not to look at her silken legs, and said, "Sure. You're setting your own pace. Doing great. But you don't want to miss too much. Set yourself back."

"Julie, I'm not going to quit. I've never felt better in my life. You and the girls have done a job on me. I'll never forget you and how hard you've worked to get me well."

To Julie her last words had the ring of a farewell address. It tore at him. She was preparing to wind things down, get on with her life. She certainly didn't need him in it, but he had to admit he wanted more of her in his. He had had few crushes on women, but his feelings now were akin to some of the torture he had felt a couple of times during grade and high school days. He had been helpless and inarticulate then. If he was to have a chance in Marti Costello's life he would have to make a commitment. The word had always braked any further action. Now, it seemed appropriate and desirable.

Marti knew his address but asked him to give her directions. She pretended surprised to learn he lived only a few blocks from her place.

He said, "Drive to your apartment. I'll walk home. You might have a little trouble finding a parking place this late."

She smiled at the gallantry. He might have been promoting an invitation into the apartment but she doubted it. She had good reasons for not inviting him in now.

She locked the car, glad to have his company in the street where the lamps threw barely enough light to illuminate the sidewalk. The night was cool and she took his arm. He made a slight move so that her hand was momentarily brought against his side. Her heart did a flip at the hint of intimacy.

Chalk it up to the wine, or maybe I wore the right dress after all.

As they walked up the three steps to the outer door she said, "I can take it from here, Julie. Thanks very much. It's been a fun evening, and I'll be back at work day after tomorrow."

There was light from the vestibule, but not a great deal. If he was going to kiss her it wouldn't be like it was a public place. Apparently he agreed with her. Putting his hand on her shoulder he exerted a light pressure and she moved towards him. His hand then slipped around to her back and he said, "I'll miss you, even for a day."

He hesitated, but she helped him out, moving her head within easy range. The kiss was tentative at first, then it became a long and complete expression of mutual involvement, not the robust one-way buss by Julie the day before. They broke apart, then joined again, even longer.

Marti knew she had to take charge and send him away. For all she knew, Phil or even Vincennes, could be in the darkness, spying on two persons too drunk from their passion to give a damn who might be watching.

She said, "Julie. I have to go in. You have to go home."

He said, "I love you, Marti. Jesus, I love you."

Billy said it once, and now, hearing it again, made her cry. Julie tried to kiss away the tears, but she broke away and lunged for the door. Over her shoulder she said, "You're sweet, Julie. I'll see you day after tomorrow."

She hurried to unlock the lobby door. God, if he followed her she would be unable to stop herself. She had to wait. This might be a last chance for real love, but at this time, for this man, she had to be free to love without fear.

57

Phillip Stanton, parked barely fifty feet away, raged.

Goddammit. He'd been right. He'd had whores who showed more emotion than she did last night. He had tried to call her after she ditched him at the suite. Then several more times, but she wouldn't answer. He thought he would drive to her apartment, apologize for chewing her out for the lousy performance in bed. She could well have been overly tired from her therapy. Now he knew why she claimed she tired. She was playing around with this guy.

He had spent the next morning working in his suite, ironing out some minor problems in the fast-food division. He tried to call Marti after lunch in the hotel's dining room with a couple of local investment bankers.

He tried to call Marti again about three, after winding up his business calls. It irritated him that she didn't have an answering service of some kind. He tried several more times after that, then ordered dinner from room service. The food was tasteless. He couldn't finish the meal, but drank the entire pot of coffee. He tried Marti's number again, then grabbed his lightweight top coat. He'd be fucked if she was going to stiff him. If she was with that kid he would break both his legs.

In the Lincoln he tried to get hold of himself. He realized he was behaving irrationally. It didn't matter. He had sent the woman a hundred thousand bucks, and he would give her whatever she wanted from Costello's stash. What was the matter with her? He had to get her out of this burg.

He had always had any woman he had ever wanted. The fact was he didn't want anyone else since first seeing Marti across the room at that silly party. It was more than a turn on. She had seduced him with a glance. There was her looks, of course, but the way she held herself, and walked, and talked, inflamed him. Their meetings in New York hadn't doused the fire. He was ready to give up his marriage for her when her husband ratted him out. He thought she had betrayed him, and it had made him sick. Her last call to his office was the happiest moment of his life. Of course he sent her the money. He would have sent her a million to get her in his arms again. He couldn't believe his excitement in seeing her last night He had felt ashamed for scolding her about the indifferent sex. Hell, of course she was tired. From fucking that therapy punk.

He had parked the Lincoln out of range of a street light, then tried her buzzer in the apartment's foyer. She wasn't home. He returned to the car, determined to sit there until she showed up if he had to wait all night.

He saw them walking toward her building through the car's side mirror. She had a hand on the therapist's arm. They were wearing date clothes. Stanton thought he recognized Marti's black dress. And those beautiful legs. She must have worn the outfit to turn the asshole on. *Where in hell had they been?*

If she invited the punk in he would tear the door down, but they just stood there looking at each other. My God, she was kissing him. And again.

She left the therapist standing there, but she didn't look like she wanted to. She disappeared into the foyer and for a few seconds Stanton sat stunned. He wanted to jump out of the car and tackle the therapist, smash him to a pulp, but he had disappeared. He stepped into the street, but there was no one in sight. And he could hear no car revving up.

Where the fuck had he gone?

He started the Lincoln and eased up the darkened street. There. Someone was walking slowly. He guided the slow moving car with his left hand as he peered through the passenger side window. Then he saw whoever it was under a street light, for a couple of seconds. It was him.

He goosed the car until it was fifty or so yards past the walker. A parking place was available and he eased into it, not having to back in. He cut the ignition and slid out of the seat. It timed out perfectly. He was on the sidewalk when Warshawsky was within about twenty feet. The area was barely illuminated.

Julie was floating, not walking, his mind on anything but outside distractions, but he saw the Lincoln glide to the curb. He slowed when the muscular man in the dark suit stepped from around the front of the car, then loomed before him. The men were between street lamps and Julie couldn't make out Stanton's face immediately, but the man's rigid stance in the center of the walk was a warning in itself.

Man, he's a big one. What's up?

Julius came to a stop a few feet in front of Stanton.

He said, "What's up buddy? You need directions, or something?"

He was prepared to turn over his wallet in the face of a gun, but he would run from a knife. No way a man built like this one could catch him.

Stanton smiled, but there were no teeth in it.

"I'm here to give you some directions, buddy. They are very simple. Keep the fuck away from Marti Costello."

Julie had been on the emotional high of his life. He hadn't felt his feet hit the walkway since the woman he loved disappeared into her building's foyer. He was a young man in love, and the certainty that his love was returned would have easily transported him on a cloud of euphoria over the next several hours. He felt he was blessed by luck he never dreamed could be his. Now he was more surprised than alarmed to have been yanked out of his state of enchantment so rudely. Later, he thought his immediate reaction hadn't been fright. He was just shocked to have his beloved's name uttered by this well-dressed thug.

Who was he? Maybe he was a replacement for the mystery guy who got shot in Marti's apartment, but what was the connection?

"Who are you, man?"

"Never mind who I am. Just get it into your pea brain that you are to make whatever excuses are necessary to drop out of Mrs. Costello's life. Don't see her again. Cut it off. By telephone, or fax, or E-mail. Do it tonight, or not later than tomorrow a m."

Julie didn't need his college education to understand the implications behind the brute man's order. He had to stay cool, use his head. It would be idiocy to react to what might be a deadly threat with a movie hero's, "And what if I don't?" or any of its variations.

Just let me get out of here. Alive and whole.

He said, "Okay. I'm cool Is that it?"

No that wasn't it. Stanton stared at the man he had decided had done him more harm than anyone or anything in his experience. The fact was, no one or no thing had ever come close. He wanted to kick the shit out of this punk who was being a smart ass. The response to his warning was flip, too quick, and obviously insincere. He would put a stop to any ambitions the punk had about Marti right now. This darkened street with no witnesses was the place to leave this asshole for almost dead. And ugly to look at. After his face was bounced off the sidewalk a couple of times Marti wouldn't want to see him again. And lover boy would be convinced that the job would be finished if he ever saw her again. Chicago had muggers and that's how the punk would explain what happened to him. Unless he preferred to die. That message would be delivered to him at his hospital bed.

He had to remember to take any cash the kid might have, and his watch. Who would ever know what happened on this dark street?

Stanton reviewed his next move. Two quick steps and the punk wouldn't know what hit him. The therapist was probably in good shape from his therapy work, but nothing would help him once his neck was in a choke hold. He would be hanging like a dressed ham. All he needed was a few seconds. Marti had to understand the punk was out of her life. Back in New York with money and clothes and a first class address, she would forget all this shit. She'd never see him again. If she tried her new boyfriend would not only be out of her life but out of this life.

He said, "Go on. Get out of here. But take care of this matter right away."

Julie stared at the man. He wanted the hood to go away, but if he lied, said he would give Marti up, the well-dressed hit man, or whatever he was, would be back.

Stanton said, "You hear me?"

Julie felt the blood rush to his face. With it came the burst of rage he remembered from a football game with Wesley hospital. A ringer picked up by Wesley for the major game, tried to block into his knee from the side. Julie pulled his leg away in time, and gave the guy a vicious elbow to the face. Only two refs worked the game. Both missed the exchange. The ringer went to the sidelines and stayed there.

He'd have to be quick, but the thug he stood in front of now could be taken. He could drop to his knees, slip his hands behind the larger man's heels, flip him, then kick him in the nuts as a momentary crippler. From that point he could do some real damage.

Trouble with that, whoever was this far into Marti's life, had resources to send another bad guy, and there might be no warning. And Marti could be in danger, too. He had to walk away from this one. Work out a plan. There was no way he was going to give up his girl.

Okay, you win this round, whoever you are, whoever you represent.

He said, "Yeah, I hear you. As I said, I'm cool. The lady is not all that important to me."

The expression on the thug's face, which had looked chiseled out of stone, eased slightly, and then the mouth snarled a dismissal.

"Okay asshole. On your way."

Stanton stepped back a step to give Julie room to pass, but not by much. As soon as Julie was a half-step past him, Stanton spun behind Julie, throwing his right arm around Julie's neck The move was the beginning of a choke hold, dangerous, even deadly if held too long. The maneuver was long ago barred from legitimate wrestling. Cops in most states were forbidden its use, even for controlling violent prisoners.

What saved Julie was the slight rustle from Stanton's silk suit. A split second before Stanton's arm got under his chin he ducked his head and shoved himself hard to his right. Stanton's couldn't complete his hold, but his hand grabbed the lapel of Julie's sport coat. He hung on, and his grip held Julie so that he could smash Julie's face with his left fist. The blow brought blood, but Julie countered with a hard right fist to Stanton's ribs. Stanton grunted, and released his hold.

Stanton hadn't wrestled since college. He still belonged to the New York Athletic Club, but business and his fondness for confining his wrestling to the more pleasurable tussles with willing bed mates had interfered with serious efforts to stay in the condition he enjoyed in undergraduate days. Still, he thought he would have little trouble handling this smaller man, and he waded forward, willing to risk taking some punches just to get his arms around the man he intended to mutilate.

The battleground was a section of sidewalk abutted to a partially wooded lot which had somehow escaped development. The little light provided by a street lamp gave the combatants almost complete privacy from neighboring four-story apartment buildings. There was no street or pedestrian traffic. Stanton was happy to have it that way. Julie longed for the sight of anyone who would hear his yells for help. He had not been in a real fight since grade school days, and squabbles back then had been quickly broken up. This thug, probably a professional hit man, had a look in his eyes Julius had never seen before, except maybe in the movies. Now he felt a fear he had never known.

He wants to hurt me bad. He might have orders to make the damage permanent. If he had orders to kill me I'd already be dead.

Julie knew he was at a disadvantage to the stronger man, but he might be in better shape, and quicker. He decided against throwing any more punches. He sensed that once the blocky man grabbed hold of a fist, or arm, the fight would go to the ground. Julie didn't want to become enclosed in those huge arms.

Who was this guy, anyway? Was he someone from Marti's past who had some kind of claim on her? Or was he representing someone? A former lover? He had been sent to give a warning. But now it was more than a warning

Whatever, Julie had to get out of here somehow, call Marti and learn what it was all about. There was no way he was going to talk himself out of this jam. He could try to run for it, but the. soles of his new loafers had no traction at all. They would slip hopelessly on the concrete sidewalk.

He was backing into the lot, mind flipping ideas on how to make a defense, when one of his feet landed awkwardly on an exposed tree root. Losing his balance he stumbled backwards. Stanton saw the misstep and moved in fast. Julie's arms clutched air. He staggered, then pancaked, landing on his back, banging his head on the hard turf. Lights flashed with the pain. Almost out of it, he was conscious enough to see the huge blob looming over him.

Stanton was sure he had wounded prey to finish off. It was time to combine some fun with smashing this asshole into the ground. He was going to do a belly "flop" on the punk, making him as easy to tear apart as soggy spaghetti.

It had been years since he had done a flop while was fooling around with some team members at Penn State. A crowd appeal move in commercial wrestling, but long since banned from amateur competition, throwing the body on top of an already stunned opponent was like hitting a beach ball with an ironing board.

Trying to clear his head, Julie still didn't have enough control of his body to twist away from this vulnerable position and fight himself back to his feet. He guessed Stanton's next move and was horrified by the mental picture of the result.

Oh no, he's going to bury me under all that bulk.

Stanton, grinning in anticipation of squashing the breath out of the much lighter man, was certain he would stun the victim, then really go to work. Flexing his knees, he left his feet in a dive. It wasn't a straight shot. His rage had only one objective. He would convert the smart ass son of a bitch into pulp. Then he would kick, gouge, and punch the shit out of the kid, doing the kind of damage to the pretty boy's face that would turn off Marti, or any woman.

To Julie, it was as if he was lying in a casket, the lid descending, implacably, irreversibly, shutting out all air and light, sealing him from life and breath forever.

Yelling a long wail of "Noooo," he flung up his right foot. It was an instinctive reflex with no plan. It was as if he was staring into a gun that was about to be fired into his face and threw up a hand in hopeless defense. Had he been deliberate with the move, and aware of the shoes he was wearing, he might have had a flash of optimism. He had worried about the new loafers he bought that afternoon to help dress him up for Peg Delaney's dinner. He already decided he might never wear the hard slippery shoes again. Right now, however, one of them rose to the occasion. The hard heel caught the diving Stanton in mid air, full in the face. Stanton's grin was instantly converted into a bloody grimace. He had never felt such pain, nor the horror of damage to his face and carefully sculpted nose. The fight was over.

Julie pushed the suddenly slack Stanton aside and scrambled to his feet. Stanton propped himself on an elbow and groped for a handkerchief.

He screamed, "You son of a bitch. I'll kill you."

Julie stood clear as Stanton used a hand to check the damage to his face. His instinct was to get away from the scene. The guy could still have a weapon. He'd like to learn more about his opponent. To do that he might have to cause more damage to the man, but his luck might not hold up. The thug was wounded, but weren't grizzley bears supposed to be most dangerous when injured? The fight was not under sanction of the Amateur Athletic Union, nor under the rules established by the Marquis of Queensberry. Whatever further damage he might do with his fists would be countered by his opponent's bulk and strength.

For Stanton, the hate had intensified, but there was no more fight in him. The blood from his nose was in his mouth, and it along with the pain, was making him sick. The punk's shoe had hurt him. Badly. He might need some stitches. His nose might be broken, his teeth loosened.

He snarled, "You got lucky, punk, but it isn't over. And the warning that you stay away from Marti Costello is still in effect. If you care anything about her you'll get out of her life."

Stanton was attempting to heave himself to his feet when Julie decided to leave the scene.

He was feeling a little queasy himself. His opponent's face was a mess. Under any different circumstances he would have helped the man over to Memorial ER, but he wasn't going to be that generous in victory.

"Memorial hospital is six blocks that way." He pointed. "You'd better get fixed up.

As for Marti Costello, we'll let her decide whether she is going to continue being my friend."

Rather cavalier, but sincere anyway. I won this fight. I'm entitled to the last word.

Not quite. As he turned away for the walk to his apartment, Stanton thug yelled after him, "You haven't heard the last from me, punk."

A totally believable promise. Julie only wanted to get away from the scene and call Marti. He had to tell her about the fight, and if possible identify the silk-suited attacker. Who was he representing with his warning? Himself? But where in hell did he come from and why now? If he had any real attachment to Marti, he should have showed up days ago.

Stanton also intended to call Marti. Back in his car, his handkerchief pressed against his face, he decided against seeking emergency room help. He was satisfied that neither his cheek bone nor his nose were broken. He'd check for further damage in a mirror. He could get patched up in the morning, if necessary.

The smart punk had driven him crazy. What did he say? "I'm cool." Shit, the punk just wanted to get out of there.

He thought it was a hold-up at first, then he thought I might be professional muscle, that I'd really mess him up. Jesus, where in the fuck did that foot come from? It was dumb. One of the first things I learned in wrestling was never leave your feet.

He drove back to the hotel, yanking the luxury car around corners and accelerating on straight stretches, running one red light. In his suite he checked his face in a mirror. There would be a hell of a bruise. He found a small refrigerator in the suite and pressed a hastily made ice-pack against his face while sipping on a huge drink Slumped down on the sofa he decided against trying to talk to Marti tonight. He might not be able to control himself after what he had seen between her and the punk. He wasn't going to lose her to a nickel-and-dime hospital worker. No other man would have this woman. He picked up the phone. He'd probably wake Brancatto up, but he wanted to make arrangements for Julius Warshawsky right now. Marti would have a choice. Go back with him to New York, or help make arrangements for her late boy friend's funeral.

58

Marti had pulled the plug on her phone. Julie might call and that could be lovely, but it might be Stanton or Vincennes, and she didn't want to talk to either man until tomorrow when she would issue her special invitation to each of them She needed the rest of the day to work out the details of her plan. She would warn Julie in the morning, then get to work.

Julie had to understand he was in danger. They couldn't see each other again until she was sure he was safe. God, she was in love. Julie had said, "I love you, and she wanted to say the words to him, but first she had to get clear of this mess with both Phil and Vincennes. She had used the words only once before, with Billy. Sweet Billy, and now she was getting a second chance to love someone as she had him. God, if there was a god, was being good to her, and she couldn't screw it up.

The first step would be to call Ross, and hope he would be available on such short notice.

Then Phil. If he was still in Chicago he would jump at her invitation. The plan had to work. If it backfired Ross would be in the clear and Stanton would be the proverbial millstone around her neck.

She was glad she went to Sergeant Carey. He was a kind man. He could have assumed she conspired with Phil to get Bob killed. He could also have assumed Bob was in her apartment to trap Vincennes, and that she was in on that, too. But he heard her story and said he would help her. He didn't think she would move this fast, but she couldn't take the chance that Ross couldn't accept her invitation, or that Phil would leave town. It was now or never.

Carey may have had his own ideas on how to move from this point. He said as she left his office, "I want to avenge the death of your husband, too, Mrs. Costello."

She had said, "Could you call me Marti?"

He said, "Sure. So long as it's social, not business."

59

The tap was off Marti's phone, so Vincennes didn't bother to ask where she was calling from. He interrupted her before she could identify herself.

"I'm in a meeting. Give me a number and I'll call right back."

She gave it and hung up.

Vincennes left the office and found a phone in a nearby bar. All agents knew their incoming calls were recorded, sometimes monitored, and whatever she said he wanted to be the only person to hear it. He didn't want to use his cell, either.

She said she was at the hospital for her workout, but she hoped she could see him that evening.

"Could you come for dinner? I know it's short notice, but I'm going back home, and I'd like to tell you my plans. I'll need some help from you to make those plans work, of course."

"Sure, of course I'll come." He had hoped her intelligence would bring her around, make her see his way was the only way. She didn't know he had come to kill her the other night, and she couldn't have been all that broken up over the death of her husband.

She started the whole mess by dropping the dime, didn't she?

Leo Carey hadn't called Vincennes since Vincennes had given his statement downtown. Vincennes was sure Marti's statement must have checked out against his, and it looked like the cops were going to agree that Costello had fired two extra shots at him in Marti's apartment Now the question was, could he get Marty back into their normal relationship? The invite looked promising.

271

He said, "You won't have anymore bogey men hiding in the kitchen, will you? It wouldn't look good for a third party to see the man who killed your husband coming over for dinner."

She tried to chuckle, but it stuck in her throat. She said, "No, but I hope you won't be coming completely alone?"

He got it. "Oh no, I'll bring something along with the flowers."

"Oh, Ross, that's great. How about six thirty sharp?"

"I'll be there."

60

She thought it might be a good idea if some appetizing smells came from the kitchen, so she picked up a seven-pound sirloin beef roast and followed the butcher's exact directions for its preparation. The aroma would fill her apartment by six.

She was forcing herself to be calm. Timing was all-important. She had rehearsed her speech twenty times and thought she had it down pat. She went over every move she would make She was dressed and ready by five-thirty. She decided against a dress. A skirt and blouse would be fine. It had been a cool day, and it was cool in the apartment, even with the heat from the oven, but she wouldn't need a sweater.

Julie had been waiting for her at the hospital that morning. He greeted her smiling shyly, not a confident lover, but she could see he was happy. He looked a little banged up, too. There was a bruise on his cheek, but he was glowing like a kid who had just won the spelling bee. He raised his eyebrows when he could see she wasn't dressed for her workout. She was ready to explain, but he didn't let her get started. He took both of her hands in his and drew her out into the hallway. She knew he wanted to kiss her. She wanted him to, but right now she had to calm him down, make him listen to her warning. They stood in a windowed alcove, down the hall from the gym door. She glanced about to see if anyone was watching, then put both of her forefingers to his lips.

She said, "Julie, I loved last night. I love you, too, but you must listen to me now. We are both in danger, but especially you. I've done some crazy things in my past, and now they are catching up with me. The shooting of my husband was part of it, but there's still more trouble, and I can't have you involved. Beginning right now we have to stay apart. I hope it won't be for long, but you can't walk home with me today, and I can't see you tonight. You have to believe me and do as I say."

No woman had ever spoken to Julius Warshawsky with more intensity. He had known few women he could classify as serious, none like this one. His female associations were with girls. Lots of girls, most of whom were happy to share some time, some laughs, a few beers which sometimes led to sex. No emotion came close to what he felt when with or thinking about Marti Costello. She was the first subject of his adoration since kid days, and he knew practically nothing about her. Except that her husband was dead, and she was free, and that he wanted her.

He wasn't going to laugh off a warning as sincere as cross bones on a bottle, but it had to be a reprise of what the big guy in the dark suit said last night. Maybe he could get the whole story here and now.

"Marti, I have to tell you. I had a street fight with a huge man last night after leaving you. I thought he wanted to kill me, but I got lucky and got away."

She gasped, "Oh Julie, I'm sorry."

"The guy threatened me, Marti, told me to never see you again. Who is he Marti?"

She had to lie. "I don't know, but he's part of my former life, what I want to leave forever and forget. I hope I can end it soon, but you are in danger. We can't be seen together."

"But this guy or someone who sent this guy must have seen us together. Right?"

"Yes."

"And that someone didn't like what he saw, and so I'm in danger?"

"Oh yes."

He stood motionless, gazing down at her, soaking up the vision of his love.

Marti stared back. She knew he wanted to handle this well, to make an intelligent response, not just say something sappy like, "I can take care of myself."

Actually, Julius didn't know what to say. He had never known fear like what he had experienced on that empty lot. That big son of a bitch had meant to kill him, at least beat him to a pulp. No one had ever looked at him before in such open hatred.

He said, "Okay, but what's the bottom line? If I stay away does that insure your safety? Can you give me a clue as to any way I can adjust to this situation or play a helpful role of some kind? What kind of a time frame are we facing here?"

He was so calm. Every word he said made her love him more.

She said, "There's a chance the problem can be ended very soon. No, there's no good role for you in this thing. Just let me go now and you just disappear. Get out of the hospital. I'll try to call you tonight. It's the best way for both of us."

She reached out to him and they wrapped arms around each other. She buried her head in his chest. He whispered in her ear. "I love you, Marti. It's forever."

She broke clear and ran for the exit, tears streaming. No man, not even Billy, had ever made her cry before. This guy made her cry every time she was with him.

In the apartment, dressed and chilling a bottle of wine, she hoped Vincennes would be on time. He had always been early for their trysts. Would he still be hopeful for sex?. Of course he would. The man's ego was unbelievable. He killed Bob and still expected her to hop into bed with him. It's the money. He thinks he can score if drops a big chunk of cash on the dinette table?

Those motel meetings with him seemed a thousand years ago. Oh, how she wished she could forget what a selfish, stupid pig she had been. Julie Warshawsky was worth a thousand Ross Vincennes or Phil Stantons. She had a chance to win him if the cards fell right in the next one-hundred minutes. She remembered another quote from high school Shakespeare. Lay on, McDuff.

She set the wine aside and picked up the phone.

61

Julie tried to think it out. For the first time in his life he was really in love, and the most beautiful, courageous, extraordinary woman he had ever met loved him. Now there was a cloud over it all. She was in trouble, and she had confirmed that he was in danger, too, then insisted he stay away and lie low until she could work it out.

It was entirely possible the man he fought last night was watching him, or had someone on his tail. He hoped Marti wasn't spotted during her brief visit to the hospital that morning. He had to take her warning seriously. Both warnings. The guy he fought with warned him, too.

Somehow he had to be near her, out of her sight but ready to help her, when she dealt with the danger linked with her past.

It had to be something involving Costello, but he's dead! Killed by marshal Vincennes.

Another figure in the mix is the guy the media calls "the fat man." He, supposedly, came to her apartment to kill her, and this was his second attempt. Now, he is still running around loose. Unable to sit in his office stewing about his helplessness, he walked into the gym. Not much doing. The girls were working with a couple of stroke patients. Cindy was helping an elderly woman try to stay on her feet. He watched for a few seconds, giving Cindy a wink to show he approved her efforts, then said, "Cindy, I'm out of here for a couple of hours. Doesn't look as if I'll be missed, but you can get me on the cell. Okay?"

She smiled. "Okay, boss. Hey, Marti Costello didn't come in. She going to miss another day?"

Good. Neither of the girls had learned of the brief hallway meeting, but they expected him to know her schedule. It's part of the brotherhood of females, he guessed.

He said, "Looks like it, but she might come in later."

He had to do something, and maybe he could pick up a clue to Marti's problem. His destination was the city's main library downtown. What he wanted might be found via a computer, but micro-filmed pages from the New York Times might even be easier.

He hadn't been to the main library since college days. All he had was the name, Robert Costello, but that might be enough. He got into his Hyundai, glancing around the hospital's parking lot to see if anyone was paying any attention to him, although a skilled watcher would be hard to spot. He aimed the car for the expressway. This time of day it might not be too bad.

It was a slow day in the huge building that housed one of the nation's largest libraries. A male attendant answered his question with a smile and a nod He was into the carefully preserved pages of the New York Times within a few minutes of his arrival.

The idea was to find something that would cause a witness to seek protection from the government. He thought he would go back a year, and then another year until he could see a story, probably involving a trial, in which Robert Costello was a major figure, probably as a witness.

He didn't have to go into the second year. The page-one story of only months ago couldn't be missed. Phillip Stanton, chairman of Stanton Industries, had been exonerated of the government's tax evasion charge. Staring back at Julie from beneath the headline were photos of Stanton and the government's key witness, Robert Costello.

Wow! Stanton. You're the bad guy.

Julie couldn't take the news sitting down. The realization that the muscular guy he had tangled with was a the prominent businessman lifted him out of his chair. He stood staring down at the monitor, a whole series of thoughts crashing together.

Marti and this guy must have had a thing going, before, during, or after her marriage to Costello. But she comes to Chicago with her husband as a federally-protected witness. A gunman shows up and shoots Marti. Then, he comes back, barging into Marti's apartment, but escapes after being wounded.

He continued the scenario. "Stanton made it clear last night he still wants Marti. He certainly wouldn't send someone to kill her. Marti wants no part of him if what we have is real, and I know it's real. I can give her nothing but my love. Stanton is a millionaire and he can have me killed for a few dollars. No wonder she wants me to lay low. She says she has screwed up her life, but she may have a plan that will make things right. I have to give her that chance.

"Stanton! The Chicago papers said the cops were looking for him. Wanted to question him in connection with Costello's death. Did they know he was in Chicago? I'll be glad to tell them, but after Marti is successful with her plan, whatever it is."

Julie worked on it further. "Obviously the Chicago police thought Stanton sent the gunman after Costello. Weird. Of course Stanton would to be under suspicion, but why would a major figure in business open himself up to such charges? Unless he thought he could arrange for an execution that couldn't be traced back to him, There's no way he wants to hurt Marti.

"He's in Chicago to get her back, but maybe Marti got to him, made promises she didn't intend to keep. Because of me. I hope."

He could have quizzed her about the entire mess except that everything happened so fast. One day he was the therapist, with what appeared a growing friendship with a dedicated, hard-working patient. There was the lunch, and the informal dinner at her place, walking her home, but no deep exchanges about personal stuff. Then pow, she's in his arms and they're in love.

He had left his phone in his car as he didn't want to be interrupted in the library. He found a public phone in the lobby and looked up police headquarters. He would ask for a Sergeant Carey. According to the news reports, Carey was handling the case, so he'd be the guy to talk to.

It was now early afternoon and Carey wasn't available. Julius left his cell number, said it was important, but declined to elaborate for the officer who took his call. The Bulls were playing at the Center that evening, but with super stars Michael Jordan and Scotty Pippen both gone, it wasn't much fun watching their replacements get mauled. He wouldn't have gone anyway, partially conscious of what an incredible decision that might have been only a few days ago. That is, pre-Marti. What in hell could he do now, but go back to the office and wait, then go home and wait some more?

Was this some kind of soap opera, or what?

62

Phil Stanton sat in his hotel room, nursing his bruised face. The injury wasn't as bad as he had first thought. A side of his face would be puffed up for awhile, but the nose would be okay. The hotel had a doctor on call for treatment last night. Stanton judged him to be in his sixties, maybe supplementing a retirement income. He peered into Stanton's face but asked no questions. Stanton thought he should say something.

He said, "I'm from New York. I had to come to Chicago to get mugged."

The doctor smiled but made no comment. He tweaked his patient's nose back into its normal position and swabbed away a lot of blood, but found no need for stitches.

He said, "You'll hurt and the face is going to puff up, but you can get by with a light-weight bandage. I'll leave some pain pills."

It was all the blood that scared him, and he had to admit the shock of the kid's move had shaken him up. He really should have continued the fight, left the kid in no shape to attract any woman.

He had never gotten in such a mess,. The awareness of powerful backing from parents who adored him was always there. In him they saw the realization of the hopes of several generations. They kept him aware of the importance of his role in their expectations, but he wasn't going to sweat it. He had satisfied his appetites per the dictates of his needs, not of the family's. The women had come and gone, but he had maintained a more than respectable family front.

It was his lust for more money, not women, that led to hiring Costello, the financial smart ass. Marti had become part of the package but it wasn't her fault her husband was a thief. He had misjudged Costello, had thought the man would never dare steal from him, much less rat him out. Now Costello was out of the picture, and the cops wanted to question him.

Sure they would, and they could. When he was back in New York. They had nothing but suspicion. No way they could trace the gunman back to Brancatto, or to him.

The fight with Warshawsky might not have been a mistake. The punk might mention the fight to Marti, and the warning he was given. If he did, she would have sense enough to warn Warshawsky of the danger he could be in. Whatever! He had to get back to New York. He couldn't be anywhere near Chicago if it became necessary to order Warshawsky dead.

It was dangerous using Brancatto's underworld ties to feed his needs, but he was safe enough in the Costello matter. He never got his chance to beat of Costello into a pulp, but dealing with Warshawsky might make up for that lost opportunity. The bastard was asking for it if he didn't disappear from Marti's life. Sure, at first he said he would follow orders and dump Marti, but after the fight he said it would be up to Marti. None of that bullshit. There was too much invested in the relationship to give her up.

Why dead? The best way. Warshawsky would be out of her life permanently, and she would forget him. She couldn't really care for the man. He couldn't be making a dime and Marti wasn't the type to give up more than a million dollars for any man, and she wouldn't risk implicating herself. She had taken his money to drop the dime on her husband. Marti would never risk heavy-duty jail time for complicity in attempted murder. The answer was money. She would go for the money and once again live the life she was destined to live in and around the world's greatest city.

He picked up the phone. He hated to have her see him like this, but he had to have her assurance she was dumping Warshawsky. And he wanted her to look him in the eye as she said so. She picked up, first ring.

He tried to play the suitor. "Can we meet for coffee and. I'm buying?"

Instead of the hoped-for chuckle he got a surprising invitation.

"Phil, I'm sorry about our quarrel. I've scheduled a workout today, but then I need to do some shopping and get my new apartment in shape because I'm cooking dinner, hopefully for you. You've tried to be good to me Phil, and I want you to enjoy a special treat."

He would change his travel plans, get out later after his dinner with Marti. He didn't want to do anything to upset her after the promise of an evening together. If it was necessary to tell her of the Warshawsky ultimatum, it would keep until tonight. He had to make up for the cracks he had made in his hotel room, keep it light, then make it clear she had to dump her boy friend and return to New York where they could resume normal relations.

She would forget Warshawsky because he would give her everything she had ever dreamed of. He would tell her he would divorce Lucia, too. That was bullshit but once in New York, with her money, she wouldn't complain about that technicality. He would pick up a nice bottle of wine for Marti's table. It should be fun. She had never cooked a meal for him. There could be many such occasions for the future. If she just used her head. If the punk was at the hospital when she showed up for her workout, he should tell her then and there. Her mood in the apartment later would tip him on whether Warshawsky gave her the brushoff.

How about that? Warshawsky couldn't have reported the fight, either to her or the cops,. Would he dump her as ordered? What was one more girl to him anyway? He probably made a practice of taking shots at attractive patients. If he was as cool as he pretended to be, he would give Marti the bye-bye and save his ass. Second thought, why not get the matter covered. Both ways.

Joseph Brancatto called his brother. "Dave, I just had a call from Phil Stanton. He wants to talk directly to the guy who broke into Mrs. Costello's apartment. Can we help him do that?"

"Joey, it's over, isn't it? Stanton never got his meeting with Costello, who is now dead. If he's up to any other mischief, we shouldn't take any part in it. From what we know now, Mrs. Costello is the only player left in his game, and Stanton isn't going to harm her. Let's cut him loose."

"Dave, I hope we don't have to do that. I really want to stay close to the man, and his business. I don't think he is going to do any harm to anyone. My guess is he wants to make sure the guy the media calls the fat man doesn't have some kind of personal agenda that could backfire. Wouldn't we want that assurance, too?"

David gave his brother's proposal a few seconds thought.

"Okay, bro. I hope it's worth your time and effort. I don't see how it fits with the family's vow to protect the Stanton family, but I'll see what I can do and call you back."

63

Marti was ready. The apartment, sweetened by tantalizing odors from the roast, was proof a great meal awaited her guests. The plan had to work. She would never have to sit across a table from Phil again. Or Ross. The goal was simple, to drive both of these men out of her life. Maybe Sergeant Carey, or Julie, if she could find him, would enjoy the meat.

She thought she had done a good acting job in the Stanton invitation. He would come with bells on. Whatever happened, she had to protect Julie She didn't have his cell number, so she called the hospital to tell him she was okay, and to repeat her warning that he should stay away from her apartment. Jane picked up his phone and said he wasn't there.

"Do you want his cell number?"

"No thanks. I just wanted to leave word that I expect to be at the gym in the morning. I don't want to miss anymore workout time."

"We don't either. See you tomorrow, then."

A few minutes later she picked up a cell call from Sergeant Leo Carey.

Carey had doubts about Marti's safety, but he admitted to himself the odds for her idea for ridding herself of both Vincennes and Stanton at the same time were favorable. He could have played it safe, and ordered her to keep away from both men. Told her to deal with them separately, by telephone. The trouble with that idea was that both Vincennes and Stanton still had an itch for her. Either man could be a danger to her if they thought she was two-timing them. Carey wasn't foolhardy, but he had never worried about taking chances if he thought the odds were decent. Obviously, the situation was a career breaker if anything serious went wrong.

He and Marti went over the final plan.

Carey said, "Both of these guys still have the big itch for you, Mrs. Costello. So I don't think you will be in harm with them both in the same room. How they react to each other is another matter. I'm going to have a squad right outside your window, and if we think it necessary we will move in fast with or without your signal for help."

The signal they agreed upon was for Marti to yell as loudly as possible and tug on one of the front window's curtains. He said he would make sure the foyer door was unlocked, but that she should leave her door unlocked.

Ross was on time. Good! She pushed the buzzer and met him at the door. He came in smiling, carrying flowers in one hand, a black valise in the other. She kissed him on the cheek and took the flowers. He held her for a second, one hand lightly on her back, checking for a wire. No matter, he would say nothing incriminating at this meeting.

He dropped the bag by the door, still smiling. *Wow, a kiss on the cheek. At least she didn't offer a hand to shake.*

Marti pointed at the recliner as she ducked into the kitchen for something to hold the roses. She called over her shoulder, "What would you like to drink?"

Vincennes sat as instructed. "Bourbon and water would be fine."

She returned with the drink, smiling. He felt his penis harden. It would be difficult to keep his hands off her. Jesus, she could have a good chunk of the money. He had brought a half million. in the valise. The rest was in the Chrysler's trunk. He took it out of the storage locker to prove to her he had it. He could promise to share it if they could resume their relationship but she shouldn't be greedy. He did all the work, took all the chances, and came up with the believable story after the apartment shooting. It should be enough to get her back on the schedule they had enjoyed before that mess.

She said, "The roses are lovely. Thank you."

"For a lovely lady. That's not all I brought."

That made her smile. She couldn't stop herself from glancing at the bag resting by the door. She had prepared a drink for herself, a Chardonay. She touched the hard back chair she had carefully positioned opposite him, and said, "For dessert?"

A hopeful note. "Right. To be opened later. Hey, something smells good. That is, besides you. What's for dinner?"

"Roast beef. The butcher said it would cook itself. I read somewhere it's hard to mess up a good piece of beef."

Vincennes nodded. "Unless you burn it up."

They laughed. She said, "I have it on a timer."

Chit-chat followed. Marti wouldn't have been able to repeat what was said for a million dollars. Somehow she hadn't broken into a sweat. Ross, she decided, was going to behave himself, at least until after the good meal he anticipated. He then would make his pitch, reveal the contents of the black bag, or both.

The sound of the buzzer startled them both. Vincennes, his glass almost at his mouth, nearly slopped the drink. Marti, on her feet was prepared with a calming remark as she moved to press the admitting button.

Thank god he's on time.

She said, "I'm sorry, Ross. Just relax. I ordered some wine for dinner."

The man who brought it didn't look like a liquor store delivery man to Vincennes. *What the hell.* He recognized Stanton from the businessman's trial pictures he examined with Lou Robbins. He struggled to his feet from the deep lounge chair.

Stanton was looking only at Marti as he entered the room. He expected a brief kiss and got it. He was extending his offerings of the wine when he saw Vincennes. He looked at Marti, with surprise and the beginnings of anger in his eyes.

"What's up? Who's this?"

Marti made herself smile. It was helped by the realization that her Julie had done some damage in his fight with her former lover. She was now into the hardest part. She had to stay calm, remember her speech, but she had to add something solicitous about Stanton's puffed-up face.

"Phil, what happened?"

Carey said she must take charge. "Don't let anything derail your plan. Each of those men want your approval. They'll hear you out."

Stanton made a gesture with his hand. "It's nothing." He advanced across the room, staring at Vincennes. Marti grabbed for the bottle of wine, spun around and deposited it on an end table adjoining the sofa. She reached for Stanton's arm and led him to Vincennes.

"Phil, come. I want you to meet someone with whom you have a lot in common.

I want you to meet United States marshal Ross Vincennes."

The men barely touched hands, and quickly, very much like heavyweights about to return to their corners before the first round. They both glared at Marti.

Stanton said, "What in hell are you up to, Marti? What do I have in common with this man?"

Vincennes thought he knew the answer and that Stanton might explode. He didn't want to be right, but he had backup if things got nasty. The Magnum was in its shoulder holster. He sized up the hard-eyed and muscular Stanton. He felt no fear, only curiosity. Obviously, Marti had brought them here to meet, and Vincennes wanted to hear it out. Then he could detain Stanton man for questioning by the Chicago cops.

"Please sit here, Phil," she said, indicating the chair she had just left.

"Sit down, Ross." The men reluctantly took their seats while she grabbed for the chair she had carefully positioned nearby. She sat before them.

She said, "Phil, Ross has a drink. Can I bring you one?"

He gave the answer she wanted.

"Hell no. Let's get on with it. What do I have in common with this man?"

She wanted to get on with it, too. She had rehearsed her next sentence many times. It was the same admission she had made to detective Carey. It had made her squirm then, but it had to be delivered now to achieve the objective of this meeting. She had to make these men, who may have thought they wanted her, to now despise her.

She said, "What each of you have in common is that each of you has been my lover."

Vincennes had guessed right. He stared at the man opposite him whose face had suddenly turned scarlet. He edged forward in the recliner. What was Marti's game? He shifted his gun hand closer to the opening in his coat.

Stanton lunged to his feet, roaring "Jesus Christ, Marti. You bring me here to announce that you're a slut. What in Christ's name is the matter with you?"

Getting to her feet almost as fast, she said, "But that's not all you have in common."

"Oh yeah?" He was livid. The Essex House look when she tried to hit him.

"Oh yeah." She would milk the lines now. She pushed her face within a few inches of his. If he didn't hate her now, he would when he heard how she had helped him part with his beloved money.

"You see, Phil, Ross has your money. He went to Minneapolis last week and stole all the money Bob stole from you."

Vincennes snarled, "Wait a minute, bitch." He was already half way out of the recliner and struggling to get on his feet. He got it now. She was setting him up. He might have to kill both of them.

She spun around to face him. "Wait for what? You covered the theft nicely by shooting Bob to death right about where Phil is standing."

Marti had more in her script, but Stanton had had enough. He moved so quickly that Vincennes, who thought he was prepared for anything, didn't have the second he needed to drag out his gun. Marti was knocked sprawling as Stanton lunged for the marshal. Vincennes threw himself to his right as he clawed for the Magnum, but Stanton was all over him.

Vincennes screamed, "Don't be a fool. She's setting us up."

Marti was stunned, but she recovered quickly as the men thrashed wildly behind her. She struggled to her knees, then to her feet, stifling a scream. She had to get to the window. She made it, leaping over the tangled bodies, and almost tore the curtain off its rod. No way would Carey and his men miss the signal.

The explosion behind her was like being hit in the back by a powerful gust of wind. She spun around to see Stanton slowly rising to his feet.

She yelled, "Noooo." Vincennes wasn't moving. Blood was pouring from a wound under his chin. Stanton, chest heaving, turned to her, eyes wild.

"It was self defense, Marti. He would have killed me. The gun just went off. You saw it."

"No. I didn't see anything. My God, Phil. We have to get a doctor."

"Forget about it. He's dead, and it's your fault. First I hear you are fucking the guy, then he has my money. I went nuts."

He grabbed her wrist, dragging her toward the door where he bent down to pick up his wrist watch, torn off in the fight. He glanced at it. "I have five after seven. What do you have?"

"Are you insane. You want the time?"

"Yes, goddammit". He grabbed her wrist, twisting it to see her watch.

"Seven oh five. Too late."

"What are you talking about? Too late for what?"

"Too late to save your pollack boy friend that's what? The first thing I wanted to know when I came in that door was whether Warshawsky had told you your fling was over. He had orders to dump you. If he didn't tell you he was out of the picture, I was going to give you until seven to tell me you'd dump him and come back to New York with me. Obviously this is news to you. Now he's in deep shit and I can't do a thing about it."

Marti screamed, "Nooooo."

Carey didn't bother to try the door knob. The door came off its hinges with a crash, nearly landing on Stanton, who jumped back into the living room.

Marti ran at Carey, screaming. "Arrest him. He killed Julius Warshawsky."

Carey grabbed Marti by the shoulders. He couldn't have slapped her to get her attention more effectively.

"What are you talking about?"

Marti flung an arm wildly in the direction of Stanton, who yelled, "She's crazy."

She yelled back, "The hell I am. You just told me you sent someone to kill Julie."

Carey's look was grim but less tense than a moment before. A pair of his men were bending over the body of Ross Vincennes. They looked up, shaking their heads.

Carey said, "Well, it had to have happened in the last thirty minutes because I found him hanging around outside and told him to get his ass out of here. He was pretty excited, but I told him he could wait somewhere else, or go downtown. He said something about the hospital and took off."

Carey made a grab for Marti, but she was past him and out the door. Carey turned to one of his men. "Let her go, Frank, but stay with her." He then reached for his cell phone.

64

The man the media had labeled "the fat man" sat patiently in the darkened Lincoln parked near the front door of Julius Warshawsky's apartment building. He had moved around the city, camping in the car, since the weird scene in the Costello woman's apartment. The media was crammed with the wild story. That he was described as a killer was no surprise, but the fact he had been pushed into the apartment by a U.S. marshal was a stunner. The son of a bitch. He would kill the man for free, even at the risk of having the federal government on his ass. He wanted to honor his deal for a do-or-not-to-do job on a Julius Warshawsky and get back home for a fix on his shoulder. Half a good fee was at risk. He was hurting from the slug that winged him, but it had passed through clean, missing bone. He was half through a bottle of pain reliever.

The phone call to find and possibly whack Warshawsky had been whispered by a male voice he had never heard before The voice, and the clown might have been trying to disguise it, used the code, also the counter to his "What do you want?' correctly, but it wasn't right. He would hang up and call his regular contact and find what this was all about. But the unknown voice stopped him with a single word. "Costello."

Shit. He then listened to the unusual request, with a deadline for a first for him, but a job was a job. He was to find Warshawsky, and whack him unless he got another call before seven that evening. Either way. He then called his regular contact and confirmed that half his usual $50,000 fee had been received. The conversation was brief. He didn't bother to ask whether the cash received from the screwed up Costello job came from the same source. At least he no longer had the more complicated job of holding the now dead Costello until the original fee payer showed up.

He was cleaning his nails with a knife better designed for cutting up large pieces of meat. The knife was normally concealed in a scabbard attached to his lower right leg. It was utilized as a back-up weapon, but its primary task was to reduce human beings into small parts.

If he was to make Julius Warshawsky disappear he had several options. Ideally, he would use the man's bathtub to dismember the body into chunks that would be transferred to the Lincoln in plastic bags and later buried in small graves. So far as he knew, none of his twenty-three victims had ever been found. To family, friends, police, the men and two women, had simply disappeared.

He glanced at his watch. Getting close to seven. He should at least try to learn whether the target was at home. Besides, the shoulder was aching. He decided to leave the comfortable car, and stuffed some plastic bags in his sport coat pocket.

In the foyer, he pushed the buzzer opposite Warshawsky. There was no response so he examined the inner door, finding the lock laughingly easy to overcome with a wallet-size case of lock picks he used regularly. A specialty of his work was waiting for his victims in their homes, motel rooms, what have you.

Warshawsky lived in what Chicago apartment dwellers call a high third, so called because the building's first floor was at the structure's second level. This called for quite a hike by the over-weight killer, who was slightly winded as he reached the top of the stairs. He took a deep breath and moved to a position in front of Warshawsky's door. He would get into the apartment, using his picks, or he would wait for his target in a convenient alcove farther down the carpeted hallway. He attached the suppressor to his Colt. His gun, modeled after the original six-shooter, was his favorite weapon, chosen over more modern handguns, because it could use a suppressor.

He was jarred from the usual air of detachment that preceded a job when he heard the police siren. There was no reason the siren signaled an interest in him but it was as good a reason as any to get out of the open area. He glanced at his watch as the zero hour had come and went Time to go to work. He shifted the Colt in its shoulder holster. He pulled out his break-in kit and stepped in front of Warshawsky's door.

He glanced again at his watch. A quarter after seven.

So, Julius Warshawsky, it's too bad for you. If you show up now, you'll usher me into your apartment for a bloody bath. With a little luck he would be on the road within a couple of hours.

How did he get into this work? Was he lucky, or what?

65

Marti was trying to run, but it was hopeless in the heels. She kicked them off, and the officer lumbering after her, picked them up.

Phil, that filthy pig. Some deal. It was give in to him or he would kill her beloved Julie. He didn't actually say Julie would be killed but that's what he meant. Oh God, she had to get to her love and warn him. Somewhere in the darkness was a killer who had to be stopped. She might have screamed at Stanton to somehow call off the killer, but Stanton would have laughed at her, told Carey she was trying to set him up, just as she must have been doing in her phony invitation to dinner. But then Carey said he saw Julie, had sent him away from his apparent watching place near the apartment.

The hope he was all right was what was driving her now, to find him and somehow protect him. She was at Memorial's side door, the one closest to Julie's office. There was always a guard there. She rushed up to the startled man.

"Did you see Julius Warshawsky? He was coming here."

The guard knew Julie but he shook his head. "Not tonight. Was he supposed to be coming in?"

Marti looked around wildly, too distraught to answer. Then she started down the hall, the policeman hurrying to keep pace. He said, "What's up?"

"I know he has a cell phone. The number should be in his office." A few seconds later she was at Julie's desk, fumbling through items and papers, not sure where to look.

The officer said, "Hey, I can get the number." He pulled out his cell.

Marti squeezed her hands together as he went to work. A few second later he said, "Thanks," and took the unit away from his face and tapped in a number. "It's three one two, two seven nine five."

Marti almost grabbed the cell from him. It was ringing.

She had him. "Julie," she yelled. "Oh God, am I glad you're all right."

The policeman saw her face light up and was happy for her. The last few minutes had been a wild finish to an otherwise ordinary day. In the woman's apartment he'd heard her yell at Carey. Something about a hit on someone with a Polish name. Now it looked as if she had found him. Some kind of protection action plan was needed.

Marti said, "I'm in your office. I was trying to find your cell number, but an officer with me got it from somewhere. Listen to me. Sit tight. Don't answer the door until we get there. You're in danger. I'll tell you all about it soon as we can get there."

She hung up and asked the officer his name.

"Frank Ellington."

"Nice going on getting that number, Frank. Can you stay with me now? I have to get to Julius Warshawsky's apartment. Then we have to get back to my place."

"I'm with you, miss," and he held out her heels. "But let's get a car over here, and add some more protection" He again opened his cell.

"Five minutes," he told Marti a few seconds later.

66

Julie heard the buzzer within a minute after Marti's call from the hospital. No way could she have covered the half mile or so in that time. He had a window on the street and he pulled the curtain to look out and down. No police car, but she said she was with a cop. Her escort could be the big plain clothes cop who shooed him away from his watch outside her apartment. Obviously the cops staked out at her place weren't going to let her run around loose.

He continued to look. No one was returning to the street from the foyer. Whoever it was still there. Why?

Because whoever it is is after my ass, that's why.

Anyone with a credit card could spring the foyer's ancient door lock. Child's play. He had done it a couple of times. He went to his door and checked the lock. Oh why hadn't he installed a dead bolt? He meant to. He had a few athletic trophies and a couple of signed baseballs that were worth a few bucks, but so far as he knew no one had ever been robbed in the building. He usually forgot to lock the door.

What in hell was that?

He had heard something just outside his door. The carpeting muffled most foot sounds in the hallway, but he had heard something.

The sound of a police siren drowned out any other sounds, and it was coming this way, its siren growing louder. Then another sound. Someone's tinkering with the door lock. Oh shit. He ran to the largest piece of furniture in the living room, a recliner, and muscled it over to the door. There was a muffled clunk as the furniture hit the door. He leaned against it for a moment, then he jumped, as if bitten by a wasp.

Ouch. What was that? Oh my God. I'm shot. I'm bleeding.

He jumped clear of the door. Then, unthinking, he screamed, "You son of a bitch. You hit me, but if you stick your head through that door I'll knock it off."

The answer was another hole in the door. *He should have kept his mouth shut. The shooter might have thought he killed him and gone away.*

There had hardly been any sound, but Julie saw the holes in the door while hearing the damage they caused in smashing a photograph of his parents on the opposite wall. He still wasn't sure where he had been hit, but it wasn't serious. It couldn't be all that bad or he'd feel something. Ouch. A burning sensation in his upper arm confirmed he'd been hit, but only grazed.

He hurried to a closet, trying to make no sound. The bastard might think he had killed him with the second shot. He had a softball bat in there. Maybe he could get a crack at the guy if he tried to bull himself in.

Another thought. To hell with playing dead. He ran to the front window, yanked it up. A cop car was at the curb, another pulling up. Marti was getting out.

He yelled, "Marti. Someone is shooting at me. Stay away."

Two cops were with her, fumbling for their guns, running into the foyer. One of the cops was putting a phone to his mouth.

Julius ran back to his door, but not straight at it. Listening, he thought he heard retreating footsteps. The shooter must have heard his yell of warning to Marti and gone back to the stairs. They were the only way out of the building from the hallway unless the bastard climbed to the roof on a ladder in the hallway utility room.

He couldn't just wait there. He grabbed the arms of the recliner, still jammed against the door. He wrestled with it until there was enough room to squeeze out the door. He charged through it, bat raised. No one there. He ran to the stairs. Two explosions, then several more. Julius ran to the stairs and scrambled down a flight. Marti was screaming. Julius reached the landing, daring to look over the banister. *Oh no, two cops down.*

And there on the stairs, barely twenty feet down from him, was Marti, staring at a gun held by a chunky man in a hat and a blue sport coat. One cop was sprawled at her feet, his weight holding her in place. The other cop, also down but trying to move, lay several steps further up the stairs.

The son of a bitch could shoot Marti, too.

Instinctively he screamed, "Here I am, you son of a bitch." He grabbed the rail with his left hand and swung himself outward as far as he could.

He had to at least distract the guy, give Marti a chance to run. He would throw the bat, something he had never done before in his life. He had just dropped them after making contact with a ball, or he tossed them aside after taking a walk and being waved to first.

It wasn't an easy angle, making a good throw while hanging over that railing. Odds makers, even ones aware of Julie's excellent athletic capabilities, might have said, "fifty-fifty on hitting or distracting the target, Twenty-five to one on doing any real damage."

Julius wouldn't have bet on himself, either. But this was a moment that made any previous association with bats or any sport trivial by comparison.

At the sound of Julie's voice, the thug swung his gun arm around. Amazing. The son of a bitch was smiling. Julius had no room or enough time to draw his arm back. With his hand on the handle he cocked his wrist and flung the bat, pouring all the strength he had ever summoned for driving a baseball.

The bat was in the air, end over end, when the killer fired. Two deadly missiles, a twenty-five ounce softball bat versus a much lighter slug from the Colt, but it was no contest if the bullet was on target.

Julius saw the muzzle flash, and instinctively realized the shot must have missed. The killer pulled the trigger again, but there was no sound or flash. He had used up the revolver's six-slug quota. The professional killer had failed to count his shots.

The bat, intended for the gunman's head, never reached its target. Instead, its heavy end hit the shooter's gun, knocking it from his hand and sending it spinning downward into the darkened stairwell. Julius saw the gunman's look of pain and alarm as he saw his tool disappear. In the beat of time he used to hopelessly look over the rail, Julie was bounding down the stairs. The hit man hesitated, then spun around and ran downward. He had decided against a hand-to-hand brawl with the bat thrower. He had his backup weapon strapped to his ankle, but he didn't think he could get the blade free in time to use it. He also knew there was no way he was going to find his Colt, and reload it, in the few seconds left before he became embroiled with and dangerously delayed from flight by the man he was supposed to kill.

So he ran, skipping over the two downed cops and the woman who was screaming her lungs out. He was out of the building in a few seconds. His goal was his car and escape. Where to he had to decide. He had spare plates for the car if the Lincoln was spotted. He might even have to ditch the car, steal another or hijack one, then hole up in the car as he had since taking the bullet in the woman's apartment.

Julie at Marti's side asked the usual, "You okay?" but his mind was on the killer. A look at the two downed officers, one moaning, the other inert and apparently dead, sickened and infuriated him.

"Marti, take care of these guys. I'm going after the bastard."

In near shock but not helpless, she yelled back, "You're not leaving me," and together they ran out the front door. Marti was still shoeless, having tossed the heels into the rear seat of Ellington's car. Julius grabbed his bat, which had bounced into the foyer. He was conscious of the availability of the officers' guns, still in their hands, but he had never fired a gun in his life. It would take too many precious seconds to pry one of the weapons free. Anyway, his would-be killer had lost his weapon and hopefully didn't have another.

Marti's hand was locked in one of Warshawsky's when they hit the sidewalk. They couldn't see the killer, although he was only a few yards away, behind the wheel of his car.

But he had problems. He hadn't given any thought to the tight supply of parking space in the usually crowded neighborhood street. His car was squeezed in its place with only inches between his car and those in front and behind. He hadn't turned on his lights, but Marti and Julie easily spotted the car by the sound of its engine and the crunch of plastic and metal as the killer first smashed into the rear of the car ahead, then did more damage as he threw the car into reverse.

"He's getting away," Marti yelled.

"Like hell he is."

Julie was running, his bat raised. His idea was to smash the window of the killer's car and drag him into the street, but he was too late by a couple of steps. The Lincoln had freed itself. With a final wrench of the wheel the killer spun free, floored the accelerator, and was gone. Julie stared after it helplessly for a moment, then ran to the nearest police patrol car, engine still running. Its door was open and its emergency lights were still flashing.

"Wait here, he yelled. Get more cops."

Marti had no intention of following that order. She was yanking at the other front door. Julie, behind the wheel, couldn't move the car without injuring her.

"Let's go," she yelled.

He would have argued with her, but the set of her face told him it would be useless. Besides, the shooter had lost his gun, and Julie still had his bat. The killer's car was a couple of blocks ahead when Julie jammed his foot on the throttle. Could he keep up with the guy? Then he yelled. The Lincoln had made a hard right.

"Hey, that's Hardwick place. A dead end. We've got him."

Marti was fumbling with the car's phone. She didn't realize she activated it, and her anguished, "Oh god, how does this thing work?" provoked an immediate response from a control desk.

A stern female voice said, "Is this call authorized?. Identify yourself at once."

Julie had spun the wheel to follow the getaway car. Marti, with a bare knowledge of where they were, blurted out, "I'm Marti Costello. Please contact Sergeant Leo Carey. We are on Hardwick place. Goodbye."

The female voice from control fired back. "Sergeant Carey will be alerted. Stop the vehicle and remain inside."

Dropping the phone, Marti used both hands to look around her for a weapon. The police on television always seemed to have them extra weapons in their cars. Julie had slowed their car to a crawl. Not finding anything usable, Marti looked up.

"Julie, don't get too close. Let's wait for help."

"He doesn't have a gun, Marti. He would have fired at us. I'm going to brain the son of a bitch. This is getting personal."

The killer had discovered his navigational error. His Lincoln, still without lights, had turned itself around in the cul de sac and was facing the patrol car. Julie could see the outline of the driver's head, still with its hat on, in the front seat. More calm than when he first decided to chase the man who came to kill him, Julie stopped the black-and-white about fifty feet from the killer's Lincoln. The narrow neighborhood street was jammed with parked cars. There was no way the hit man could drive out. He was trapped.

But Marti was sure he was not helpless.

"Be careful, Julie. The man is huge."

Bat in hand, Julie advanced purposefully toward the Lincoln, certain the killer would have showed a second gun, if he had one, back on the apartment stairway.

Why doesn't the bastard come out? If he doesn't, I'll use my bat to smash the window and drag him out.

Marti had no more use for the car phone. She wanted to be at Julie's side and help him if she could. She was a few steps behind him when the killer's car door opened. She was frightened by the menacing movement of the big man leaving the car.

It's as if he's meeting friends. Why doesn't he run? He must know the flashers will attract someone. Carey and more of his people are at my apartment, only a few blocks away.

The face of the killer was still partially hidden by the rim of his hat and in shadow from the weak light. Marti thought it seemed to be wearing a smile.

Shoving the car door closed, he spoke in a flat midwestern voice.

"You're pretty good with that bat, buddy. I guess you figure on subduing me, huh?"

Marti, seeing Julie inch forward, called, "Don't get too close, Julie."

Julie wanted to get close enough. If the guy tried to run he wanted to bring him down right then and there.

The killer said, "Oh, I'm harmless enough. You knocked the gun out of my hand, remember?"

He took a couple of steps towards Julie. "I don't want to slugged with that bat.

What say we just wait here till the cops show up. Okay?"

Marti thought the man was giving up too easily, also that he was too close to Julie. Julie thought she was too close, too. He turned his head slightly to warn her to stay further away when the man moved forward with the speed of a pro-bowl linebacker. Marti saw the glint of something in his right hand.

She screamed, "Look out, Julie."

She was too late. Julie saw the move. He could have tried to evade it, but instead he instinctively tried to parry the thrust with his bat. He felt he could then counter with a horizontal smash to the killer's head.

He misjudged both the speed of the attacker's lunge and the length of the killer's custom-built blade, but his bat did prevent the thrust that would surely have impaled him. His bat deflected the knife so that it raked across his stomach instead of puncturing it, but the shock from the penetration froze him. Horrified by the wound, he froze, dropping the bat. Instinctively he tried to cover his stomach with his hands. He felt he might be dying. Blood was seeping through his fingers. The overwhelming fear of a follow-up thrust made him turn away from the attacker. He fell to the pavement. He wanted to roll under a car, somehow delay another slash by the long knife. Panic was joined by raw terror.

There was embarrassment and deep chagrin, too. He, a good athlete, had been suckered and beaten by a faster man. And Marti. The son of a bitch would kill her, too. He had to get up, put up some kind of fight. Maybe one of the residents in the apartment buildings surrounding the scene would help.

The few seconds of Julie's agony and self-criticism were filled with calm pleasure by the knifer, and horror by Marti Costello. The fat man knew the cop car requisitioned by the crazy couple would be followed by others, but he could still get away, melt into the darkness between the apartment building. He could swipe a car, probably in the next street. He wanted to earn the rest of his fee, too. The grounded and terrified kid would die with one more thrust. He should run for it. As a professional killer he should have conceded he was out of time, but for those few seconds his rage took over. He had to bury his knife in this man, who not only had fucked up his job, but had been a threat to his life.

Marti was screaming from the moment Julie went down.

"Oh my god." She would have run to his side, but the killer warned her away with an impatient flick of his knife. He would make his move and get out of there. He ignored her and advanced on his victim. Julie yelled, "Run Marti" as he struggled to role under one of the parked cars.

Marti, too frozen in fear to scream, looked around frantically. She had to stop this fiend. Then what she later described as a gift from the almighty. Julie's bat lay at her feet. There was no question about what she must try to do with it, but was there enough time? She was still in her stocking feet, which may have added a couple of milliseconds to the speed with which she snatched up the bat.

Raising it sideways as if she was again a batter in a childhood ball game took another immeasurable iota of time. The movement threw a flicker of shadow across the killer's back. Sensing interruption, and more annoyed than concerned, he swung his head toward Marti. She had felt no animosity for the man who had accidentally shot her in the bungalow's basement, but now her brain had room only for fury and hate. His expression in the split second he had to see what she was up to changed to horror as Marti swung in a vicious arc. Only an instinct to turn his face away from the blow saved it from bloody obliteration. Marti's horizontal stroke across her body was delivered with all the new strength she had gained from her rehab workouts. The bat landed flush against the side of the killer's head. The sickening crunch signaled that some real damage had been done.

She dropped the bat and fell to her knees besides Julie. He managed to twist himself to a sitting position and leaned against the car he hoped to roll under. He tried to smile as he saw the unconscious killer.

"Wow, Marti, you really creamed him."

"Oh Julie, how badly are your hurt?"

"I dunno. Maybe not as bad as I first thought. I don't think he got anything vital."

He pulled up his sweater which covered a T-shirt. He pressed the garments, soaked with blood, against the wound.

"Help me get my handkerchief out of my pocket. It'll help stop the bleeding."

Cop car sounds and flashers now complemented the scene. Someone had spotted the fight from their apartment window and called 911, but a squad car was already in the street. Carey, still in Marti's apartment, had relayed the report on Marti's desperate call. Another car was already searching the neighborhood after finding the carnage in Julie's stairway.

With the flow of blood under control, Julie and Marti sat in the back seat of the patrol car. Marti took a last look at the fallen hit man. Lots of blood. He hadn't moved since she had delivered her blow.

The driver said, "Sergeant Carey is waiting at your apartment, Mrs. Costello, He wants you there right away." He jerked his head toward Julius. "He'll have a medic there to take care of that cut, too."

Julie put the arm that hadn't been nicked by the killer's bullet around Marti's shoulders.

"Marti, we make a hell of a team, and you swing a good bat. How do you think you'd be with a rolling pin?"

It sounded like a veiled proposal, and it thrilled her, but she wasn't sure he would follow through after the next thirty minutes in her apartment.

She said, "Julie, you are about to hear some nasty stuff about me. I'm not going to blame you for any reaction you might have, but I'm hoping you will understand I'm not the same woman who came to Chicago with her husband several months ago."

Julie grinned. "I know. You are in a lot better shape."

She couldn't smile. She said, "I love it when you tease me, but you'll need more than your sense of humor when you learn what a damn fool I've been."

67

A police department medic took charge of Warshawsky as soon as their car pulled up in front of Marti's apartment. Julie tapped her arm. "Go," he said. "I'm okay."

Marti hurried into the apartment. She had to know about the officers on Julie's stairs.

A grim Carey said, "Frank Ellington will be okay but Bill Harris died at the scene."

Marti said, "Oh no. That's horrible. I'm so sorry."

She received several admiring glances and nice goings in the crowded apartment. Someone said, "You must be some kind of ballplayer the way you swing a bat."

She said, "I haven't played baseball since grade school. It was instinctive, I guess. The man was about to stick Julie again and I just went kind of crazy."

Julie, naked above the belt but swathed in bandage, arrived in the living room grinning. He, sobered immediately when Marti went to him and whispered the news about officer Harris.

One of the officers had thrown a jacket over his shoulders.

He brightened up again in response to his share of quietly-delivered congratulations from the officers still crowding the small room. He was feeling better with both of his wounds tended. He was now convinced neither the bullet nor the knife had done serious damage.

He said seriously as if reporting his recovery from the measles. "All the blood squirting out of my stomach scared hell out of me. I've never been knifed before."

His audience, including Marti, laughed as he had intended them to.

Leo Carey had a handshake for Julie. He was happy for the lovers, but an officer with eighteen-years service had died.

The ambulance taking Ellington to Memorial had stopped by Marti's building, and the heavily-bandaged Ellington described what had happened in Warshawsky's building.

He said, "Bill ran in ahead of me, and the son of a bitch cut us down from the top of the stairs. We didn't even hear the shots. We got off a couple only after we were hit. What happened after that?"

Carey told him. "A pretty lady cold-cocked the bastard with her boy friend's baseball bat."

Ellington smiled through his pain.

Carey hadn't heard everything about Julie's exploit with the bat on his apartment stairway until Marti explained his heroics.

To Carey's "Nice going," Julie said, "It was incredible luck I hit the gun. I was aiming at his head."

Vincennes's body had been removed, but Phil Stanton sat glowering on the edge of Marti's recliner. He had demanded to see a lawyer, but Carey told him he was not under arrest.

"If and when you are, you can call every shyster in New York. Now shut up."

Marti would not look at Stanton as she excused herself.

She said, "Be right back," and she ducked into the kitchenette, returning with a disk she held up as if it was a court-room exhibit. She took two quick steps and slid it into the DVD on a shelf just below the room's television set.

She said, "Now we'll see if this thing works."

Stanton growled, "What in hell is she talking about?" but awareness of what he was about to see was in his eyes.

Using the remote control she pressed a button; then another. Stanton, Carey, Julie, and several cops stared at the television screen.

Marti said, "Phil, I didn't see your fight with Ross. You knocked me down, and I went to the window to signal for help. You said Ross tried to kill you and that you acted in self defense. Fortunately, per Sergeant Carey's great idea, we might be able to see the whole show.

The lighting wasn't perfect, but the focus was excellent. A camera installed by specialists Carey had referred Marti to, picked up Vincennes as she led him into her living room. Other hidden equipment recorded every sound, even their footsteps.

She looked at Julie. "There's a lot of it I'd wish it didn't pick up, but it's the price of getting this mess cleared up."

Vincennes's exchanges with Marti followed until they reacted to the buzzer announcing Stanton's arrival. He was shown walking to the chair Marti had designated for him. The lens had been adjusted to cover the entire width of the room. All three of the subjects were in frame as they took their seats.

The immediate and intense dislike of the men for each other was startlingly clear. Then, when Marti confessed her affair with Vincennes, and how he had hijacked the Stanton money originally stolen by Robert Costello, the action that followed was faster than any director would have asked.

Julie murmured, "Wow." It was the only sound to accompany the crashing of furniture and the thrashing men. What took place was clear. Vincennes had managed to get his gun clear and was trying to get off a shot, but Stanton had both of his hands around Vincennes's gun hand as the men crashed to the floor. He was the stronger of the pair. He worked Vincennes's gun as if Vincenne's was offering only token resistance and in only a few seconds the Magnum was under Vincennes's jaw. The explosion caused Marti to shriek, "Oh my god."

Julie, standing next to her, grabbed her around the shoulders.

Marti murmured, "You murdered him."

Stanton yelled, "No. It was self defense."

Carey nodded to his aides, and they started to lead Stanton out of the apartment, when Marti yelled, "Hold it."

She jumped in front of her former lover and slapped him across the face with all the new strength she had acquired in Julie's gym. Stanton reeled back, stung and furious.

Marti yelled, "You once told me nobody could hit you, but I just did."

Stanton's stare of hate contrasted with Carey's grin as Carey's aides took Stanton away.

"Read him his rights in case we charge him tonight," Carey called after his aides.

Carey retrieved the disk from the DVD, and he reached for Marti's hand.

"You did everything perfectly. I didn't want you in the same room with those guys, but you were right. It could only have worked per your gutty performance.

"It's too bad Vincennes thought he should bring his gun to your dinner. We hoped our plan could get him out of your life. Now he's out of his. As for Stanton, the film will be useful in ridding you of him, too. His attorneys will yell about entrapment, but I'll never tell them whose idea it was to rig your apartment with the state of the art video system. Will you?"

"Are you kidding, Sergeant? I'll brag about it to my grandchildren."

Carey said, "As for Mr. Stanton, however he's judged, he will learn that I will personally kill him if any harm comes to you. And on an official note, I'd like you both to come in tomorrow and give your statements. There will be a certain amount of crap to go through, including news people you'll probably want to dodge, but it will go away. In this town there's another big story every day."

Marti and Julie walked the big cop to the ruined door and watched him amble down the hall. Julie led her to a chair. He said, "Let me get you a drink."

Marti was still pale from the horrifying replay of Ross Vincennes's death. She also was still tingling with satisfaction from the way she had ushered Phillip Stanton from her life.

Julie returned with some of the rye Marti thought Phil might have asked for. She sipped and looked up at him. It had worked out, but he had seen the film, too, and now knew of her affairs with Vincennes and Stanton.

He grinned down at her, then sank to his knees and took her hand.

"Look. When I fell in love with you I knew it was with a woman, not a girl whose experience with men might have been limited to fraternity party beer bashes. We are both experienced adults with a chance to start over. I want my new life to be with you. Forever.

"I've just been fooling around with life, Marti. One friend told me I was playing it like it was all a big game. Now I want to grow up and really begin to live. With you."

He took a breath. He had never dreamed he could make such a speech.

She placed the glass on an end table. "Hold me, Julie."

Epilogue

Marti and Julius Warshawsky launched their marriage with the help of $500,000 they found in the black bag Vincennes dropped inside Marti's apartment door. Marti also had most of the $100,000 sent by Phil Stanton. She sent a check for $50,000 to the Chicago Community Fund as an anonymous donor, and another check of the same size to her parents.

The replay of the Stanton-Vincennes fight did not prove Stanton's intent to kill Julie. When Stanton went to retrieve his watch in the apartment foyer he was out of camera range and the sound was keyed only to what the camera picked up. Chicago's District Attorney got an indictment for first degree manslaughter against Stanton, but Stanton's legal counsel, directed from New York by David Brancatto, helped uphold Stanton's plea of self defense. The Brancattos thus maintained their grandfather's edict to protect the Stanton family. David also counseled Stanton to not implicate Marti in the betrayal of Bob Costello. Or attempt to retrieve any of the cash stolen by Bob Costello.

The "fat man,." ultimately identified as Tom Whitaker, a runaway out of Detroit, never recovered his full mental capacity after Marti's crushing blow. He was sent to a prison for the criminally insane for the rest of his life. His connection with Phil Stanton was never proven.

The half-million in cash Vincennes delivered to Marti's apartment enabled Marti and Julie to found the Warshawsky Fitness Academy, which helped by their recently achieved notoriety, was a success from its beginning. The couple have two children, a boy and a girl.

Marti also sent her mother the $32,000 found in Bob Costello's brief case Then, when the sales of the New York condo and the Chicago bungalow were settled, she sent her mother another $50,000. The rest she sent to the Columbia University business school in the name of alumnus Robert Costello. She kept her late husband's Buick.

Philip Stanton played no further role in Marti's life. He was sued for divorce and lost control of Stanton Corp. to a group formed by his wife and Joseph Brancatto's nephew, Carmine Ambrosia. Carmine achieved his dream, and that of his uncle, by becoming President and Chief Executive Officer of the Stanton Corporation. He funneled generous amounts of financial counseling fees to his uncle. The Brancattos never revealed their family's pledge to protect the Stanton family. When Philip was subsequently arrested and tried for fraud in a bogus real estate scheme, David Brancatto represented him, but lost the case. Philip was sentenced to ten years in prison.

Jody Vincennes was humiliated to learn of her husband's infidelity, but was comforted by the discovery of nearly $2,600,000 in his automobile after it was impounded. She remarried, and her two daughters went on to careers in law and finance.

Leo Carey accepted his lieutenancy and part-time work at a desk, but he didn't permit it to be confining. He also became a regular customer at the Warshawsky Fitness Academy as well as a close friend of its owners.